# SECOND CHANCE TO DIE

## A Pharmaceutical Mystery

MIKE GRINDSTAFF

Jan-Carol
Publishing, Inc

Second Chance to Die
Mike Grindstaff

Published July 2023
Little Creek Books
Imprint of Jan-Carol Publishing, Inc.
All rights reserved
Copyright © 2023 by Mike Grindstaff
Cover Design: Tara Sizemore
Cover Photos: Adobe Stock
Author Photo: Dana Grindstaff

ISBN: 978-1-954978-94-2
Library of Congress Control Number: 2023942807

You may contact the publisher:
Jan-Carol Publishing, Inc.
PO Box 701
Johnson City, TN 37605
publisher@jancarolpublishing.com
jancarolpublishing.com

*Dedicated to Papaw.*
*Without him, Destiny would never have existed.*

# AUTHOR'S NOTE

In the beginning, my first novel, *Moon Over Knoxville*, was just a bucket-list item. It took an embarrassingly long time to complete, but the sequel, fortunately, was written in a much shorter period.

I am a pharmacist (quasi-retired), who has always loved to read and dreamed of writing a book one day. My life—and the characters in this book—have been shaped and molded by pharmacy, baseball, and rock and roll.

As some of you may know, baseball is wrapped in superstitions. When a hitter gets on a hitting streak, he is likely to try to duplicate his daily routine, such as eating the same foods, wearing the same socks and underwear (unwashed, of course), sitting on the same place on the bench, et cetera. I played baseball as a youth until the field size outgrew my talent level. As an adult, I coached my children in both baseball and softball until they went on to high school, where I couldn't coach any longer. I could no longer be a coach, but I started umpiring so I could still be around the game I love and cherish.

The point is that I am superstitious. So much so that there is no chapter thirteen in either of my novels! Please don't contact the publisher about a missing chapter—it was skipped intentionally.

While this is a work of fiction, the characters are near and dear to my heart. If you, the reader, think it's appropriate, there may be a third, and final, book in the future.

# PROLOGUE

"Come in," the aging man directed weakly.

"Hey, Mr. Stanford. How's it going?" asked the bubbly young woman.

"Hey, Honey. Come on in. I'm feeling pretty rough today," the man responded, not getting up from his chair.

"Oh, I'm sorry. What's wrong?" the woman asked, obviously concerned.

"I just feel like crap. I'm really weak today, and I've been having hot flashes. It feels like my heart is going to pound out of my chest."

"Let me go get the nurse. I'll be right back."

"No, I'm sure it's nothing. Probably just another glorious day in old age," the man said, trying to make a joke of it.

"I doubt it, Mr. Stanford. You aren't old at all."

"I'm sure as hell not young!" the man refuted.

"Look, let me go get a nurse," the woman implored again.

"No, just sit here with me for a while. I'm actually feeling a little better since you came in."

"Great!" the woman smiled, obviously pleased. "If you feel up to eating, I brought some of the cheese and crackers you love so much."

"Maybe that would make me feel better. I haven't eaten much today. I just haven't felt like it, but I do love that cheese. How 'bout I pour us a glass of Chianti and we can play a game of Scrabble while we eat your delicious cheese?"

"Oh, Mr. Stanford, you do have a way with women," the woman joked.

"Nah, you just bring out the best in me. I wish I had met you fifty years ago," he stated boldly.

"Oh, you! You better watch it. I might just have to ditch my boyfriend!"

"I couldn't do you any good at this point, but I can kick your butt at Scrabble. Set up the board, and I'll pour the wine," he said with more energy than he'd had in days.

"OK, you're on!" the young woman said.

A short time later, the woman complained meekly, "Dang, you've won two in a row! You are really on your game today, Mr. Stanford."

"I told you that I could kick your butt," the man replied, smiling broadly.

"I'm just glad you're feeling better," the woman said, returning the smile.

"Best I've felt in three days," the man affirmed. "I think it must be either your company or that marvelous cheese you bring. Therefore, I am requesting that we continue with this therapy indefinitely," he suggested with a devilish smile.

"OK, but you gotta let me win a game occasionally," the woman pleaded.

"Like hell," the man laughed.

"OK, I gotta get. I'm glad you're feeling better. I'll see you in a few days."

"Thanks for coming by. I always look forward to your visits."

"I enjoy them, too. See ya soon," the woman said, turning to leave.

# CHAPTER 1

Destiny Lawson sat on the edge of the bleachers, leaning forward, obviously tense. "This makes me so nervous," she said to Bradley Jinswain without turning to look at him.

"He's got this," Bradley replied calmly.

The two were at Willow Creek Park on a sultry Saturday night in July, watching a friend's fourteen-year-old son play a travel baseball game.

"Steeeerike one," said the umpire as the catcher caught the inside pitch three inches off the plate.

Bogie stepped out of the batter's box and risked a disgusted glance at the umpire. He quickly surveyed the situation in front of him. It was the bottom of the sixth inning, and his team trailed 6–5. There were runners on second and third with one out.

"Let's go, batter," the umpire pressed.

As Bogie dug back into the box, he heard Bradley say, "C'mon kid. There's nobody better. Don't be an umpire. Be a hitter! Let's go! You're looking middle-away."

The pitcher delivered a ball in the dirt, and Bogie immediately held up his left hand, signaling the runner at third base to stay as he saw the catcher expertly block the ball with his chest. "Three balls, one strike," the umpire announced to the crowd.

"You sure that wasn't a strike, Blue?" Destiny asked sarcastically.

Ignoring the jab, the umpire instructed Bogie to get back into the batter's box.

"Your pitch right here," Bradley called out.

The pitcher delivered the pitch, an 80mph fastball. It was belt-high on the outside part of the plate, and Bogie unloaded on it, ripping it just inside the first base bag and down into the corner.

As the winning run from second base crosses the plate, Bogie's teammates mob him between first and second base. "Whoo! You rock! Hell yeah!" his teammates scream as they dogpile on top of Bogie.

The celebration finally ended as the coaches pulled the players off Bogie and gave him high-fives as he dusted himself off. "Way to stay disciplined, Kid. That was an awesome job of going with the pitch! I'm super proud of you! Now, get your stuff together, and I'll see you on the bleachers," Bogie's manager said.

After collecting his gear, Bogie sat on the bleachers with his teammates as the coaches discussed the good, bad, and ugly parts of the game. His excitement was palpable as he replayed the game-winning hit in his mind over and over. Bogie was so lost in his thoughts that he didn't hear the manager giving him accolades.

"Uh, Bogie, you with us?" the manager asked, smiling.

"What? Oh, yeah. Sorry, Coach. I was just, uh . . ." Bogie responded sheepishly.

"Yeah, I know what you were doing, and I don't blame you! Everybody in," the manager said. "Bogie, you count it down."

As the players all put one hand on top of another, Bogie screamed, "Who are we?"

"Eagles!" the players responded.

"Who are we?" Bogie repeated louder.

"Eagles!" the team responded just as loudly.

"One, two, three . . . Go Eagles!" Bogie shouted at the top of his lungs.

As the players broke up and headed to their respective cars, Bogie saw Bradley and Destiny standing at the end of the bleachers.

"Great job, Honey," Destiny said, hugging Bogie.

"Uh, thanks," Bogie replied.

"Awesome job, Kid!" Bradley offered, extending a fist.

Bogie pounded the fist and said, "Thanks, Mr. Jinswain."

"That was a great job of hitting. You waited for the pitch that you could take the opposite way and then you drilled it! Your dad would be so proud!"

"Thanks. I just wish he was here to see it," he said, tears welling up in his eyes.

# CHAPTER 2

Jackson Montgomery thumbed idly through the myriad of channels on his television, not really focusing on anything on the screen. It was a Saturday night in late July, and he was exhausted from a day of yard work and car washing. Earlier, he had ordered a pizza from Stefano's, driven down to Cumberland Avenue to pick it up, and finally made his way sluggishly home to eat in solitude. After downing two Sweetwater 420s, he sat in a vegetative state in his recliner, flipping blindly through the channels.

With eyes growing heavy, he vaguely recalled seeing a baseball game on the previous channel. Switching back, he found the Rockies hosting the world-champion Red Sox in an interleague game. While not an avid baseball fan, Jackson decided to settle on the game as opposed to old re-runs of *What's My Line* or the latest episode of *Love It or List It*.

As the game went to a commercial in the bottom of the fifth inning, a picture of the Rocky Mountains appeared on the screen. It triggered something in Jackson's exhausted brain, and he called his son, Cody, who lived in Wyoming.

Listening to the phone ring in his ear, Jackson realized he hadn't talked to Cody in almost a month. Cody and his fiancée, Sandy, were expecting their first child in three weeks or so, and Jackson mentally chastised himself for not keeping in touch with Cody and Sandy better. He just couldn't seem to get his shit together since his wife, Madeline, committed suicide last October.

"Hello," Cody finally answered breathlessly.

"Hey, Bud. How's it going?"

"Oh, great, Dad. I was just helping Sandy with her Kegel exercises," Cody responded.

"Uh, sorry. I didn't mean to interrupt anything," Jackson said bashfully. "I thought Kegel exercises were to strengthen the vagina," he added slowly.

"Yep, they are. Sandy lets me help her out sometimes," Cody told him. "Actually, it's about the only time I even get to see her 'down there', anymore," Cody added jokingly.

"I understand. When your mom was pregnant with you, she was sick for the entire nine months. I hardly even got to see her naked, much less help with anything 'down there'," Jackson said, laughing.

After chit-chatting about mostly inane subjects, Cody finally asked, "So, Dad, how are you really doing? Have you gotten back into the groove at work? Are you getting out of the house, or have you become a hermit?"

"I'm fine!" Jackson thundered, ire instantly rising. "I am not a hermit. I go to work every day. I work in the yard. I even played golf once this summer."

"Once?" Cody asked incredulously. "You used to play golf once a week with Marwin. Get back to that. You've got to be more active. You've gotten sedentary since—uh, over the last year or so. You, as a doctor, know the dangers of becoming sedentary."

"I am not sedentary!" Jackson said emphatically. "I get plenty of activity, but I don't play golf as much as I used to. As you know, Marwin is not here to play golf with anymore," he continued sadly.

"I know, Dad, and I hate that for you. I remember how much you enjoyed playing golf with him."

Changing the subject, Cody asked, "How's work these days?"

"Work kinda sucks, really," Jackson replied forlornly. "With Marwin gone, I have had to go back to prescribing all the medications for my patients."

"Well, that sounds rough, but isn't that what most doctors do every day?" Cody asked sarcastically.

"Bite me! I really became dependent on Marwin doing it, and I got out of practice, I guess. I never realized what a huge help he was all these years."

"Look, Dad, I gotta go. I will let you know how Sandy is progressing as we get closer to the due date. Please take care of yourself. We love you."

"I'm fine. Don't worry about me. You just take care of Sandy and get ready to take care of that new baby."

"I love you, too," Jackson added sadly after Cody disconnected.

# CHAPTER 3

"Thanks for the ride, Destiny," Bogie called over his shoulder, climbing out of the SUV.

"Anytime, Buddy," Destiny replied, turning off the vehicle. "I'll walk you in."

Bogie dug in his bat bag. "You don't have to. I have my key."

"I don't think your mom would be happy if I just dumped you on the curb. Come on. Let's get you inside."

The door to the simple split-level house opened just as Bogie was reaching for the knob. Bogie's mom, Lindsey, said, "Hey, Bud. How'd it go?"

"Great! We won, and I got the game-winning hit!" Bogie returned, already reliving the magical moment.

"Awesome! Way to go!"

Suddenly realizing that Destiny was still standing in the doorway, Lindsey said, "Thanks for taking him, Destiny."

"No problem. I enjoy baseball and love to watch him play," Destiny replied. "I'll be happy to take him anytime."

"Thanks, but I doubt that will be necessary," Lindsey said defensively. "I hate to miss his games, but with this deadline for my major project at work, I didn't feel like I could take three to four hours off."

Eyeing Lindsey, Destiny said, "I understand completely. Sometimes work just takes precedence."

"Nothing takes precedence over my children!" Lindsey returned fiercely.

"Whoa!" Destiny said, holding up her hands. "I wasn't implying anything. I just meant that I know how work can interfere with life sometimes. Again, I will be happy to help any way that I can, especially since Marwin isn't—"

"Thanks. I'm sorry," Lindsey said sadly. "I didn't mean to jump on you. You helped me out tonight, and I'm acting like a bitch. I don't know what's wrong with me."

Instantly softening, Destiny said, "Hey, it's OK. Is there anything I can do?"

Lindsey started to reply, but then just stared. Finally, she said, "No, I have a lot going on right now. Especially with Marwin being . . ." She trailed off. "I'll get it together sooner or later."

Noticing Lindsey's omission of Adam, her husband, Destiny wondered what had happened in Lindsey's life. She had her own problems to deal with, though, so Destiny offered, "Let me know if you need to talk or if I can help with the kids. I've come to really love your kids, you know."

Staring painfully at Destiny, Lindsey said, "I know. They love you, too." She put her hands on her hips and smiled. "I've got to get back to work. Thanks again for taking Bogie tonight."

"Sure. Good luck with your project," Destiny said as Lindsey closed the door.

# CHAPTER 4

Jackson's head slumped to his chest, and he jerked himself awake. Glancing blearily at the TV, he saw the baseball game had been replaced by the talking heads recounting the day's sports activities. He stood unsteadily on his feet and stumbled toward the stairs, preparing to ascend to his bedroom. Just as he turned the light out, his phone rang.

*Who in the hell is calling at this time of night?* he thought.

Glancing at his phone, he saw it was 12:14 a.m. He answered the phone warily.

"Hey, it's me," came the response.

"Helen? What's wrong?" he asked, now wide awake.

"Nothing," she said innocently. "Everything is fine. I just called to see how you are doing."

"At 12:15 in the morning? Bullshit. What's going on?"

"Well, actually, I saw your lights on, so I thought you might still be up."

"You saw my lights? How?" Jackson asked, befuddled.

"I was out driving around, and I came by your house," Helen confessed.

"What are you doing driving around at this time of night? You need to . . . where are you exactly?" he inquired.

"Uh, parked in front of your house," she replied with a nervous giggle.

"What? Uh, well, do you want to come in?" Jackson asked stupidly.

"Oh, no, it's getting late," Helen said. "I should be heading home."

"Look, you're already here, and I'm already up, so you might as well come in and let me know what the hell is going on. I'll open the door for you."

"OK, but just for a few minutes." She smiled as she disconnected the call.

* * *

DESTINY'S CELL PHONE RANG just as she pulled to the curb in front of the two-story house which sat completely in the dark. A sense of worry spread over her beautiful face, and she answered the phone distractedly.

"Hey, Des. I was just making sure you got home OK," Bradley said.

"Uh, actually, I just pulled in," Destiny said, eyeing the dark windows of the house.

"Oh, I thought you would have already been home before now."

"I ended up staying at Lindsey's longer than I anticipated," she replied.

"Was there a problem?" he inquired.

"No, everything was fine. Look, I gotta go. I'll talk to you later. Thanks for coming to watch Bogie play. I know it meant a lot to him to have you there."

"No problem. He's a good kid with a great future in baseball if he'll work at it."

"You really think so?" Destiny asked, recalling Bradley's own short-lived career in the minor leagues.

"Yeah, I think so. If he doesn't get hurt or burnt out."

"Well, hopefully, he will put in the necessary work if it is something that's important to him. Thanks for checking on me. I'll talk to you later." Destiny ended the call, climbing out of the car and walking up the concrete path.

As she sorted through the keys on her keyring, the front door opened.

"It's about damned time!" Marwin Gelstone slurred.

# CHAPTER 5

"Hey, Baby. I thought you were in bed since all the lights were off," Destiny said, stepping up to kiss Marwin.

Marwin looked around uncertainly and discovered that the lights were, indeed, off. Swaying on his feet, Marwin lurched toward the wall and swiped his hand along it in search of the light switch. His hand, unfortunately, found only a framed picture of the kids which was dislodged from its hanger and plunged to the floor.

"Shit! Where the hell is the…" Marwin mumbled as Destiny reached past him and flipped on the switch.

Startled by the bright light, Marwin emitted another curse, then shuffled from the room, leaving Destiny in the doorway. Watching Marwin stumble toward the kitchen, Destiny closed and locked the front door, took a deep breath, and prepared to enter the battle she had been dreading for quite some time.

\* \* \*

"So, TELL ME WHAT in the hell you're doing driving around Knoxville at midnight," Jackson implored.

"Do you have any wine?" Helen asked, completely dodging the question.

"Uh, yeah, sure. Red or white?" Jackson replied, again looking at the clock.

"White would be great, thanks."

Jackson opened the bottle of Edna Valley Pinot Grigio and fetched a stemless wine glass from the bar. He handed the glass to Helen and returned the bottle to the fridge without pouring any for himself.

"Well?" he asked, watching Helen curiously.

Again dodging the inquiry, Helen said, "Pour yourself a glass. I'll be on the back deck."

Jackson stared, dumbfounded, as Helen exited the kitchen.

*Shit,* he thought. *Why does she always prance in here and order me around?* Grudgingly, Jackson poured himself a small dollop of wine and followed Helen out into the sultry July night.

Helen was perched on a lounge chair with her head tilted back, apparently staring into the heavens.

"OK, Helen, tell me what in the hell is going on," Jackson demanded.

"I love sitting under the stars," Helen replied, yet again refusing to answer Jackson. "It's incredible how many stars you can see and how far away they really are," she continued like a fascinated eight-year-old.

"Uh, yeah," Jackson stammered, wondering what was wrong with the Girl Friday from his office.

"Did you ever wish upon a star as a kid?" Helen asked, completely oblivious to Jackson's growing irritation. Not waiting for his answer, Helen continued, "We grew up out in the country, and my sister and I would catch fireflies and put them in a jar. We would sit in the pasture and watch the stars twinkle and the fireflies light up, talking girl-talk for hours. We dreamed of moving to the big city, marrying rich doctors, having a dozen kids, and living happily ever after."

"Helen, where is all of this going?" Jackson asked, almost pleading.

Helen glanced at Jackson and finally recognized his bewilderment. She pointed to the chair next to her lounge and said, "Come sit with me."

"I don't want to sit! I want to know what in the hell is going on," Jackson all but yelled.

A pained look crossed Helen's face. She sighed and said, "I need to talk to you, Jackson. I have to let you know what I'm feeling. Can you please just come and sit with me?"

Seeing the hurt on Helen's face, Jackson walked slowly over to the chair and sat beside her. Helen set her nearly empty wine glass down and took both of Jackson's hands in hers. She gazed into Jackson's face, backlit by the kitchen light, and said, "Let me have my say. Please don't interrupt me before I am done, or I may lose my nerve."

Jackson nodded numbly, wondering what was happening.

"My sister got an academic scholarship to Northwestern, ended up going to law school, met the man of her dreams, got married, and has two perfect children. Her husband is in real estate, and she practices corporate law. Her kids are on the honor roll every semester and both are sports stars in multiple sports. She couldn't have dreamed of a better scenario." Helen stopped and drained her wine glass, disappointed that it was already empty.

"Now, for me. My story is the antithesis of my sister's. My grades were mediocre, and I didn't know what I wanted to do, so I decided to go the community college route until I could figure things out.

"Well, I met this guy there who was a couple of years older than me, and he swept me off my feet. He doted on me and treated me like none ever had before. He was so sweet and attentive. I fell completely head-over-heels in love. We did everything together, and I thought he was 'the one'. He was starting med school in the fall, and I had just applied to nursing school. We planned to get an apartment together, and it looked like our lives were on the happily-ever-after trail."

Helen stopped again and reached for her wine glass, seeming to have forgotten that it was empty. Frowning, she returned the glass to the table and continued, "One day, near the end of summer, we were supposed to meet some friends at the lake for a get-together before school started again. I was working that day, so we drove separately. I got off work and drove to the lake, but when I got there, he wasn't there. No one had heard from him. This was thirty years ago, and neither one of us had a cell phone.

"At first, I didn't worry that much. I assumed he had car trouble and would be along shortly. But, after a couple more hours went by and he still wasn't there, I began to freak out. A friend of mine took me to look for him. We drove the route that we thought he would most likely have taken if he was coming from his apartment. We made it all the way back to his apartment and never saw any trace of him.

"By this time, I was completely frantic. I had never really been much of a worry wart, but that day I just knew that something was horribly wrong.

"I made my friend take me to the police station. When we arrived, I burst through the doors, ran to the first cop that I saw, and started babbling about my missing boyfriend. My friend came over and tried to help explain the situation to the cop as I was nearly incoherent. The cop eventually calmed me down enough to answer some questions. I gave him my boyfriend's name, address, car description, et cetera.

"As I gave the cop my boyfriend's name and description, a look crossed his face and he left, saying that he would be right back. My hysteria immediately returned, and by the time he came back with a second cop, I was freaking out again.

"The second cop was a detective and he informed me that my boyfriend had been killed in a jewelry store earlier that day. Apparently, he had been in the store when a kid came in and tried to rob the store. My boyfriend tried to wrestle the gun away from the kid, and it went off, killing my boyfriend.

"I remember going numb. My hands and feet were tingling, and my head was ringing. It was decades ago, but I can still remember it like it was yesterday."

"Oh my god, Helen. I'm so sorry. That's horrible!" Jackson said, immensely glad that Helen had made him pour himself some wine.

Looking into Jackson's eyes, Helen said, "Hush, let me finish. I'm almost done. I need to be able to get all of this out."

Jackson shuddered in spite of the sizzling July night and drained his wine, silently praying that Helen's tale wasn't about to get worse.

"The next several days were a blur," she went on. "There was a funeral that I can only vaguely remember, even now. I didn't go back to work. I didn't eat. I didn't sleep. I didn't even shower. I cried until there were no more tears.

"One day, about two weeks later, my boyfriend's mom and dad showed up at my house. I looked like hell, as you can imagine, and I didn't want to see them. I had no idea what to say to them.

"They sat on the couch and tried to make small talk. They looked worse than I did, and I felt so sorry for them. None of us knew what to say, but my boyfriend's father finally reached into his pocket and pulled out a small box. He held it out to me and told me that they wanted me to have it. Inside was a small diamond ring. My boyfriend had bought it right before he was killed. Apparently, he intended to propose to me that day at the lake, but he never got the chance," Helen finished, her voice trailing off.

Jackson was speechless as he watched Helen relive her long-ago nightmare. He suddenly realized that he didn't really know Helen, even though she had worked for him for the last eight years.

"Jesus," he finally whispered. "I, uh, don't know what to say. I'm so sorry," he offered miserably.

"I know. Me, too," Helen said sadly. "The rest of the story, as Paul Harvey said," Helen continued, showing her age in the reference, "is that I almost didn't go to nursing school. I ended up dropping out of college and became a hermit for the next couple of years. I worked odd jobs in fast food and grocery stores just to have enough money to help out at home. I experimented with drugs but, thank God, I didn't care for any of them. I didn't date or go out with another guy for over two years—I just couldn't. I was a *hot mess*, as young people say nowadays.

"My parents were sick with worry. They tried to get me into a church, but I wasn't much interested. They finally got a shrink for me to try to help me cope, but I had no interest in talking to a stranger about the crap in my life. I couldn't understand how God could be so cruel, and I didn't want to hear a bunch of psychobabble from the shrink.

"I stayed in a pathetic state until I received a visit from my boyfriend's mom, almost three years after his death. I hadn't seen her in forever. My boyfriend's parents had tried to keep in touch, but I had shunned them. I just couldn't deal with them. It was too painful. So, when she showed up one night, alone, I was shocked. I later found out that my mom had asked her to come to talk to me since nothing else had helped and my mom was getting desperate.

"Anyway, she basically told me to get my shit together and to start living again. She said that I was throwing away the life that I had dreamed of and that wasn't going to bring my boyfriend back. She told me that he would have been devastated to know that I was wasting my life. At first, she was calm, but eventually, she really let me have it!

"Of course, I was pissed and hurt that she was attacking me like that. I told her to get out, and I never wanted to hear from her again. After she left, I got into a screaming match with my mom, and I stormed out of the house. I drove around aimlessly for a long time before I realized that I was near a park that my boyfriend and I used to hike in. We would pack a backpack with sandwiches and wine or beer and find a secluded place to picnic. It was *our place.*

"I got out of my car and ran up the trail blindly until I was out of breath and exhausted. I wasn't thinking about where I was going or what I was doing. I finally saw a large rock that we used to picnic on, and I sat down, completely out of breath. The memories of all of our previous times together flooded over me, and I lost it.

"I cried until I couldn't cry anymore, and then I screamed. I screamed at my boyfriend, the punk who shot him, and God. When I was almost completely hysterical, I heard my name being called. I looked around wildly and there sat my boyfriend on the rock behind me. I was dumbfounded!

"He spoke so kindly to me with such love in his voice that I calmed down almost instantly. He told me that I had to go on with my life and not give up on my dreams. He said that I deserved to be happy and that he was sorry that he wouldn't be the one to spend his life with me, but that God had other plans. As I started toward where he was sitting, he told me that he would be watching me and that he loved me. Then he was gone."

Jackson stared at Helen, again speechless. Sensing that Jackson was beginning to question her sanity, Helen smiled and said, "I know, I don't believe in that shit either. I know he wasn't really there with me. I'm sure it was my subconscious projecting or something. It doesn't really matter, anyway. The main thing is that I had an epiphany.

"I drove home and told my parents that I was moving out and that I loved them. I even thanked Mom for contacting my boyfriend's mom. My parents began to protest, but I just slinked away to my room and went to bed. I slept like I had never slept before—or since—really. I woke with a clear vision of my life's plan.

"Unfortunately, everything didn't go exactly per my vision," Helen chuckled.

"I couldn't get into nursing school since I dropped out of college. So, I decided I could still help patients and be around medicine by working in a doctor's office.

"At first, I couldn't find a job. I did some candy striping in a nursing home and eventually saw an ad in the paper for a receptionist at the local practitioner's office. I applied, and even though I was young and had no medical experience, the old guy hired me. After six months or so, he realized my passion for medicine.

"One afternoon, after work, he handed me a piece of paper with a time, date, and location on it. When I asked him what it was for, he told me that it was my interview time with the dean of the local nursing school and that I had better not miss it since he put his butt on the line for me. The rest, as they say, is history." Helen sat back in her chair, exhausted, but obviously relieved.

After a moment, Jackson said, "I'm so glad that the old geezer gave you the job because you are the best nurse I have ever worked with. I guess people are right when they claim that everything works out the way it is intended. I never really subscribed to that theory, though." Jackson's face fell at the thought of his wife's suicide, just eight months prior.

Taking a deep breath, Helen said simply, "Well, everything didn't work out perfectly. I did get into the medical field and I love my job, but I never found Mr. Right.

"After I got my crap together, I started dating again. I even had two long-term relationships, but I bolted when the guys got serious. I couldn't make a big commitment. I never felt the guys were *the one*." Taking Jackson's face in her hands, Helen added, "Until now."

# CHAPTER 6

Destiny followed Marwin as he weaved his way toward the kitchen. Having better luck finding the light switch, Marwin turned on the lights and looked around, dazed. He finally spied the Rabbit Hole bottle and set off to pour another drink.

"Hey, why don't we go sit outside? It's a beautiful night," Destiny said, grabbing Marwin's hand before he could pour his drink and hoping to derail his drunken train.

"Sure, why don't you pour a drink, too?" Marwin replied, pulling his arm away and pouring the bourbon almost to the rim.

"Nah, it's late and I'm tired. I think I will take a raincheck. Thanks, though."

"OK, I'll just have one for you," Marwin said as he stumbled onto the deck. "So, how was the game?" Marwin slurred.

"It was awesome! The Eagles won and Bogie got the game-winning hit in the last inning."

"Atta, kid!" Marwin exclaimed.

"Bradley said that Bogie had a great at-bat. He thinks he has the potential to play college ball if he keeps working at it," Destiny told him.

"*Bradley?* What the hell was he doing at my son's baseball game with my girlfriend?" Marwin exploded.

"He was doing what his father should have been doing!" Destiny spat back, then instantly regretted it.

Marwin looked as if he had been slapped. "Really? You know I can't go out. I'm not—"

"You're not what?" Destiny fired back. "You're not able to leave the house? Who says? Certainly not your doctor. He gave you a clean bill of health a month ago."

"Does this look like a clean bill of health?" Marwin screamed, pointing above his ear at a six-inch-long scar on the side of his head.

Feeling a pang of guilt, Destiny quickly suppressed it and said, "That's a cosmetic scar. It didn't affect your brain, supposedly."

"I can't believe you!" Marwin yelled.

"Mar, wait," Destiny said, taking a deep breath. Before Marwin could speak again, Destiny continued, "I know you suffered a terrible trauma. I can't imagine what you went through. You were very lucky. You could have been killed. Fortunately, God spared you and I am so thankful that He did. I don't think I could live if something happened to you. However, with all that being said, you've got to get your life together. It's been over six months since Shoehorn tried to kill you. You aren't working. You aren't attending your kids' functions. You're drinking way too much. You aren't even gambling! You are a shell of your former self."

Taking a deep pull from his bourbon, Marwin scoffed, "You don't understand. You don't know shit about what happened in Shoehorn's office!"

"You're right. I don't know what it was like to almost die at the hands of a crazy doctor. But, I do know what it's like to watch the love of my life slip away from me. I'm scared, Mar. I need you. The kids need you, too."

Seeing tears glistening in Destiny's eyes rocked Marwin. He started to retort but suddenly stopped. Staring at Destiny, Marwin's hands trembled, and the glass slipped to the deck, shattering. Finally, Marwin emitted a low cry and said, "I'm scared, too, Des."

Marwin's pitiful condition removed all the vitriol from Destiny, and she engulfed him in her arms. "It's all right, Baby. Everything will be fine," she whispered against his chest.

Marwin said nothing. He clung to Destiny with all the strength he possessed and silently sobbed.

* * *

A SHORT TIME LATER, Marwin and Destiny sat in the study, each drinking a bottle of water. Destiny had cleaned up the broken glass on the deck. When she finished, she found Marwin talking on his cell phone. He had called his ex-wife, Lindsey, in hopes of talking to Bogie about the game. Lindsey immediately recognized Marwin's inebriated state and told Marwin that Bogie had already gone to bed.

"Look, Linds, I need to talk to him. I tried his phone, but he didn't answer. I know I've been drinking, but I also know that he isn't asleep at this time on a Saturday night," Marwin implored. "Please. It's really important."

Hearing the out-of-character desperation in Marwin's voice, Lindsey relented. "OK, hang on a second."

"Hello," Bogie said tentatively a moment later.

"Hey, Bud. How's it going?" Marwin asked.

"Uh, good, I guess," Bogie replied.

"Great. Destiny just told me that you guys won tonight and that you got the game-winning hit. That's awesome!"

"Yeah, it was pretty cool. I wish you could have seen it. Mr. Jinswain said that I did a great job of being patient and going with the pitch."

"I wish I could have seen it, too," Marwin said sadly. "You'll just have to do it again at the next game."

"You're gonna be at my next game?" Bogie asked hopefully.

"You betcha!" Marwin said, giving Destiny a wan smile.

"Really? That's awesome! I have a game Tuesday night at six. It's just against a scrub team, though."

"Hey, don't take anyone too lightly," Marwin admonished. "You know anyone can beat anyone else on any given day, especially if one team doesn't take it seriously."

"Yeah, I know, but these kids aren't nearly as good as we are," Bogie said cockily.

"You better check that attitude, Bud. Those 'scrubs' might just kick your butt."

"No chance," Bogie said, laughing.

The conversation soon lagged, and Bogie gave the phone back to Lindsey. "Thanks, Linds, I really appreciate you letting me talk to him. I'll see you tomorrow night."

"No problem, but Marwin, you've got to get your crap together. Everyone is really starting to worry about you. The kids are very concerned."

"I know, I know. I need to get it together. I've already heard how I am becoming a loser," Marwin snapped, looking at Destiny.

"That's not what I said, Marwin," Lindsey replied.

"Yeah, OK. I'll see you tomorrow night. Thanks, again," Marwin said, tiredly disconnecting the call.

"I never said you were a *loser*," Destiny stated, turning to face Marwin. "I said you need to get your shit together. We are all just worried about you, Honey. There is no need to take it out on Lindsey. She is just concerned about you."

"Jesus, is this gang up on Marwin day? Neither of you knows what it's like to almost die! No one was there except me. When Shoehorn tied me up and placed that pillow over my head, all that I could think of was that I had failed *you*. I was scared that I would never hold you in my arms again or see my kids again. I thrashed with all my might and there was this searing pain in my head and then just blackness," Marwin said, voice shaking. "I know it sounds crazy, but I'm scared," he added, slumping down on the couch.

Destiny sat beside Marwin and placed her arm around his shoulder, trying to pull him to her. Marwin tried to resist and pull away, but Destiny whispered, "Don't. Come here."

Marwin slumped over and rested his head on Destiny's shoulder. Stroking his hair, Destiny continued in a whisper, "I'm sorry, Honey. You're right. No one knows what you went through. We are all here for you and love you. We'll do whatever it takes to get you back on your feet."

The two remained in their embrace until the alcohol, fight, emotions, and events of the last six months overwhelmed Marwin and he snored softly against Destiny's chest.

# CHAPTER 7

Marwin awoke to the sound of running water. He opened his eyes and was surprised to see he was on the couch in his study.

He sat up, and his head immediately exploded as if the hangover had been biding its time until he was alert enough to experience the full force of it. He rose unsteadily and was rocked by waves of nausea and dizziness.

The events of the previous evening began to slowly penetrate his consciousness while his back muscles tried to unwind. As he tried to stretch, his lower abdomen sent a sharp pain through him and he doubled over, instantly bringing about another bout of dizziness.

Using the wall to steady himself, he walked toward the bathroom. Unable to stand erect and swaying in front of the toilet, Marwin thought it prudent to sit. As the urine drained slowly from his distended bladder, the pain receded from his abdomen.

Sitting with his elbows on his knees and his head in his hands, Marwin muttered, "Shit."

Having finally finished his extended bathroom visit, Marwin shuffled his way to the kitchen. Knowing that he had not set the automatic coffee maker the night before, he was surprised when the aroma of coffee penetrated his befuddled senses. As he poured the steaming beverage into his favorite UT mug with hands shaking like a wino in detox, Destiny's voice sounded from behind him.

"Good morning."

Turning, Marwin saw Destiny standing in the doorway dressed in a burgundy, terry-cloth bathrobe, knotted at the waist. Her hair was wrapped in a towel on her head.

Suddenly embarrassed by the events of the night before and his current state, Marwin looked down at the floor and said, "Morning."

"How're you feeling?" Destiny asked gleefully.

"Like I was shot at and missed and shit at and hit," Marwin replied with a groan.

"Uh-huh, that's what I figured," Destiny returned cheerfully.

Glancing at the clock on the microwave, Marwin saw it read 7:18 a.m. Realizing that Destiny had already taken a shower, he asked, "Why are you up so early on a Sunday morning?"

"Because church starts at 9:30, and I thought it might take you a little longer than normal this morning," she said, smiling.

"What? Uh, no, Des. I don't think I'm going to church today," Marwin said, trying to recall the last time he had gone there.

"Yes, you are," Destiny stated matter-of-factly. "Today is the first day of the next stage of your life, and you are going to start it in church."

The two sips of coffee along with the ten minutes in an upright position caused Marwin's stomach to turn over. He started gagging, setting the mug on the counter, and lurching back toward the bathroom.

Destiny followed and found him kneeling in front of the toilet with his arms on the toilet and his head resting on them. Wetting a washcloth with cold water, she instructed, "Hold this on your head and call me if you need me."

Marwin placed the cold cloth on his neck and silently prayed for his nausea to pass. When it appeared that his stomach's contents were going to remain in place, he rose on shaky legs and made his way back to the study. Just as he sat down and leaned his head back on the couch, trying to overcome another wave of nausea, Destiny appeared in the doorway and said, "Don't even think about sitting down. Go get in the shower."

"Des, I feel like shit. I need to throw up or die or something," Marwin complained.

"Well, go throw up, and then take a shower. I don't want to be late for church," Destiny said, her skill as a district attorney shining through as she turned away from him.

\* \* \*

"HELLO," JACKSON SAID GROGGILY, answering his cell phone. Seeing it was still completely dark outside, his heart rate kicked up immediately. The time on his phone read 4:37 a.m.

*Shit*, Jackson thought, his pulse continuing to climb.

"Dr. Montgomery, this is Ilene Kendrick from Forever Young. I'm sorry to disturb you at this hour, but your patient, Wilson Stanford, was just transferred to Fort Sanders Hospital. He was here in the infirmary earlier but went into cardiac arrest, so they called the ambulance. I knew you would want to be made aware of the situation."

Now, completely awake and relieved that it wasn't a family member in danger, Jackson's tachycardia started to abate. His brain processed the information and he said, "No problem, Ilene. I appreciate you letting me know. I'll head over to the hospital right away." Almost as an after-thought, he added, "Damn, this is the second patient this week."

"Yes, sir, I know," Ilene said sadly. "Hopefully, he will pull through. I know you lost a patient earlier this week."

"Thanks again for letting me know, Ilene," Jackson said before he hung up.

After pulling on a pair of khaki pants and a golf shirt, Jackson was suddenly weary. While his mind was wide awake, his fifty-five-year-old body was exhausted.

It was after 2 a.m. when Helen finally left. His mind had raced inces-santly, and he had been unable to go to sleep. The last time he remem-bered looking at his phone, it was 3:45 a.m. He apparently had drifted off only to be awakened by the call from the retirement home less than an hour later.

Jackson pulled on his brown Sperry shoes, grabbed his keys, and went quickly to the garage where his 2018 Mercedes convertible sat waiting. The garage door rose, and the pre-dawn Knoxville summer air rushed in, already near eighty degrees. Jackson rolled out of the garage with the top down in hopes that the wind would keep him awake on the twenty-minute drive to Fort Sanders.

*At least there will be no traffic at this time of night*, he thought as he headed toward I-40.

Traveling down Campbell Station Road and in search of something stronger than the wind to keep him awake, he saw a sign for Dunkin' Donuts. He whipped his car across two lanes and into the parking lot.

After ordering a black coffee, he drove mindlessly toward the hospital. His thoughts turned to the bizarre events of the previous night.

He hadn't known that Helen had suffered so much tragedy in her life. Even crazier was her confession of her desire for a personal relationship with him. He didn't know what to make of that. His wife had just died eight months ago, and he hadn't thought about another woman since. The fact that his son, Cody, had accused Helen of trying to move in on him immediately after his wife's death suggested that others must have been able to see Helen's intentions all along. Even the author of his wife's fake suicide note had insinuated that he was having an affair with Helen.

*Was I that blind?* he wondered. *Could she have exhibited signs of interest in the past?*

Before any answers came to him, Jackson pulled into the parking lot, and his mind changed over to his ill patient. Mr. Stanford was in his mid-seventies and had also recently become a widower. His wife had lost her battle with breast cancer, and he had decided to move into Forever Young. He seemed to have adjusted fairly well to his new life. Jackson had done his yearly physical two weeks ago, and he was in good health for a man of his age.

*Shows what doctors know*, Jackson thought as he entered the hospital.

* * *

"THANKS FOR COMING WITH me," Destiny said, entwining her fingers with Marwin's as they left the church.

"I didn't know I had a choice," Marwin joked.

"You didn't," Destiny said, smiling. "You feeling well enough to eat something?"

"You offering something?" Marwin asked with a leer.

"You perv. You must be feeling better. I meant food."

"Yep, food would be good. Nothing too adventurous, though. Maybe Jacks?"

"Sounds good. You think you are sober enough to drive now?" Destiny asked.

"Might still be over the legal limit, so I'll let you drive," Marwin replied as another wave of dizziness swept over him.

\* \* \*

JACKSON ENTERED THE EMERGENCY room at Fort Sanders Hospital and was able to locate his patient in the ICU quickly. Upon entering the room, Jackson saw a frail-looking man in obvious distress. Mr. Stanford's face was an ashy pale and his eyes were mostly sunken back into his skull. Quickly checking the monitors above the bed, Jackson noticed that Mr. Stanford's blood pressure was 212/105 and respirations were at 48. Intravenous fluids had been started in both hands, and multiple bags of fluids and medications were running into him.

"What's his status?" Jackson asked the attending physician at the patient's bedside.

Recognizing Jackson, the doctor replied, "Not great, I'm afraid. We still haven't been able to get his pressure down, as you can see. He coded on the way in. Stat labs showed elevated cardiac enzymes and the EKG confirmed the MI. His kidney function is also poor. They got him stabilized with hydralazine and labetalol, but then the blood pressure skyrocketed again. We just started the nitroprusside, but that hasn't had much effect either."

As the doctor finished explaining, the monitors began beeping loudly and the screen flashed red.

"Shit," the doctor said, turning away from Jackson.

Jackson glanced at the screen and saw the BP was now 250/128. Mr. Stanford jerked wildly in the bed, and his eyes rolled back in his head.

"He's seizing! I need 2mgs of Ativan, now!" the doctor shouted.

As the nurse pushed the Ativan into Mr. Stanford's IV, the monitor emitted a steady beep, and the EKG went flat. The doctor grabbed the defibrillator and shocked Mr. Stanford—once, twice, three times—but the monitor continued to show the flatline. They continued working on Mr. Stanford for another ten minutes before pronouncing him dead.

After thanking the doctor and the nurses for their efforts, Jackson walked slowly back to his car, overwhelmed by sadness.

# CHAPTER 8

Marwin and Destiny sat eating their subs, looking out at the light foot traffic on Seventeenth Street. In a little over a month, thousands of orange-clad students would be present. Today though, only a few were milling about on Sunday morning.

"Mmm, good call on lunch, Dr. Gelstone," Destiny said savoring her steamed steak and cheese sandwich.

"Yep, not bad," replied Marwin, enjoying his usual ham and smoked cheddar sub. He had eaten tentatively at first, trying to decide if his body was going to accept what he was offering. After a few shaky bites, his stomach relented, and Marwin was able to enjoy his food.

Marwin and Destiny made small talk while they ate, each intentionally avoiding the previous night's debacle. Finally, Marwin said, "I've been thinking, and you're right. I haven't been myself since the shooting. I've neglected the kids, my job, my friends, and most of all, you." After a brief pause, Marwin added, "I'm sorry."

Destiny felt a pang of guilt but quickly shook it off. "You should be sorry! We need you. I need you! I love you with all of my heart, but I can't be with the person that you've become."

"What do you mean?" Marwin asked, alarmed.

"I mean that I need *my* Marwin back," Destiny answered, looking directly at Marwin.

"OK, I-I will get it together, "Marwin stammered, fearful for their relationship.

"Honey, I know it was a terrible experience for you, but it's time to try to put it behind you. The good Lord spared you, so make the most of it and get back to living your life."

Encouraged by the softening of Destiny's words, Marwin said, "Let's call Jackson and see if he wants to come over for dinner tonight. I haven't talked to him in almost two weeks, so he might tell me to take a hike."

Smiling, Destiny said, "He might tell you worse than that."

"True, and it would be deserved," Marwin admitted. "Since we are trying to get back to the *old Marwin*, you wanna go back to the house and fool around? The kids won't be home until six tonight."

"Let's call Jackson and see about dinner first, you perv."

As Destiny drove toward West Knoxville, Marwin called Jackson. At first, the conversation was strained and somewhat awkward, but eventually, the two long-time friends and colleagues fell into their adolescent poormouthing.

After Marwin disconnected, Destiny asked, "What did he say?"

"He said he would bring the beer since beer goes with everything," Marwin answered, chuckling.

"Was he glad to hear from you?"

"I think so, but he sounded a little distracted, though. He seemed preoccupied with something, actually."

"He was probably just in shock from hearing from you," Destiny offered, only half-kidding.

"Bite me!" Marwin snapped.

"Maybe later, if you're lucky."

* * *

AFTER STOPPING AT KROGER where they picked up bison meat, bacon, cheese, buns, and a carton of red potato salad, Marwin and Destiny returned to his house. Marwin fried the bacon and sautéed some onions. He crumbled the bacon with the onions and added some extra sharp cheddar cheese and mixed all of it into the bison meat. He patted out six burgers and topped them with seasoning before covering them with plastic wrap and putting them in the fridge for later.

Destiny had turned on REO Speedwagon radio on Pandora and was busy slicing tomatoes and onions for the burgers. Marwin and Destiny sang along to Foreigner's *Cold as Ice* as Marwin came up behind her and nuzzled her neck. She tilted her head toward him, forcing him away, so he quickly changed sides and kissed the other side of her neck.

"Ooh, you better stop," Destiny advised but that only made him more insistent.

He continued to kiss her neck and throat, caressing her breasts through her sundress. "Did it work?" he asked in a whisper against her ear.

"Of course it worked," she replied breathlessly, referring to her hard nipples.

"So, I haven't lost my touch?" Marwin asked, spinning Destiny around.

Looking into her eyes, Marwin felt the raw desire that he hadn't seen in quite some time. Destiny's hunger caused him to immediately harden, and he pressed against her, kissing her deeply.

Destiny's tongue wrestled fiercely with Marwin's, and a soft moan escaped her throat. He lifted the dress over her head and quickly unsnapped her bra. He bent his head and suckled her left breast before licking southward, dropping to his knees.

He roughly pulled her panties down and put his tongue into her honey hole, licking ferociously. Grabbing her buttocks, Marwin plunged his tongue into her as far as it could go, causing Destiny to emit a guttural groan.

Pulling Marwin's head up, Destiny instructed, "Now!"

She pushed herself onto the island and scooted to the edge. Laying back, she spread her legs, sending him the ultimate invitation.

Marwin quickly disrobed and walked toward her, his bulging erection leading the way. He gave Destiny's mound one more tongue-lashing before inserting his throbbing member.

She immediately began thrusting to match his pace and was soon emitting more guttural sounds. As Destiny's rhythm increased even more,

Marwin suddenly felt the air begin to leak out of his member. Shocked, he held his breath and tried to concentrate, but the lack of circulating oxygen finished deflating Marwin, and he slipped limply out of Destiny.

At first, she was unaware of what had happened and continued to try to finish. Finally, she recognized the situation and looked up at Marwin.

"I'm sorry," he said sheepishly. "Let me finish you." He dropped his head between her legs.

"No," she said softly, pulling his head up.

"Please," Marwin implored, trying one more time to get back between her legs.

"Come here," Destiny instructed, holding her arms out to Marwin.

Marwin couldn't look at her as he stepped miserably into her arms. "I'm sorry. I don't know what happened."

"Shhh, just hold me. There is nothing to be sorry for."

Marwin laid his head on Destiny's shoulder and tried to murmur more apologies. Destiny ignored them and clung tightly to him. Finally, she said simply, "I love you."

Hearing those magic words, Marwin's spirits lifted, even though his member didn't. "I love you, too, Des."

"Good, now let me down. This granite is cold on my ass!"

* * *

MARWIN AND DESTINY SPENT the rest of the afternoon listening to music and talking idly. Every time that Marwin passed by Destiny, he reached out to touch her. He grazed his fingers across her arms, hips, and butt, and told her that he loved her.

His over-attentiveness eventually grated on Destiny's nerves, and she said, "Stop touching me!"

"I can't help it. I've missed you."

"Well, I've missed you, too, but you're wearing my skin off."

"I'm sorry. I seem to be screwing everything up today. Except you," he added sadly.

"Stop it," she said. "You haven't screwed up anything. I'm glad you like to touch me, just try to do it a little less." She put her finger to her chin and smiled. "Maybe we can even pick up where we left off later."

"That sounds awesome! Hopefully, my friend will behave better the next time," Marwin said, glancing in the direction of the offending member.

"Your friend behaved just fine," Destiny said as the doorbell chimed. "Sounds like Jackson is here."

Jackson entered the kitchen carrying a 12-pack of Sweetwater IPA and a bottle of Edna Valley Pinot Grigio. "Hey, good looking," he said to Destiny, giving her a quick hug.

"Oh, hey yourself," replied Marwin. "Nice of you to notice my outfit," he continued, referring to his Hawaiian shirt and white shorts.

"Hey, Marwin. I didn't even know you were here," Jackson replied with a straight face.

"Bite me!" Marwin snapped playfully.

"I hope you've got something better than that for dinner," Jackson responded.

The three friends grabbed drinks and Destiny's iPhone and headed out to the back deck. While the afternoon temperature was near ninety, the deck was comfortably shaded by large oak trees.

As Marwin sang along to .38 Special's *Fantasy Girl*, Jackson said, "Destiny, can you please put on some good country music so Elvis over there won't be able to sing along?"

"My singing happens to turn Destiny on," Marwin quipped.

"Maybe so, but it isn't doing anything for me, and the neighbor's dogs are starting to bark," Jackson shot back.

"Bite me!" Marwin suggested again. "You love it when I sing, right Baby?" he asked Destiny.

"Uh, yeah, but Jackson is right. I do hear some dogs barking," she giggled.

Before Marwin could respond, Jackson asked, "So, what are we eating tonight?"

"Buffalo burgers," Destiny told him.

Jackson nodded. "Sounds good."

"Well, technically, we are having *bison* burgers," Marwin chimed in.

"Whatever. Same thing," Jackson commented.

"No, bison and buffalo are not the same things," Marwin explained. "Bison have large humps on their shoulders and buffalo do not. They also have large beards and buffalo do not. Buffalo have large, long horns and bison have short, sharp-pointed ones."

Jackson cracked, "Of course. Thank you, Mr. Wikipedia."

"No problem. Anything else you would like to know?" Marwin asked with a grin.

"Yeah, I wanna know when you're getting off your ass and going back to work," Jackson replied.

"Why?" Marwin asked, alarmed. "Is something wrong? Is Sam not taking care of things?"

"Sam is great. I'm just afraid you are going to burn him out by making him work all these hours. He's working at the pharmacy, covering the nursing home, and doing some consults for me. I'm pretty sure he would appreciate some help. Plus, if you stay away much longer, you won't know anything anyway. You know, if you don't use it, you lose it."

Glancing at Destiny, Marwin said, "Don't I know it! Actually, I am going back to work full-time tomorrow, as it has recently been brought to my attention that I need to *get my shit together*."

"Really?" Jackson said. "There seems to be a lot of that going around lately. I was just told the same thing about myself by two different people."

"I guess we're just a couple of fuckups," Marwin opined.

Destiny intervened. "You guys are not fuckups. You are both wonderful men who have suffered terrible traumas in the last few months. If anyone can get their shit together, it would be you two. I have complete faith in both of you." Destiny hugged Jackson and reached for Marwin. Before they could embrace, her phone rang.

"Hey, Brad. What's up?"

"I was wondering when you would be able to go over some stuff for Shoehorn's case. The assistant DA, Simon, wants to get together with you, Marwin, and me as soon as possible since the trial is approaching soon. He just wants to make sure that we are all on the same page and ready to put that quack away."

"He mentioned that to me on Friday." Glancing at Marwin, she said, "I'm with Marwin and Jackson right now. I'm sure they wouldn't mind if we got together here tonight."

Marwin nodded and pointed to the grill, and Destiny took that as her cue to further extend the invitation. "Why don't you guys come over for burgers around 5:30?"

"OK, that would be great. Let me check with Simon, and I'll let you know shortly."

"Is Brad coming over for dinner?" Marwin asked after Destiny hung up.

"Possibly. Simon McKinney, the assistant DA in charge of Shoehorn's case, wants to meet with us to make sure we're ready for the trial."

At the mention of the upcoming trial, Marwin's pulse immediately jumped. "Oh, I thought it was just Brad. I didn't know someone else would be with him."

"Does it matter?" Destiny inquired, irritated for seemingly no reason.

"We might not have enough food," Marwin said weakly.

"I doubt that. You always have enough food to feed an army."

"I like to eat," Marwin confessed.

"We can tell," Destiny replied, looking at Marwin's protruding belly.

"Hey, that's not nice!" Marwin complained.

"Sometimes, the truth hurts," Destiny said, dismissively. "I think you're just afraid to talk about the trial."

Marwin was surprised by her venom. "Bullshit!" he snapped. "I'm not afraid to talk about the trial. I can't wait to see that piece of shit put away for the rest of his miserable life."

"Great," Destiny said, smiling. "That's the Marwin that we all know and love."

# CHAPTER 9

"This is the one we've been looking for," Helen said to her niece as she unloaded the last box from the U-Haul truck.

"Thank God," Kristen Cantore replied with a tired smile. "I'm about beat."

"Let's get this last box inside and unloaded before Mr. Gatti's delivery person gets here with our pizza."

"Sounds good. I'll check the wine that I stuck in the freezer earlier." Frowning, Kristen said, "I have no idea where the glasses are. I guess they are in one of these *kitchen* boxes, but I have no idea which one."

"Never fear. This isn't Aunt Helen's first rodeo," Helen said, pulling a bag containing red plastic cups, paper plates, and paper towels from the front seat of the truck.

"Sweet! You rock, Aunt Helen."

Helen and Kristen sat on the faded paisley couch, using boxes for a table upon which to eat. As their energy ebbed with each passing minute and swallow of wine, Helen looked around the messy apartment and said, "You've got your work cut out for you."

"Yeah, but it's OK. School doesn't start until next month, so I should be able to get this place in shape."

"I'll come by tomorrow after work," Helen offered.

"You don't need to do that. You've done more than enough already. I can't begin to thank you, Aunt Helen."

"No thanks necessary, Honey. That's what family does," Helen said, smiling.

"Well, apparently, not all family," Kristen said glumly. "Mom and Dad should be moving me, but I guess their jobs are more important."

"Your mom and dad do have important jobs," Helen said, defending her sister and brother-in-law. "Your mom is in the middle of a huge tort suit."

"Yeah, she is always in the middle of something. She's never available when we really need her," Kristen stated sadly.

"Oh, Honey, that's not—" Helen started but changed her mind. "You're right, Kristen. Your mom and dad should be here helping you. I guess they have their priorities a little out of whack."

"Always, have," Kristen affirmed.

"Well, it's their loss. They missed out on this gourmet dinner that I prepared," Helen said with a laugh.

"Damn straight, Aunt Helen!" Kristen said, touching her cup to Helen's.

* * *

JACKSON, DESTINY, AND MARWIN spent the afternoon on the shaded deck, catching up. It was the first time that they had spent any appreciable time together since Marwin had gotten shot. Both Destiny and Jackson had tried to get Marwin to socialize more over the last couple of months, but each time he refused and crawled further back into his hole.

Marwin had become reclusive. He hadn't worked a full day since the shooting in April and had only consulted on a handful of cases over that same period. Marwin felt bad that his partner, Sam, had been stuck with all the work, but he just couldn't force himself back into the daily grind of pharmacy and all the people he had to see.

As Marwin reflected on the shooting and the terrible days that followed, Jackson said, "Uh, Earth to Marwin."

"What?" Marwin asked, confused.

"We've been talking to you for five minutes. I was afraid you had slipped into a coma."

"Sorry. I guess I was lost in my thoughts. What did you say?"

"I was just telling Destiny how I've lost three patients this summer that all appeared to be in good health," Jackson explained.

"It sounds to me like *you* might not want to go back to work, for your patient's sake," Marwin suggested with a grin.

Jackson seemed hurt. "I can't believe you're making jokes when I have lost three patients recently."

"You're right, there's nothing funny about people dying," Marwin conceded. "Sorry, my bad."

"Were these patients young or old?" Destiny asked.

"They were all between sixty and seventy-five years of age, but as I said, they were all in good health."

"I guess their numbers were just up," Marwin suggested.

"Undoubtedly," Jackson affirmed. "It just doesn't make sense. Three seemingly healthy males entering the final stage of their lives just drop dead without any apparent reason. I have numerous patients that are ill with various disorders, but these three were overall healthy. It makes me wonder if I might have missed something when I checked them over," Jackson said morosely.

"Maybe, but I doubt it," Marwin replied. "As they say, 'shit happens.'"

"Well, I feel much better after your philosophical words of wisdom," Jackson replied snidely.

"No problem." Marwin flashed another grin. "Glad I could help."

"Speaking of helping, do you think you could get your ass back to work and help Sam take care of my patients?"

"I just told you. I'm going back to work tomorrow," Marwin snapped. "You having trouble dosing your own patients since I have been gone?"

"Of course not!" Jackson said defensively. "I have been taking care of my patients since you were just a twinkle in your daddy's eye." He softened his tone, approaching the issue from a different angle. "It's just that I have more time to spend with my patients if you take care of all the medications. I really think it improves their care."

Shocked by Jackson's verbal acknowledgment, Marwin said, "I'm glad you think so because I do, too. I plan on being in bright and early tomorrow and will try to help Sam get caught up on everything. I can look through the consults that Sam did for you if you want."

"Nope, not necessary. I agreed with almost all of his plans and the ones that I saw differently, we discussed and are going to monitor the patients closely. I have as much confidence in Sam as I do in you."

"Uh, OK. Great," Marwin stammered. "Would you like for me to look over the charts of the three patients who passed recently?"

"I think they're all relatively simple, but sure," Jackson said, even though he wondered if he had missed something.

"OK, just have Helen email their charts to me, and I'll look at them first thing tomorrow."

Clapping Marwin on the shoulder, Jackson said, "Thanks, I really appreciate it."

"No problem," Marwin said easily. "I'll be right back. I think Brad and Simon are here."

Marwin returned a couple of minutes later, followed by Bradley and Simon McKinney. Each chose a beverage and settled onto the deck chairs, enjoying the late autumn afternoon.

"So, you want to discuss the shooting?" Marwin asked Simon abruptly.

"Yes, but we need to talk about the entire case, not just the shooting," Simon replied.

"Let me sum it up for you," Marwin snapped nervously. "Dr. Ernie Shoehorn caused several area women to commit suicide, including Jackson's wife, Madeline. Then, he tried to kill both Destiny and me. Brad's partner shot him, and now he's in jail. The end."

"Well, that was certainly succinct," Destiny said. "But, as the district attorney, I believe the jury will want just a few more details."

"Why? That's exactly what happened," Marwin barked.

"Take it easy, Mr. Gelstone," Simon said coolly. "You, Destiny, and Dr. Montgomery endured a terrible ordeal. I need you to be able to provide specific, clear details that will enable us to put Dr. Shoehorn away for the rest of his life. You are the only one who can provide all the information. I know it's painful to talk about, especially since you have been trying to learn to forget it, but we need to go through the entire thing to make sure we present an airtight case to the jury so that they have no choice but to convict Dr. Shoehorn."

Visibly shaken, Marwin protested, "You don't understand."

"Make me understand," Simon calmly challenged. "Plus, pretend I'm the jury and help me understand what he put you through."

Reaching for his beer but finding that he had traded it for a bottle of water, Marwin took a deep breath and relived his nightmare.

# CHAPTER 10

"Last October, your boss and I drove up to my family's cabin on Boone Lake. We went up on a Friday evening, intending to stay for a week or so. It's beautiful there in the fall, and we both needed some time away.

"We were awakened in the early morning hours on Saturday by a phone call from Jackson. He let us know that his wife, Madeline, had committed suicide the previous night.

"Of course, we were shocked and returned to Knoxville on Saturday afternoon. When we got back, we found Jackson in a terrible state. He was completely blindsided by his wife's death. They had been preparing to celebrate their twenty-fifth anniversary. Madeline was an active socialite in the Knoxville community and was in good health, so her suicide was hard to believe.

"The day after her death, Jackson received a call from Winston Browne, supposedly a reporter from the Sentinel. The man asked a lot of questions about Madeline's death and seemed to have information that the police hadn't released. Jackson reported it to the police, and they discovered that the Sentinel didn't have a reporter by that name. This caused the Knoxville PD to send Detective Bradley Jinswain out to look into the suicide. On the evening of the visitation at the funeral home, Jackson received a note in the mail."

Glancing painfully at Jackson, Marwin paused. Jackson gave a slight nod of his head and then turned away. After hesitating a little longer, Marwin finally continued, "The letter blamed Jackson for the suicide.

It implied that he was having an affair with his nurse, Helen, and he neglected Madeline's needs."

"This letter came in the mail?" Simon asked.

"Yes, it was in the stack of mail that Jackson pulled out of the mailbox that night." Pausing, Marwin added, "I'm not sure if it was post-marked or not, though. I guess someone could have just put it in Jackson's mailbox."

"The letter was mailed from East Knoxville," Bradley confirmed. "There were lots of fingerprints on the letter and envelope, but as expected, Madeline Montgomery's were not found."

"Meaning that she neither wrote nor mailed the letter, correct?" Simon inquired.

"That's what we determined, but she could have worn gloves," Bradley answered.

"Why would she try to hide her identity if it was her suicide note?" Simon asked, perplexed.

"We concluded that she wouldn't have," Bradley stated matter-of-factly. "I do have more information about the note, though."

"Just hold onto it for now, please. Let's allow Mr. Gelstone to finish his recollection of the events," Simon instructed, as if he was already in the courtroom.

"OK, after the note was found," Marwin picked up, "everyone was completely flabbergasted. No one believed that Madeline had written that note or that any of the details were true." He glanced at Jackson. After receiving a thin smile from Jackson, Marwin continued, "Because the suicide was so far-fetched, Destiny asked me to look into it."

Looking from Destiny to Marwin, Simon asked, "Why would she ask you to look into it? You're a pharmacist, not a detective. Why would the DA ask you to investigate a suicide?"

Immediately taking offense, Marwin snapped, "Because, I'm a drug expert. She thought that maybe some of Madeline's medications had contributed to her suicide."

"Again, I have to ask why?" Simon said.

Marwin scrubbed his face. "She was just grasping at straws, I think. As I said, the whole thing was crazy and didn't make any sense from the start. The imposter of a reporter called, along with the fake suicide note, and everyone was just looking for answers." Turning to look at Destiny, Marwin continued, "Destiny believes in me. She knew that I would find something if it was there to find."

"And did you?" Simon inquired as if Marwin was sitting on the witness stand.

"No, not really," Marwin stated glumly. "I found a bunch of herbal supplements and allergy medications in the bathroom. None of which would have contributed to her suicide. However, Jackson found a packet of the powder in her purse while he was looking for her checkbook."

"What kind of powder?" Simon asked.

Suddenly nervous, Marwin looked at Bradley. As if reading his thoughts, Bradley said, "It's cool, Marwin. All the official lab requests are in order."

Simon glanced from Marwin to Bradley and back again, obviously baffled.

"Uh, we went through some *unofficial* channels early in our investigation," Bradley admitted. "We might have skipped some of the processes to save time. I called in some favors."

Frowning, Simon studied Bradley for a moment and then asked, "So, what was in the powder?"

"Chlormethiazole," Marwin responded. "It's a sedative-hypnotic used to detox alcoholics in other countries. It isn't available in the United States."

"So, the lab found out it was a foreign sedative-hypnotic powder in Mrs. Montgomery's purse?" Simon asked, bewildered.

"Actually, I figured it out before the lab results came back," Marwin replied proudly. "The Knoxville lab couldn't identify the powder, so they sent it to the FBI lab in Langley, Virginia. While we were waiting on the results, I figured out what was in the powder. The lab later confirmed that I was right."

Simon raised his eyebrows. "Wait a minute. You mean you were able to come up with the name of a powder that is only available in other countries, and the Knoxville lab couldn't?"

"Yep," Marwin said, grinning.

"Please explain that, if you don't mind," Simon instructed.

"Well, as I said earlier, I'm a drug expert! I'm blessed with a great memory. Some people claim that it's eidetic, but I just think that I can remember what I want to."

"Anyway, while I was listening to Rock 104 one day, they were playing a block of songs by The Who, and the DJ was talking about Keith Moon, the incredible drummer that played with the band. Somehow, it triggered a memory from pharmacy school. We were told a story about Keith Moon and how he overdosed on the drug that they were trying to detox him with. That drug happened to be chlormethiazole."

"H-Hold on," Simon stammered. "How could you possibly think that was what was in the powder in her purse?"

"Because of the side effects that chlormethiazole produces. It causes severe allergies, sneezing, runny nose, watery eyes, and halitosis. When we went through Madeline's medicine cabinet, we found several different boxes of allergy medications and a couple of bottles of mouthwash. Jackson thought that she was suffering from an allergy to ragweed at the time and didn't think much about it."

Simon took a deep breath, and his voice rose as he spoke. "Still, there is no way that someone would think that a drug that is only available in foreign countries would be in the purse of a socialite in Knoxville, Tennessee, who abruptly committed suicide."

"Maybe," Marwin said nonchalantly. "But chlormethiazole has one more major side effect, and that is suicide, especially with the abrupt discontinuation of the drug."

"Wow! I'm impressed that you were able to piece together all of that given the circumstances," Simon admitted.

"It's what I do," Marwin said with a shrug.

"Well, why in the world did Madeline Montgomery have a packet of this strange drug in her purse?" Simon asked.

"Because her gynecologist, Dr. Ernie Shoehorn, gave it to her," Marwin explained.

"Why? Wouldn't he use an FDA-approved drug to treat her with?" Simon asked, befuddled.

"Because he was trying to kill her!" Jackson interjected vehemently.

Taken by surprise by the venom in Jackson's response, Simon looked from Marwin to Jackson and back again, obviously trying to decide the best way to proceed. Finally settling on Marwin, Simon asked, "Could he really kill her with that drug?"

Mindful of the pain the conversation inflicted on Jackson, Marwin took a long minute before responding. Eventually, he replied, "If he gave her a huge dose, it could have killed her, just like what happened to Keith Moon. However, a prominent socialite dying of an overdose from an unknown drug would have led to an autopsy and investigation. What Shoehorn did, and I have to give that asshole credit, was actually brilliant. He gave Madeline the chlormethiazole mixed with another drug that inhibited the breakdown of the chlormethiazole in the liver, thereby leading to excessive blood levels of the chlormethiazole. After several weeks, Shoehorn abruptly stopped the chlormethiazole and gave her another drug that rapidly removed the chlormethiazole from her system. This induced suicidal ideation and ultimately led to her taking her own life. Because it was a suicide, no one suspected that anyone else was involved. If not for his arrogance, he likely would have gotten away with it. In fact, I believe he has murdered several other patients in the same manner over the last couple of years."

"No, if not for your perseverance and extensive knowledge," Jackson said, "that son-of-a-bitch would have gotten away with it, just like he did with all those other women."

Marwin gave a small smile but said nothing.

"That is an incredible story," Simon remarked. After a long pause, he continued hesitantly, "I'm not going to sugarcoat things. It will be extremely difficult to get a jury to believe that Shoehorn intentionally set out to cause his patients to commit suicide. However, I believe we have a great shot at doing just that. Can you tell me how you went from discovering the contents of the packet to getting shot in Shoehorn's office?"

Marwin picked up the water bottle, again wishing for something stronger, and looked around for Destiny. At first, he didn't see her on the deck, but then she emerged from the door carrying a half-full tumbler of amber liquid. She handed him the glass and kissed him softly.

"You can do this," she whispered before returning to her chair.

Although he dreaded finishing his tale, Marwin smiled, overcome by the love spreading through him. "Thanks, Des," he said gratefully. "You're the best!"

"I know. That's what I've been told before," she replied playfully. "Get on with your story so you can start cooking. I'm starving."

Marwin grinned and took a small sip from his glass. He immediately felt the bourbon trace a trail to his belly. Bolstered by Destiny's support much more than the liquor, Marwin finished his story.

"Once we figured out what the powder was, we hypothesized that Shoehorn intentionally tried to induce Madeline to commit suicide. Jackson found a series of numbered dates in her calendar as well as multiple visits scheduled with Shoehorn over the previous four months. Jackson had not even known that Madeline was seeing Shoehorn. Apparently, she changed from her regular gynecologist over to Shoehorn based on a friend's recommendation.

"Anyway, Jackson confronted Shoehorn about Madeline's excessive visits, but he was unable to get any information out of the quack." He shot Jackson a sideways smile. "It may be because he tried to beat the shit out of him in Ruby Tuesdays."

Jackson held up his glass in a mock toast, acknowledging his role in the assault.

"Our hypothesis was far-fetched," Marwin said, "so we didn't officially go to the police. Bradley agreed to help us on the side, and we came up with a plan."

Pausing for a sip, Marwin continued, "I had several verbal encounters with Shoehorn when he called my pharmacy."

"What kind of verbal encounters?" Simon pressed.

"On several occasions, Dr. Shoehorn tried to prescribe incorrect dosages for some of his patients. When I tried to get him to correct them, he became arrogant and tried to force me to fill them as he had written them. He threatened to report me to the pharmacy board if I didn't fill them as he wanted. I ignored his threat and told him to spell my name correctly when he made his report to the board.

"The day after one of our verbal sparring sessions, I went to his office to ask him some questions about Madeline. As you can imagine, that didn't go very well. I certainly didn't get any information from him, but I did succeed in pissing him off.

"A short time later, Bradley, Jackson, Destiny, and I conspired to snare Shoehorn. We had Destiny make an appointment with Shoehorn and fake having menopausal symptoms."

"Menopause? Isn't she a little young for menopause?" Simon asked, looking at his boss.

"I'm a *lot* too young, thank you," Destiny snapped. "However, I have an acting background. I played Snow White in a play in kindergarten, so I figured I could fake it with a little help from Marwin and Jackson's coaching."

Simon chuckled and shook his head, wondering if this tale could get any stranger.

"On Destiny's first visit," Marwin resumed, "she told Shoehorn that we were lovers and that her symptoms were interfering with our sex life. Shoehorn felt her up under the guise of an exam and then gave her a bunch of vitamins to take.

"We sent her back a couple of weeks later for another visit. She told Shoehorn that I had proposed and that we were going to be married. She told him that her symptoms had gotten worse, and she was worried about not being able to have a healthy sex life. Shoehorn became enraged at Destiny for constantly talking about my pharmacy prowess as well as the great sex life we had before the onset of her symptoms.

"Destiny finally *begged* him to help her. He gave her more vitamins and also some packets that contained chlormethiazole with a very specific schedule as to how to take them."

"So, Shoehorn gave Destiny the same drugs that you propose he gave to Madeline to induce suicide?" Simon asked incredulously.

"Yep, exactly," Marwin confirmed. "That was exactly what we were hoping he would do. We finally had proof that he had given Madeline the drugs as well as the schedule in hopes of leading her to commit suicide.

"We still had some problems, though. We needed to prove that Madeline actually ingested the drugs, so we had her body exhumed. We had a hair analysis done, and it showed that she did, indeed, have chlormethiazole in her system. We were still wary that a jury wouldn't convict him of murder since it was under such bizarre circumstances.

"After the hair analysis confirmed that Madeline had chlormethiazole in her system, Bradley was able to get a warrant for me to wear a recording device. I paid the good doctor a surprise visit in hopes of getting him to talk about chlormethiazole. Bradley was outside listening in and was supposed to intervene if things went south. Unfortunately, he didn't make it in time, and Shoehorn tried to kill me."

Marwin's hand shook on the glass, but he steadied it. "He placed a pillow over my head and shot me, but fortunately, I thrashed and turned my head at just the right time, so the bullet only cut a superficial trench in the side of my head instead of blowing my brains out." Marwin sat back, visibly exhausted, his previous jolly demeanor now gone.

"Wow! It sounds like you are lucky to be alive," Simon commented.

"Absolutely," Marwin concurred.

"We're all lucky that he is alive," Destiny said, walking over and wrapping her arms around Marwin.

Marwin closed his eyes and allowed himself to be completely engulfed. Simon let the embrace play out naturally before saying, "Uh, OK, Detective Jinswain, could you take us through the events following Mr. Gelstone's shooting, please?"

"Sure," Bradley said. "My partner, Dan Jennings, and I were parked just down the street from Shoehorn's office. We were able to listen to Marwin's conversation. Everything was going as planned, but then Shoehorn pulled a gun on Marwin. We called for backup and ran to the office. We didn't wait for the elevator but took the stairs to the third floor, so it took a minute to get there."

"You sure you didn't stop to grab a beer?" Marwin asked.

Ignoring the jab, Bradley continued, "We crashed the front door and saw Shoehorn running out the back door. Jenkins took off after him, and I looked for Marwin. I found Marwin on a table with a pillow over his head, lying in a pool of blood. I called it in and tried to get the bleeding stopped. I stayed with Marwin until the ambulance got there and then went looking for Jenkins. I had heard over the radio that he was in pursuit on foot, so I took off after him.

"I found him two blocks over. Shoehorn was on the ground. He had been shot in the leg, and Dan was cuffing him when I arrived. Apparently, Shoehorn fired at Dan a couple of times, and Dan returned fire, hitting him in the leg. An ambulance transported Marwin to the hospital, and another one was dispatched for Shoehorn."

"OK, great," said Simon. "Thank you for those details. Earlier you said that you had some info regarding Mrs. Montgomery's suspected suicide note. Could you please share that with everyone along with any other ends that might need tying up?"

# CHAPTER 11

Kristen Cantore walked slowly, with no purpose at all, around the grounds of Windover Apartment Complex. The July heat had dissipated some, but the humidity was still as stifling as it was earlier in the day.

She and her aunt had finished the large Mr. Gatti's pizza and the bottle of pinot easily. Her aunt had left, and now it was up to her to straighten up the disaster that now served as her new home. Kristen had opened a box labeled "bedroom" in search of sheets to put on her bed, which her aunt had helped her assemble before she left. The box contained pillows and a comforter, but no sheets, so she opened another identically labeled box. This one contained a mixture of flip-flops, tennis shoes, and a vibrator that she had hastily shoved in and sealed up while her aunt was out of the room.

*Shit*, she thought, walking back to the kitchen.

She opened the refrigerator and seemed shocked to find it empty except for a lone bottle of Kendal Jackson Chardonnay. Wondering why she opened the fridge anyway, having just finished eating pizza, Kristen decided to open the wine and explore her new surroundings.

Pouring the Solo cup half full, she searched for her keys. After a couple of irritating moments, she located them under the pizza box on the bar.

Grabbing her keys and wine, she locked up and trudged down the stairs, immediately wondering why she was going anywhere but bed. Kristen meandered past the playground and picnic area and headed toward the pool which was still teeming with people on a hot afternoon. She watched as kids splashed, jumped, and screamed while parents sat reading and drinking, paying little or no attention.

Just past the pool, she found a path. With no idea where the path led, Kristen entered the narrow opening. The path was bordered by low shrubs intermixed with dogwood trees that would provide a great deal of shade during the day. The sounds of the pool soon faded, replaced by the chirping of crickets and cicadas.

Gnats swarmed around Kristen's head and mosquitos buzzed in her ears. Swatting the bugs and cursing, Kristen was ready to turn back when the path opened up to a large pond. Surveying the scene, Kristen saw a one-acre pond with benches spaced evenly around the edge at multiple locations. Two sets of picnic tables were visible, one at each end of the large pond. Posted signs warned swimmers to stay out of the pond and asked tenants to catch and release any fish they caught. The setting sun was glittering on the water, and Kristen marveled at what a beautiful, serene place she had stumbled upon.

She thought about her new life in Knoxville. She was excited to start nursing school at the University of Tennessee but was even happier to finally be on her own and out from under her self-absorbed parents. She silently wondered if they had even realized that she had moved out.

Kristen's daydream was interrupted by the sound of voices which startled her as the pond was devoid of people. Looking around, at first, she didn't see anyone. The sounds were emanating from the far end of the pond, and Kristen stared into the glittering water, finally seeing a young woman sitting in the shadows on a picnic table, talking on a cell phone.

The woman, spotting Kristen, motioned for her to join her. Having been raised in a big city, Kristen instantly stiffened and started to turn back to the path.

"Hey, it's all right. I won't bite you," the woman said across the pond. "I think we are neighbors."

Having not met any neighbors, Kristen backed away.

"Damn, do I look like an ax murderer or something?" the woman chuckled as she climbed off the picnic table and walked toward Kristen.

Kristen's pulse ticked up, and she prepared to run. She had been all-state in track in high school and was confident she could make it back to the pool area before the woman caught up to her.

Sensing Kristen was about to bolt, the woman stopped advancing and said, "Take it easy. We really are neighbors. I saw you moving your stuff in 2231-E earlier. I live right across the hall in 2231-F."

Bewildered, Kristen frantically tried to remember her apartment number as she backpedaled a few more steps, never taking her eyes off the woman smiling at her. Realizing that her apartment number was 2231-E, Kristen stopped retreating momentarily.

The woman seemed pleased that Kristen had stopped. "I didn't realize that I looked so threatening. Hell, I thought I looked kinda cute."

The woman's assessment of herself caused Kristen to really look closely at her for the first time. She appeared to be in her mid-twenties, about five feet, six inches tall. She had sandy-brown hair pulled back in a ponytail and wore running shorts and a tank top that barely contained her large breasts.

*Hell, she can't run with those breasts. They would knock her unconscious in the first fifty yards,* Kristen thought.

Noticing Kristen's body language, the woman advanced a little more and said, "My name is Polly, Polly Hampton."

"Hey, I'm Kristen, Kristen Cantore," Kristen answered nervously.

"Nice to meet you, Kristen," Polly said with a big smile.

"Uh, yeah. Nice to meet you, too," Kristen replied, relaxing more.

"This is my favorite place," Polly said, gesturing to the pond. "I come down here to enjoy some peace and quiet. Occasionally, someone is fishing or there might be a couple of teenage kids down here smoking pot, but usually it's just me and the bugs."

Somehow, her fear had made Kristen forget about the bugs, but now they returned with a vengeance, swarming around her head and getting into her eyes. "Well, I can see why you like it. It is beautiful and secluded. It would be a great place to relax."

"Yep, excepted for the damned bugs," Polly said, smashing a mosquito on her arm and leaving a bloody smear.

53

"Uh, I'm glad I had the chance to meet you, Polly, but I really need to be unloading boxes instead of drinking wine with the mosquitos, so I gotta get back."

"Ah, screw it. The boxes will be there tomorrow. Let's go back to my place and have another glass of wine, without the bugs," Polly suggested.

"Uh, I don't know," Kristen said, trying to make a logical excuse.

"Look, if you really wanted to unpack boxes, you wouldn't be out here wandering around," Polly observed. "I'll even come over in the morning and help you before I go to the retirement center."

"You work at a retirement home?"

"Yep, I work at a few of them in the area. Tomorrow, I have to go to Forever Young out on Chatman Highway."

"Wow, that's crazy! I'll be going to Forever Young as a student nurse on some nights and weekends."

"That is crazy!" Polly agreed. "Let's go get some wine, and I'll tell you all about Forever Young."

"OK, cool," Kristen said, her unpacked boxes completely forgotten.

* * *

BRADLEY SIPPED HIS DRINK and said, "We obtained a warrant for Shoehorn's house. We confiscated a home computer, a laptop, and a tablet. Our technicians found a deleted Word document of the suicide note on the laptop. The paper that the note was printed on matches the paper in Shoehorn's printer. Shoehorn had a laser printer, and the note was printed on a laser printer. I'm not sure if they have definitively shown that the note was printed on Shoehorn's printer, but I feel confident that they will. The note was mailed from a post office near Shoehorn's house but didn't contain any of his fingerprints. Of course, as previously noted, Madeline's prints weren't on it, either."

"Could the defense argue that someone else could have used Shoehorn's computer to write the note without his knowledge?" Marwin asked, suddenly going into Perry Mason mode.

"You've been reading too much John Grisham," Jackson remarked. "Any jury will know that he faked the note."

"Both of you are probably correct," Destiny interjected. "I'm sure the defense will argue that there is no proof that Shoehorn actually wrote the note or even had any knowledge of it. However, I agree that the jury will assume that he did write it."

"Put the bastard on the stand and ask him!" Marwin chimed in.

"We'll have to wait and see if the defense elects to put Shoehorn on the stand or not," Simon said. "Plus, someone who would induce suicide in his patients would have no trouble lying under oath."

"True," Marwin said, exhausted.

Seeing doubt and weariness engulf Marwin, Destiny said, "Relax, Baby. Simon is going to make sure that Shoehorn pays for everything he has done." Turning to Bradley, Destiny asked, "Were you able to prove that Shoehorn impersonated the reporter from the newspaper?"

"No, not yet. Honestly, I think that may be a dead end. We know the call was made from an old pay phone in East Knoxville, but there is no way to prove that Shoehorn actually made the call. Plus, impersonating the reporter doesn't prove that he tried to kill Madeline."

"Obviously, if he made that call so soon after her death, he would have had to have some knowledge of the suicide, though," Bradley said thoughtfully.

Glancing uneasily at Jackson, Destiny asked, "How did Shoehorn know that Madeline committed suicide? We know he was trying to induce it, but how did he know that she actually went through with it?"

"That's a good question," Bradley said.

"That's why I am the district attorney," Destiny said with a smile that quickly dropped away.

"Did she call Shoehorn that day?" Marwin asked gingerly.

"Why the fuck would she call that prick?" Jackson exploded before realizing the answer to his own question. "Oh, my god! She might have reached out to him for help. She should have called me if she was think-ing about killing herself. Jesus . . ."

Jackson's voice dissolved into sobs as he turned away from the group. Destiny was the first to react. She put her arm around his shoulder and tried to pull him to her. She fought his initial refusal until he finally slumped into her.

After a few awkward moments, Bradley said, "I'll check her cell phone and your home phone to see if she made any calls to Shoehorn over the last few days before her death."

Jackson stared numbly over Destiny's shoulder at Bradley and said, "Thanks."

Releasing Jackson with a comforting squeeze of her hand, Destiny said, "What about Shoehorn's office? Did you find his supply of chlormethiazole?"

"Actually, we did find a few packets with a white powder in them," Simon responded. "They have been sent to Langley for analysis. We are assuming that they contain chlormethiazole."

"Did you check all of his patient charts?" Marwin asked.

"Well, not the active patients, as doctor-patient confidentiality is an issue," Bradley explained. "However, we did pull the archived charts and are looking at the deceased patients for similarities to Mrs. Montgomery and Destiny's charts. That should be enough to bolster our case without having to fight the confidentiality mess."

"Maybe, but what if there are other patients out there right now who are receiving the same *treatment* as Madeline and Destiny? They could be contemplating suicide right now!" Marwin exclaimed.

Choosing his words slowly, Simon said, "Since Shoehorn has been in jail for three months, his patients haven't been seeing him. So, whatever was going to happen, likely has already happened."

"All the more reason to get those active charts," Marwin demanded. "There might still be someone who could be saved."

"Shit," Simon sighed.

"Marwin's right," Bradley said. "We need to check his active patients on the chance that someone is being treated with chlormethiazole and hasn't taken their own life. I'll get to work on the confidentiality hurdle and let you know what we can do."

"I say to just confiscate all his charts, now," Marwin reiterated. "Even if we can't use it against Shoehorn, we might save a patient."

"Settle down, Sherlock," Bradley admonished. "Let's see if we can do it the legal way before we start thinking about going rogue."

"We can't afford to take too long," Marwin reminded him.

"OK, I think we've covered most everything for now," Simon said. "I'm not going to lie to you guys, it will be a difficult conviction to acquire. I'm not sure that there is a precedent out there for a doctor inducing suicide. However, I feel like we may be able to send him away for the rest of his life!"

"You sure seem more confident than anyone else," Jackson said forlornly.

"I have an excellent mentor," Simon said, glancing at Destiny.

# CHAPTER 12

Kristen followed Polly into her apartment, which appeared to mirror her own, sans the boxes piled everywhere. Scanning the space, Kristen saw a black leather couch and loveseat bracketed by dark oak end tablets covered in glass.

A stunning painting hung over the leather couch. A grown woman in the fetal position appeared to be floating in the water, her long hair spread across the surface.

"Wow, that's an amazing picture," Kristen murmured.

"Thanks," Polly replied, obviously pleased that Kristen had noticed one of her prized possessions.

"Where did you get her?"

"I bought it in New York at a gallery. The artist is Robyn Chance, and she is amazing! I hope to be able to buy some more of her pieces soon, but they are all very expensive. This is all I could manage right now."

"How pricey, if you don't mind me asking?" Kristen asked, shocked at her own nosiness.

"I paid eight thousand for it last summer," Polly stated easily.

"Holy crap! That's a lot of money to just hang on your wall."

"It's only money," Polly said flippantly. "I plan on making plenty more."

"At Forever Young?" Kristen asked.

"Yeah, right now. I just meant with my company. We're still a new company, so we will be growing fast over the next several years. Since I started on the ground floor, so to speak, I hope I can ascend the big ladder as the company grows."

Polly pointed to the kitchen. "You ready for that glass of wine? I've also got some killer cheese that you'll love."

"Sure, I guess so. But only one glass, and then I've got to go," Kristen said without much conviction.

"Cool, I'll be right back. Make yourself at home where you ought to be," Polly joked.

Polly returned a few minutes later carrying a tray containing two wine glasses, a bottle of Edna Valley chardonnay, a plate with what looked like cheesecake, and a half loaf of French bread. "Take your pick of glasses and pour us some wine while I cut the bread and spread the cheese."

"Cheese? That looks more like cheesecake," Kristen noted, referring to the two-inch thick, pale-yellow slice resting on the plate.

"I know, right? It is actually a French cheese called Boursault. Here, taste this." Polly handed Kristen a piece of bread covered in creamy cheese.

"Oh, my god!" Kristen murmured, still chewing. "That's the best cheese I have ever tasted. Where did you get that from?"

"It comes from northern France. I originally brought some back when I visited with a friend, but I like it so much that I order it now and have it delivered."

"It's amazing," Kristen reaffirmed, marveling at Polly's apparent wealth.

"Eat all you want. I have plenty."

"Thanks, it really is delicious. I might have to order some of that for myself if it isn't too expensive."

"Oh, it's only money," Polly repeated gleefully. "You'll make plenty of it when you become a nurse."

"I sure hope so. I dream of being able to support myself and maybe travel and see the world one day."

The girls sipped wine and munched on the cheese, and the conversation eventually lagged. Kristen put down her empty wine glass.

"I need to get home," she said.

"Before you go, let me tell you what I do at the retirement centers and nursing homes," Polly offered. "Maybe you might be interested in working with our company one day after you get out of school."

"Shit," Kristen replied. "I'm just starting. I can't even think about finishing yet."

"It will fly by. Trust me. You'll be a registered nurse in no time and making the big bucks like me."

"So, you're an RN?" Kristen inquired.

"Nope, never had to go to nursing school. I started with this company shortly after I got out of high school."

"I don't understand. What exactly do you do?" Kristen asked, understandably confused.

"I'm basically a playmate for the residents," Polly answered cheerfully. "I visit, play games, and sometimes watch movies with them. A lot of the time, I just listen to them talk. Most of them are lonely. Many have lost their spouses, so they miss having someone to talk to or hang out with."

"Are you serious?" Kristen asked incredulously. "You get paid to babysit old people?"

"Basically, yes. I am a certified nursing assistant, so I make sure they are taking their meds correctly and that their vital signs are stable, but for the most part, I don't do anything related to nursing or patient care as you would think of it."

Now completely baffled, Kristen said, "No offense, but why would someone pay you to be a companion to residents in a nursing home? Who is footing the bill? No insurance company is going to pay for a babysitter."

"The homes actually have a contract with our company, so they pay us for the services."

"But that makes no sense since you aren't providing nursing services. The homes still have to pay the nurses and CNAs to care for the patients. I don't see what value the homes are getting from your company."

"We provide *very* valuable services!" Polly snapped, obviously offended. "Our residents are much happier than those residents in homes without our services, so they tend to live much longer, meaning more revenue for the homes. It's really a brilliant plan."

"Huh," Kristen said, trying to process the information. "Well, I guess it must work or your company wouldn't stay in business, much less be growing like you said."

"Yep, the owner of our company is really prescient. A true visionary!" Polly said proudly. "He is conducting research to document the value of our services."

"Damn, I wish I was smart enough to come up with something like that," Kristen lamented.

"I don't know all the details, but apparently, our owner was very close to his grandfather. After his grandmother passed away, his uncle put his grandfather in a nursing home and basically forgot about him. His parents seldom visited, and his uncle and aunt never went back after dropping him off. They just left him there to die. Obviously, his grandfather became very depressed and withered away. Our owner vowed to never let elderly people suffer the same circumstances."

"Wow," Kristen remarked, letting the idea sink in. "That is really cool."

"Yep, he fully believes he is making a difference in people's lives and that the facilities will see the financial benefits, too."

"Well, he might just be right. Look, I gotta go." Kristen rose from her seat. "Thanks for the wine and that amazing cheese. I'll see you later."

"No problem, it was nice to meet you. I'll come by tomorrow and help you unpack if you'd like."

"OK, that would be great! See you tomorrow."

# CHAPTER 14

Jackson had been exhausted when he returned from Marwin's house. He came home and trudged upstairs to his bedroom, got undressed, and crawled into bed.

He tried to resume reading the latest Dean Koontz book lying on his nightstand, but his eyes grew too heavy, and the book kept slipping out of his hands. He turned off the lamp and was asleep before his head settled all the way down onto the pillow.

He slept soundly until awakened by his bladder, so he stumbled into the bathroom to relieve himself and then ambled back. Glancing at the clock, he was shocked to see that it was only a little past midnight.

*Sweet,* he thought, elated that he had six more hours to sleep.

Snuggling down, he closed his eyes and was soon disappointed as he was unable to return to sleep. Apparently, his brain had flipped a switch while he was urinating, allowing all the previous few day's events to parade in front of his mind's eye.

Hearing Marwin recount the events surrounding Madeline's death was torturous. Her death was now almost a year prior, but the wound was as fresh as a knife slice. The fact that it was a fellow physician that had caused her to take her own life refused to let the wound heal. Jackson could not fathom what he would do if Shoehorn was found innocent of Madeline's murder. In fact, he didn't want to contemplate it.

Jackson's mind then turned to Helen and her profession of love for him. *What the hell am I supposed to do about that?* he thought.

Then he focused on Cody and the approaching birth of his first grandchild. Jackson had unexplained anxiety over the child's birth. Cody's wife, Sandy, was doing well, and everything was on track, according to the OB/GYN. The baby was growing at a normal rate, and all the genetic tests were negative. Still, Jackson couldn't shake the doomsday feeling. He supposed it was his years of experience as a physician and all the maladies that he had witnessed that were responsible for his feelings of dread.

Jackson's anxiety led him to the deaths of the seemingly healthy patients he had seen recently. At first, he was sure he hadn't missed anything, but doubt had crept in.

He tossed and turned in the bed. Each time he turned over, he saw a different face-Madeline, Shoehorn, Marwin, Destiny, Cody, Sandy, Helen. Each image rolled past like pictures in a Viewfinder.

"Shit!" he exclaimed to the empty bedroom as he got out of bed and trudged tiredly down the steps.

He turned on the television in his study and scrolled mindlessly. He stopped on the Weather Channel long enough to see that it was going to be another scorcher.

He finally settled on an old M.A.S.H. rerun. As Klinger petitioned for a Section Eight once again, Jackson slumped in his recliner, mentally and physically drained.

* * *

MARWIN ROLLED OVER AND switched off the alarm. It still had twelve minutes remaining before it sounded.

He had slept fitfully, at best. He tried to go to bed early in anticipation of his first day back at work but had been unable to sleep. His mind whirled with thoughts of Shoehorn, Madeline, and most of all, Destiny. She had laid her cards on the table and informed him in no uncertain terms that he had to get his shit together—sooner rather than later. His mind fashioned multiple excuses for his recent behavior but ultimately decided that Destiny was right. He had to straighten up before he lost the most important person in the world to him. Once Marwin settled on that realization, he spent the rest of his non-sleeping nighttime hours plotting out the steps to right his sinking ship.

His grandiose plans quickly vanquished sleep, and he spent the rest of the night picturing multiple scenarios where his life took an immediate Pollyanna turn while everyone lived happily ever after. He finally discarded most of that nonsense and worked on more realistic solutions.

He vowed to throw himself back into his pharmacy work and give Sam a break. He swore that he would be a better father to Bogie and Morgan before he lost them. Lastly, he committed to devoting his whole being to Destiny and asking her to marry him. For real this time. The struggle in his mind, while preventing sleep, did allow him to pursue a course of action.

Marwin jumped out of the bed with more energy than he felt and headed to the bathroom. Freshly showered, he grabbed a Tervis tumbler full of strong, black coffee and a plain bagel and headed off to work, full of hope and with a more positive attitude than he'd had in weeks.

Unfortunately, the eastbound morning traffic on I-40 quickly began to eat away at Marwin's mood. He switched the radio over to WIMZ and listened to the inane ramblings of John Boy and Billy before turning on Pandora. He scrolled through his stations and finally settled on Triumph Radio which was currently airing *Magic Power* by the station namesake. He sang along with Rik Emmett as he slowly inched eastward.

Trying hard not to let the concrete jungle squash his mood, he turned his mind to the week ahead. He planned to work every day this week and let Sam take some much-needed time off. Bogie had a game on Tuesday, so he needed to check with Sam to see if he could close that night. He also planned to have a special evening with Destiny when he could propose to her.

*Might not be the best time, right now,* he thought as he finally reached thirty miles per hour on the interstate. *Ah, screw it! I'm going to go for it.*

The gridlock eventually relented and Marwin arrived at the pharmacy shortly before eight o'clock. Although an hour later than he intended, he still had an hour before he had to open. Unlocking the door, he stepped inside and was greeted by the insistent beeping of the alarm.

As he turned toward the keypad, Marwin froze. He suddenly couldn't remember the code to disarm the alarm system.

*Shit,* he thought. *I'm gonna set the damned alarm off.*

His mind still perplexed, he punched in a four-digit code and cursed again when the alarm continued to beep. "That was your bank code, dumbass!" he chastised himself. "Think."

Just as he finally remembered the code, 4768, the siren exploded in the early morning air, causing Marwin to jump. "Damnit," Marwin muttered as he punched in the correct code, silencing the alarm.

As Marwin made his way to the office, the store phone rang. "Damn, people, it's barely eight o'clock," he grumbled to himself, his earlier jolly mood now almost completely gone.

"Community Pharmacy," Marwin answered.

"This is AT&T. We received a report of an alarm breach," a woman said.

"Yeah, I screwed up the code," Marwin said bashfully. "I haven't worked in a while, and I punched in the wrong code. When I finally remembered it, it was too late."

"What is your name, sir?" the woman asked.

"Marwin Gelstone. I'm the owner of the store."

"Mr. Gelstone, can you supply the emergency code word, please?"

"Pennywise," Marwin responded after another moment of panic.

"OK, thank you, Mr. Gelstone. Have a great day."

"Thank you, too. Sorry for the inconvenience," Marwin said, hanging up.

"What a way to start the day," he murmured, heading to his office.

# CHAPTER 15

"Checkmate!" proclaimed the young woman.

"Damnit, you beat me again. Are you sure that is checkmate?" Jill Jennings asked, exasperated.

"Yep, gotcha again, Jill," the woman said, smiling.

"I don't know why I get up this early just so you can kick my butt in chess. I could have stayed in bed and been dreaming about Tom Selleck."

"You would be dreaming, 'cause you couldn't do anything with Tom Selleck at your age," the woman joked.

"Such abuse," Jill replied. "Ah, hell, you're right. I'm way too old to do anything but dream anymore."

"Well, at least you still have your dreams. Hold on to those as long as you can," the woman advised. "I'll go make you a bagel while you clean up the board."

"OK, that's a deal," Jill said. "Did you happen to bring any of that fabulous cheese with you that you had the other day?"

"I sure did," the woman replied. "I'll spread some on your bagel after I get it toasted."

"Great. Would you mind putting a dollop of Baileys in my coffee this time? I need something to help me cope with my loss."

"Sure, no problem, but you should be used to losing to me by now," the woman joked.

"Ouch! That hurts," Jill said, feigning offense. "I'm glad the home pays for your services, and it doesn't come out of my pocket."

The woman toasted two everything bagels and poured a large shot of Baileys Irish Cream Liqueur into Jill's mug. Once the bagels were toasted, she removed two containers of the creamy cheese from her bag. Selecting one, she spread the cheese over a bagel. She washed the knife well and spread the cheese from the other container onto the second bagel. She immediately took a bite out of the bagel and then carried the two bagels and two bananas back into the small living room where Jill had just finished putting the chess set away.

"Here you go," the woman said, handing Jill the untouched bagel and a banana. "I'll be right back with your coffee."

"Don't forget the Baileys," Jill reminded her.

"Already got it loaded," the woman replied.

Returning with the liqueur-laden coffee and a black cup for herself, the woman said, "I have about fifteen more minutes before I have to go. Is there anything you need me to help you with or do for you?"

"No, Honey. I really do appreciate you coming by and sitting with an old lady. I hate to admit it, but I enjoy you kicking my butt in chess."

"Well, I really enjoy kicking your butt, too," the woman said, patting Jill on the shoulder. "I'll get your morning meds for you, and then I need to spread my good cheer down the road."

Taking the woman's hand in her own, Jill said, "We are so lucky to have you here. You really brighten our day. I don't know if all these old people would last very long if you didn't visit us. You are truly a bright spot in our darkening days."

"Thanks, but don't you start getting all sappy on me," the woman said. "Your days are plenty bright enough. If I have anything to say about it, you have many good years ahead of you and more butt-kickings at chess."

"I doubt I have that many years left. I'll be eighty-three in March. As for the butt-kickings, I'm gonna surprise you next time. Maybe a different foot will kick a different butt."

"You can certainly try," the woman returned, smiling. Holding out her hand, she continued, "Here's your Prozac, Tenormin, and meloxicam. Do you need anything else?"

"Actually, yes. Would you bring me a couple of Sudafed? This ragweed is killing me."

"Sure, be right back," the woman replied, a smile spreading across her face.

* * *

KRISTEN OPENED HER EYES slowly, momentarily unsure of where she was. Her view consisted of stacks of boxes, an empty pizza box, and a coffee table just inches from her face. Still confused, Kristen finally recalled that she had slept on the couch, too tired and drunk to make it to her sheet-less bed when she returned from Polly's the previous night.

As she became more oriented, she was aware of the insistent ringing of the doorbell. Standing unsteadily, she weaved toward the front door, catching her little toe on the edge of the couch.

"Shit!" she cursed, now hopping the rest of the way to the door. Kristen opened the door to find Polly holding two Starbucks cups and a bag.

"Good morning, Sunshine!" Poly said exuberantly before taking in Kristen's disheveled appearance. "I was beginning to wonder if you were dead. I've been ringing the bell for five minutes."

"Funny," Kristen grumbled, stepping back to allow Polly to enter.

"I brought breakfast," Polly said, holding out the bag and handing one of the cups over.

"Umm, that smells delicious," Kristen said, withdrawing a banana nut muffin from the bag.

"Eat some of the muffin first to get your blood sugar back up before you eat the breakfast sandwich," Polly instructed.

"What? Are you my mom?" Kristen asked testily.

"Nope, just trying to help with your hangover," Polly replied. "All that wine you drank last night drove your blood sugar down so that's why you're shaky and queasy with a headache this morning."

"I'm not hungover," Kristen protested weakly, stomach already souring.

"Eat," Polly pushed.

As Kristen grudgingly nibbled on the muffin, Polly moved boxes around based on the descriptions on the outside. "You weren't kidding. This place is a mess."

"Thanks for noticing," Kristen mumbled, mouth full of muffin.

"Anytime," Polly replied, smiling.

"I'll be right back."

"Going to go throw up?" Polly asked cheerfully.

"Maybe. I'm not sure yet," Kristen said. "But I *am* sure I need to pee, brush my teeth, and do something with this mop on my head. You don't have to wait on me, just put stuff wherever you want to. I'll find it one day and move it if I don't like it."

"OK, will do," Polly said, opening the first box.

* * *

DESTINY ROLLED OVER, STRETCHING languidly, awakening her muscles from top to bottom. Seeing that the clock read a little past six, she climbed out of bed. She felt more refreshed than she had in weeks.

Last night was the best she had slept in recent memory. Maybe going over the Shoehorn case and hearing Simon's determination allowed her to relax. Perhaps she was relieved because she had finally confronted Marwin about his recent behavior. Whatever the reason, she was grateful.

She padded to the window and raised the shade. Seeing the sun just breaking the horizon, she opened the window to allow the warm air to enter. As she watched the rapidly spreading daylight, she wrapped her arms around herself, silently wishing Marwin's arms were around her instead.

While Marwin had responded positively to her ultimatum and promised that he would get his life together post haste, she knew that their relationship still hung on the edge of an abyss. She closed her eyes and silently prayed that the Lord would hold Marwin and her together and allow them to have the life they longed for. Before ending her prayer, she thanked God for the life that he had provided for her. Realizing that she should have been thankful before she asked God for a favor, she begged for forgiveness and wondered if He was tired of humans with all their requests and so little of their service.

As she headed to the shower, she thought of calling Marwin but decided to surprise him at work later as she had nothing pressing at the office before noon.

# CHAPTER 16

Jackson awakened to a distant beeping sound, but he had no idea where it was coming from. Opening his eyes, he saw Laura Ingalls milking a cow on the farm.

*Which is worse, milking a cow or doing a prostate exam first thing in the morning?* he wondered as he rose slowly from his recliner, muscles protesting violently.

As he slowly walked toward the restroom, the beeping continued, no closer than before. *Shit, that's the alarm clock on my nightstand,* he thought, detouring toward the stairs. Reaching the base of the stairs, he smelled the aroma of coffee and detoured, yet again, toward the kitchen, temporarily ignoring the alarm and his bladder.

With a steaming mug in his hand, Jackson ascended to his room and killed the alarm, if only for today. He took his mug into the bathroom. He stepped into the large walk-in shower, allowing the hot water to pound his aching muscles.

As the water worked its magic on his body, his mind turned to Helen, and he wondered how he was supposed to act around her at work. Crazily, he wished Madeline was there to ask her what he should do.

*What the hell is wrong with you?* He asked himself. *If Madeline were here, I sure as hell wouldn't be asking her how to deal with Helen wanting a personal relationship with me! What a dumbass I am.*

Of course, if Madeline were here, Helen likely wouldn't have professed her love for him. Sadness settled over Jackson as he exited the shower.

"Oh, Madeline!" he wailed to the bathroom they'd once shared. "I miss you so much. I don't know how I can keep doing this. I'd give anything to have you back."

Jackson stood, dripping, and bowed his head before toweling off and getting dressed. He desperately fought the urge to crawl back into bed.

On his drive to the office, he played several scenarios for his first face-to-face interaction with Helen. Realizing that trying to play it out in his mind was pointless, he decided to call Cody and check on Sandy.

"Hello," came the groggy answer from fifteen hundred miles to the west.

"Hey, Bud. How's Sandy doing?" Jackson asked, oblivious to Cody's sleepy voice.

"Uh, she's fine, Dad. What's wrong?"

"Nothing's wrong. I was just checking on Sandy."

"She has her visit this morning, so I'll let you know what the doctor says. Of course, they don't open for four more hours."

"OK, let me know if she has dilated any," Jackson said, completely missing Cody's jab.

"Are you sure you're OK?" Cody asked.

Immediately, Jackson's thoughts turned to the fast-approaching meeting with Helen. There was no way he could mention Helen's confession to Cody. He already suspected Helen of trying to move in on Jackson.

*Shit. What am I gonna do?* he thought. *I don't want to lose Helen as my head nurse, but I don't have any personal feelings for her. Do I? Hell, I don't know what I feel anymore.*

"Dad? You still there?"

"Uh, yeah. I'm sorry, I was woolgathering there for a minute," Jackson replied weakly.

"Tell me what's going on!" Cody demanded.

"Nothing, Son. Everything is fine. I'm headed to work and just wanted to check on Sandy."

"Bullshit, Dad. You don't call at five-thirty in the morning just to check on Sandy. What's going on with you?"

"What?" Jackson stammered. "Oh, crap! I forgot about the time dif- ference. Did I wake you?"

"It's all good, Dad. Now, tell me what's wrong. It's not like you to be so distracted."

"I'm not distracted. I'm just anxious about Sandy and the baby," Jackson replied, realizing that he had just passed his exit off I-40. "Look, I gotta go. Let me know about Sandy after she sees her doctor this morning, please."

"Dad! What the hell is going on?" Cody virtually screamed.

"I'll talk to you later," Jackson replied, hanging up and leaving Cody perplexed.

* * *

MARWIN TURNED THE LIGHT on in his office and concluded that the office had been broken into by a neat freak.

"What the hell?" he asked aloud as his eyes roamed the normally cluttered office.

His desk was almost spotless. Usually, it was covered in papers, half- full Mountain Dew bottles, and at least two coffee cups containing black sludge. On the top of the desk lay only one group of file folders, arranged neatly in the corner, a keyboard, a flat-screen monitor, and a wireless mouse.

The two file cabinets that were normally littered with stacks of papers were clean. Opening the drawer of one of the cabinets, Marwin found an array of folders, each with a different color tab.

*What the hell?* he wondered again.

As he was about to investigate the folders, he heard the bell above the door tinkle, announcing a visitor. Sure that he had locked the door back after the alarm debacle, Marwin went quickly toward the front of the store.

"Hey, Marwin! I didn't know you were coming in today," Sam exclaimed.

"Yeah, I thought I would surprise you. I'm gonna try to be productive instead of being a worthless slug for a change."

Sam shook his head once. "Hey, you aren't worthless. You have every right to take as much time as necessary after what you went through."

"Yeah, well, it's time to get back at it," Marwin said, turning to the office.

"That's awesome!" Sam followed slowly behind.

"So, it looks like we had a hurricane come through and blow all my papers away," Marwin said lightly.

"Uh, no, all your stuff is here," Sam said shyly. "I just organized it a little."

"Yeah, *a little*," Marwin said laughing. "It looks great. I can't promise that it will stay this neat, but I appreciate you straightening up."

"Thanks." Sam visibly relaxed.

"I just want to know when you had time to do all of this with all the other stuff you had to do."

"I did most of it after hours on a couple of nights," Sam explained. "Actually, I had some help."

"Who helped you?" Marwin wanted to know.

"A friend of mine came by after I closed up, and we got everything organized and labeled."

"What's her name?" Marwin asked, grinning.

"Dawn," Sam answered, returning the smile.

"And who exactly is this *Dawn?*"

"She's a pharmacist at Bi-Lo. She's really sharp, too."

"I imagine she's hot, too?"

"Uh, yeah, she's hot!" Sam confirmed.

"I figured. Well, if you are going to violate HIPAA, it might as well be with a hot woman," Marwin joked.

"Uh, we didn't—shit. I didn't even think about HIPAA, Marwin."

"I don't blame you. HIPAA would be the last thing I would be thinking about if I had a hot woman in my office. Don't sweat it. I doubt that she would do anything with our patients' information, anyway. Please give her my thanks for cleaning up my mess. In fact, why don't you thank her properly over dinner tonight," Marwin suggested, handing Sam an envelope.

"Uh, I'm not sure that will work. It'll be after seven before I get out of here, and I am usually cooked by that time. What's this?" Sam asked, waving the envelope.

"It's a drop in the bucket for what I really owe you, but it's all you are getting right now," Marwin replied.

"I don't understand. You've been paying me, so you don't owe me anything."

"Bullshit. I owe you more than I will ever be able to pay back. Money won't replace all the time you lost here while I was at home having a pity party, but it probably won't hurt either."

Opening the envelope, Sam's eyes widened when he saw the check. "No, Marwin, I can't take this."

"You can and you will," Marwin said. "I really appreciate all you've done while I was out." He extended his right hand.

"I don't know what to say," Sam stammered, finally shaking Marwin's hand.

"Say 'thank you,' dumbass! That's what I would say if someone gave me a check for 10-k."

"Thank you," Sam said before adding, "Dumbass."

At this, Marwin burst out laughing. "You're welcome. Now get out there and get ready to retrain me."

\* \* \*

As MARWIN AND SAM readied the pharmacy, the phone rang. It was still five minutes before opening, but it was the back line, so Marwin answered, "Community Pharmacy."

"Well, I'll be damned," came the reply.

"Shouldn't you be checking a prostate or something?" Marwin asked Jackson.

"Not this early, I hope. I hate it when my day gets off to a shitty start," Jackson deadpanned.

"Nice."

"I was just calling to see if you actually dragged your ass out of the bed like you said you were going to," Jackson confessed.

"Yep, I'm here and ready to save lives and stamp out diseases."

"I hope Sam is there to help show you around," Jackson said.

"He's here, but I am sending him home after lunch."

"You sure about that? You will probably need a nap by lunchtime. Better have him stay until you wake up," Jackson suggested.

"Funny," Marwin countered. "I gotta go. My patients need me. Please don't tie up this line any longer. I have important business to conduct."

"Kinda early to be calling your bookie, isn't it?" Jackson said, laughing.

"Goodbye, Dr. Montgomery."

"Oh, Marwin?"

"What?

"I'm glad you're back," Jackson admitted.

* * *

THE MORNING STARTED AT a frenetic pace, and Marwin had to continually explain his past absence to his customers. Shortly after ten, the bell above the door tinkled, announcing a new arrival. Marwin looked over the shoulder of the lady he was talking to and saw Destiny. Her tanned skin glowed against her canary-colored dress, and a brilliant smile spread across her face as she locked eyes with him. Destiny walked slowly down the analgesic aisle and back up the cough and cold aisle while waiting for Marwin to finish with the lady.

"Good morning, ma'am. Is there anything that I can help you with?" Marwin asked, smiling.

Surprising Marwin, Destiny leaned across the counter and kissed him softly. "You already have," she said after breaking the kiss.

"Yeah, Jackson called to make sure I showed up, too. I guess you guys don't have much faith in me anymore."

"Au contraire, we all have faith in you," Destiny replied, her smile spreading to her eyes.

"Thanks, Des. I appreciate you kicking my ass. I needed it."

"No problem. That's what I'm here for. To give you what you need," Destiny said demurely.

"Not sure you can do anything right now, but I might let you know later exactly what I need," Marwin returned.

"I'm gonna hold you to that, Dr. Gelstone. Have a great day and I'll see you tonight."

As Destiny turned to leave, Marwin said, "Hey, Des? I love you."

"Love you, too," Destiny replied beaming.

Just after noon, Marwin finished counseling a patient and turned to his technician, Miranda. "What the hell is going on around here? That is the fourth or fifth time that I've filled scripts for gabapentin, hydrocodone, and Xanax and it is barely lunchtime."

"Yep, everyone seems to bring them in lately," Miranda agreed. "Dr. Foster, the internal med guy, had to leave his practice due to family issues, and a new doctor, Dr. Wisebaum, took over for him. He believes everyone needs to be loaded all the time."

"That's horseshit! Many of these patients are young with no history of neuropathy or diabetes. In fact, most of the diagnosis codes for the hydrocodone prescriptions just list chronic pain for the diagnosis. There can't be that many thirty-year-olds with chronic pain. This guy is a drug supplier!"

Miranda nodded. "It sure looks that way."

"Has Sam called this guy?" Marwin asked, irritated.

"Uh, I'm not really sure," Miranda said vaguely.

"OK, we need to call him and find out what the story is. We're not going to supply a bunch of dope to our patients."

"That's just it. Many of these are our regular patients who used to see Dr. Foster. This new guy comes in and starts giving them a bunch of crap," Miranda complained.

"I'm gonna talk to Sam, and we are going to stop this before it gets worse," Marwin asserted.

"This has been going on for a couple of months at least," Miranda offered hesitantly.

Marwin scanned the store and located Sam at a table measuring a patient's blood pressure. When he finished and returned to the pharmacy counter, Marwin said, "Sam, I need to talk to you, please."

"What's up?" Sam asked.

"Marwin, the phone is for you. It's Dr. Montgomery," Miranda called before Marwin could answer Sam.

"OK, thanks." Picking up the phone, Marwin said, "Que pasa?"

"I just called to see if Sam had you retrained yet. I need some info and didn't know if I needed to speak to Sam or if you could handle it." Jackson chuckled.

"I doubt there is anything you could ask me that I would need to get Sam for, but go ahead and we'll see," Marwin retorted.

"All right, Hotshot. I have a new patient that used to see Dr. Foster for his alcoholism. He said he had been controlled on Campral, but he stopped taking it for a few years because he had quit drinking and didn't need it any longer. He attended AA meetings and did well for several years until his son was killed in a plane crash, and he relapsed. He's back in AA, but he wants to start the Campral again, and I know nothing about it or how to use it."

"Well, you've called the right place," Marwin offered as his brain began to search for the obscure drug.

"I figured. Lay it on me," Jackson instructed.

As Marwin's brain tried unsuccessfully to retrieve the needed information, a pallor descended over his face. His ears buzzed, and his heart rate skyrocketed. Marwin rifled through the thousands of mental folders with increasing speed, a panic beginning to set in.

*Shit!* He thought. *I've drawn a blank. I can't remember anything at all about the drug!*

"Hello. Earth to Dr. Gelstone," Jackson said in his ear. "Did you go to lunch and forget me?"

"Uh, no, I'm still here. I just … I'm not … I can't seem to remember the drug," Marwin admitted pathetically.

"What? The great drug expert, Dr. Gelstone, can't remember a drug? Holy shit! Someone write this down," Jackson howled.

"Wait a minute, damnit! It'll come to me," Marwin protested.

"I'm glad I didn't ask you the dose of Ativan for someone in status epilepticus," Jackson said, obviously enjoying Marwin's struggle.

"Four milligrams IV. Repeat in ten to fifteen minutes, if necessary," Marwin immediately fired back. "But that doesn't answer your original question," Marwin added sadly.

"Hell, maybe I should have just asked Sam," Jackson said, pouring it on.

"I doubt he will know, but I will ask, "Marwin said. Turning to Sam, who had been watching the whole scene, Marwin asked, "Do you know anything about Campral and how to dose it?"

With no hesitation, Sam replied, "Sure, six hundred sixty-six milligrams three times a day with meals. It is only available as three hundred thirty-three milligram tablets, so the patient takes two tablets three times daily with a meal."

Marwin stared dumbly at Sam and then repeated the information to Jackson.

"Tell Sam that I appreciate it," Jackson said.

"Yeah, sure," Marwin replied dully.

Finally becoming aware of the impact on Marwin, Jackson offered, "Hey, Kid. Don't sweat it. No one's perfect. Even the best swing and miss occasionally."

Recalling the previous day and his erectile dysfunction, Marwin said, "Don't I know it. If you need anything else, just call Sam on his cell. I'm sending him home."

"Nah, I'll just call you if I need anything else today. No way you would miss two in a row," Jackson replied, trying to assuage Marwin's ego.

"Yeah, right," Marwin said, hanging up and wondering what had happened to him.

# CHAPTER 17

Jackson pulled his Mercedes into his garage, turned off the motor, and slumped heavily against the seat. On his drive home, he realized he hadn't laid anything out for dinner. No matter, really, as he didn't feel much like eating anyway.

What a shitty day! Helen acted as if nothing had happened over the weekend. She didn't mention her late-night visit to his house and subsequent profession of love for him. He, in turn, tiptoed around her all day as they both tried to ignore the elephant in the room. Their interaction, or lack thereof, was so awkward that he had trouble concentrating on his patients.

Initially, the second call he made to Marwin didn't have an impact on him. Usually, Marwin readily supplied pharmaceutical information, so he assumed that Marwin was just a little rusty and didn't have his brain fully engaged yet. However, upon reflection, he wondered if the extended time off and excessive drinking had affected Marwin's knowledge. Jackson immediately discounted that thought and turned his mind to the latest patient he had lost over the weekend.

Jackson had spent a half-hour with the patient's daughter, trying to explain why her father suddenly dropped dead. Ultimately, he fell back on the theory that her father's number came up. That had led to a tirade and questions as to why anyone would ever go to a doctor if they were just destined to die when God pulled their number. To that, Jackson hadn't been able to give a satisfactory answer.

The daughter had demanded an autopsy and seemed to imply that Jackson had missed something at her dad's last check-up. Jackson tried to assure her that her father was in good health for his age and that his death had shocked Jackson as much as anyone. Thinking of Marwin's offer to review the patient's chart, Jackson explained that he had already arranged for a peer review of the patient's chart. While that seemed to calm the man's daughter somewhat, Jackson felt bad for stretching the truth. Still, he was confident that he hadn't missed anything and that Marwin's review, while not exactly a peer review, would bear that out. The man's daughter had finally left, but not before intimating that litigation was still a possibility.

Jackson finally realized he was still sitting in his car in the garage as the engine softly ticked and the garage-door light extinguished. *Can't sit here all night,* he thought as he opened the door and walked slowly inside.

He placed his briefcase on the table and headed upstairs to change. His mind faintly registered the flashing red light on the answering machine as he passed his study.

After changing into gym shorts and an Under Armour tee shirt, he padded back downstairs, barefoot, in search of something to eat. His search of the fridge for anything meaningful was fruitless except for the Dogfish IPA. He opened the ale and took a long pull from it, closing the door in disgust. Moving to the pantry, he spied a bag of Cheetos, which appealed to him. Grabbing the unopened bag, he headed toward the study but detoured to the fridge for a second beer.

*No need to have to make another trip,* he reasoned. Jackson carried the beers and Cheetos to the study and sat down to listen to his messages.

The first message was from someone telling him that the warranty on his vehicle had expired. The second message was a hang-up. The third message was from Cody. Cody's voice made Jackson realize he had never talked to Cody after Sandy visited the doctor.

*Crap!* he thought. *How could I have forgotten about her visit? I wonder if I am developing early-onset dementia.*

"They said it's not really a big deal," Cody's voice said from the machine.

"Shit," Jackson muttered and rewound the message he had apparently missed while pondering his mental status.

"Hey, Dad, it's me. Just letting you know that Sandy's blood pressure was up this morning. It looks like she may be developing pre-eclampsia. They said it's not really a big deal, and they're monitoring her. She's on house arrest for now. She wasn't dilated or effaced, so she's still right on track. We just need to keep a check on her blood pressure. I love you, and I will talk to you later."

*"Damnit! I knew something was wrong,* Jackson thought irrationally. He dialed his son.

"Hey, Dad," Cody answered.

"Why didn't you call my cell or the office?" Jackson chastised.

"I didn't want to bother you at work. Sandy's fine. The baby's fine."

"How high was her blood pressure?"

"They took it several times, and it averaged about 170/95."

"Does she have edema? Swelling in her feet or legs?" Jackson asked, developing his own differential diagnosis.

"Well, she is pregnant, so she does have some swelling. It's a little more today than it has been, but it doesn't look excessive."

"Since when did you become a doctor? How about her urine? Is she spilling protein?"

"Uh, yep, she did have a significant amount of protein in her urine," Cody confirmed.

"Shit!" Jackson exclaimed. "They need to start her on meds right away."

"Relax, Dad. They started her on meds. We're monitoring her pressure, and I'm charting the readings for the doctor. I'll give them the report in the morning."

"If her pressure stays up, you take her to the emergency room," Jackson commanded.

"I will, Dad. I just took her pressure right before you called, and it was down to 135/82, so I think the meds are working just fine."

"OK, good," Jackson said, visibly relaxing. "Tell her that I love her. Keep me up to date if anything changes."

"I will. She loves you, too, Dad."

Jackson clicked off and fell back in the chair, completely drained.

* * *

"HAVE A GOOD NIGHT, Joe," Marwin said, clapping the last patient on the shoulder.

"Thanks for waiting on me, Marwin. I can't believe that I fell asleep this afternoon. Martha really needs her medicine, though, so I am grateful that you waited for me."

"No problem. I was going to be here late anyway."

"Oh, we are really glad you are back, too," Joe said and waved.

"Thanks, Joe. I'm glad to be back."

Marwin locked the door, turned off the main lights, and trudged to his office. His first day back was in the books. It had seemed impossibly long, and he was physically and mentally exhausted.

The day was eventful, though. He had discovered a new drug-supplying doctor had moved into the area and was pumping everyone full of opioids, gabapentin, and anxiety meds. He learned that Sam was becoming an excellent pharmacist. Not only had he kept the store afloat, but he had helped it prosper in Marwin's absence.

Unfortunately, he received a lesson in humility from the pharmacy gods. He was disgusted with his inability to give Jackson the information he needed. While he hadn't faltered on any of the other questions throughout the day, as far as he knew, his mind seemed slow, and the answers came grudgingly.

Once, Miranda had asked him for the brand name of phenelzine, and Marwin's mind was initially blank. Just as panic was returning, he blurted out, "Nardil." Miranda thanked him and didn't appear to notice how long it had taken him to answer. Or if she had noticed, she didn't let on.

Reflecting, Marwin realized he hadn't asked Miranda why she was inquiring about Nardil. It wasn't even used any longer. He knew they hadn't filled a prescription for it because he would have verified it.

Wondering if the pharmacy had any of the drug in stock, he walked to the shelf and searched for it. After several seconds, he finally spied a lone bottle of Nardil fifteen milligram tablets. He picked it up, and the label told him the bottle had been there for two years and was set to expire soon.

*Crap! We need a prescription for this before it expires,* he thought, returning the bottle to the shelf. Making a mental note to ask Miranda why she was interested in Nardil, Marwin returned to his office to check the consults that had come over that day.

Shuffling through the fax referrals, Marwin pulled out one from a gastroenterologist. After a quick scan, he decided that one required his immediate attention. It concerned a sixty-four-year-old male with a history of COPD and ulcers. The GI doc had done a breath test, and the man was positive for Helicobacter pylori, the bacteria associated with causing ulcers.

The doctor had started the patient on a regimen of clarithromycin, amoxicillin, and omeprazole. His current med list included two inhalers for his COPD, Daliresp, and metoprolol. Four days after beginning the H.pylori regimen, the man's wife called and said he was suffering from severe diarrhea and headaches, and he refused to eat. He had lost five pounds in four days. She also stated that his normal bubbly disposition had disappeared, and he appeared depressed.

Marwin picked up the phone and dialed the number at the bottom of the referral.

"Mike Kingsly," a voice said.

"Hey, Mike. It's Marwin Gelstone. How's it going?"

"It's not going. I'm sitting in the middle of I-40, going nowhere fast. You got something for me?"

"Yes, sir. Your COPD patient you are treating for H. pylori is toxic on the Daliresp. The clarithromycin is inhibiting the metabolism of the Daliresp. Let's stop the clarithromycin and change it to azithromycin. Give him one gram daily for three days and have him continue taking the amoxicillin and omeprazole. His symptoms should improve, but it'll take a few days as Daliresp has an active metabolite with a long half-life."

"Damnit, I should have checked on the Daliresp, as I don't know much about it," Mike conceded.

"I understand completely," Marwin said.

"Thanks for helping and getting in touch with me tonight. I'll call in the new order while I'm sitting here doing nothing. I'll call the wife and let her know, too."

"All right. Let me know if this doesn't work or if I can do anything else for you," Marwin offered, hanging up, his earlier doubt dissipating like fog on an August morning.

# CHAPTER 18

"I can't believe it!" Kristen exclaimed. "I think this is the last box I need to unpack. I was sure I was going to be here all week unpacking this crap. Let me grab a shower, and I'll take you out for a beer and a burger. It's the least I can do after all of your help."

"I'd love to, but I have to go back to Forever Young," Polly said. "I have an appointment with a patient at five o'clock."

"OK," Kristen said, slightly dispirited. "Well, I owe you big time. Let me know when you're free, and we'll go. Since all my stuff is unpacked, I'd like to go out and explore the city. I need to map out the best route to school, too."

"Uh, you're gonna need more than one route. Traffic blows around here," Polly responded. "I tell you what, let me see this patient, and I'll come back and pick you up. We can ride around the city so you can get familiar with the areas that you will be in. We can stop by a couple of cool bars, too."

"Are you sure you'll feel like it?" Kristen asked.

"Sure. Sleep is overrated anyway." Polly laughed. "We can all sleep when we're dead."

"All right, cool. But I want to drive. I need to get familiar with the streets."

"Fine by me. You drive. I'll drink," Polly said as she left.

Kristen stacked up the last cardboard moving boxes and headed to the shower. As the water cascaded over her tired body, she exhaled heavily and smiled, thrilled that the next stage of her life was off to such a great start.

She had been extremely nervous when she left the comfort of her parents' house to travel hundreds of miles to a city where she only knew one person. The thought of living on her own was both exciting and terrifying.

She had been told that nursing school was very difficult. While she had always been a good student, the fear of failing and having to return to her parents' house was terrifying.

*No way in hell I'm going back there,* she thought.

Turning off the water and exiting the shower, Kristen's mind turned to Forever Young and her new job there. She had little or no experience with nursing or with old people in general. In fact, old people kind of creeped her out.

She hoped she could help Polly's company and pick up some extra cash if she could find the time. Money would be tight, as her nursing assistant job only paid ten dollars an hour. That wouldn't buy many groceries, much less many bottles of chardonnay. Having toweled off, she pulled on a lightweight peasant top and her favorite dress shorts. She decided to pour a small glass of wine and walk back down to the pond where she had met Polly.

* * *

As the woman drove down Mabry Hood Road, the late-afternoon sun threatened to blind her. Flipping the visor down, she squinted against the sun. Traffic was already heavy, and the lack of visual acuity was disconcerting.

The woman's cell phone chirped from the center console, and she instinctively glanced down. After she saw the text message and sender, a strange sense of excitement spread quickly through the woman. She looked up just in time to avoid rear-ending the car in front of her and whipped into the parking lot of a local insurance company. She put her car in park and left it idling. Grabbing her phone, she read the text message again.

*Check in ASAP*, the message read.

The woman dialed a long-distance number from memory as she was forbidden to store it in her contacts.

"Good afternoon," said a man's pleasant voice. "I appreciate your promptness. First, let me commend you on a job well done. Everything appears to have gone splendidly."

"Thank you, sir," the woman replied, beaming.

Ignoring her, the man continued, "Please, give me an update on the status of your current assignments."

"Yes, sir," the woman said, hoping her nervousness didn't travel across the airwaves. "I have two active assignments; the rest are still in the passive phase."

"I'm well aware of your assignments since I am the one who assigned them," the man snapped. "I need a status report. How are things progressing?"

"Oh, of course. I'm sorry," the woman stammered. "J.J. is progressing very nicely. She enjoys the food and developed allergies, so we have begun Sudafed therapy."

"Excellent! We will need this assignment completed before the end of the month. Please ensure that occurs," the man instructed.

"Of course. That should not be a problem."

"Your other assignment?" the man asked impatiently.

"That one, uh, is going a little slower," the woman confessed. "The patient doesn't enjoy the food. He won't even touch it."

"I see. Do I need to get someone else involved?" the man asked.

"No! I can handle it. I've already got a plan that I will be implementing tonight. Don't worry. I've got it under control."

The pretense of kindness disappeared, and the man stated, "You better have. I will not hesitate to remove you if necessary."

"You can count on me." The woman replied, but the line was already dead.

The woman dropped her iPhone on the center console and sat shakily against the seat. Trying to calm her nerves, she closed her eyes and took several deep breaths. After several moments, her heart rate decreased, and her head cleared. While she claimed to have an alternate plan for her assignment, in reality, she was stumped. Slipping her car back into gear, she hoped she had an epiphany soon.

\* \* \*

JACKSON SAT IN HIS RECLINER, head lolling to one side, in front of a television showing old reruns of game shows. A distant chiming caused him to stir, and he looked around, bewildered. The chiming resumed, and he realized someone was ringing his doorbell.

As he went to the front door, he glanced at the grandfather clock and noted that it was almost eleven o'clock at night. This caused his heart rate to shoot up, and his mind started to worry about bad news that would inevitably be on the other side of the door.

Looking through the peephole, Jackson spied Helen smiling sheepishly back at him. *Oh, shit, not again! I don't have it in me tonight,* he thought. He took a deep breath and opened the door.

"Hey, sorry it's so late," Helen began. "We need to talk." She strode past him and headed to the back porch.

"Uh, OK." Jackson followed her like a puppy.

The still-warm summer night greeted them, and Helen took the seat she had occupied just a few nights prior.

"Uh, would you like something?" Jackson offered.

"No, thanks, I'm good. Let me get this over with so we can both go to bed. Today was very uncomfortable at work for both of us. I didn't mean to mess things up, but I had to let you know how I feel about you."

Helen paused and looked into Jackson's eyes before continuing, "Maybe I shouldn't have said anything, but life is too short, and I'm not getting any younger, so I figured I might as well lay it all on the line. I love you, Jackson Montgomery."

Unsure of what to say, Jackson looked away, and the silence stretched out painfully. Finally, he murmured, "I know."

Helen offered nothing else. She just waited for Jackson to continue. Eventually, he did. "Helen, you have been my Girl Friday for eight years, and I don't know what I would do without you. I would never do anything to hurt you, and I certainly don't want to lose you, but I don't know if I can reciprocate your feelings."

Seeing the hurt in Helen's eyes, Jackson rushed on, "Madeline's death is still too fresh. I haven't thought about loving anyone else in over twenty-five years. I'm flattered that you are interested in me, but all this has caught me off-guard. I'm still trying to process losing the love of my life. I am not ready for anything new right now."

Now it was Helen's turn to let the silence drag out. After a moment, she said, "I understand, Dr. Montgomery. I will do my best to maintain a professional relationship at work and continue to run the office to the best of my ability. However, I will never come to you in this manner again. If you can process Madeline's death and decide that you can be interested in someone else, you will have to come to me." After a beat, Helen added, "Don't wait too long, though."

Helen got up and walked back into the house. "Don't bother," she called over her shoulder. "I'll show myself out."

Jackson sat, perplexed, as his mind searched for answers. Unable to find any solution, he said, "Shit!" to the mosquitos and crickets, who seemed unaffected by his plight. Rising, he ambled to bed and dreaded going to work in eight hours.

# CHAPTER 19

Marwin and Destiny sat on the back deck, each sipping a William Hill Pinot Grigio. Destiny had brought over a giant chicken salad, and Marwin heated some garlic knots for their fare. As the heat of the day slowly dissipated, they ate quietly, speaking infrequently, each happy to be gaining some degree of normalcy in their relationship.

"So, how'd your first day back go?" Destiny asked.

"Pretty well, I think. I don't think I killed anyone."

Marwin replayed his day in painstaking detail as Destiny listened, sipping her wine. She smiled at Marwin's returning enthusiasm.

"I knew you wouldn't miss a beat," she said when he finally finished recounting the day.

"Actually, I did miss a beat," Marwin replied morosely, enthusiasm suddenly gone.

"What happened?"

"I brain-locked," Marwin said simply.

After he told her about his inability to provide Jackson with information about a certain drug, Destiny grabbed his hand and said, "Don't sweat it. No one can know everything all the time."

"No one but me!" Marwin refuted loudly.

"I hate to break it to you, but you may just be human after all," Destiny poked lightly.

"Damn, I hope not," Marwin said, squeezing her hand.

Destiny smiled and leaned into Marwin, kissing him gently at first, then more passionately. The kiss increased in length and fervor before Bogie interrupted it.

"Um, sorry, Dad," Bogie said, slightly embarrassed.

"What's up, Bud?" Marwin asked easily.

"Uh, I was just wondering if you were, uh, gonna be able to come to my game tomorrow night?" Bogie stammered.

"Damn right! I'll be there," Marwin replied with his previous enthusiasm.

"Cool, it's a scrub team, so we should smoke 'em," Bogie asserted.

"Careful, talking like that can bite you in the butt. Never take any opponent lightly. You guys better give a hundred percent and not take the other team for granted."

"Ah, Dad. They suck. We'll kill them!"

"I hope so. What time do you need to be there?"

"I need to be at the batting cage at 4:30. The game starts at six. I can just catch a ride with PC," Bogie told him.

Bogie seemed unsure, and Marwin saw an opportunity to strengthen his relationship with his son. "You know, I'd love to watch during BP. Maybe I could drive you, PC, and anyone else that needs a ride."

"Really?" Bogie said excitedly. "That would be great! I'll text PC and MP and let them know that we'll pick them up. Thanks, Dad."

Feeling the happy energy from Bogie, Marwin turned to Destiny and said, "Thanks for smacking the shit out of me when I needed it."

\* \* \*

THE WOMAN KNOCKED ON the door of apartment 106 and waited to be invited in. When there was no response, she pounded on the door.

"Damn, why don't you knock the door down and come on in?" the grey-haired man said as he opened the door.

Non-plussed, the woman smiled and strode past the man into the living room of the small apartment. "Well, it took you long enough to answer the door," she chided. "I knocked so long, my knuckles are red."

"Oh, I guess I didn't hear you. I was in the bathroom getting ready."

The woman glanced at the man dressed in cotton slacks and a paisley button-up Oxford shirt with a pair of loafers. "Oh, looks like someone has a hot date!" she exclaimed.

"Damn right, I do, so I don't have time for you tonight," the man explained. "I'm going over to have dinner with Gladys. I think we are going to watch a movie, too."

"You taking one of your porno movies?" the woman joked.

"That's not a bad idea," the man returned.

"Well, it's your lucky day," the woman said, reaching into her bag.

"I hope it's gonna be my lucky night," the man admitted with a Cheshire grin.

She opened a plastic container and handed the man a small blue tablet.

"What's this?" he asked.

"It's a new supplement that I want you to start taking. It's crammed full of vitamins and minerals that will put some pep in your step."

"I already take a multivitamin every morning, so I don't need another one," the man replied, handing the tablet back to her and crossing his arms.

"I know you do, but this one is different. Try this one for two weeks, and if you don't see a difference, go back to your other one." She took a notepad from her bag and added, "I'll contact your doctor and let him know what you're doing."

"OK, whatever. I've gotta go. I can't afford to be late for anything at my age 'cause I never know how long I have," the man joked.

"You're not dying anytime soon," the woman assured him.

"What? Are you God now?" the man asked sarcastically.

The woman looked up from the notebook and said, "You never know. Here. Start taking the vitamin tonight, and then you can just take one every morning with your regular meds starting tomorrow. Have you already taken your evening meds?"

"Hell, no. I can't remember anything anymore," the man replied, disgusted.

"Let me go get them," the woman offered.

She returned with the man's pill box and handed it to him. "The morning doses of metoprolol and isosorbide are still in here, too."

"I told you. I can't remember shit."

"Well, maybe the new vitamin will help your memory, too," the woman suggested.

"I'm sure," the man scoffed. "Now, get out of here so I can take my drugs and get over to Gladys's apartment before she dies of old age."

"All right, all right. I'll see you Thursday."

"I can hardly wait," the man said, practically pushing the woman out the door.

* * *

MARWIN AWOKE TEN MINUTES before his alarm went off. After the requisite trip to the bathroom, he headed downstairs to get coffee.

Coffee in hand, he retrieved the morning edition of the Sentinel from the front porch. Glancing first left, then right, he couldn't locate the newspaper. As the first curse of the day was preparing to cross his lips, Marwin stepped on the paper lying directly in front of the door.

*Must have a new delivery boy,* he mused.

Taking the paper and coffee to the back porch, Marwin smiled as the first light of day appeared around him. He felt more refreshed and alive than he had in weeks. Maybe it was because he hadn't gotten hammered the night before. Maybe it was his return to work. Maybe it was his peaceful interaction with Bogie as opposed to the normal contentious one. Likely, it was the improved trajectory of his life and the resurrection of his relationship with Destiny.

Marwin recalled the period of time shortly after Madeline's death last year. He and Destiny had bickered and fought frequently. Luckily, that hadn't lasted very long as it made Marwin ill. He and Destiny had returned to normal until he decided to become a drunken recluse after Shoehorn tried to kill him.

*Thank God she didn't give up on my dumb ass*, he thought.

Marwin sat quietly, enjoying his coffee, paper unopened on his lap as the world continued to brighten around him. He listened to the birds communicate until the door opened, and Morgan bounded onto the deck.

"Morning, Dad," she said.

"Hey, Honey. What are you doing up so early?"

"Patrick's mom is taking us rafting today. I guess I am too excited to sleep."

"Rafting? I didn't know you were going rafting with Patrick," Marwin snapped.

"Yes, you do. Remember, you said it was OK last week?" Morgan said timidly.

"I did no such thing!" Marwin thundered but instantly wondered if he had permitted the outing.

"Dad! You told me I could go!" Morgan said, trying not to cry. "You can call Mom and ask her. She knows it's been planned for over a week."

He planned to tell her he didn't need to check with his ex-wife to confirm anything, but Marwin stopped and stared sadly at Morgan. Instead of a fiery retort, an apology suddenly escaped his lips, "I'm sorry, Honey. I guess I musta forgotten. It's fine. You can go. Bogie has a game at six, so we won't be home until close to nine."

"I know, Dad. Mom said I could spend the night with her tonight. She'll pick me up from Patrick's house when she gets off work. I thought you already knew that."

"Apparently, not," Marwin said sorrowfully. Smiling, he continued, "Have a great time! Just be careful. I'll see you tomorrow after work, and you can tell me all about it."

A smile burst onto Morgan's pretty face, and she hugged her dad fiercely. "Thanks, Dad." Pulling away, she continued, "I've got to go fix my hair and decide what swimsuit I'm going to wear."

"Make sure it is one that covers you up," Marwin instructed, smiling.

Marwin skimmed the paper, then headed upstairs to get ready for work. Passing through the kitchen, he left Bogie a note to mow the grass and take the garbage to the curb to be picked up.

Twenty minutes later, Marwin was out the door with a bagel and a second cup of coffee. Traffic was shockingly light, and he arrived at work an hour and a half before opening time.

He went straight to his office to handle the rest of the referrals from the previous day. After an hour of dosing calcium channel blockers, ACE inhibitors, and statins, Marwin hit the restroom and prepared to open.

Checking the clock, he decided to see if he could catch Dr. Wisebaum in the office. Marwin's pulse ticked up as he waited for someone to answer the phone. After pushing a series of numbers and drifting through several menus, he was prepared to leave a message when a voice surprised him, "Internal Medicine. This is Katie."

"Oh! Hey, Katie. It's Marwin Gelstone from Community Pharmacy. How are you this morning?"

"I'm good. How 'bout you?" Katie returned amicably.

"So far, so good, but it's early yet," Marwin replied, chuckling. "There's plenty of time for things to go in the toilet."

"Don't I know it," Katie said, joining Marwin in a laugh. "What can I do for you this morning, Marwin?"

"I'd like to talk to Dr. Wisebaum, so if you could leave a message for him to call me, that would be great."

"Sure. No problem. Is it concerning a specific patient?" Katie inquired.

"No, not really. I just thought I would introduce myself," Marwin said evasively. "I've been on, uh, leave for a few weeks and I have seen his name on several prescriptions since I got back. I just wanted to see if I could be of any help to him."

"Oh, OK. Gotcha. What's your number, Marwin? I'll leave a note for him to call you when he gets in."

Before Marwin could give Katie his number, she said, "Wait, he just walked in the door. Let me see if he has time for you right now."

The line switched to Katy Perry singing about kissing a girl, and then Katie cut back in, "Marwin? Hold on. Dr. Wisebaum will be right with you. Have a great day!"

"Thanks, Katie. You, too." Marwin said, his pulse increasing a few more beats in preparation for the upcoming battle.

While on hold, Katy Perry was replaced by Kelsea Ballerini, singing about the first time on WIVK. Marwin added the choice of music to the list of reasons not to like this doctor.

"Who listens to this crap?" he wondered aloud as the other end of the phone came to life.

"Well, I'm more partial to older country music than I am to today's country," a smooth male voice said with a small laugh. "Today's country isn't really country music. It's just pop music if you ask me."

Startled by the conversation, Marwin stammered, "Uh, I'm not really into anything but rock and roll."

"You must mean before 1990, then," the voice suggested.

"Actually, I mean exactly that. There hasn't been any good music since the eighties ended," Marwin affirmed, grudgingly beginning to like the doctor.

"I hear you," the voice said pleasantly. "I love music, but I assume you didn't call just to talk about the lack of sensible lyrics from artists with substance with me. What can I do for you this morning?"

"I was calling to introduce myself and see if you had time to discuss a couple of patients. If you don't have time now, call me back at your convenience."

"Now is good. What's up?"

Not really expecting to have an intense discussion so soon, Marwin was momentarily at a loss.

"Hello? Mr. Gelstone? Are you still there?"

"Uh, yeah. Sorry," Marwin stumbled. "I'm here. I was telling Katie I have been gone for several weeks, and I noticed your name on some prescriptions when I got back. My partner told me that you took over for Dr. Foster. I just wanted to introduce myself and see if I could be of any service to you." He thought it was best to ease into the conversation.

"Well, thanks for calling, Mr. Gelstone. I appreciate you taking the time, as I know you must be busy. I am Dr. Steven Wisebaum, and I did take over Dr. Foster's practice. I'm sure we will be in touch, as your pharmacy is listed in several of Dr. Foster's patients' charts.

"It's nice to meet you. Thanks again for calling," Wisebaum said, dismissing Marwin.

"Well, I did have a couple of questions," Marwin interjected quickly. "I've noticed that several of our patients are now on gabapentin and hydrocodone. None of them were on these previously. I wasn't aware of them getting diagnosed with a condition warranting such therapy."

"Well, sure, Mr. Gelstone," Dr. Wisebaum said easily. "I place many of my patients on that combination. All of my patients who suffer from painful conditions receive that combination of drugs. I have found them very effective, and the patients feel much better on them than they did previously."

"I have seen patients with back pain or neuropathy on that combination," Marwin told him. "But all the ones yesterday were young to middle age and had diagnoses of hypertension, dyslipidemia, et cetera. They had nothing related to pain at all, but they all received your combination of drugs with a listed diagnosis of chronic pain. Plus, that is a bogus diagnosis anyway."

"Excuse me? Who are you to question my diagnosis?"

"I'm the pharmacist trying to look out for my patient's well-being," Marwin answered firmly.

"At least you got that right, you are the *pharmacist*, and I am the *doctor*. I do the diagnosing and treating, and you dispense the medications I prescribe to treat the condition."

"That's great, as long as the patient actually has that condition," Marwin said, voice rising.

"Listen, you have no right to question my diagnosis or—"

"I have every right if the treatment is harmful to the patient," Marwin interrupted.

"That's enough! I will not debate this with you any longer. I have patients to see. Goodbye, Mr. Gelstone."

"Actually, it's *Dr.* Gelstone, and I promise you that I will be discussing your therapy with each one of your patients. If they don't need this crap, I will suggest that they toss the prescription and find a better doctor."

"You are overstepping your boundaries. I'll report you to the pharmacy board," Wisebaum threatened.

"You do that. Just make sure you spell my name right! It is M-A-R-W-I-N G-E-L-S-T-O-N-E, license number 16102, in case you need it," Marwin said, slamming down the phone.

"Looks like that went well," Miranda said from behind Marwin.

"Yep, 'bout as well as I figured it would. I didn't even know you were here."

"Well, it is time to open," Miranda replied, pointing at the clock.

"I see that. I guess I was having so much fun that I didn't notice the time. Let me get the lights, and I'll tell you about my conversation with the good doctor."

# CHAPTER 20

"Dr. Montgomery?" Helen asked as Jackson left the exam room. "For god's sake, Helen. Stop calling me Dr. Montgomery!"

Helen shot eye daggers at Jackson, and the debate raged on her face. Finally, she exhaled loudly and said, "I'm sorry, *Jackson*. University called and said that Tom Richardson died last night."

"What? How?" Jackson stammered.

"They brought him into the ER about ten last night. He was visiting his girlfriend and passed out. The girlfriend called the nurse on duty, and she called 911 when she determined he was unresponsive. I don't have all the specifics, but it looks like his blood pressure bottomed out, and he suffered multiple organ failures. He expired about two o'clock this morning."

"Why the hell didn't I get a call?" Jackson thundered.

"I'm not sure, Jackson. I asked the administrator, and he couldn't give me a solid answer. Looks like someone dropped the ball."

"Dropped the ball?" Jackson asked incredulously. "A man died, and no one thought to contact his treating physician? Bullshit!"

"It wouldn't have changed the outcome," Helen offered haltingly.

"I—" Jackson started. He took a deep breath. "I know, Helen. I just can't believe that we lost another patient. What the hell is going on?"

Seeing the despair on Jackson's face, Helen placed her hand on his arm and said gently, "I don't know. We have never lost this many patients in such a short time. I guess it's just a bad stretch."

"A bad stretch? I'm not a baseball player in a hitting slump! I am a doctor who has lost a year's worth of patients in the last six weeks.

Something is wrong here. Either I suddenly suck as a doctor, or something is fucked up! Did Marwin ever review those charts that you gave him?"

"I haven't seen anything from him," Helen replied quietly.

"Well, call his ass, and tell him I need them reviewed *right now*! Go ahead and send him Tom Richardson's, too."

"Will do," Helen said, turning away.

\* \* \*

MARWIN'S DAY ROLLED ALONG nicely. It was late summer, and many people were out of town until school began again. Colds and flu hadn't started yet, so only the approaching ragweed season added to the normal pharmacy day. He was dismayed that he had received several more opioid prescriptions from Dr. Wisebaum and some from his colleagues in the same practice.

The morning dissolved quickly away, and Marwin realized that he had really missed being at work. When Sam arrived at one, Marwin filled him in on his conversation with Wisebaum.

Laughing, Sam said, "So, another doctor reporting you to the pharmacy board, huh?"

"Guess so," Marwin replied. "At least they'll know how to spell my name when they issue the Pharmacist of the Year award to me."

"Good point!" Sam said with a grin.

"Hey, why don't you and—what's your lady friend's name?"

"Dawn."

"Yeah, Dawn. Why don't you guys come over for dinner on Saturday?" Marwin offered. "Maybe we could play some games, and I could fill her in on all the stuff she needs to know about you."

"OK. Let me check with her, and then I'll let you know. You better get outta here. You don't want to be late getting Bogie to his game."

"I've got plenty of time," Marwin said, glancing at the clock. Marwin spent the next half hour going through faxes and referrals. He said his goodbyes and headed for the door.

"Telephone, Marwin," Miranda announced just as Marwin was exiting the door.

"Shit!" Marwin exclaimed. "Tell them I have already left for the day."

"Uh, it's Helen from Dr. Montgomery's office," Miranda replied.

"Crap, I'll get it in the office," Marwin said, turning back around.

"Hey, Helen. What's up?" Marwin asked, taking a seat behind his desk.

"Hi, Marwin. Jackson asked me to check with you to see if you had reviewed the charts of his patients that recently passed away. Have you found anything important?"

Momentarily lost, Marwin searched his brain before saying, "No, not yet."

"Have you reviewed them all?" Helen inquired pointedly.

"Not all of them," Marwin replied evasively, as he was unable to actually locate any of the charts that Helen had supposedly sent over. "Hold on one second, Helen."

Walking to the pharmacy counter, Marwin asked, "Sam, have you seen any charts from Jackson's office for recently deceased patients?"

"Yeah, they're on your desk."

"Where? I didn't see them."

"In the tray on the corner marked *urgent*," Sam said.

"Shit," Marwin grumbled, finally seeing the black tray on the corner of his newly organized desk.

*When did that get there?* he wondered.

Scooping up the charts, Marwin responded, "I'll get my preliminary report to Jackson tomorrow."

"OK. I will let him know," Helen said. "Marwin, I am sending you another chart as we lost another patient last night."

Stunned, Marwin said, "What is going on, Helen?"

"I don't know, but Jackson is very upset, so please let him know as soon as you can get through all of them."

"I will, Helen. Tell Jackson to relax. I'm sure it's just a crazy run of bad luck."

"I sure hope so. Thanks, Marwin, see ya."

Marwin picked up the stack and began to read. After a while, he was interrupted by Sam.

"Hey, you still here? You're gonna be late for Bogie's game."

Looking at his phone, Marwin jumped up and said, "Oh, shit! I gotta go!"

Grabbing the charts, Marwin sprinted for the door.

\* \* \*

THE EARLY, NON-EXISTENT TRAFFIC had been replaced by the ubiquitous road construction on I-40. As Marwin sat silently cursing in the stop-and-go traffic, his low-fuel light turned on.

"Damnit! I don't have time for this!" he swore to the empty SUV.

He didn't want to make Bogie late to the game, but he was also responsible for his teammates' tardiness. The guilty thoughts forced Marwin to whip down the emergency lane to the West Hills exit. Praying there were no cops nearby, he tore off the exit ramp to the Wiegel station and filled up. After putting just enough gas in to get him where he needed to go, he screeched out of the parking lot and fought to Kingston Pike.

Marwin finally pulled into his driveway to find Bogie and his teammates dressed in their uniforms, each with a look of despair on his face. He had let them down.

"Dad, we're gonna be late!" Bogie screamed as they climbed into the SUV.

"Nah, we'll make it," Marwin replied with more confidence than he actually felt.

"Coach is gonna be pissed," MP said to PC in the back seat.

"Yep, I know. We are screwed," PC affirmed matter-of-factly.

"Dad, Coach Mike is gonna kill us!" Bogie fired at Marwin.

"It'll be all right. Only one person can hit at a time," Marwin offered, knowing Bogie was right.

As all students of Murphy's Law can attest, anything that can go wrong will go wrong. Marwin caught every red light and got stuck behind a bus disembarking passengers twice.

The appointed time of 4:30 came and went with Marwin and the boys over two miles from the field. A gloom settled over the car, and only the DJ on WIMZ could be heard promoting a double shot of the Scorpions coming up after the break.

"OK. We finally made it. Grab your stuff and run for the cages. I'll go talk to your coach," Marwin instructed the boys. "Oh, you guys take out your frustration with me on the baseball tonight!" Marwin added, trying to fire the boys up.

The boys grabbed their bat bags and flew toward the batting cages. Marwin took his stadium chair and scoped out a good vantage point down the third base line. He had a scrawny butt, so it was difficult to sit on the hard metal bleachers. He always brought along his Tommy Bahama beach chair. After setting up his chair, he grabbed a water bottle from the concession stand and headed to the cages to watch Bogie hit.

As Marwin neared the cages, he spied three boys jogging around the outfield fence, each dressed in Eagle uniforms. "Ah, shit," Marwin said aloud as he noticed the boys suffering the consequences of his crime.

As the boys drew near, Marwin offered, "Sorry, guys."

PC and MP didn't break stride or even look in Marwin's direction, but Bogie narrowed his eyes at Marwin and said, "Yeah. Thanks for the ride, Dad."

Marwin watched silently as the boys made five more laps around the field before finally going to the batting cages. He hesitated before slowly walking over to the cages. At best, Bogie's hits were mediocre. Marwin slipped quietly back to his seat, where he found Destiny sitting in his chair, playing on her phone.

"Hey, beautiful," Marwin said. He bent down to kiss her neck.

"Umm. Hey, yourself," Destiny purred.

"I wasn't sure if you were gonna make it," Marwin said. "I would've brought another chair for you."

"I've got one in my trunk. I'm not sure if I will be able to stay or not. I've got some crap from work to deal with. Hopefully, I can resolve it over the phone. If not, I will have to go back to the office."

"Give me your keys, and I will get your chair," Marwin offered.

After returning with the chair, Marwin and Destiny chatted about the day's events. Marwin recounted his conversation with Dr. Wisebaum and informed Destiny about the newest patient Jackson had lost.

"Wow! That's crazy that he has lost three seemingly healthy patients recently."

"Actually, I think it may be four now. It does seem crazy, though," Marwin agreed.

The two watched the teams warm up, and Destiny asked, "What's wrong with Bogie? He looks pissed off."

Marwin explained the boys' lateness and the consequences.

"Well, that's crappy," Destiny stated. "It wasn't their fault that they were late. It was yours."

"I know, but stuff happens," Marwin said nonchalantly.

"Does it? Or was this something that could have been avoided?"

"I got held up at work and then had to get gas," Marwin explained. "Then traffic sucked. Everything just went against us."

"Well, if you had already reviewed the charts like you were supposed to, you wouldn't have left work late. If you knew you needed gas, you should have stopped on the way to work this morning. And traffic always sucks so that is no excuse," Destiny replied, refuting Marwin's excuses.

"Hey, whose side are you on?" Marwin asked irritably.

"Bogie's," Destiny said simply.

"Damn, Des. Cut me some slack here, why don't you?"

Looking at Marwin, Destiny's eyes softened, and she said, "I know you're trying, but you have got to get your crap together."

The game started, and the Eagles played sloppily. PC struggled on the mound, walking several batters. The defense was poor behind him, and they made several errors. Before anyone knew what was happening, the supposed superior Eagles team was trailing 7–1 after three innings. Bogie had a poor first at-bat, taking two fastballs down the middle and then swinging at a curveball that bounced in front of home plate.

During the next two innings, the Eagles rallied as their opponents played as poorly as expected. Going to the seventh and final inning, the

Eagles lead 8–7. The top of the inning got tense quickly as the opposing team loaded the bases with two outs. Coaches were yelling instructions from both sides of the field, and fans were oohing and awing with every pitch.

The batter ripped a hard ground ball straight to Bogie at third base for the would-be last out, but Bogie lifted his glove, and the ball shot directly between his legs and down the left field line, allowing two runs to score. The Eagles were stunned and went quietly in the bottom of the seventh inning, securing a 9–8 loss to a reportedly inferior team.

The post-game meeting was very different from the joyous one just three days prior. The coaches railed the boys for their sloppy play and seeming inattentiveness. After what seemed like forever, the team was released to their parents.

"Tough game, Buddy," Destiny consoled as Bogie slumped over to them.

Bogie said nothing, almost on the verge of tears.

"Hey, don't be rude," Marwin admonished.

Glaring at Marwin, Bogie turned to Destiny and said, "Thanks for coming to watch me play. I hate that I lost the game for us." After a beat, he added, "It was really Dad's fault, though."

"Bullshit!" Marwin thundered. "You can't blame me for this. I'm not the one who took the other team too lightly."

"You're the one who made us late and that caused us to have to run laps. PC was probably too tired to pitch effectively. And maybe that is why I missed that last ball," Bogie finished, jaw clenched.

"Really? Stop making excuses! Yes, I made you guys late and you had to run. I'm sorry. I have already apologized to your coach. But that had nothing to do with taking the other team lightly and not being ready to play.

"Did your running cause you to take two meatballs right down the middle and then swing at one that bounced in the dirt? You couldn't help that I made you late and maybe you think that it wasn't fair that you had to run for something that I did."

Marwin stared at his son. "Guess what? Life isn't fair! You better learn that concept and quick. You need to control what you can control and not worry about the rest."

Bogie's tears threatened, so Marwin inhaled deeply and said, "Look, that was a tough game tonight. The kid ripped the ball to you, and you couldn't handle it. Give him credit for doing his job. Next time, maybe you will be able to do *your* job, and we'll get a different result." He patted him on the back. "Don't let it get you down. You are a very good player who had a bad game. Unless you decide to quit tonight, you will have other bad games, too. Are you gonna quit?"

"Hell, no! I'm not quitting!" Bogie said, eyes blazing.

"Atta, Kid," Marwin said, cuffing Bogie on the shoulder. "Let's get some food. I'm starving."

# CHAPTER 21

"Keep up the good work, Myrtle," Jackson instructed his patient as he left the exam room. "I'll see you in a year unless you need me before then."

Jackson walked to the breakroom and poured his third cup of coffee. Unwrapping a granola bar, he glanced at his watch and saw that he had thirty minutes before his next appointment.

He decided to call Vince Adkins, the Knox County medical examiner, to see if he had the results of Wilson Stanford's autopsy. He dreaded the conversation for a couple of reasons. First, Adkins was a gruff old goat who was difficult to talk to. Second, Jackson was fearful the autopsy would reveal that he had made a mistake that contributed to Mr. Stanford's death. Dialing the number, Jackson broke out in a sweat like a patient receiving their biopsy results.

"Coroner's office," said a pleasant voice. "This is Sara. How can I help you?"

"Hey, Sara. This is Jackson Montgomery. Could I speak to Vince, please?"

"Let me check, Dr. Montgomery. Actually, he is in his office right now. Let me transfer you."

"You calling 'bout your patient's results, I assume?" Adkins asked without preamble.

"Yes, I was hoping you had them ready," Jackson replied.

"Well, it looks like he exploded inside," Adkins said simply.

"What do you mean, 'he exploded'?" Jackson asked incredulously.

"Just what I said, *he exploded*. He had a cerebral hemorrhage and a myocardial infarction. His liver was extremely congested, and one of the renal arteries ruptured. Like I said, he exploded on the inside."

Stunned, Jackson murmured, "What the hell would have caused that?"

"Not sure yet," Adkins said. "I don't have the toxicology results back. However, based on the myoglobin in his urine, the muscle rigidity he experienced in the ER, and the hyperthermia that occurred, I would say that he died of hypertensive crisis, secondary to serotonin syndrome."

"Serotonin syndrome?" Jackson asked weakly. "Uh, hold on a second, Vince," Jackson said, frantically trying to access Mr. Stanford's electronic chart.

"I don't have time to hold on. I have other dead people besides yours," Adkins groused.

"Just give me a second. I'm trying to get into his chart," Jackson grumbled.

"Why? It ain't gonna bring him back, and I don't care what meds you had him on. I'll let you know what the tox screen shows." Adkins said, hanging up.

* * *

"YOU WANT TO GO grab some lunch?" Polly asked from the chair where she had been lounging, idly watching Kristen rearrange the kitchen.

"Yes, but no," Kristen responded. "I gotta watch my money. I'll just make a sandwich here."

"Don't worry about the money. I'll pay for it," Polly offered.

"Nah, you've done too much already. I'll make us both a sandwich if you'd like."

Rising from the well-worn chair, Polly said, "I'm in the mood for one of Jack's steamed sandwiches."

"Really, Polly? I can't afford to eat out all the time. I don't make the big bucks like you do."

"Funny you should mention that. Yesterday, I talked to my boss about you. I suggested that maybe you could work a few hours for us from time to time."

"What? When? I'm going to nursing school and working at Forever Young already. I don't have any more time for a second job."

"Yes, you do. Come on, let's go eat, and I will explain it all to you," Polly said, herding Kristen toward the door.

After a brief hesitation, Kristen's willpower disintegrated, and she said, "What the hell. Let's go."

"That's my girl," Polly said, grinning.

* * *

"BIT? YOU AWAKE?" MARWIN asked, knocking on Morgan's door.

"Sure, Dad. Come on in," came the reply.

Morgan was sprawled on her bed with a book closed in front of her. Her blond hair fell easily over her shoulders, and her face glowed a pretty shade of pink.

"Forget your sunscreen yesterday?" Marwin asked, noticing the reddened cheeks.

"No, I used it. I just didn't put any on my face. I didn't want it to give me pimples."

"Well, melanoma lesions look worse than pimples," Marwin replied.

"Oh, Dad," Morgan groaned.

"Don't 'oh, Dad' me. You've got to take care of yourself."

"Like you've been doing?" Morgan asked without thinking.

"Hey! Watch your—" Marwin started. He decided to approach it from another angle. "Touché. When did you get so smart?"

"Long time ago," Morgan answered confidently.

Marwin chuckled. "How was the rafting, anyway?"

"It was awesome! Patrick's mom packed us lunch, and we had a great time."

He had no idea where Morgan had gone, so Marwin asked, "Uh, what river did you guys float?"

"We went to this place close to Gatlinburg and floated down the Pigeon River. It was really cool!"

"I'm glad you had a good time. Maybe we can all go again before winter gets here," Marwin suggested.

"Even Patrick?" Morgan asked doubtfully.

"Yep, even that old boy," Marwin said, smiling.

"Great. That would be awesome!" Morgan replied, wearing out her favorite adjective.

Changing the subject, Marwin asked, "You got any dirty clothes in your hamper? I'm getting ready to start a load of laundry."

Morgan jumped off her bed. "I'll bring them down in just a minute."

"Nah, you keep reading. I'll get them. What are you reading, anyway?"

"It's called *The Hunger Games*," Morgan said.

"I've heard of that! Isn't it kinda dark, though?"

"You mean kids having to kill each other to survive? It's just fiction, Dad."

"I'm glad you know the difference between real life and fiction, Honey," Marwin said, picking up Morgan's hamper and heading downstairs.

Having already grabbed Bogie's hamper, Marwin sorted the clothes in the laundry room. He made separate piles based on colors while idly thinking that life seemed on the upswing.

Maybe it was his going back to work. Maybe it was the peaceful interactions with his kids. Hell, maybe it just involved pulling his head out of his ass.

Thinking that was the most likely explanation, Marwin loaded the clothes into the washer. He stopped abruptly while dropping Morgan's cut-off jeans into the washer. Pulling the shorts out, he dug his hand into the front left pocket and withdrew a small purple lighter.

"What the hell!" he said aloud.

Leaving the laundry room without starting the washer, Marwin headed back upstairs. Before he had climbed two steps, his phone rang from the kitchen.

"Shit!" he exclaimed and reversed his course.

Picking up his phone, he saw it was Destiny calling.

"Hey."

"I thought I was going to have to leave a message," Destiny said.

"Yeah, sorry. I was headed upstairs, and my phone was in the kitchen. What's up?"

"Funny you should ask. I think we should get together soon and see what comes up," Destiny replied with a giggle.

"Uh, yeah, sure. Sounds good," Marwin said, obviously distracted.

"Well, don't get too excited," Destiny returned irritably.

Hearing her agitation, Marwin said, "Hey, I'm sorry. I gotta go take care of something. Let me call you back in a little while, and we can work out some plans."

"Is everything OK?" Destiny asked, concerned.

"I'm not really sure. I'll call you back."

# CHAPTER 22

*Call me*, the text demanded.

*Shit*, the woman thought. *I can't call right now.*

Mind whirling, the woman searched for a solution. Seeing a Shell station ahead, she whipped in front of a car and shot into the parking lot.

"Something wrong?" the woman's passenger inquired.

"Uh, no. I just realized that I needed gas, and my company credit card is a Shell," the woman replied, adlibbing. "Would you mind pumping? I need to pee."

"Sure. No problem."

The woman used the credit card at the pump and hurried inside the restroom. After ensuring that both stalls were unoccupied, she dialed the number and locked the restroom door.

"I want to commend you on the job you are doing," the man's voice said.

"Thank you, sir," the woman replied, acknowledging the anticipated increase in her heart rate in her chest.

"When you told me you had a plan, I didn't expect it to work so quickly. The speed at which you carried out your assignment was impressive."

Beaming, the woman replied, "Thank you."

Just then, the restroom door rattled, and a woman's voice said, "What the heck?" The door rattled again as the other woman pushed against it. Finally, there was a rapid knock on the door.

"Shit," the woman whispered.

"Excuse me?" the man asked.

"Uh, sorry, sir," the woman whispered.

"Is everything all right?"

"Yes, sir. Did you need me to do anything?" the woman asked, trying to push the conversation along.

"No, I just wanted to commend you, and let you know that there will be a bonus in your account tomorrow. Also, there are no other assignments at this time so you may revert to maintenance mode."

"Open up!" someone cried outside the door, followed by more insistent knocking.

"I really appreciate it," the woman said into the phone.

"I'll be in touch," the man said, disconnecting.

The woman quickly unlocked the door and was greeted by the manager holding a ring of keys. The manager eyed the woman and asked, "What were you doing in there? Why was the door locked?"

"I was using the restroom, thank you," she answered indignantly.

The manager again looked the woman over, sniffed the air, and said, "I doubt it. You need to leave, and don't bother coming back here."

The woman strode past the manager and the frustrated restroom patron and hurried to her car.

"Everything ok?" her passenger asked.

"Yeah, everything's fine. I just needed to pee, and some crazy bitch locked the door so I couldn't get in. I finally gave up and just left. I guess I will hold it until we get to the restaurant. Thanks for filling up."

"No problem, but it only took four gallons to fill it up," the passenger said, looking curiously at the woman.

*Fuck!* thought the woman. "Really? she asked incredulously. "I swear the gas gauge said I was almost on empty."

"Apparently not."

"Hell, maybe I'm going blind," the woman said, forcing a chuckle.

* * *

114

As Marwin ascended the stairs, his cell phone rang again. "Damnit! What now?" he said to the ringing iPhone.

Jackson's name stared up at him from the screen. "What's up?" he asked curtly.

"I wondered if you had reviewed my charts?"

"Not yet. I haven't had time."

"Shit," Jackson said, disgusted. "Just forget it. I'll call Sam and see if he can look at them for me. Maybe he can tell me how my patient died from serotonin syndrome."

"What? Wait! What are you talking about? Serotonin syndrome?"

"Have you forgotten what that is, too?" Jackson sniped.

No answer came forth from Marwin and Jackson realized that he had hit below the belt.

"I'm sorry. That was a low blow."

"No, it wasn't," Marwin said sadly. "I deserved it. After I was unable to help you the other day and then I left your charts unreviewed, I don't blame you for your lack of trust."

"Whoa! Who said I didn't trust you? I only keep bugging you because I want you to look at them. Something is wrong. There is no way that patient developed serotonin syndrome."

"Why do you suspect that he did?"

Jackson recounted his conversation with Vince Adkins, and Marwin said, "He's a piece of work."

"He's a piece of something, all right." Jackson agreed.

"Look, I have the charts with me. I have a situation to deal with, and then I will sit down and go through them with a fine-tooth comb," Marwin promised.

"You gotta call your bookie?" Jackson scoffed.

"No, I wish that was it. I gotta go kick my daughter's ass then I will get to your charts."

"Oh, OK. Have fun with that, and let me know when you're through with the charts."

"Will do."

Marwin started up the stairs the third time, then retreated and placed his cell phone on the table in the hallway. Not to be denied this time, he climbed the stairs and knocked on Morgan's door while simultaneously opening it.

"Dad! I could've been naked," Morgan protested.

"Oh, well. I've seen you naked before," Marwin replied, tossing the lighter toward Morgan.

Morgan instinctively caught the lighter, and the color drained from her face.

"What the hell is that?" Marwin thundered. "Don't say, 'A lighter,' or I will beat your ass!"

Morgan sat still, eyes cast down to the floor, not speaking.

"Well?" Marwin all but screamed. "Don't even think about lying. Just tell me the truth," he demanded.

Morgan lifted her eyes, pulled her shoulders back, and said, "I was smoking yesterday."

Flabbergasted, Marwin stared at his precocious daughter. "What the hell were you thinking? Was Patrick smoking, too?"

Morgan formulated a lie but finally just replied, "Yes, Dad. Patrick and I were both smoking."

"Where was Patrick's mom?"

"She and Patrick's dad took their picnic to a different spot. Patrick and I took ours down to a secluded place by the river," Morgan confessed.

"Do you have any idea how stupid that was?" Marwin asked, still fired up.

"Come on, Dad. What's the big deal? Everyone tries cigarettes when they're young."

"Bullshit! Everyone doesn't try smoking when they are young," Marwin refuted angrily, but he knew Morgan was right.

"Well, if it makes you feel any better, it made me so dizzy that I thought I was going to throw up."

"Morgan, you have no idea what kind of damage cigarettes do to your body."

"Dad, it was just a couple of cigarettes. It's not like I am addicted to them or anything."

"Not yet, but nicotine is one of the most addictive substances known to man. It's very difficult to stop once you get hooked."

"If it's so addictive, why is it legal?" Morgan wondered.

"It's not legal for twelve-year-olds!" Marwin snapped, completely side-stepping the question. "I assume Patrick's older brother bought them for you guys?"

Morgan didn't answer. She just stared defiantly at Marwin.

Marwin glared back and said, "I'll be talking to Patrick's parents and Patrick, too. Would you like me to tell them anything for you since you won't be seeing or speaking to them anytime soon?"

"Dad!"

"Forget it! You're grounded until further notice."

# CHAPTER 23

Dawn Anderson strode down the familiar hallway of the east wing of Forever Young, bags of groceries weighing her down. Her grandmother had been a resident at the facility for five years, moving in after her husband of forty-seven years had succumbed to pancreatic cancer.

At first, her grandmother, Gladys, had kept to herself, rarely leaving her room except to take her meals in the dining room. She regularly declined offers from other residents to play Canasta and Bridge or to work on jigsaw puzzles in the common room.

Dawn had worried that her grandmother was slipping into depression and had spoken to her physician about starting a low-dose antidepressant. Gladys had adamantly refused the medication, stating she was fine.

Dawn continued to worry about her grandmother until the day she discovered her in the common room playing checkers with a grey-haired gentleman. Dawn had stood at the doorway and observed the two elderly people enjoying each other's company. Gladys won the game and let out a squeal of delight as the man pushed back from the table, cursing.

Gladys had rounded the table and had planted a light kiss on the man's lips. "Better luck next time," she had said with a grin.

"You're the one who will need luck next time," the man grumbled.

Gladys had noticed Dawn leaning in the doorway. "Hey, Honey. I didn't know you were here."

"I just got here," Dawn fibbed.

"Come meet my friend, Tom."

"Friend, huh?" Dawn joked.

"Well, he's not my enemy, so I'll just call him a friend," Gladys said, approaching a blush.

"Nice to meet you, Tom," Dawn said, extending her hand.

"Likewise," Tom replied, bringing Dawn's hand to his lips.

Momentarily stunned, Dawn said to Gladys, "I see why you are friends."

"Tom is quite the philanderer," Gladys affirmed.

"Guilty," Tom said, smiling.

Remembering the day things seemed to turn around for Gladys brought a smile to Dawn's face. Gladys had settled in and appeared to be happy at Forever Young now. Dawn knocked on the door of her grandmother's apartment, and she was instructed to come in by a weak voice.

"Hey, Memi. How's it going?" Dawn asked, entering the room.

Gladys was seated in a faded recliner, her lap filled with wadded-up tissues.

"Memi, what's wrong?" Dawn asked. Alarmed, she placed the groceries on the table.

Gladys burst into tears. Her sobs rattled her body.

"Memi, what is going on?" Dawn implored, kneeling beside the recliner.

"Oh, Honey. It's Tom. He passed away last night," Gladys told her, choking on her tears.

"Oh, no. What happened?"

"I really don't know. He came over, and we had dinner. He seemed fine, but when he got up to go to the restroom after dinner, he passed out. He stood up, took a couple of steps, and then just collapsed. I ran over to him and saw that he was unconscious, so I called the nurses' station. They came down and worked on him but ended up calling an ambulance since they couldn't get him to come around. The ambulance took him to the hospital, but he passed away. It was horrible!"

"Oh my gosh. I'm so sorry, Memi," Dawn responded, stunned.

"I just can't believe that he's really gone," Gladys said mournfully, rising from the chair.

Dawn pulled her diminutive grandmother into her arms and held her for several minutes as the grief poured out. Finally, Gladys broke the embrace and said, "Thanks, Honey. I really needed that."

Wiping her tears away, Gladys blew her nose and asked, "What's in the bags?"

"Oh. I just picked up a few things for you at the grocery store."

Ever the food enthusiast, Gladys said, "Let's see what goodies you brought me today." Opening the bags and removing items, Gladys murmured, "Bologna, eggplant, M&M's, hamburger meat." Reaching into the last bag, Gladys withdrew a rectangle of cheese and emitted a small squeal, "Ooh, my cheese! Since when does Kroger carry this type of cheese?"

"They don't. I ordered some for you. I know how much you love it. I was going to give it to you next month for your birthday, but this morning I decided to go ahead and give it to you now."

"Oh, Honey. You are the best granddaughter I have."

"I know, Memi. I'm the only granddaughter that you have."

Smiling weakly at Dawn, Gladys said, "Help me put the groceries away, and I will get us a small glass of wine. Then we'll sample your amazing cheese."

"Memi, I brought the cheese for you. I don't want to eat it," Dawn said.

"Honey, you are the only family I have left. If I can't share it with you, who am I going to share it with?" Gladys said morosely.

\* \* \*

MARWIN STOMPED DOWN THE stairs, picked up the charts, and headed toward the back deck. Changing course, he detoured to the fridge for a Sweetwater and then to the pantry for a bag of pretzels. Once on the deck, he settled into his favorite chair, opened his beer, and read.

For no reason known to him, he had arranged the charts in the chronological order in which the patients had died. The first patient was a sixty-eight-year-old female who had been a resident at Forever Young for eight months. She had been a recent widow whose medical profile was unremarkable except for well-controlled dyslipidemia and mild depression, which didn't begin until after her husband had passed. Her med list was short, consisting only of atorvastatin 20mgs daily, citalopram 20mgs daily, and a multivitamin. Her yearly labs had just been done and were all within normal limits. Her BMI was slightly elevated at 26, revealing that she was marginally overweight. Flipping through the pages, Marwin came to the report from the hospital when the woman had passed.

She had been admitted with hypertension, and her blood pressure had been recorded at 185/110. She'd shown signs of tachycardia with a heart rate of 124 BPM and tachypnea with sixty respirations per minute. Her body temperature had been 102, and she was sweating profusely. Her muscles were rigid. Despite attempts to control her blood pressure, her condition deteriorated, and she finally suffered a massive stroke and died.

Marwin placed the papers on a table and picked up his beer, now wet with condensation. "Damn," he muttered as he flipped back through the chart. Seeing nothing new of significance, Marwin went on to the second chart.

As he read, Marwin noticed similarities. This patient was a recent widower who had only been a resident at the facility for a few months. His medical history was also mostly unremarkable, with only hypertension listed. The medicine list was short, containing only furosemide and amlodipine. Labs showed mild renal insufficiency, not uncommon for his age. This patient's demise closely mirrored the previous patient.

The patient was admitted with severe hypertension, muscle rigidity, and elevated body temperature. He eventually suffered a heart attack as the doctors had been unable to control his ever-rising blood pressure, and he passed a few hours later.

"What the hell?" Marwin asked the backyard cicadas while reaching for his beer. *What were the chances that two seemingly healthy—although elderly—patients had died in almost an identical manner?* he pondered.

Not a believer in coincidences, Marwin re-read the second chart and came to a conclusion—something stunk! There was no way that two patients with basically benign medical histories had died from hypertensive crisis and resultant stroke and heart attack. Marwin considered exchanging his empty beer for a full one but thought better of it and reached for the third chart.

The third patient was also a recent widower who resided at Forever Young. He was the patient that Jackson had told Marwin about the previous weekend. According to his autopsy, the patient had died from serotonin syndrome.

His medical history was positive for epilepsy for several decades' duration. He had recently developed mildly elevated blood sugars. His med list contained carbamazepine, metformin, and citalopram. Labs were normal except for a slightly elevated hemoglobin A1C and fasting glucose. According to the chart, the patient had not had a seizure within the last ten years, so the epilepsy was well-controlled. According to the notes, Jackson had suggested discontinuing the seizure meds, but both the patient and the neurologist had refused.

On the evening of his death, the patient developed severe hypertension and muscle rigidity. His body temperature was 103. The course of this patient's demise was much the same as the previous two patients.

Marwin sat back in his chair, stunned. His mind picked through the meds and diagnoses, searching for a cause. He quickly decided there was no rational reason for the patient to have developed severe high blood pressure. Theoretically, the patient could develop serotonin syndrome from the combination of carbamazepine and citalopram, but it seemed far-fetched to Marwin.

Marwin looked for the autopsy report but found it was not in the chart. He had hoped to find something that would shed light on the strange situation.

As the day's events began to overwhelm Marwin and his eyelids sagged, he decided that it would serve no purpose to continue, so he gathered the charts and headed inside.

# CHAPTER 24

The woman pulled into the parking lot of Forever Young. Dropping the car into park, she took a couple of calming breaths and tried to still her nerves. Her mission today wasn't normally required. She had only had to carry this out on two other occasions.

Closing her eyes, she visualized the next fifteen minutes. After running and re-running the dialogue internally, she stepped into the sultry August evening and walked calmly into the facility.

Dressed casually in Lululemon running shorts, a tee-shirt, and Asics tennis shoes, her purse slung easily over her shoulder, she smiled at the nurse behind the desk and said, "Hey, Tracey, how's it going tonight?"

Looking up from the computer where she was either working or playing a game, the brown-haired nurse replied, "Oh, hey. It's going, I guess. You here to check on Gladys?"

"No, actually. I need to see Tom for a minute. I left my planner on his table last night."

"Oh, I guess you haven't heard. Tom passed away last night."

"What? That can't be. I just saw him last night. He was on his way over to Gladys's for dinner and a movie. He seemed perfectly fine when I left."

"Well, I'm afraid it's true," Tracey said. "He passed out in Gladys's room and was taken to the hospital, but he didn't make it."

"Oh, my gosh. That's awful!" the woman lamented.

"Yeah, I really like Tom. He was a great, fun-loving guy, even if he seemed grouchy sometimes. That is the worst part about working here," Tracey said sadly. "Someone is always dying."

"I know what you mean. I hate it when I lose a patient." The woman replied earnestly. "I get attached to them, and it is really hard when they pass away."

"It's been a tough stretch lately," Tracey admitted. "We've lost several patients recently."

"I know. I've lost some, too." After a brief pause, the woman asked hesitantly, "Is Tom's room open? I know exactly where I left my planner. I can be in and out in less than a minute."

"No, I locked it this morning after we found out he had passed. It was unlocked when I went by this morning. I guess he didn't lock it last night before he left."

"Is there any way you could give me the keys? I hate to bother you, and I know you are busy in the evenings."

Before Tracey could answer, the phone rang. Answering the call, she held up her finger to the woman, asking her to wait. The woman smiled and turned away from the desk. After a couple of minutes, Tracey said, "Hey, this is gonna take a while. Just take my keys. Make sure you lock the door when you leave."

Smiling broadly, the woman said, "Sure, no problem. I will bring your keys right back."

After getting the keys from Tracey, the woman walked down the hallway toward Tom's room, stopping to chat briefly with some residents. Reaching the door, she slipped the key in the lock and stepped inside the recently deceased person's apartment.

Locking the door behind her, she flipped the lights on and went straight to the bathroom. She removed the bottle that she had left for Tom the previous night. Dropping it into her purse, she retraced her steps, extinguishing the lights as she exited. She locked the apartment door and walked calmly back to the nurse's station, forcing herself not to skip gleefully down the hallway.

Seeing that Tracey was off the phone, the woman said, "Thanks, Tracey. I really appreciate your help. It's hard to believe that Tom is gone."

"I know. We're gonna miss him," Tracey said sadly. Almost as an afterthought, she added, "Did you find your planner?"

"Yep, right here," the woman replied, pulling the planner from her purse. "I would be lost without it."

"I understand that. Have a great night," Tracey said, turning back to her computer.

As the woman fired up her car, she cranked the air conditioning to the max to dry the sweat that soaked her. Taking a deep breath, she felt the tension drain away.

Waiting for the anticipated text message, she tuned the radio to WIVK and sang along to the latest Luke Bryan song, *One Margarita*. Before she got to the chorus, her iPhone dinged, and a text message appeared.

The message read: *Success?*

*100%*, the woman texted back.

Thinking of the perfectly timed phone call, she added, *Thanks for the assist.*

*Anytime*, came the immediate reply.

The woman deleted the texts, dropped her phone in the cup holder, put the car in gear, and drove off in search of a celebratory margarita.

*  *  *

STUMBLING TOWARD THE STAIRS, almost too exhausted to climb to his bedroom, Marwin reached for his phone and saw it was after eleven.

*Shit*, he thought. *I didn't call Destiny back.*

Debating whether it was worse to call this late or not call at all, he finally decided to risk waking her up.

"Everything all right?" she asked with no greeting.

"Yeah, I'm sorry it's so late. I had to deal with Morgan, and then Jackson called about the charts. I reviewed them for him, and I guess time got away from me. I'm sorry."

"It's fine, Babe. What's going on with Morgan?" Destiny inquired.

"Stupid teenage-wannabe shit that I am not ready for," Marwin said dejectedly.

"Ah, I see. You wanna tell me about it?" Destiny asked quietly.

Marwin recounted the smoking incident as well as the resultant conversation and grounding.

"Ouch! Starting the school year grounded is never good," Destiny opined after Marwin had finished.

"Sneaking around smoking with your wannabe-boyfriend when you're only twelve is never good either," Marwin returned.

"True, but don't be too hard on her. She's a kid, and kids are going to try all kinds of stuff. Hopefully, she won't like cigarettes, and you can cross smoking off the worry list."

"*Don't be too hard on her?*" Marwin imitated indignantly. "She's lucky that I didn't beat her little ass!"

"Do you think that would keep her from doing it again?" Destiny asked calmly.

"I doubt it, but it might have made me feel better," Marwin said irritably.

Sensing that she couldn't assuage Marwin's anger, Destiny changed the subject. "You want to see if Sam and his new friend want to come over on Saturday for dinner?"

Sighing, Marwin said, "Yeah, that sounds great. The kids are at Lindsey's this weekend so maybe you and I can spend some quality time together."

"Quality time, huh? Maybe some quantity, too?" Destiny suggested.

"That does sound good," Marwin agreed. "Plus, I owe you."

"I plan on collecting," Destiny said huskily.

"I can't wait. I'll let you know what is on the menu—besides me—when I figure it out."

"OK, but you're the only item I am really interested in," Destiny cooed.

"You better stop talking like that or you're gonna get a midnight visitor."

"Come on. I'm waiting," Destiny offered.

Thoughts of naked flesh flashed through Marwin's mind, causing a pleasant stirring. "I wish I could," he declined. "I'll talk to you tomorrow. Love you."

"Bummer. Maybe I'll just start without you. Love you, too."

Marwin disconnected and thought briefly of starting without Destiny, too, but saw the stack of charts and remembered he had promised to call Jackson back.

*Shit,* he thought tiredly.

Bracing for Jackson's tirade, Marwin gathered the charts and the empty beer bottle and went inside.

"It's 'bout damned time," Jackson answered irritably.

"I know. I'm sorry," Marwin apologized again.

"I hope you found something important since you are calling in the middle of the night."

"It's not exactly the middle of the night," Marwin protested meekly.

"Close enough. What did you find?"

"Uh, nothing," Marwin confessed. "There is no pharmacy reason as to why these patients should have died in the manner that they did. So, you're off the hook."

"Damn, I was almost hoping you had found that I had screwed up," Jackson admitted reluctantly.

"I never thought that I would find any such thing. However, I'm gonna pick through them again in the morning when my mind is clearer just in case I missed something."

"Well, while you're picking back through them, you can look through another chart. I just lost another patient last night," Jackson said miserably.

"What? Are you serious?" Marwin asked, stunned.

"I'm afraid so. This patient lived at Forever Young, also, oddly enough."

"Did this patient die unexpectedly, too?" Marwin asked.

"Yes, he dropped dead after dinner," Jackson confirmed.

"Geez! What the hell is going on? There is no way all these patients just dropped dead like that, even if they all were elderly," Marwin concluded. "Something is wrong over at Forever Young."

"Great, just what we need. Another mystery."

# CHAPTER 25

Marwin sat parked in the middle of I-40, half listening to the inane ramblings of John Boy and Billy on WIMZ. He felt like hell, as sleep had eluded him until the wee hours of the morning. His mind had been overwhelmed by all the day's events, and it wouldn't turn off and allow the Sandman to take over.

While waiting for sleep, he replayed his altercation with Wisebaum, Bogie's game, Morgan's smoking, and Jackson's patients suddenly dying. The only pleasant memory from yesterday was Destiny's randiness.

Sleep had finally overtaken his whirling mind sometime after 4 a.m., and his alarm clock had sounded at 5:30. He had intended to get to work early to review the charts again along with the new one that Jackson said he had sent over, but the August heat had been joined by a monsoon, so traffic piled up much earlier than normal.

Reaching for his phone, Marwin wondered if the state-wide hands-free law applied if your car was parked on the interstate and not actually moving. Deciding he didn't care either way, he dialed his ex-wife, Lindsey, to let her know about Morgan.

After he detailed the previous night's events, Lindsey said, "Great. You grounded her while she'll be with me. Thanks a lot!"

"What did you want me to do?" Marwin yelled.

"You could've checked with me first. I had planned to take the kids on a hike in Cades Cove and then go into Gatlinburg for the weekend."

"Well, sorry I didn't check your calendar before I disciplined my daughter," Marwin snapped.

"*Our* daughter," Lindsey immediately corrected. "You should have talked to me before you handed down your sentence, Marwin. Instead, you ranted and raved and punished her without getting my input."

"I did what I thought was necessary," Marwin said defensively, an edge of doubt pushing at his mind.

"Of course you did. You always think you know what is best, Marwin."

Before Marwin could respond, Lindsey continued, "Look, this isn't about Morgan's punishment or my plans. This is about communication between us. We have always been able to talk things over regarding the kids, but recently, you've been shutting me out."

"I have not," Marwin retorted.

"Marwin, stop! Whether you want to admit it or not, you've been a different person since you were shot. I'm not saying that's unexpected. I'm just stating a fact."

Lindsey waited for Marwin's rebuttal, but when none came, she finished by saying, "For what it's worth, I have no problem with Morgan's punishment. I probably would have busted her ass and then grounded her."

\* \* \*

JACKSON LEANED BACK IN his chair, taking a sip of his long-cold coffee. Making a face, he went to the microwave to revive his java and stretched his aching back. He had been unable to sleep, so he had gone to the office at 6 a.m. On the way, he grabbed a bagel and a donut from Dunkin' along with a thirty-two-ounce black coffee. Rain was pounding down, forcing the rush hour traffic to start earlier than usual, so he had forgone the interstate and was traversing the side roads.

Once at his office, he perused Lexicomp and Micromedex in search of information on serotonin syndrome. Finding nothing of use, he turned to Medline, where he again struck out. Finally, in desperation, he searched WebMD. Once again, he gained no new information, so he childishly deleted his search from his computer.

Frustrated, Jackson took his revived coffee from the microwave and returned to his desk, sitting down heavily. An idea had occurred to him earlier, but he had brushed it off as foolish. Now, with his frustration threatening to boil over, he revisited the idea.

Picking up his iPhone, he scrolled through the contacts until he found the one he needed. He pressed the blue call button, but before he heard it ring on the other end even once, he disconnected the call with the red button and dropped his phone onto his desk.

"You idiot," he mumbled aloud.

Almost immediately, Jackson's phone rang. Seeing the name and number pop up caused him to emit a curse. The phone continued to ring as Jackson's finger hovered over the discard button. Finally, for reasons unknown, his finger pressed the green answer button before his brain could stop it.

"Hello," he answered tentatively, trying to act as if he hadn't just dialed the number.

"Hey, Jackson. Did you need me?" Detective Bradley Jinswain asked.

\* \* \*

MARWIN'S MOOD, WHICH WAS already headed south, deteriorated rapidly upon opening the store. His main technician, Miranda, had called out due to a migraine, and his order was delayed because of the rain. Two patients were already waiting on items that were supposedly in the delayed order, and neither of them understood the reason for the hold-up. The phones were unusually active for that time of the month, and prescriptions were pouring in left and right.

With no one to go out to get lunch, Marwin was relegated to digging into his emergency food drawer or else succumbing to hypoglycemia. Foregoing water, he opened a Mountain Dew and ate stale peanut butter crackers between phone calls. As he typed a prescription while he waited for the insurance agent to explain why they would only cover fifteen Ambien tablets per month, Marwin glanced up to see Sam coming through the door.

"Hallelujah!" Marwin said.

"Aw, thanks for missing me," Sam quipped.

"Yep! Glad to see you today," Marwin admitted.

Quickly surveying the carnage on the counter, Sam checked the computer to find that Marwin had already filled one hundred twenty-five prescriptions before one o'clock. "Holy crap! You've been busy today."

"Uh, a little bit," Marwin deadpanned. "Plus, Miranda is out with a migraine. It's just been Rachel and me this morning."

"Oh, shit! You should've called me," Sam admonished. "I would've come in early."

"Ah, we made it. Didn't we, Rachel?"

"Yeah, we made it," Rachel replied with a wan smile.

"I'll be right back. I'm about to float," Marwin said, heading to the restroom. When Marwin returned, a doctor was holding on the phone for him.

"This is the pharmacist," Marwin answered.

"Hey, Marwin, it's Alain. I gotta quick question."

"OK. Shoot," Marwin said.

"I'm having a brain fart today. I have a patient who had two stints put in during his catheterization. I started him on Brilinta but forgot to tell him to take a daily aspirin, too. When I called his wife to tell her to have him take an aspirin every day, she asked if a baby aspirin was OK. I hate to admit it, but I blanked. I couldn't remember how much is in a baby aspirin."

"Eighty-one milligrams," Marwin supplied immediately.

"OK, cool. Then that's just what he needs," Alain said. "Thanks for your help, Marwin."

"Whoa. Wait a minute, Alain. If he's on Brilinta, he needs more than one hundred milligrams of aspirin for the Brilinta to work effectively."

"What? Are you sure? I thought we couldn't exceed a hundred milligrams?"

"No, I'm pretty sure you have to have more than that," Marwin replied.

"OK. I guess I'll let him know," Alain said slowly.

"Marwin, that's not right," Sam said.

"Yes, it is," Marwin argued defiantly.

"What's that?" Alain asked, confused.

"Nothing. I was talking to Sam."

"Marwin, you've got it wrong. A patient cannot take more than one hundred milligrams of aspirin with Brilinta, or the Brilinta will not work. They should always be on baby aspirin," Sam stated matter-of-factly.

Overhearing the conversation, Alain asked, "Which is it, Marwin?"

Marwin's mind raced along with his heart as self-doubt rushed in.

"Marwin?" Alain asked.

"Uh, hold on, Alain."

He eyed Sam steadily. "Are you positive?"

"Absolutely," came Sam's immediate reply.

Marwin's face flushed as he told Alain, "I had it backward. The patient cannot exceed a hundred milligrams of aspirin with the Brilinta, so a baby aspirin is what he needs."

"OK. Thanks, Marwin. I'll see you later."

"Don't thank me, thank Sam. He's the one who saved my ass and the patient," Marwin said morosely.

"OK. Tell Sam I said thanks," Alain said, disconnecting.

Marwin hung up the phone slowly, avoiding eye contact with Sam. "What the fuck is wrong with me?" he asked no one in particular.

"Nothing is wrong with you," Sam offered quickly.

"Obviously, there is," Marwin huffed. "This is twice in two weeks that I have screwed up."

"That we know of," Sam joked and immediately regretted it. "Look, don't sweat it. Your brain would have gotten it straightened out, and you would have called Alain back. Nothing would have happened to the patient."

"It seems to me that your confidence in me is misguided," Marwin said glumly.

"Nah. You're still the best," Sam said, trying to boost Marwin's confidence.

"Bullshit. If I'm the best, the rest of the pharmacists must suck," Marwin said, turning to his office.

The pharmacy gods flipped the magic switch, and the flood of prescriptions and phone calls seemed to stop abruptly. Marwin brooded all afternoon and had difficulty concentrating on the work at hand. He was not used to making mistakes, and he always knew the correct answer to the requested information.

His mind replayed the almost disastrous conversation with Alain over and over. His brain would not accept that he had given out the wrong information. Thank God Sam had overheard the conversation and stopped him from possibly harming a patient as well as damaging his reputation with a trusted physician.

Marwin decided to look over the last chart Jackson had sent over for the latest patient that had passed. Thinking of the previously deceased patients, Marwin assumed this patient died similarly but forced himself to start at the beginning rather than skip ahead to the hospital report.

The latest patient was a seventy-nine-year-old widower with a history of angina, hypertension, and anxiety. He'd suffered a heart attack four years prior, but recent EKG and lab work was normal. His meds included metoprolol 50mgs twice daily, lisinopril 10mgs every morning, isosorbide 60mgs twice daily, and doxazosin 4mgs at bedtime. He also had diazepam to take on an as-needed basis. Expecting another hypertensive crisis, Marwin was shocked to find that the patient had suffered severe low blood pressure with resultant multiple organ failure.

"What the hell?" Marwin said aloud.

The cause of death was exactly opposite from the other patients. Returning to the previous charts, Marwin searched again for an explanation to explain the bizarre deaths. All the patients were elderly but in seemingly good health. All had relatively recent yearly check-ups that were satisfactory. None had any recent issues, and all their lab work was good. Medications were surprisingly few considering the patient's ages.

After several minutes of staring blankly at the pages, Marwin discovered a couple of similarities in the patients. All had lost a spouse, and all of them resided at Forever Young.

Marwin's search was interrupted by Rachel. "Line one is for you, Marwin."

"If it's a doctor, let Sam get it," Marwin replied disgustedly, even as he reached for the receiver.

"This is the pharmacist," Marwin answered in a tired voice.

"Hello, pharmacist. This is the DA. You wanna bring me some medicine?" Destiny asked with a chuckle.

"Oh. Hey, Des,"

"Well, don't sound so thrilled to hear from me," Destiny replied, picking up on Marwin's somber mood.

"Oh, it's not you. It's all me."

"What's wrong? Are you all right?"

"I don't want to talk about it right now, but I'll tell you all about it later," Marwin said.

"It's not more trouble with Morgan, is it?"

"No, not that I know of anyway. Like I said, it's all me."

"Oh, OK. I was just calling to see if you had confirmed everything with Sam for Saturday," Destiny asked.

Marwin slumped. "No, it's been crazy here today."

"Well, don't forget to ask him so we can make plans," Destiny instructed.

"OK. I will. Look, I gotta go. I'll talk to you later. Love you."

"OK. love you, too," Destiny said, already starting to worry.

\* \* \*

"OH. HEY, BRADLEY. I, uh, accidentally dialed your number. Hope I didn't wake you," Jackson stammered.

"Nope, I've been at work since six. I'm actually working on stuff for Shoehorn's trial. Everything all right with you?"

"Yeah, I guess. I'm still trying to get used to the daily grind again. I guess I sorta liked not having to deal with all the bullshit every day while I was away."

"I can understand that," Bradley agreed. The conversation lagged, and Bradley said, "Well, I saw where you called me, and I wanted to make sure you didn't need me. I'll talk to you later."

"Yeah, OK. Sure," Jackson said, pushing himself to say what was on his mind. "Bradley, you haven't heard of a bunch of people dying in nursing homes or assisted living homes lately, have you?"

"What? I don't really recall hearing anything like that. Why?"

At first, Jackson didn't reply. Instead, he closed his eyes and leaned back in his chair, hesitant to voice his concerns. He could feel his pulse in his ears as he finally said, "I think someone is killing my patients."

# CHAPTER 26

The rain had vanished, leaving a gray, steamy late afternoon in its wake. Traffic was tolerable on I-40 as Marwin headed west, having left Sam to close the store.

Driving with one hand, he scrolled through his phone until he found Triumph Radio on Pandora. Listening, Marwin sighed heavily as Getty Lee belted out *Working Man* before giving way to The Scorpions who declared *There's no one like you.* Marwin turned up the volume and sang off-key as the rock and roll began to hammer through his dark mood.

Absorbing the lyrics from the Scorpions song, Marwin realized, yet again, that for him, there was no one like Destiny. She was the light to his darkness, the bread to his pudding, and a million other silly romantic quotes. She was the absolute best thing that had ever happened to him.

After his divorce from Lindsey, Marwin was introverted, going only to work and returning home without socializing. He quit playing golf and rarely spoke to anyone outside of work.

As Marwin's eyes watched the road, his mind replayed the long-ago afternoon at work when a stunning woman entered the store. She walked down one aisle and then back up the adjacent aisle, obviously in search of a product.

Coming out from behind the counter, Marwin asked, "Can I help you find something?"

The woman, dressed in a bright red dress that hit just above her knees and clung to all the important parts, looked up sheepishly and said, "I'm looking for your laxatives."

"OK. They're right over here," Marwin offered, walking to the end of the aisle. "Any particular one that you are looking for?"

"Uh, no," she answered. "Not really. I'm not sure what I need."

"OK. Let's see if we can figure it out," Marwin said, immediately falling into his clinician role. "First, how long has it been?"

The woman stared blankly back and him, so Marwin said, "One day? Two? More than two days?"

Again, the woman looked quizzically at Marwin, unsure of what to say.

"OK. Let's take a different approach. When was the last time you pooped?"

"Oh, I'm sorry. I wasn't sure what you were asking," the woman replied with an embarrassed laugh. "Let me see. I think it was about four days ago."

"Four days ago? Holy crap! No pun intended, but that is way too long. You need to go every day."

"Yeah. Well, I have IBS. I don't have everyone else's normal habits."

"Gotcha. Are you uncomfortable or hurting?" Marwin asked.

"Not yet, but I don't want to get that way. What do you suggest? Keep in mind, I don't want to swing the other way either."

Marwin looked at the beautiful woman, and something deep inside him changed. He made a split-second decision. "Do you have a few minutes, Mrs.—?"

"Actually, it's *Miss* Lawson, Destiny Lawson. Nice to meet you, Mr.—?"

"Uh, Gelstone, Marwin Gelstone," Marwin said, unable to take his eyes off the woman.

"I have some time before I am due in court. What did you have in mind?"

A part of Marwin's long-dormant desire had several ideas, none of which had anything to do with constipation. "I thought we could go into the counseling room and sort this out."

"Awesome! Let's see what you can do. However, if this is a first date, I expect a nice chardonnay," Destiny said with a brilliant smile.

* * *

BRADLEY JINSWAIN HUNG UP the phone, perplexed. Jackson had suggested that someone was intentionally killing his patients, but it was hard to digest.

Based on his conversation with Jackson, all the patients were elderly, living in a nursing home or assisted living facility. Each one had a condition—albeit minor—which could have contributed to their deaths. None of the patients were extremely elderly, but all were over seventy, so they were approaching the natural end of their lives anyway.

Bradley picked up the file he had been working on before Jackson called and read through it for the umpteenth time. The file was part of the case against Ernie Shoehorn and contained details on all the patients that Shoehorn may have killed.

Shoehorn was a local OB/GYN who had killed several patients, including Jackson Montgomery's wife, Madeline. Imagine the irony of a doctor killing his patients, including the wife of another doctor, who now thinks that someone is trying to kill his patients. It was too much for Bradley, and he closed the file on his desk.

Bradley reached into one of his desk's drawers and extracted a worn baseball. He sat back, closed his eyes, and rotated the baseball in his hand. He effortlessly changed from a two-seam fastball grip to a four-seam grip, and on to a curve ball, a slider, and finally to a change-up before starting over again.

While his hand rotated through the rote grips, his mind tried to find a link, if there was any, between Shoehorn's case and Jackson's wild accusation of someone harming his patients. The obvious connection was Jackson Montgomery. His wife had been killed, and his patients were dying. However, Shoehorn couldn't have had any direct link to the deaths as he had been incarcerated a few months prior.

As Bradley continued to idly walk the baseball through different grips, he wondered if Shoehorn could have enlisted someone to help him. While Shoehorn and Jackson had graduated from the same medical class at Duke University, Bradley was unable to uncover any motive for the attack on Madeline. He made a mental note to dig into that further. Could Shoehorn have hated Jackson so much that he not only killed his wife but also had someone kill his patients?

*Not very likely*, Bradley mused.

According to Jackson, he barely even knew Shoehorn in med school. He remembered he was a bottom-of-the-barrel student, and Jackson had little or no contact with him outside of class or rotations. Jackson had offered no motive for Shoehorn killing Madeline, and so far, Bradley had failed to unearth one.

With no motive for the initial murder, it seemed unlikely that Shoehorn would be involved with whatever may or may not be happening to Jackson's patients. Bradley stopped rolling the ball across his fingers and dropped it back into the drawer, its leather now slightly warm.

# CHAPTER 27

The rest of the week dissolved in a blur of prescriptions and consultations. Fortunately, Marwin did not experience more episodes of brain fog, and he settled into the daily grind of pharmacy.

His home life was reasonably calm as Morgan had been on her best behavior since her grounding, even cleaning her room without prompting. Bogie had been putting in extra work off the hitting tee and seemed to have recovered from his disastrous game.

Marwin hadn't seen much of Destiny as she was busy helping Simon prepare for Shoehorn's trial. He looked forward to entertaining Sam and his new girl. The kids were gone again for the weekend, and Marwin was excited about some adult time.

He finished his second cup of coffee and a bagel on the back deck as the August heat started to skyrocket the mercury in the thermometer. He had Phil Steele's college football guide and his notebook on the table and was starting his calculations for the upcoming season. He was way behind in his preparation as the season kicked off in three weeks, but he was determined to get back into the groove. As he began calculating the estimated yards per point for each team in Division One, his phone rang.

"Good morning, Counselor," Marwin said, answering after just one ring.

"Good morning, Doctor," came Destiny's canned reply.

"What's up?" Marwin asked.

"Nothing yet, but I hope you will change that later," Destiny purred.

"Oh, yeah? What did you have in mind?"

"I'll show you what I have in mind when I get over there."

"Well, what are you waiting for? Get over here," Marwin said, feeling a familiar stirring.

Aware of Marwin's obsessive planning, Destiny asked, "You got everything in line for today?"

"Yep, I believe so. I thought I would grill barbecue chicken with corn on the cob and green beans. How's that sound?"

"Sounds great to me. Have you got everything you need?"

"No, I have to run to Kroger and pick up a few things. Anything special you need for tonight?"

"When are you going to the store?" Destiny asked, ignoring the question.

Glancing at his gambling stuff, Marwin said, "Uh, I've got some work to do here, and then I'm gonna head up there."

"So, you're finally getting back to gambling, huh?" Destiny asked with a chuckle.

"Very funny," Marwin replied without denying it. "Why don't you come by at one and help me get everything ready?"

"What time is Sam coming over?"

"I told him to come around four, so we could play cornhole before dinner."

"OK. I'll be over around noon," Destiny responded cheerfully.

"Uh, OK. I guess I'll postpone my work and go to the store."

"All right. I'll see you in a little while. Love you."

"Love you, too," Marwin said, closing his football notebook.

He jumped through the shower and pulled on a pair of gym shorts and a Margaritaville tee shirt. Grabbing his shades and the grocery list, he headed out the door.

The sun was brilliant as he drove down Cedar Bluff Road. He mentally surveyed the groceries and their upcoming preparation but kept losing his train of thought.

He couldn't get Destiny out of his mind. His mind quickly forgot about beans and corn and turned to various positions into which he could try to get Destiny. As always, everything went perfectly in his mind, and never once did last week's power outage enter his mind.

Marwin was lost in his fantasy. Not only did he develop a noticeable erection in his gym shorts, but he also mindlessly turned onto I-40 East rather than continuing past to Kingston Pike.

"Shit! Where am I going?" he asked aloud. He exited West Hills and backtracked back down Kingston Pike to Kroger.

Exiting the car, he checked for any sign of his previous arousal and walked into the store. He was dismayed to see a million people shopping on Saturday morning.

Pushing his way through the throngs of shoppers, he picked up corn, some half-runner green beans, and a large pack of chicken. He had intended to skip dessert but changed his mind and picked up a key lime pie from the freezer section. Rounding out his shopping, he grabbed a twelve-pack of Hazy Little Thing IPA, two bottles of St. Michelle chardonnay, and two different flavors of Stubbs Barbecue Sauce. After paying, he cranked up Pandora and rocked out to Bob Seger as he sang *The Horizontal Bop*, hoping it was a harbinger for later in the day.

Once home, he listened to Pandora play the golden songs of the eighties while unpacking the groceries. As he prepared to snap the green beans, his doorbell rang.

Opening the door, he found Destiny looking back at him, dressed in Lululemon running shorts and a white Tennessee Vols tee shirt. Marwin's eyes danced across her uncovered nipples as they tried to push through the cotton fabric. He forced himself away from her tempting breasts and looked into Destiny's green eyes. He almost commented on her risqué outfit, but he stopped when he felt raw hunger radiating from her.

Destiny walked past Marwin, purposely brushing her left breast against his arm. Marwin closed the door, locked it, and followed Destiny. She headed straight up the stairs.

Marwin's heart rate ticked up, and he hurried up the stairs behind Destiny. Catching her just before she reached the top of the stairs, Marwin grabbed her hips.

Destiny stopped but didn't turn around. Instead, she leaned forward, bracing herself on the top step, and pushed her butt back into Marwin.

A guttural moan escaped Marwin, and he pulled the running shorts down and eased Destiny onto the steps. Wrapping his arm around her, he grabbed a breast and gave a rough squeeze while pushing against her from behind and kissing the back of her neck.

Destiny groaned and ground her bare butt against Marwin's bulging erection. Marwin pushed roughly back against Destiny, causing her to emit another moan, this one deeper than the other. Marwin's shorts went down to his ankles as Destiny arched her back, showing Marwin her opening.

Marwin smacked her ass, causing her to release an almost primal roar. He licked his fingers and smacked her ass again before plunging into her.

She moaned loudly and rocked back and forth furiously. Marwin tried to match her rhythm but seemed to zig when she zagged. As he concentrated on matching Destiny's frenetic pace, he felt the air leak out of his balloon. As panic set in, Marwin thrust wildly, silently willing his erection to hold on.

"Fuck!" Marwin exclaimed, breathless, as his flaccid member slipped out of Destiny. Seeing the hunger still in Destiny's eyes, he tried to roll her over and plunge his head between her legs.

"No, don't," she said but didn't pull Marwin's head up.

Marwin never hesitated. He ignored Destiny and assaulted her womanhood with his tongue.

"Marwin, stop," she said without conviction and opened her legs wider. "Oh, Honey. Stop. It's, uh, oh . . ." Destiny's voice trailed off, and her hand grasped Marwin's hair at the back of his head, forcing his mouth further into her.

Marwin's tongue worked overtime, and Destiny bucked her hips until a large groan and several spasms went through her. As the spasms subsided, she smiled and looked down at Marwin.

"Thanks. I needed that."

Marwin stood, pulled up his shorts, and replied sadly, "No problem."

Sensing Marwin's black mood, Destiny said, "Hey. It's fine. Don't make a big deal out of it."

"Don't make a big deal out of it?" Marwin asked incredulously. "That's easy for you to say!"

"Honey, take it easy. Don't worry about it." The look on Marwin's face sent pain through Destiny's soul, so she added gently, "Plus, you did me good. Isn't that always your goal?"

Stepping past Destiny, Marwin replied sourly, "Yeah, at least there is that. I'm going to take a shower. I'll be down in a little bit."

* * *

WHEN MARWIN ENTERED THE kitchen, Destiny was seated at the bar with the green beans spread out on a newspaper before her. Her iPhone played an Eagles tune as she idly tore the strings from the beans and broke them into small pieces.

She had slipped into a yellow and orange sun dress with white sandals. Marwin's heart swelled as he watched Destiny work. She was absolutely stunning, even dressed so simply and doing domestic chores.

His dark mood lightened as he watched her. He wrapped his arms around her and kissed the back of her neck. Destiny tilted her head, grabbed Marwin's arms, and pulled herself deeper into his embrace.

"Ummm," she sighed.

"Thanks for starting on the beans," Marwin said, grudgingly pulling away from her luscious neck.

"No problem. I'm almost done. Anything else I need to do?"

"No, not really. I'll season the chicken and put it in the marinade. Could you shuck the corn for me? After that, we can grab a beverage and chill for a little while before Sam and his date get here."

Marwin prepped the chicken and added lump charcoal to his Big Green Egg. He grabbed a Michelob Ultra for Destiny and a Hazy Little Thing for himself.

He watched Destiny finish rinsing the silk from the ears of corn. Marwin, again, was struck by a strange feeling. He grabbed Destiny's hands and gazed at her. "I love you."

Destiny's smile spread to her eyes, and she replied, "I love you, too," before kissing him softly.

As Marwin tried to break the kiss, Destiny slipped her tongue gently between his lips and ran her hand through his hair, preventing him from escaping. The two kissed gently but progressed on a deeper level before settling down and finally stopping.

"Wow! That was awesome," Marwin said like a teenage boy receiving his first real kiss.

"Glad you liked it. There's plenty more where that came from," Destiny said, beaming.

"Let me see," Marwin said, pulling Destiny back to him.

Destiny kissed Marwin deeply and pulled him tightly to her, feeling him harden against her. Just as Marwin dropped his hands to her butt, Destiny broke the kiss and said, "Let's have that beverage now."

"Uh, OK," Marwin stammered. "What should I do with this?" he continued, pulling his engorged member from his shorts.

"Hmm," Destiny said, bending over to kiss the head of his penis. She swirled her tongue around the tip and then quickly engulfed him. As a moan escaped Marwin, Destiny popped up, grabbed her beer, and turned to go to the back deck.

"Hey, where are you going?" Marwin asked, exasperated.

"Outside," Destiny replied, smiling.

Marwin finally managed to get his penis back into his shorts, so he grabbed his beer and followed Destiny onto the back deck. The two spent the next hour talking, sipping their beers, and enjoying the much-needed time together. As the doorbell sounded, Marwin said, "That's probably Sam. I'll be right back."

"OK," Destiny replied, pulling up her sundress to reveal she wasn't wearing panties. "I'll be waiting."

Marwin, Sam, Destiny, and Dawn made their introductions, grabbed drinks, and headed into the backyard, where the corn hole boards were set up. The sun beat down on the browning, late-summer grass, and the four tossed the bean bags. Marwin and Destiny won three of the five games before Marwin declared that he needed to cook.

The four settled onto the back deck with fresh drinks, talking easily as if they were lifelong friends. While Destiny was in the restroom, the conversation naturally turned to medicine between the three pharmacists.

"Did you get a chance to review those charts for Jackson?" Sam asked.

"Yep, I didn't find anything really," Marwin replied.

"Well, I didn't think you would find anything indicating that Jackson was responsible for the deaths," Sam said.

"What deaths?" Dawn inquired, eyebrows arching above her blue eyes.

"Jackson Montgomery is a local doctor we work closely with," Marwin explained.

"I know Dr. Montgomery," Dawn responded. "Sam told me you guys do all the dosing for his patients. I think that is awesome!"

"Yeah, we're really fortunate that Jackson lets us be so involved with his patients," Marwin agreed.

"So, what's the deal with these deaths you were referring to?" Dawn asked again.

"Jackson has had four patients die in the last couple of months, and none of them had any issues that would explain their unexpected deaths. All the patients were elderly, living at Forever Young, an assisted living facility. Three of them suffered a hypertensive crisis and died of a stroke or heart attack. The fourth patient suffered multi-organ failure secondary to severe hypotension."

"Did you say Forever Young?" Dawn asked, sounding alarmed.

"Yes, do you know the facility?" Marwin asked.

"Sure, I'm out there two to three days a week visiting my grandmother. Actually, my grandmother's boyfriend just passed away." Her hand went to her mouth. "Oh, my gosh! I bet Tom is the patient you just mentioned who died from severe hypotension," Dawn concluded, stunned.

"Probably," Marwin agreed. "If you visit so often, do you know the nursing staff well?"

"Oh, yes. They have some excellent nurses there. Why do you ask?"

"Just curious. I wondered if there could have been some serious medication mix-ups that led to those deaths."

"Well, the patients there use their own pharmacies for their meds as Forever Young doesn't have an on-site pharmacy. Unless they are on the hospital side, Forever Young doesn't supply their medications."

"Oh, well. I doubt all these patients happen to use the same pharmacy," Marwin mused. "I guess we could always track that one, though."

"What are you tracking down now, Dr. Gelstone?" Destiny asked, returning from the restroom.

Marwin explained the unlikely theory that all the deceased patients used the same pharmacy and that there had been a major medication mix-up that led to unexpected deaths.

"Oh, I thought you had disposed of your detective hat," Destiny joked.

"I have," Marwin confirmed quickly.

"Detective's hat?" Dawn asked quizzically.

"Marwin played detective a few months back," Sam said cautiously.

Dawn looked expectantly at Marwin, eyebrows raised.

"Ah, shit. Let me get a glass of wine, and I'll tell you about it," Marwin said grudgingly.

* * *

"THAT WAS DELICIOUS," DAWN said, rising from the table. "That was the juiciest chicken I have ever eaten."

"Thanks, it's all because of the Egg," Marwin beamed. "Greatest grill ever!"

"Maybe you need to get one," Dawn said to Sam.

"Are you ready for Sam to start cooking for you?" Marwin asked jokingly.

Dawn eyed Sam and smiled. As the smile spread upward to her eyes, she said, "Sure, he can cook for me anytime."

Luckily, Sam's face already had a red tint due to the alcohol, so his blush didn't show. Trying to recover, he looked at Dawn. "I will be glad to cook for you any day." Before Dawn could respond, Sam added, "Or every day."

"Whoa, did you just propose?" Marwin asked. "Are you guys getting married?"

"Who's getting married?" Destiny asked, returning from the kitchen.

"Uh, no. I don't know. That's not what I said," Sam stammered, his face flushed.

"So, you don't intend on marrying me?" Dawn asked, clearly enjoying watching Sam squirm.

"No, I mean, yes. Can we talk about this later?" Sam pleaded.

Dawn flashed a brilliant smile, took both of Sam's hands in hers, and kissed him softly on the lips. "Sure," she said with a wink.

"You guys up for playing some cards?" Marwin asked, trying to help his partner out.

Sam and Dawn agreed. "Absolutely."

I'll get the Rook cards, and we'll kick your ass at that, too," Marwin said arrogantly.

"We'll see," Sam fired back.

The conversation turned to the upcoming trial while they played. "So, is Shoehorn gonna be tried for murder?" Dawn asked.

"Yes, he has been charged with murder in Madeline's death. According to Simon, the assistant DA, there is no precedent for charging someone with the inducement of suicide, but he believes the case is strong enough to set a new precedent. The fact that Shoehorn copped a plea to attempted manslaughter in my shooting will likely help in the murder trial. It will at least show his propensity for violence and lack of respect for human life."

"That's game," Sam said, circling the one-thousand-point total on the paper. "Who kicked whose ass?" he continued defiantly.

"Well, you kept the Rook up your ass the whole night," Marwin said disgustedly.

"You're just jealous," Dawn piped up.

"We want a re-match," Destiny chimed in.

"You got it, but not tonight," Sam said. "I think we better get home."

"You better stop at the jewelry store since you have already proposed," Marwin laughed.

"Marwin!" Destiny scolded.

"Funny," Sam said, taking it in stride.

"Thanks for a great day and a fabulous dinner. It was nice to meet you guys," Dawn said, extending her hand.

Ignoring the hand, Marwin hugged Dawn and whispered in her ear, "You're a lucky girl." Pulling back, he continued, "I'm glad to finally meet you as well. We'll do it again soon, but next time we get to have the Rook some."

"Not if I can help it," Sam said, holding a fist out.

Pounding the fist, Marwin said, "You guys drive safe. Who's driving?"

"I am. I've only had three drinks since we got here, so I'm good," Dawn confirmed.

After Sam and Dawn left, Marwin and Destiny retreated to the kitchen to finish the clean-up. "I really like Dawn," Destiny offered.

"Yeah. I do, too. She seems very nice, and Sam says she is a great pharmacist. It looks like Sam likes her quite a bit, also."

While Destiny wiped down the countertops, Marwin loaded the coffee pot, setting it to come on at 8 a.m. Turning to face Destiny, he took her by the shoulders and kissed her gently. "You're the best, Des."

Emotion brightened Destiny's face, and she entwined her fingers with Marwin's before she pulled him upstairs to the bedroom.

# CHAPTER 28

Kristen trudged up the stairs slowly. Closing her door behind her, she chucked her keys in the direction of a wooden bowl residing on the counter but missed badly and watched disinterestedly as the keys slid off the counter and out of sight.

Opening the fridge, she found little of interest except for a Woodbridge Chardonnay, which she left untouched as she closed the door. Walking to the bathroom, she stepped out of her clothes, leaving an apparel trail behind her.

Kristen turned on the shower but then changed her mind and plugged the bathtub in favor of a soak. As the water began to rise, she decided the chardonnay wasn't such a bad idea and padded naked into the kitchen to retrieve it. Just as she closed the door to the fridge, there was a loud knocking at the door.

"Shit," she cursed.

Starting to the door, she remembered the running water and trudged back to turn it off, emitting another curse as she went. As she covered herself with a towel, the knocking resumed, louder this time.

Kristen ran to the door and stepped on her wayward keys, forcing a larger epithet from her mouth. She hopped to the door on one foot and peered through the peephole. Polly stared back at her.

"Took you long enough," Polly said as she strode into the apartment. Seeing Kristen's disheveled appearance, Polly asked, "What the hell happened to you?"

"Uh, I was getting in the tub when you knocked on the door and— Never mind. It's been a long day."

"Yeah? So, you made it through your first day of nursing school unscathed?"

"I guess so. We had work to do in all our classes today. I expected to get the syllabus, meet the teacher, et cetera, and go on my merry way. Nursing school is different."

"Not surprised. It is a short, three-year program and there's a ton of information to learn. Do you have any real classes or are they just Intro to Nursing?"

"I have some intro classes, but I also have Pathophysiology as well as Clinical Immersion, whatever that is."

"Cool. Did you have your introduction at Forever Young today, too?"

"Yeah, I just got back from there. I was at school at 7:30 this morning, left at noon, grabbed a burger, and was at Forever Young by one. I left there at six, and traffic sucked ass, so I got home ten minutes ago."

"Have you eaten?" Polly inquired.

"No. It looks like a gremlin came in while I was gone and cleaned out my fridge," Kristen joked.

"Well, get your ass dressed, and we'll get some food," Polly ordered.

"Nah, I can't afford to eat out. I've got to watch my money. I won't be getting a check from Forever Young for a month, so things are gonna be pretty tight."

"Well, you said you don't have any food," Polly pointed out. "Eating out looks to be the only option, other than starving to death."

Thinking of the wine, Kristen said, "I'll make do. I've got a little money in the bank, so I will go to the store soon and pick up some food."

"So, you are gonna go to school in the morning and come home and be Rachel Ray? You look like you can barely stand up after the first day."

"I'll be fine," Kristen said indignantly.

"Yeah, you probably will be, but for tonight, get your ass dressed, and we'll go get something to eat," Polly told her. "Plus, I'm buying since I got a fat bonus today."

"Damn! Another bonus? Didn't you just get one recently?" Kristen asked, amazed.

"A little while back," Polly answered evasively.

"Wow! Maybe I need to get a job babysitting old people," Kristen laughed.

"They're not just old people," Polly chastised. "They are people who have been able to live a long life, many of them without their spouses. If you plan on becoming a nurse, you might want to take a compassion class."

Seeing the look on Polly's face, Kristen said, "You're right. I'm sorry. I shouldn't have said that."

"You're fine. You'll be amazed at how quickly you become attached to your patients. They're like family in no time."

"I hope I like them more than *my* family," Kristen replied sullenly.

"You will. Now, get dressed or you're going to be the talk of the school tomorrow after you're seen tonight at Calhoun's wearing only a towel."

\* \* \*

MARWIN'S MORNING PEACEFULNESS TURNED straight to chaos. For some unknown reason, the pharmacy was slammed. Prescriptions poured in for allergy meds to combat the onset of ragweed. He made two simple, but time-consuming compounds. He went round and round with a podiatrist regarding the use of oral vancomycin for a patient's toe infection. Apparently, the doctor didn't understand that oral vancomycin wasn't absorbed into the systemic circulation and was only useful to treat a specific infection in the gut.

He opened a protein bar as Miranda announced, "Doctor Montgomery is on the phone for you, Marwin."

"OK. Thanks." Marwin sighed.

Deciding that Jackson could wait a minute, Marwin crammed the remainder of the protein bar in his mouth and chewed slowly. After swallowing the bar, Marwin answered, "This is the pharmacist," as if he didn't know who was waiting for him.

"Did you finish your lunch?" Jackson asked, forever prescient.

"Uh, no. I was busy saving lives and stamping out disease. Thank you," Marwin retorted.

"Uh-huh. I bet. All you've been doing is trying to stop people from sneezing," Jackson replied as if he had been in the store.

"Can I help you, Dr. Montgomery? I am a very busy man, and I don't have time for idle chit-chat right now."

"OK, whatever, Dr. Gelstone. I was wondering if you had heard anything from Destiny."

"No, but it's early yet. They should have started jury selection about an hour ago, though."

"I know. I was just wondering if she had called you."

Recognizing the pain in Jackson's voice, Marwin said, "Des said it would probably take a couple of days for them to select a jury. She'll let me know when there's something to know. Are you going to the trial?"

"Damn right I'm going! I want to see that son-of-a-bitch fried for what he did to Madeline."

"I know, Buddy," Marwin soothed. "You do know that it is going to be a rough road, though, right?"

"What do you mean? Has something changed? Is Simon waffling now?" Jackson asked.

"No, Simon is all-in. He thinks he can get a conviction. Otherwise, he wouldn't push for the trial, especially since Shoehorn is already in jail for the next seven years."

"Seven years isn't enough for that monster!" Jackson raged. "I want him to rot in jail before he rots in hell."

Silence filled the line before Jackson said, "Hey, I gotta go. Will you let me know if you hear anything from Destiny, please?"

"Of course. Is Alain covering your patients so you can go to the trial?"

"Yeah, he and Wisebaum are gonna cover for me for however long the trial runs," Jackson confirmed.

"You're letting Wisebaum take some of your patients?" Marwin asked, stunned.

"Yeah. Why not? He is new to the area, and one of my colleagues recommended him. I don't know much about him, though." Jackson confessed.

"Well, he's a drug supplier," Marwin stated bluntly and then recounted his conversation with Wisebaum and told Jackson about the increase in opioid prescriptions lately.

"Ah, shit!" Jackson swore. "I'm gonna kill the guy who recommended him. Let me go. I gotta fix this before all my patients become dope addicts."

* * *

JACKSON TRIED TO FIND someone else to cover his patients. He instructed Helen to cancel and reschedule as many patients as possible, and then he called Dr. Wisebaum to inform him that he wouldn't need his services. Wisebaum was curious about the sudden change of plans, but Jackson expertly side-stepped his questions.

Preparing to leave for the day, Helen stopped Jackson and told him he had a call waiting for him on line one.

"Dr. Montgomery," Jackson answered in a tired voice.

"Vince Adkins here," came the gruff reply.

"Hey, Vince, what's up?" Jackson said, suddenly not as tired.

"I got the toxicology report on your patient, Wilson Stanford. He had significant amounts of amphetamine in his system at the time of his death. This further solidifies my diagnosis of hypertensive crisis, secondary to serotonin syndrome. I will be signing his death certificate today with that diagnosis."

"Wait! What? Why would he have amphetamines in his system?"

"I'm not sure, but I'll go out on a limb and say that he probably ingested them," Adkins replied sarcastically.

Ignoring the jab, Jackson asked, "Are you *sure* it was amphetamines? Could it have been a false positive test from something like Sudafed?"

"It's possible, but not very likely based on the serum and urinary concentrations as well as the muscle rigidity and severe hypertension he experienced. I would bet my license that he ingested amphetamines."

"Any other odd findings?" Jackson asked.

"Actually, yes. There was an unexpected finding in his urine. It contained ammonium chloride."

"What the hell?" Jackson asked, befuddled.

"I have no idea, but I can tell you that the ammonium chloride would have increased the urinary excretion of the amphetamines, for whatever that is worth."

Jackson sat back, his mind whirling, unable to understand why his elderly patient might have taken amphetamines.

Eventually, Adkins said, "If you have any more questions, let me know."

Jackson hung up and accessed Wilson Stanford's chart. As he scrolled through the chart, Helen said from the doorway, "You going home soon?"

Jackson didn't respond and scribbled notes.

"Is everything all right?" Helen asked. Receiving no response, she walked to Jackson's desk and laid her hand on his shoulder, startling him.

"What?" Jackson asked, obviously unaware of her presence.

"What's gotten you so intrigued that you didn't hear me from five feet away?" Helen asked, glancing at the screen.

"Uh, sorry. I just got the tox report on Wilson Stanford. It showed significant amounts of amphetamines in his blood and urine, and I have no idea why."

"Amphetamines? Mr. Stanford? That's crazy."

"I know," Jackson agreed. "You can go ahead and leave. I'm going through his chart again, and then I'm gonna call Marwin to see what he thinks."

Jackson's stress level was up, so Helen gave his shoulder a light squeeze. "OK. I'll lock the door. Let me know if I can help in any way."

Jackson went through the chart twice more before he gathered his notes and called Marwin.

"This better be good," Marwin grumbled after answering. "You interrupted my favorite REO Speedwagon song."

"Oh, no. Pardon me. Turn that shit off, and listen to me," Jackson commanded.

155

Jackson's tone forced Marwin to bite off his retort. "What's up?"

"Vince Adkins called with the toxicology report on Wilson Stanford. His blood and urine were positive for amphetamines. His urine also contained ammonium chloride."

"Whoa! A seventy-five-year-old man with amphetamines in his system? That's crazy!" Marwin stated. He completely forgot about Kevin Cronin Riding the Storm Out.

"I know. I've been going back through his chart for over an hour. I can't find a plausible explanation, other than he must have been taking speed, I guess. I've never done a drug screen on him, never even considered it." Jackson put his head in his hand.

"Don't beat yourself up," Marwin consoled him. "I don't think any physician would do a drug screen on a patient like him. It would be a waste of insurance money, if they even paid for it."

"How can I not beat myself up? If I had ordered a drug screen, this patient might still be alive!"

"Don't be ridiculous," Marwin said. "No one would have considered doing a drug screen on a patient in this demographic and having this medical history."

"I still wish that I had, though. Do you have time to listen to my notes to see if you can come up with a reasonable explanation?"

"Sure, this is the patient with a history of epilepsy, diabetes, and recent depression, right?" Marwin asked, his eidetic memory shining through.

"Uh, yeah. How do you do that?" Jackson was always amazed by Marwin's ability.

"I'm just that good," Marwin said simply.

"OK, Mr. Memory, what meds was he on?" Jackson asked, even though he knew that Marwin would be able to tell him.

"I remember him being on carbamazepine 200mgs three times a day, citalopram 20mgs daily, and metformin 1000mgs twice daily. I think his last carbamazepine level was around 8, his A1C was 8.4, and his fasting glucose was 170ish. Everything else was within normal limits, I think."

"Damn, that's impressive," Jackson remarked, flummoxed.

"Hey, it's what I do. God blessed me with the ability to remember what I want to."

"Well, that's great, but did He give you the ability to figure out how the hell this man got amphetamines and ammonium chloride in his system?" Jackson asked.

"Sure," Marwin said simply. "He was poisoned."

# CHAPTER 29

As the sun sank slowly below the West Knoxville horizon, Marwin sat, exhausted, on his back deck. A wine glass and a bowl that once held chicken alfredo sat empty beside him. His notebook and the Phil Steele magazine resided beneath his chair, unopened.

The chaotic life of retail pharmacy had kicked his butt this week, and his mind was full of issues: Shoehorn's upcoming trial, the possibility that Jackson's patients were murdered, the new school year starting, Morgan's—hopefully brief—foray into cigarette smoking, his brain fog issues at work, and his erectile dysfunction. He felt completely overwhelmed.

Marwin carried his dirty dishes inside and exchanged his wine glass for a Yeti of ice water, hoping to keep his exhausted mind as clear as possible. Returning to the deck with his water, he spied the unopened football book beneath his chair. Checking the time on his phone, Marwin got a wild hair and decided to call his bookie.

The phone rang in his ear for a long time. Marwin prepared to hang up, but just before he disconnected, a voice said, "Yes, sir?"

"Uh, yeah. Eighty-eight," Marwin said, giving his assigned number.

"Yeah, man. Where you been? I was beginning to think you were dead."

Thinking of his close call in Shoehorn's office, Marwin shuddered and said, "Almost. Hey. I was wondering if I could play a baseball game or two tonight."

"Sure, but everything is online now. I just need to get you the website and passwords. I have already set your account up. You can lose money twenty-four hours a day now," the bookie joked.

"Online? I hate computers! You mean I can't call you anymore? Marwin whined.

"Nope, I'm not taking anything over the phone any longer. My partners have created this secure site that you can access anytime you want. It has a ton more betting options than I ever gave you, so you can lose —I mean win—a lot more money now. We'll just settle up in person whenever necessary."

"Shit," Marwin said, disgusted. "Maybe I'll just quit."

"I'll bet you," the bookie replied, laughing at his pun.

Marwin took the betting information along with his untouched Yeti inside his study. He made several attempts to access the website, all without success.

"Screw it!" he said aloud as Morgan stuck her head in the doorway.

"What's wrong, Dad?"

"Oh, uh, nothing, Honey. I was having trouble getting on this site on the computer."

Entering the study, Morgan offered, "Let me see what I can do. I'm pretty good with technology."

"No, that's OK. It's not a big deal," Marwin stammered, trying to hide the paper behind his back.

"Dad, just give me the paper," Morgan said, and then her eyes widened. "As long as it isn't a porn site."

"It is definitely not a porn site," Marwin said indignantly.

"Gimme," Morgan said, reaching for the paper. She scanned the contents. "Your bookie is finally getting into the twenty-first century?"

"Apparently, but I don't like it."

"How do you know you don't like it?" Morgan rolled her eyes. "You haven't even tried it yet. You don't like change, Dad, but change is sometimes necessary for growth. Take a caterpillar, for instance."

Reflecting on Morgan's experiment with tobacco, Marwin said sternly, "Not all change is good or better. Some things should remain the same, though, like my wonderful, innocent daughter."

"Ah, Dad, I'm still your wonderful daughter," Morgan replied with a smile, much older than her years.

The fact that Morgan left out *innocent* in her description was not lost on Marwin, but before he could comment, Morgan said, "You're in, Dad! Wow, you have a ten-thousand-dollar limit!"

"What? Where do you see that?" Marwin asked, dumbfounded.

Morgan spent the next ten minutes walking Marwin through the various dropdown menus on the site.

Marwin shook his head in disbelief. "Holy crap! I didn't know you could bet on ping pong."

"Yeah, looks like it. Remember, though, most people lose money gambling," Morgan replied as if she was the parent and not the child.

"That part I do understand well," Marwin said with a smirk. "So, what's up, Bit?"

Morgan's previous ease and confidence vanished, and she said, "I was wondering if you thought I might be able to, uh, possibly, uh–"

"Spit it out, Kid," Marwin interrupted, wondering where this was headed.

Gathering herself, Morgan said, "I want to try out for the middle school softball team."

Shocked, Marwin asked, "Softball team? You've never played softball in your life."

"Yeah, I know, but I have played catch in the yard with Bogie lots of times. He says that I have a cannon for an arm."

"OK. But having a strong arm and playing catch in the yard is not the same as playing competitive softball, Honey," Marwin said gently.

"I know that, Dad. I'm not stupid. I wouldn't have much chance of making the team, but I really want to try."

"Are you sure you want to put yourself through that? It could be rough if things don't go well."

"Yes, I do. Do you think you could try to help me?" Morgan asked hopefully.

Thinking of the upcoming trial and the current chaos in his life, Marwin started to beg off. However, looking into his beautiful, precocious daughter's eyes and feeling responsible for her trepidation, he changed his course.

"Sure, Honey. I would be glad to work with you. Someone recently told me that change is good and allows growth, so we'll see how it goes."

"Oh, Dad! Thank you!" Morgan hugged him, and her embrace was worth more than all the money he could win on the gambling site.

* * *

THE LOW VIBRATION CONTINUED for roughly twenty seconds, ceased, then immediately began again. Eventually, the sound penetrated Marwin's consciousness, and he began to stir. Opening his eyes, he spotted his iPhone dancing across the nightstand. He reached for the jitterbugging phone and knocked his cholesterol medicine bottle onto the floor. As he answered the call, his befuddled brain registered that it was 3:21 a.m., and Jackson was calling him.

"Hey, Jackson. What's wrong?" Marwin asked, instantly awake.

"Sandy had the baby about an hour ago," Jackson told him.

"That's awesome. Congrats, Grandpa." He could already sense something was amiss.

"Yeah, thanks, but it looks like there might be a problem," Jackson said shakily. "The baby's Apgar scores were eights."

"Eights aren't bad," Marwin offered. When Jackson didn't respond, Marwin continued, "You know the scores can be subjective. One nurse might rule it an eight, and another one might say it's a nine."

"Or they could say seven," Jackson said sadly.

"Come on, Jackson. You know there is zero reason to worry about Apgars of eight."

"Yeah, maybe, but Cody said the baby was lethargic, too."

"Again, that could just be Cody's perception. His observation might be based on watching newborn babies on Grey's Anatomy reruns," Marwin suggested.

"I doubt it," Jackson said.

"All right. Hang up and get Delta on the phone. Fly out and see for yourself that the baby is fine." It was the best suggestion to help alleviate Jackson's fear.

"I'd like to, but the trial is set to begin. I want to see that sonofabitch fry!" Jackson spat.

"Actually, Destiny told me today that the start has been pushed back until Monday, so you can fly out, see your grandchild and get back for the trial."

"Why the hell didn't someone let me know the trial was going to start on Monday?" Jackson thundered.

"It was late when Destiny called me. I assumed you had already been notified."

"Hell, no! No one told me shit," Jackson yelled, fully enraged.

"I'm sorry, Jackson. Hey, it doesn't matter anyway. Just take the extra time to welcome your grandchild."

"It does fuckin' matter!" Jackson said, unable to let it go.

"You're right. You should have been contacted. I'll find out who dropped the ball, but in the meantime, see Cody, Sandy, and your new grandkid."

"OK. I will," Jackson sighed. "I'm sure I'll feel better once I hold him or her in my arms."

"Yep, I'm sure you will. Have a great trip and call me when you get back. Tell Cody and Sandy that I said congratulations."

"OK. Will do."

"Oh, Jackson. One question: What's the kid's name?" Marwin asked.

Jackson sat, stunned momentarily, then laughed and said, "Hell, I have no idea. I'll let you know when I find out."

\* \* \*

THE WOMAN LOUNGED LAZILY by the pool, unaware of the blazing sun beating down on her reddening skin. Her iPhone resided on the chair next to her, her earbuds were in place, and her eyes were closed behind her Maui Jim sunglasses. The Eagles played softly in her ears as she dozed off and on.

Her Pandora was briefly interrupted by an incoming text message, but the woman slept, her head lolling painfully to one side. Sixty seconds later, a second text message interrupted the music but failed to wake her. A minute following that unnoticed text, her phone rang in her ear. The second ring punched a small hole in her awareness before the third ring finally woke her. Glancing at her phone groggily, the woman sat bolt upright after seeing the caller's number.

"Hello," she answered, making herself sound normal.

"Why were my texts unanswered?" the man asked.

"Uh, I didn't see them, I guess," she stammered. "I was away from my phone for a few minutes." Her heart raced.

"Have you forgotten that you should never be away from your phone?" the man asked menacingly. "I expect to be able to reach you at *all times*. This is unacceptable."

*Oh, shit!* The woman thought, trying to formulate a plausible excuse. Finally, giving up, she said, "Yes, sir. I'm sorry. It won't happen again."

"See that it doesn't. I have a new assignment for you, and time is of the essence. I am faxing the details to you in exactly three minutes. I expect a report from you within forty-eight hours. No later."

As the call disconnected in her ear, the woman was already cramming her feet into her flip-flops and stuffing her towel into her bag. She flew back to her apartment.

\* \* \*

MARWIN'S WEEKEND WENT BY in a blur of softballs, baseballs, and heat. Bogie's travel team played in a tournament in Bearden, having two games on Saturday and one on Sunday. Thankfully, the Eagles played poorly on Sunday and were knocked out early. Between the games, Marwin worked with Morgan in the batting cages and on empty adjacent fields on hitting, fielding, and throwing.

Physically, Morgan was athletic, but she had poor throwing form, couldn't judge a fly ball, and was unlikely ever to be able to hit live pitching. Still, she had worked tirelessly in the sweltering heat without whining. As the sweaty trio loaded into the SUV, Morgan asked, "So, what do you think, Dad?"

She was enthusiastic, even though she was tired, and it caused Marwin to temper his answer. "Well, you have a great arm and are very fast, so that will be attractive to them."

"I doubt anyone is going to think she is attractive," Bogie offered with a sneer.

Before Marwin could chastise Bogie, Morgan slugged him in the arm. "Shut up, Butt-face!"

Bogie shoved her back, so Marwin had to referee. "Hey! Don't touch your sister or any other woman for that matter!"

"She's not a woman. She's a pipsqueak," Bogie replied.

"That's enough! Watch your mouth," Marwin advised. "Actually, you can mouth off all you want while you mow the grass when we get home."

"Dad, no! I just played three games in twenty-four hours. I don't want to mow the yard today."

"I don't want to listen to you whine either," Marwin said irritably.

"I'm not mowing the yard," Bogie grumbled.

"You might want to reconsider that last statement," Marwin returned evenly.

No other sound was forthcoming, so Marwin turned up WIMZ, and they rolled on home.

* * *

DELTA FLIGHT 230 TOUCHED down at Laramie Regional Airport, and Jackson trudged wearily to the closest rental car kiosk. After securing a Ford Explorer, he stopped at a sandwich shop, picked up a sub that felt like it weighed five pounds and a Coke, and hit the road. According to the navigation system in the SUV, it was a twenty-minute drive to the hospital.

As he drove, Jackson's mind turned to a multitude of subjects. He was excited to meet his new grandchild but worried there might be some medical problem. He couldn't believe that someone might be purposely harming his patients. He couldn't wait for the trial to start so he could watch that bastard, Shoehorn, fry. He missed Madeline intensely and was saddened that she would never see their grandchild.

The lack of sleep and the mental anguish caused Jackson to sink lower in his seat. Glancing in the side mirror, he saw a line of cars backed up behind him. A glance at the speedometer told him he was driving at 30mph.

"Shit," he said aloud as he mashed the accelerator.

Once at the hospital, Jackson found his way to the maternity floor and approached the nurse's station.

"Can I help you?" a woman dressed in blue scrubs asked pleasantly.

"Yes, I'm looking for my new grandchild. He or she was born last night." Jackson explained.

"OK, sure. What's the name?"

"Uh, I have no idea," Jackson responded, laughing. "My son called and said the baby had been born, and I jumped on a plane and got here as fast as I could. I never thought to ask the name, and I didn't tell my son I was coming."

"That's all right," the nurse said, smiling. "What's your daughter-in-law's name?"

"Sandy, Sandy Montgomery. No, that's not right. They haven't gotten married yet. Hell, I don't know. I'm too tired to think. I can't even remember Sandy's last name," Jackson finished pathetically.

The nurse looked oddly at Jackson, trying to decide if there was a lunatic loose on the ward. "OK. Wait right here. I believe we only have one Sandy up here right now. Let me check. I'll be right back."

Jackson nodded and said, "Thank you."

Realizing that he probably looked like a patient who escaped from the psych floor, he decided to find the restroom and try to freshen up. As he reached to open the door, Cody exited the bathroom.

"Dad? What the hell are you doing here?" He embraced Jackson in a big hug.

"Thought I would check out the newest member of the family," Jackson replied, relishing in the embrace.

As Jackson and Cody walked past the nurse's station, the nurse said, "Looks like you found someone you know."

Jackson smiled and kept walking.

"What was that about?" Cody asked.

"I'll tell you later," Jackson replied as the two entered Sandy's room.

Sandy was holding the child to her breast, but she glanced up when she heard the door open.

"Dad! What are you doing here?"

Jackson turned toward the wall and repeated his previous answer. "Just thought I would check up on the newest member of the family."

"I'm so glad you are here. Come over here and meet her in person." Sandy said.

"Uh, go ahead and feed her. I'll see her in a few minutes." Jackson tried to hide his awkwardness.

"She's done. I actually think she has fallen asleep. I guess my breast isn't that exciting." Covering herself, she handed the baby to Jackson. "Here, take her, Dad."

Jackson took the tiny, seemingly perfect baby off Sandy's chest and held her in his arms. The previous chaos melted from his mind, and his heart swelled to a height that he wasn't aware was possible.

Blinking back tears, he asked, "What's this beauty's name?"

"Maddie Olivia Montgomery," Cody answered, coming to stand by his father. "We wanted to name her after Mom but didn't want it to be Madeline. So, we went with Maddie and made her initials spell MOM."

Jackson was overwhelmed with emotion, and tears spilled from his tired eyes.

* * *          —

KRISTEN STEPPED OUT INTO the late-afternoon sun and was immediately smothered by the humidity. She had dressed in a tee shirt, running shorts, and tennis shoes and intended to go for a late-day jog. Seemingly, school and work—but certainly not the chardonnay—had added a few pounds on the scale since she had moved to Knoxville.

The stifling heat and humidity were causing her to second-guess the jogging outing. Standing on the sidewalk in front of her apartment, she waffled back and forth. Before she could decide, Polly emerged from her apartment.

"What's up?"

"Not much, just trying to decide if I really want to try to run or not. It's hot as hell out here."

"I can answer that for you," Polly offered. "You don't want to run. Your shoes would melt on the asphalt."

"Maybe, but I need to run. My ass is getting fat," Kristen confessed.

"Nah, your ass looks fine. You need to take it easy. You've been burning the proverbial candle at both ends and in the middle, too. I haven't even seen you all week," Polly lamented.

"I know. I really don't have a life. Just school, work, and repeat." She wiped the sweat from her brow and decided to follow her friend's advice. "You want to come over for a glass of wine?"

"I would love to, but I have to go to Forever Young. Maybe I'll stop by when I get back."

"OK, sure. Are you playing chess, Scrabble, or cards tonight?" Kristen asked with a chuckle.

"I'm not sure. This is a new client for me, so I don't know anything about her yet."

"Well, have fun babysitting," Kristen said.

"Beats the hell out of running in the ninety-five-degree heat," Polly replied, heading to her car.

* * *

DAWN ENTERED THE SLIDING doors of Forever Young and was instantly grateful for the reprieve from the scorching heat. She walked toward her grandmother's room, silently praying she was feeling better. Tom's death had taken a toll on Gladys, and she seemed to have reverted to the state when she first moved to the facility. The door opened as Dawn reached the room, and a young woman exited.

The woman was dressed in navy slacks and a lightweight blouse, carrying a black bag that was somewhere between the size of a purse and a suitcase.

The young woman smiled brightly. "Hi! How's it going?"

"Fine, thanks. I'm Dawn Anderson, and this is my grandmother's room," Dawn said, eyeing the woman.

"Nice to meet you, Dawn. I work with Geri Assist, and Tracey asked me to stop in and visit your grandmother," the woman explained. "She told me your grandmother lost her friend and has been really taking it hard, so I stopped by to chat with her and see how she was doing. She seems like a very sweet lady."

"Tracey's right," Dawn confirmed. "She hasn't been doing well since her boyfriend passed suddenly. Thanks for stopping by to see her."

"No problem. I'll see her two to three days a week until we get her back on track."

Dawn's eyebrows shot up. "I'm sorry, I don't understand. What exactly do you do?"

Before the woman could answer, Gladys opened the door and said, "I thought I heard voices out here. Why are you standing in the hall, Dawn? Come on inside."

Dawn stepped past the woman, and a cold shiver ran through her as she brushed against her.

# CHAPTER 30

Marwin was awakened by a loud clap of thunder at 4:48 a.m. Groaning, he rolled away from the pounding rain outside his window, but to no avail, as lightning lit the room, followed immediately by a house-shaking blast of thunder. The alarm was set for five o'clock, so he decided to get up. The kids had to get ready for their first day of school, and Shoehorn's trial was starting, so it was likely to be an eventful day.

Marwin made his way downstairs, switched on the coffee pot, and retrieved Bogie's lunch from the fridge. He quickly clicked onto his gambling site and discovered the Red Sox had gotten blasted by the Orioles, and his wager had gone up in flames.

*That's a great start to the day*, he thought sarcastically.

He debated the safety of showering during the storm but was spared the decision as the house was rocked again, and the lights went out. "Shit," he said, disgusted, and took his coffee into the study. Seated at his desk, he listened to the rain pounding on the roof, and his thoughts turned to the upcoming trial.

*What a shitty year Jackson has had*, Marwin thought sadly. His wife of twenty-four years had committed suicide, likely assisted by her psychotic doctor, and now some other psycho was trying to poison his patients. He could think of no other explanation for why an elderly patient with no history of drug abuse had amphetamines and ammonium chloride in his system.

Ammonium chloride was not a commonly found substance. It was an ingredient in licorice, but someone would have to ingest ridiculous amounts of it for the inorganic compound to appear in appreciable levels in their body.

The significant number of amphetamines in the man's blood was the deciding factor for Marwin. He deduced that someone was giving the man amphetamines and then trying to mask it with the ammonium chloride that would speed the elimination of the amphetamines.

*Damn,* he thought, *it would have to be someone with extensive medical knowledge to concoct that mixture of drugs.*

*Who would have daily access to a patient in an assisted living facility?* Jackson was the man's doctor, so he obviously didn't poison him. Marwin had no idea what pharmacy the man used, but he couldn't fathom a pharmacist intentionally poisoning the man.

*Maybe a drug error occurred?* He supposed a nurse saw him every day at Forever Young, but the man was in good health and took few meds, so that seemed unlikely. It seemed improbable that a nurse would be able to feed him amphetamines and ammonium chloride every day.

Marwin continued to ponder the situation before realizing the kitchen lights were back on. Listening, he heard only silence as the pounding rain was gone. He jumped through the shower and dressed in khaki pants with an aqua-blue golf shirt.

Slipping on a pair of Docksiders, he woke the kids as there had been no sign of life from either of them. Remarkably, he rousted the kids out of bed with minimal effort and headed downstairs for more coffee. Marwin watched Bogie board the bus and gave Morgan instructions to start a load of laundry before her bus arrived.

Having accomplished quite a bit in his mind, Marwin climbed into his SUV and headed off on the thirteen-mile trip to the Knoxville courthouse. The earlier deluge caused water to pond on the interstate, and that, combined with the normal Monday morning traffic, turned the commute as black as the morning sky. He barely maintained 20mph and grew nervous as court started promptly at 9 a.m.

He and Destiny had planned to meet at eight, but that looked unlikely now. Feeling his frustration build, he decided to try to be productive, so he called Bradley Jinswain. For once, he abided by the hands-free law and used his Bluetooth to call through his car.

"Good morning," Bradley answered.

"Morning, Bradley. You got a minute?"

"Sure, I'm eating breakfast and trying to get motivated to clear some of this paperwork off my desk. What's up?"

"I wanted to bounce something off you. It might be crazy, but it might not either."

"Uh-oh. I remember the last time you had a crazy idea," Bradley said, referring to Marwin's theory that Shoehorn had caused Madeline to kill herself.

"Yeah, and I was right," Marwin said somewhat defensively.

"Yeah, I just hope they can prove it in court over the next week or so," Bradley remarked. "What you got this time?"

"I think someone is poisoning Jackson's patients," Marwin stated.

"Whoa! Are you talking about the patients of his that have died recently?"

"You know about that?" Marwin asked, surprised.

"Yeah, Jackson called me a few days ago and told me that he had lost several patients unexpectantly and for no foreseeable reason."

"A foreseeable reason could be that they are being poisoned," Marwin offered.

"Poisoned? What are you talking about?"

Marwin explained that the autopsy results showed hypertensive crisis, serotonin syndrome, and the presence of amphetamines and ammonium chloride in the man's system.

"Wow! Amphetamines? That seems unlikely to me in an elderly man, but I guess nothing surprises me much anymore. Everyone seems to be on some drug—legal or illegal—these days."

"True," Marwin said, thinking of the increase in narcotics and anxiety drugs in his patients at work. "But, based on the ammonium chloride, I feel certain he was being poisoned with the amphetamines and then given the ammonium chloride to try to speed the removal of the drug."

"Wait, I'm confused. Why would someone poison somebody with a drug and give them another drug to remove it faster? That makes no sense to me."

"Sure it does," Marwin said confidently. "The plan is for the amphet-amines to do the damage and the ammonium chloride to remove them, so they will likely go undetected."

"Well, if you put it that way, I guess I could see it," Bradley admitted. He still sounded unsure, though. "So, what do you want me to do with this theory of yours?"

"I'm not certain, really," Marwin confessed. "I doubt you can open an investigation based on a seventy-year-old man having amphetamines in his system."

"You would be correct about that," Bradley agreed. "Let me think about it, and I will get back to you."

"OK, thanks. You coming to the trial?" Marwin asked.

"No, probably not today. I am on standby if things progress faster than anticipated, but it will likely be at least Wednesday before I have to testify."

The courthouse parking lot stretched out in front of Marwin, and every space seemed filled. He wished Bradley better luck with his day as he searched for a place to park in the sea of vehicles.

It was time to face his would-be murderer, and Marwin was ready to help put Shoehorn away for the rest of his life.

* * *

IT WAS 8:25 A.M. before Marwin secured a parking spot and found Destiny inside the courthouse. She was talking to Jackson, who looked like he had been on a three-day bender. Destiny looked beautiful in a simple navy dress that brushed her knees. Marwin wondered for the unknownth time why she was attracted to him. He had clearly outkicked his coverage!

Marwin came up behind Destiny and nodded at Jackson over her shoulder. He resisted the urge to pat her on the butt but grabbed her shoulders and kissed her lightly on the cheek.

"Umm," Destiny said, tilting her head to the side.

"You didn't even know who was kissing you!" Marwin groused.

"I'd know your kiss anywhere," Destiny returned with a smile.

Jackson watched the exchange. "Get a room."

"We've got a room, a courtroom. Now, let's go put that bastard away for good," Destiny said, eyes blazing.

Marwin and Jackson followed Destiny into a room they had never seen. It was still fifteen minutes before the trial was set to start, but most of the seats were already filled. Destiny sat beside Simon at the prosecutor's table, and Marwin and Jackson sat behind her in the front row.

The jury was already seated and consisted of seven women and five men. Simon was pleased with the extra female juror, assuming that women would be appalled at a gynecologist taking advantage of his patients. He hoped it would be easier for the jurors to believe the same doctor had intentionally harmed his patients.

After the judge was seated, Simon was given the floor to make his opening statement.

"Good morning. My name is Simon McKinney, and I will represent the State of Tennessee in this extraordinary case.

"Over the last few years, a local doctor has gone astray. Not only has he broken the oath to do no harm, but he has broken the law in the most serious manner possible. We will show that the doctor abused his relationship with his patients, made inappropriate sexual advances, and even coerced some patients into committing suicide.

"Members of the jury, we will provide witnesses who will testify to the inappropriate actions of the doctor. We will show you evidence of how he imported a drug from another country with the sole purpose of causing his patients to commit suicide. You will hear from a local Doctor of Pharmacy how this man caused his trusting, unsuspecting patients to kill themselves.

"The defense will ask you to believe that the doctor was provoked to the point that his mind snapped, but we will prove that he is far from insane. In fact, he devised a brilliant, almost foolproof, plan to get rid of his patients who confided in him about their sexual problems.

"Lastly, we will show irrefutable proof that the doctor is violent, as he is currently serving seven years in prison for attempted manslaughter of the very same Doctor of Pharmacy mentioned previously. At the conclusion of the evidence, we ask that you return a guilty verdict and prevent this doctor from doing more harm. Thank you."

Simon returned to his seat with a calm, confident look on his face. The defense attorney rose and sauntered toward the jury.

"Good morning, ladies and gentlemen. My name is Lawrence Wellborn, and my colleagues and I represent Dr. Ernie Shoehorn." Wellborn turned slightly and pointed to Shoehorn who sat dressed in a black suit with a grey tie.

Shoehorn's face was haggard, and he appeared to have lost twenty pounds since incarceration. His green eyes, once striking, were now sunken in their sockets.

"Dr. Shoehorn," Wellborn went on, "sits there, wrongly accused of murder. Dear Members of the Jury, this case represents a travesty of justice, an outright attack on a respected physician in our area who has effectively treated thousands of patients for over a decade.

"The prosecution mentioned that Dr. Shoehorn is brilliant, and on that point, they are correct! We will show how Dr. Shoehorn developed a cutting-edge drug regimen that treated the most difficult patients. You will hear from multiple patients extolling the benefits of Dr. Shoehorn's treatments. We will show that this case is frivolous and based on a jealous pharmacist's frustration at his inability to prescribe drugs himself."

At those words, Marwin sat on the edge of his seat, appearing ready to refute the attorney. Destiny turned slowly to Marwin and gave a slight shake of her head. Marwin's jaw clenched, but he saw Destiny's wan smile and settled back in his seat, his eyes throwing daggers at Wellborn.

"We will show that this rogue pharmacist went so far as to try to entrap Dr. Shoehorn, even enlisting the help of our own district attorney. The evidence will show that not only did Dr. Shoehorn help his patients, but he also went above and beyond the normal scope of practice to provide a better life for his patients. Once you have heard the evidence, you will determine that the state cannot meet the burden of proof and return a verdict of not guilty. Thank you."

* * *

THE WOMAN SAT ALONE on her couch, her bare feet propped on the coffee table. She sipped a glass of white wine and tried to formulate a plan for her latest assignment.

Sifting through the details she had received from her boss, she found that the target was a woman in her seventies who was relatively new to the Forever Young assisted living facility. Like her other recent targets, she was a widow with a large, lump-sum insurance policy. Her policy had a cancer clause, and she was believed to have lung cancer, so she needed to be eliminated before the diagnosis was confirmed by a doctor. Her death would prevent the policy's payout.

The target's medicines included a thyroid tablet, a diuretic, and a low-dose blood pressure tablet. She also used two inhalers for COPD. None of the medicines provided a quick and easy demise with the woman's usual method of elimination. Completely stumped, the woman paced around the room, her mind searching for any way to eliminate the target while making it look like a natural death.

The woman's labs indicated lung cancer as her CEA, RBP, and 1-antitrypsin levels were all through the roof. Fortunately, the company had an employee at the lab who was stalling the release of the information to the doctor. However, the results could only be delayed for so long without suspicions arising. Once the doctor made the diagnosis, the company would be forced to pay out the considerable lump-sum policy. At least the patient had not had an x-ray or lung biopsy, so there might still be time to eliminate her.

The woman finished her wine and refrained from refilling her glass in hopes of having an epiphany. A sense of panic edged in as she paced around the room. With each lap around the furniture, her anxiety level ratcheted up. She prided herself on her control and adaptability.

A small idea tickled her mind as she passed the closet. She opened the closet door, eyed the hidden refrigerator, and allowed the idea to blossom. Unfortunately, she doubted the plan would act quickly enough to eliminate this woman before the lab work returned and the doctor ordered x-rays and a biopsy that would confirm the cancer. The woman sighed. Unless another idea came soon, she would have to roll the dice with what she had. She opened the fridge and went to work.

* * *

KRISTEN CARRIED HER PLASTIC wine tumbler with her as she walked to the front of the apartment community to check her mail. She had not checked her mail since school had started, so she dreaded the bills she might find. The sun was finally sinking, but the heat and humidity persisted, and Kristen's shirt was quickly spotted with sweat stains. She retrieved her mail and was elated to find only the Xfinity bill with numerous pieces of junk mail.

Returning to her apartment, she noticed Polly's car parked nearby. Wondering why Polly hadn't come by for a glass of wine, she knocked on her door.

No answer came, so she glanced back toward the car, determining that the vehicle was Polly's, and knocked on the door again. Several seconds passed, and no one answered the door, so Kristen turned to leave. As she walked away, Polly opened the door, appearing somewhat frazzled.

"Hey, Kristen. What's up?" Polly asked.

"Not much. I saw your car and wondered if you were still interested in having that glass of wine. I knocked on the door a couple of times. I didn't think you were home."

"Uh, I was busy," Polly said sheepishly. "You know, a little afternoon delight," she added, grinning.

"Oh! I'm sorry," Kristen stammered, blushing.

"It's all good. Let me clean up, and I'll be right over."

"OK. Cool."

Even after her explanation, Polly's behavior and appearance seemed strange. Kristen had experienced some pretty wild nights, but none had ended with a creamy substance on her like the one she had seen on Polly's face and arms.

\* \* \*

COURT RECESSED FOR LUNCH, and Jackson and Marwin met outside the courtroom. Destiny remained behind to discuss the case with Simon. The two friends conversed about their interpretations of the morning session.

Simon had produced two women who were once patients of Shoehorn's but left his practice after becoming uncomfortable with his repeated physical exams. Both women were in their forties and reasonably attractive.

After that, the Assistant District Attorney introduced the charts of two now-deceased patients who were under Shoehorn's care when they committed suicide. One of the patients dived off the bridge into the Tennessee River, and the other patient swallowed the entire bottle of her antidepressants. Both charts referenced their complaints about poor sexual performance. Unfortunately, there was no mention of chlormethiazole, the strong, foreign drug Shoehorn had given Madeline and Destiny, or any special treatment in the charts.

Before lunch, Simon had introduced Madeline's chart into evidence. Like the previous charts, it referenced dissatisfaction with her sex life. Simon produced the dates of the office visits for Madeline, showing the frequency with which she saw Dr. Shoehorn. Next, he presented her computer calendar as evidence. Her calendar matched the previous visit dates exactly. The word *Start* appeared on Madeline's calendar, and Simon suggested it identified the date Madeline started her chlormethiazole therapy.

Destiny stepped out of the courtroom a few minutes later and joined the other two. As the rain had stopped, they walked the short distance to Stock and Barrel for lunch.

Jackson waited until they were seated to talk to Destiny about the trial. "What do you think, Des? You're the lawyer here."

"I thought everything went according to plan," she replied without hesitation.

"Well, I assume you guys put together a good strategy. I'll take that as a positive."

The three sat in a booth, ordered sandwiches and water, and tried not to mention the upcoming afternoon session.

Marwin said, "I called Bradley about your patients and told him my theory that someone is poisoning them. He is going to do some digging and let me know where we can go from there."

"Poisoning? What are you talking about?" Destiny asked around a bite of her Club sandwich.

Jackson and Marwin took turns bringing Destiny up to date on the deceased patients from Forever Young. Marwin hadn't had the chance to tell her the particulars about what he'd speculated.

Destiny sipped her water, and the ice clinked against the glass. "Well, if Marwin is right, it would almost have to be a doctor, pharmacist, or nurse behind it."

"Could that bastard Shoehorn be involved?" Jackson asked.

"I doubt it. He's been locked up for the entire time frame in question. If he is involved, he would be working with someone on the outside."

"I agree with Des. It seems unlikely that Shoehorn is involved."

"Yeah, you're probably right. The son-of-a-bitch probably doesn't have any friends he could work with," Jackson concurred.

"So, am I just the unluckiest fucker on Earth?" Jackson asked miserably.

Marwin clapped him on the back and tried to lighten the mood. "You're not unlucky. You have Destiny and me as friends!"

Jackson didn't bother to say anything. He drank some water, looking like he wished he had ordered scotch to go with it.

"So, let's figure out our next step," Marwin suggested, pushing on.

"Whoa! Dr. Gelstone, you're not putting your detective hat on again, are you?" Destiny asked, smirking.

"Well, maybe," Marwin returned sheepishly. "I am the drug expert, so it only makes sense that I try to figure this out."

Destiny knew Marwin too well. With a bright smile, she said proudly, "That's my Baby!" After a brief pause, her eyebrows jumped, and she added, "So, you've started gambling again, huh?"

\* \* \*

DURING THE AFTERNOON SESSION, Jackson took the witness stand. He was visibly unsettled and couldn't take his eyes off Shoehorn sitting calmly at the defense table. Sensing Jackson's unease, Simon walked him through some easy questions. Jackson quickly relaxed and gave a passionate testimony.

He told the court about the packet of powder in Madeline's purse. He explained how he allowed Marwin to go through their medicine cabinet, and Marwin discovered multiple allergy medications and vitamins. Jackson described Madeline's horrible breath and uncontrolled sneezing that lasted for a couple of weeks and then cleared up, seemingly overnight, about two weeks before her death.

Simon allowed Jackson to explain that chlormethiazole frequently caused sneezing and bad breath as a side effect of treatment. Before Simon finished with Jackson, he asked, "Dr. Montgomery, can you please tell us the most severe side-effect of chlormethiazole?"

Jackson took a slow, deep breath, looked directly at Shoehorn, and answered shakily, "Chlormethiazole can induce suicide if stopped abruptly."

One juror audibly gasped, and several others shifted uneasily in their seats.

Upon cross-examination, Wellborn asked Jackson, "Isn't it true that you physically attacked Dr. Shoehorn in a local restaurant?"

Jackson didn't answer immediately, but after the judge's prompting, he said, "I never hit him."

"Dr. Montgomery, did you reach across the table and physically grab Dr. Shoehorn by his coat, causing drinks to spill?" Wellborn asked.

Jackson shifted the target of his daggers from Shoehorn to Wellborn. "Yes."

"So, you obviously have an intense dislike for the defendant," Wellborn said.

"Of course I do. He forced my wife to kill herself!" Jackson asserted.

"Your Honor?" Wellborn pleaded.

"Dr. Montgomery, please answer the questions as they are asked and refrain from further comments," the judge admonished.

"Yes, Your Honor," Jackson replied easily.

Wellborn hammered away at Jackson, asserting that Jackson had hated Shoehorn in medical school and looked for someone to blame for his wife's death. Jackson stated that he hardly knew Shoehorn at Duke and only remembered him as a mediocre student who finished near the bottom of their class.

Moving on, Wellborn focused on Madeline's chart and delved into her sexual problems.

"We weren't having any sexual problems," Jackson barked.

"So, your wife was able to reach climax every time you had sexual relations?" Wellborn asked.

"Objection! Irrelevant, Your Honor," Simon said, standing.

"Your Honor, Dr. Shoehorn treated Mrs. Montgomery for depression and sexual dissatisfaction. We are trying to establish the rationale for the treatment," Wellborn offered.

"Overruled. Dr. Montgomery, please answer the question."

Jackson pressed his lips together and scowled.

"Dr. Montgomery?" the judge pressed.

"I doubt Madeline climaxed every time we made love, "Jackson finally admitted.

Wellborn pounced. "You *doubt* it? You don't know? You didn't care enough to ask or try to find out?"

"Objection! Your Honor, the defense is badgering the witness!" Simon roared. He stood and pointed at Wellborn.

"Sustained. Mr. Wellborn, please ask a question and allow the witness to answer."

"Yes, Your Honor," Wellborn said, stifling a smile.

He turned to Jackson. "One last thing, Dr. Montgomery. Please tell us about your illicit affair with your head nurse."

# CHAPTER 31

Bradley sat back in his chair and stretched, his back popping and cracking in protest of the last three hours. He grabbed a protein bar from his desk drawer and gently rubbed his eyes.

His day had been split between an active investigation of a murder by a drug-crazed eighteen-year-old and an endless amount of paperwork for an armed robbery that had resulted in two people being shot, including the perpetrator.

The paperwork had taken much longer than it should have as his mind wandered to Shoehorn's trial and Jackson's theory that someone was trying to kill his patients. Ignoring his distended bladder, Bradley picked up the phone and dialed.

A gruff voice answered after the fourth ring. "Coroner's office."

"Hey, Vince. It's Bradley Jinswain. Have you been promoted to answering the phones?" Bradley laughed.

"Fuck off, Jinswain. I'm busy. Do you want something, or did you call just to piss me off?" Vince Adkins barked.

It was pointless to beat around the bush. "I was wondering if you had analyzed the stomach contents for Wilson Stanford."

"Who?"

"Wilson Stanford. He was the elderly patient of Dr. Montgomery's who died unexpectedly recently. I believe your diagnosis was a hypertensive crisis, secondary to serotonin syndrome."

"Oh, yeah. I remember him. His body basically exploded," Adkins said callously. "What do you want with the stomach contents? You investigating something?"

"It's been suggested that Mr. Stanford may have been poisoned."

"Did a little bird land on your shoulder, shit, and then whisper that in your ear?"

"Actually, Marwin Gelstone, a pharmacist, suggested it as a possibility," Bradley said slowly.

"Ah, shit! Not him again. What does the pharmacist-turned-Dick Tracey think happened to this poor slob?"

Bradley's face heated. "Look, I just need the stomach contents, Vince."

"My official report will be ready in a couple of days. You can get them then."

"No, I can get them right now, Vince. I suggest you try being a little more cooperative when I call," Bradley threatened.

"Hey, you said we were even," Adkins replied, voice shaking and bravado gone.

"You can give me the results or report me to my boss for reneging on my promise. I can still turn you in for illegal gambling."

"You're an asshole, Jinswain!"

"Everybody's gotta be somebody," Bradley replied, laughing. "The stomach contents?"

"OK, hold on a minute. Let me get them."

Bradley listened to classical music in his ear as he waited for Adkins to return, finally feeling as if he had accomplished something. Within a minute, Adkins rattled off the information he'd requested.

"Sausage—probably summer sausage—bits of cracker, a white creamy cheese residue, grape skins, and a light red tint, likely a red wine," Adkins reported.

"Do you have his blood alcohol content?"

"No, I would never have thought to check that," Adkins scoffed. Before Bradley could respond, Adkins continued, "It was 0.04 percent. Anything else I can do for you?"

"No, that's it for now." He decided to try to smooth things over a little. "I really appreciate your help, Vince."

The only response was an audible click as Adkins hung up the phone.

* * *

"I'VE NEVER HAD AN affair!" Jackson thundered. He started to rise.

"Keep your seat, Dr. Montgomery," the judge admonished.

"Dr. Montgomery, didn't your wife suggest the contrary in her suicide note?" Wellborn asked as Jackson slid back down.

"My wife didn't write a suicide note!"

"Dr. Montgomery, please answer the questions civilly. Inside voice, please," the judge instructed.

Jackson glared but said, "Yes, Your Honor. I'm sorry."

"Please proceed, Mr. Wellborn."

"We have your wife's note right here." Wellborn waved a piece of paper. "Your Honor, the defense would like to read the note aloud, if the court will allow it."

"As you wish," the judge said.

Wellborn cleared his throat and began reading, "*Dearest Jackson, I never imagined writing a letter like this, much less what I am about to do. However, as they say, 'Never say never.' I feel that I have no choice but to end my life. I've been unhappy for months, and you haven't noticed or didn't care. I am sick of doing for everyone else and no one doing for me. I guess you will have to learn what to do for yourself now or maybe some other woman can help you. I feel that you have used me for years. I made all the appearances with you so that you could look like the happy doctor, but you ignored me when we got home. You haven't wanted sex in months. I guess you're being taken care of somewhere else. You never worried about my wants or needs, but you sure expected me to take care of yours. I know my death will be an embarrassment to you, but not as embarrassing as being the trophy wife of a local doctor. Well, your trophy is broken. Goodbye, Madeline.*"

Jackson visibly shrunk in his seat as Wellborn read the supposed suicide note. Seeing Jackson's discomfort, Wellborn asked, "Dr. Montgomery, were you having an affair?"

Jackson looked to Simon, expecting an objection, but Simon sat placidly, looking on. "No. I've told you. I've never had an affair. I also told you that Madeline didn't write that note."

"It is clearly signed by your wife and contains details of your relationship no one else would know."

"Bullshit!" Jackson roared. "There is no signature, and every detail is a lie."

"Dr. Montgomery, you will watch your language, or I will hold you in contempt of court," the judge said firmly.

"I believe there is plenty of truth in the details," Wellborn pushed.

"Objection! Is the defense going to ask a question or hypothesize?" Simon asked, standing.

"Sustained. Mr. Wellborn, stick to asking questions of the witness and save your hypothesis for your closing argument."

"Yes, Your Honor. I have nothing else for Dr. Montgomery," Wellborn said, striding back to the table.

* * *

"HEY, TRACEY. HOW'S IT going?" the woman asked the nurse as she strode past the nurse's station.

"Oh, hey. It's going, I guess," Tracey replied with a weak smile.

"Hang in there. It's almost Friday."

"Uh, it's only Tuesday," Tracey said, frowning.

"That's a technicality. You can act like it's almost Friday," the woman replied glibly.

"I wish I could be as upbeat as you seem to be all the time."

"What's not to be upbeat about? I love my job!" the woman stated enthusiastically.

"Apparently, more than I love mine," Tracey admitted.

"By the way. How's Gladys doing?" the woman inquired.

"Oh, she's about the same, I guess. Still seems really down."

"All right. I'll stop in and check on her."

The woman proceeded to an apartment door and was greeted a minute later by a small, grey-haired woman. She was hunched at the waist and had a pained expression.

"How are you today?" the woman asked.

"All right, I guess," the elderly woman said tiredly, turning back into the room.

"Are you sure you're OK? You don't look like you feel well."

"You're right. I don't feel well. I've been sweaty today, and my skin is clammy. I think something is going on with my heart. It feels like it's about to pound out of my chest."

"Huh, let me take your blood pressure and listen to your heart," the woman said, withdrawing a stethoscope from her black bag.

The woman listened to the elderly woman's heart and was delighted to hear it galloping. She placed her fingers on the artery in the woman's wrist and counted forty beats in fifteen seconds.

*Excellent!* she thought.

Next, the woman observed the other woman's breathing and mentally noted that her respirations were almost eighty breaths per minute.

*Perfect!*

Attaching the cuff, she measured the blood pressure and was thrilled to find that it was 185/100.

The woman removed her stethoscope and smiled. "Well, everything sounds good. Your pressure is a little bit elevated, but nothing to worry about. Have you eaten anything today? I brought some more of the cheese you ate yesterday since you seemed to enjoy it."

"It was delicious. I've never had cheese like that before," the elderly woman agreed.

"Let me get you some. Would you like a small glass of wine or anything? You know, the wine might help you relax, which could bring your blood pressure down," the woman offered.

"No, thank you. Just a glass of water and that wonderful cheese, please."

*Crap. You can't win them all,* the woman thought as she headed to the kitchen.

She returned a few minutes later and found the elderly woman slumped in a recliner, sweating profusely and ghostly pale.

"Here's your cheese," the woman said happily as if nothing was wrong.

"Not sure … not sure I can, uh," the elderly woman started to say but gasped instead.

"Nonsense, this will make you feel so much better."

She moaned, grabbing her chest. "Help me. Call the nurse."

"OK, hang in there. I'll be right back," the woman replied, going to the door.

After locking the door, the woman returned and sat beside the elderly woman, taking her hand. She was repulsed at the cold, clammy hand, drenched in sweat.

"Oh, oh," the elderly woman said again, grabbing her chest.

"I'm right here," the woman assured her gently.

The older woman slumped sideways in the chair, barely conscious. Taking the cheese, the woman inserted a large gob of the creamy substance into the older woman's cheek. The drug inside the cheese was rapidly absorbed through her cheek, bypassing the liver and obtaining maximum effects.

She moaned softly but was too weak to move. The woman re-checked her pulse, and it had increased to over two hundred beats per minute. She smiled and sat back on her chair beside the elderly woman who had finally ceased to moan. Twenty minutes passed, and the woman checked for a pulse, but this time there was none.

With the expected outcome realized, the woman worked quickly, removing the residue of the cheese spread from the older woman's mouth. She then moved her to her bed, tucking her in neatly. Picking up the plate with the cheese and crackers, she stuffed it all into her large black bag. She retraced her steps to the kitchen, making sure that there were no remnants of the cheese. After washing the knife and returning it to the drawer, she checked the dead woman's pulse one last time before leaving the apartment.

"See you later," the woman said as she passed Tracey's desk.

"How's Mrs. Westmoreland today?" Tracey asked, glancing up.

"She's fine. She didn't want to play any games, though. She said she felt like taking a nap, so I tucked her in, and she was out before I even got out the door."

"I wish I could take a nap," Tracey lamented.

"Nah, there's plenty of time for that when you're dead." The woman laughed as she walked out the door.

\* \* \*

MARWIN SAT AT HIS desk, eating pizza, staring blankly at the gambling site on the screen. He was exhausted. He didn't know a trial was so tiring, especially when he wasn't presenting or testifying.

The constant back-and-forth between the lawyers was incredible. He had been disgusted by the lawyers who would lead a witness into an answer and then cut the witness off and twist the words around.

*I'd hate to be a juror trying to decipher what the truth actually is,* he thought.

Marwin scrolled through the baseball standings and noticed the Yankees had lost three games consecutively. They were only a small favorite over the surging Angels, so he bet fifty dollars on the Yankees to win. He resisted the urge to bet on more games and closed the computer to go in search of his children.

He located Bogie in his room, muffled rap music emanating from his earbuds. Bogie gave a half-hearted wave at Marwin but didn't remove his earpieces.

Marwin pointed to his ear and waited for Bogie to remove the earbuds. "How was school today?"

"Good," Bogie replied, reinserting the earbuds.

Marwin walked over to Bogie and pulled the buds from his ears. "Don't be rude."

"What? How was I rude?"

Marwin ignored the questions. "What classes do you have this semester?"

"Same old classes, math, science, English, history."

"What math do you have this year?" Marwin persisted.

"Calculus II," Bogie said with a groan.

*Great*, Marwin thought. Calculus had almost killed Bogie last year. He even started skipping school to avoid going to class. Marwin had finally gotten a tutor, and Bogie survived with a C.

"OK. We want to stay on top of that one. We can get some outside help if we need to. What about science? Do you have chemistry?"

"Yeah," Bogie answered, clearly uninterested.

"I loved chemistry when I was in school," Marwin offered.

"Cool," Bogie replied, eyeing the earbuds still in Marwin's hands.

Changing tactics, Marwin asked, "Did you watch Morgan's tryouts?"

"Yeah, but the field was flooded, so they just went into the gym and let the girls throw and hit some soft toss into nets."

"How'd she do?"

"She did good, but you may be getting a bill from the school," Bogie said cryptically.

"Ah, hell. Let me go find out what happened. Get some rest."

"OK. Good luck tomorrow, Dad."

Stunned, Marwin looked back at Bogie. He had purposely kept the details of Shoehorn's trial from his kids. They hadn't shown much interest, and Marwin didn't want to trouble them. He was shocked that Bogie knew he was taking the witness stand the next day.

"Thanks, Bud," he said simply as he left the room.

Marwin found Morgan sitting on the side of her bed, firing a softball into a glove. She was listening to Carrie Underwood sing about carving her name into the leather seats of some cheater's car.

"Hey, Bit. How was your day?"

"It was awesome! My teachers seem really nice, and Mariah is in two of my classes." Morgan replied enthusiastically.

"Great. How'd tryouts go?"

"Well, the field was too wet to get on, so we went to the gym. We did some throwing and hit balls into nets. I think I did fine."

"Cool. Maybe you guys will be able to get on the field tomorrow so you can show off your speed."

"Yeah, Coach Dalton said I have a cannon," Morgan said, beaming.

"You do. Sometimes it's a loose cannon, though," Marwin said with a chuckle. "I heard I might be getting a bill from the school for some damages?"

Morgan's eyes widened. "Bogie is such a butthead! It wasn't my fault, Dad. The girl didn't catch the ball, so it went off the tip of her glove and ricocheted into the janitor's room window."

"I see. So, maybe next time, get the throw down into her chest," Marwin suggested, ever opposed to excuses.

"All right," Morgan replied dourly.

Marwin ruffled her hair. "Hey, I'm really proud of you for trying out. Keep working hard."

"Dad, my hair!"

"It's OK. There's a brush in the bathroom," Marwin said, laughing. "See you in the morning."

"Good night, Dad, and good luck tomorrow in court."

\* \* \*

MARWIN RETURNED TO HIS study and tried to find the Yankee game on the television. He considered pouring himself a merlot but opted for Crystal Light instead. After scanning the variety of channels available and coming up empty on the Yankee game, he settled for the Braves and Brewers game.

As the game played, Marwin thought about his upcoming appearance on the witness stand. After watching the defense try to destroy Jackson's testimony without even a hint of sympathy for his loss, Marwin dreaded how they would attack him.

To the layperson, his story about Keith Moon and chlormethiazole would sound crazy. Unfortunately, all the jurors were laypeople, so that didn't bode well. Marwin's recent nemesis, self-doubt, began to creep in, and he reconsidered the merlot.

Scores scrolled across the bottom of the TV, and Marwin noted that the Yankees were down 5-1 in the seventh inning. Emitting a curse, he turned the TV off, leaned his head back, and closed his eyes. Within mere seconds, Marwin drifted off and was softly snoring.

Sometime after midnight, Marwin awoke with a stiff neck, momentarily dazed at his surroundings. He stumbled upstairs, not even turning off all of the lights. He set his alarm, crawled into bed, and was instantly wide awake.

Instead of sleeping, his mind raced with thoughts of the trial. He tossed one way, then another, before finally giving up and going downstairs. It was 3:14 a.m., and he was exhausted and frustrated. On a whim, he decided to review the chart of the patient who had possibly been poisoned.

The patient was on two medications that could increase serotonin activity, citalopram and carbamazepine. He had been stable on the combination for quite some time, so it seemed unlikely that excessive serotonin developed overnight. Of course, if the man truly took amphetamines, it would explain the serotonin effects, hypertension, stroke, and heart attack. Marwin dug through his mental filing cabinet until he located a definition.

*A hypertensive crisis often occurs due to uncontrolled high blood pressure. It can also occur with severe kidney disease or the use of recreational drugs such as amphetamines or cocaine. Drug interaction with monoamine oxidase inhibitors could also lead to a hypertensive crisis.*

The patient did have amphetamines in his system, but there was no hint of illicit drug use, according to Jackson. He was not taking a monoamine oxidase inhibitor, so that pathway was out. Frustrated, Marwin closed his mental filing cabinet and covered up on the couch with a throw. As his mind slipped slowly into sleep, an idea formed.

# CHAPTER 32

The day dawned with a dense fog engulfing Knoxville. Visibility was less than a quarter mile, and traffic crawled at a snail's pace. Fortunately, Marwin rose at 5:30 a.m., showered, and dressed quickly in blue khaki pants and a light-blue, short-sleeved, button-down Oxford shirt.

He had only slept for a couple of hours but felt more refreshed than normal. He silently wondered if it was due to his choice of beverages the previous night.

He got the kids up and out the door and commuted to the courthouse, eating a chicken biscuit on the way. Before leaving, he had checked the baseball scores from the previous night and was shocked to see the Yankees rallied and won 6–5. He took it as a good omen for the day.

The fog was dense but dissipated as the autumn sun began its assault. Marwin's grandfather always said that for every big fog in August, there would be a corresponding large snowfall during the winter. Marwin had never kept up with his theory and had no idea if there was science to back it up. However, if the theory held, Knoxville was in for a helluva snowstorm that winter.

As he entered the courthouse, Marwin broke out in a sweat. Destiny talked with Simon. She was dressed in a bright green dress, her long brown hair lying easily across her shoulders. *Oh, my,* Marwin thought, mesmerized as always by Destiny's beauty.

"Hey, Hottie," Destiny said, spying Marwin. She gave him a quick kiss. "You ready?"

"I hope so," Marwin replied, forcing a smile.

"You'll be fine. Just be your normal, confident self. Remember, you are the reason we caught Shoehorn to start with." She took his hand in hers. "I believe in you."

"Thanks, Des. Let's go fry that bastard!" Marwin said, visibly puffing up.

After swearing in, Marwin took his seat on the witness stand, and Simon asked, "Dr. Gelstone, will you please describe for us how you came to be involved in the investigation of Madeline Montgomery's death?"

"Yes. Dr. Montgomery and I have had a collaborative agreement for several years. He diagnoses the patients, and I handle the drug therapy. After Madeline's death, he was searching for answers to explain her—uh—irrational behavior. Even though he knew that Madeline didn't take many medications, Jackson asked me to look through her medicine cabinet to see if anything could have caused problems."

"I see," Simon said. "And what did you find?"

"Absolutely nothing, except for a bunch of allergy medications and a drawer full of vitamins and herbal supplements that we later learned came from Shoehorn. There was nothing that suggested she would end her life."

"Was that the end of your involvement?" Simon asked.

"No. Really, it was just the beginning." Marwin took a deep breath and steeled his nerves. He recited how Shoehorn had given Madeline the chlormethiazole in a specific regimen designed to cause her to harm herself.

"Did you know Dr. Shoehorn before Mrs. Montgomery's death?" Simon inquired.

"Sort of. I had some discussions on the phone with him regarding his prescribing habits. On several occasions, Dr. Shoehorn prescribed inappropriate dosages of medications."

"Objection, Your Honor. The witness is offering an opinion that wasn't requested," Wellborn said, standing. "He is disparaging my client."

"Your Honor, the witness has a Doctorate of Pharmacy. He is a drug expert and is certainly qualified to know if a dosage is correct," Simon refuted.

"Overruled," the judge decided.

"What happened when you questioned the doctor's dosages?" Simon asked, returning to Marwin.

"He immediately adopted a god complex. He told me that I was just a pharmacist, and my job was to dispense whatever medication he prescribed in the exact manner he had prescribed it."

"Did you agree to do that?" Simon asked, already knowing the answer.

"Of course not. I would never give one of my patients a dosage that was potentially harmful or insufficient to help their conditions."

"Did Dr. Shoehorn agree to change the prescriptions to your recommendations?"

"Sometimes. Sometimes not. He frequently threatened to report me to the pharmacy board."

"How did you respond to that?" Simon asked.

"I gave him my license number and spelled my name for him," Marwin stated, grinning. "I wanted the board to know which pharmacist was doing such a good job."

Simon waited for the chuckles to die in the courtroom before asking, "So, you only spoke to Dr. Shoehorn on the phone?"

"No, I visited him at his office once. I wanted to ask him about all the weeds and seeds he had given Madeline."

"Weeds and seeds?"

"Natural herbal supplements," Marwin explained, straightening up in his seat. "It seems that Dr. Shoehorn prefers to treat his patients with products that have not undergone rigorous testing as opposed to FDA-approved products."

"Your Honor, the witness is judging my client," Wellborn objected.

Frowning, the judge said, "Mr. Wellborn, the witness has a professional judgment that he has earned. You will have the opportunity to challenge his judgment upon cross-examination if you would like."

"Did Dr. Shoehorn give you the requested information?" Simon asked.

"No. He cited confidentiality laws, became irate, and threatened to have me arrested for trespassing once he uncovered my identity."

"Did that end your investigation?"

"Hell, no. It made me determined to find out what was going on."

"Dr. Gelstone, please refrain from cursing," the judge instructed.

"Sorry, Your Honor," Marwin replied sheepishly.

With Simon's help, Marwin walked the jury through how Destiny had posed as a patient of Shoehorn's, claiming to have sexual problems. He explained how Shoehorn had given Destiny the same powder containing chlormethiazole that he had given Madeline. He finished by describing the process of the administration of high doses of the drug and then the abrupt withdrawal and how that could lead to thoughts of suicide in some patients. Marwin hypothesized that was the cause of Madeline's suicide.

"Dr. Gelstone, why would Dr. Shoehorn want to harm our district attorney?" Simon asked, sounding shocked.

"Because she told him that she and I were getting married. After he gave her the packets with the chlormethiazole, she pretended that her sexual problems were resolving. She told him that she achieved multiple orgasms every time we made love. Shoehorn threatened to withhold the drug if she didn't submit to multiple pelvic exams. He also made her watch pornography and have another pelvic exam under the guise of needing to check her ability to create vaginal secretions. The old pervert just wanted to feel her up."

"Objection, Your Honor!"

"Sustained," the judge replied instantly. "Dr. Gelstone, please keep your personal opinions to yourself. Please strike Dr. Gelstone's last statement."

"Can you please tell us how you wound up in Dr. Shoehorn's office, tied to an exam table?" Simon continued.

Marwin visibly shrunk in his seat and didn't answer.

"Dr. Gelstone, please answer the question."

Marwin tried to speak, but the horror in his mind prevented his mouth from opening. He closed his eyes and finally recounted that fateful day in April. When he opened his eyes, the courtroom was not visible. Instead, he saw himself clearly as he pushed into Shoehorn's office at closing time. Watching the nightmare in his mind's eye, he saw himself follow Shoehorn down a hallway and into his office. Shoehorn pulled a gun from his desk and pointed it at him.

Marwin's heart rate ticked up, just like in Shoehorn's office. He watched Shoehorn tie him to the exam table. The doctor admitted he had killed his patients with chlormethiazole and had tried to kill Destiny, too. Shoehorn placed the pillow over Marwin's face and fired into it as Marwin thrashed wildly on the table. A black veil covered Marwin's vision before slowly lifting, leaving the courtroom again visible.

"Thank you, Dr. Gelstone. No further questions."

"Mr. Wellborn, you may cross-exam."

"Mr. Gelstone, I understand that you proclaim yourself a drug expert. Is that correct?" Wellborn asked snidely.

"It's *Doctor* Gelstone, and I am a drug expert," Marwin replied with an icy stare.

"To prevent confusion for the jury, you do not have a medical doctorate. Correct?" Wellborn pushed.

"Of course not. I'm a pharmacist. I have a Doctorate in Pharmacy."

"Good. So, it's clear that you are not a medical doctor."

"Objection, Your Honor," Simon cut in. "Is Mr. Wellborn going somewhere with this? It is well established that Dr. Gelstone is a pharmacist."

"Sustained. Move along, Mr. Wellborn."

"OK. Mr. Gelstone, please provide proof of your expertise to the court?" Wellborn said. He persistently ignored Marwin's rightful title.

"Objection! Your Honor, the witness is not on trial here," Simon protested. "He doesn't have to prove anything."

"Mr. Wellborn, I suggest you ask specific questions of the witness or dismiss him," the judge admonished. "Also, please properly address him."

"Mr.—uh—Dr. Gelstone, could you please tell us the maximum dose of acarbose?" Wellborn fired, seemingly off the cuff.

Marwin shifted in his seat, but before he could answer, Simon stood and objected, "Your Honor, the witness should not have to pass some test that the counselor has made up."

"It depends on the patient's weight," Marwin said before the judge could address the objection. "If the patient weighs over sixty kilograms, the maximum dose is 300mgs daily. If the weight is less than sixty kilograms, the maximum is 150mgs per day. The higher doses in patients weighing less than sixty kilograms often leads to elevated liver enzymes."

Watching Marwin transform, Simon slowly returned to his seat. *Wellborn is gonna prove my case for me,* he thought.

"All right. Very good, Mr.—Dr. Gelstone. What is the half-life of Prozac?"

Simon wanted to object again, but Destiny placed a hand on his arm and shook her head. "Let him go," she whispered.

"Fluoxetine, or Prozac by the brand name, has a half-life of one to three days initially but may increase to four to six days with chronic administration," Marwin answered. He sat fully erect in his seat.

"I believe you are incorrect on that, Dr. Gelstone," Wellborn snapped. "The correct answer is up to sixteen days."

"No, that is norfluoxetine, the active metabolite of fluoxetine," Marwin corrected smugly.

"Are you sure?" Wellborn asked, blanching.

"Of course, but you can ask Dr. Google if you would like," Marwin shot back.

Wellborn turned his back on Marwin and nodded to his assistants at his table. Gathering himself, he turned back to Marwin and asked, "Are you familiar with the drug Parnate?"

"Of course."

"Please tell us the half-life and route of elimination," Wellborn directed, continuing to search for a way to discredit Marwin.

"Tranylcypromine, or Parnate, by the brand name, has a short half-life, about two hours, but the clinical effects can last up to a week. It is metabolized by the liver into multiple metabolites, some of which have pharmacologic activity. Originally, it was thought that amphetamine was one of the metabolites of Parnate, but later investigations refuted that," Marwin finished, an odd look coming across his face.

"All right, Dr. Gelstone—"

"Your Honor, this is all very fascinating, but does counsel have anything in mind besides verifying the validity of Dr. Gelstone as a drug expert?" Simon asked.

"Agreed. Mr. Wellborn, please move along. No more pharmacy quizzes for the witness."

Disappointed in his failure to discredit Marwin, Wellborn abruptly changed directions. "Dr. Gelstone, you testified that Dr. Shoehorn shot you. Did you see him pull the trigger?"

"Uh, no, it is difficult to see anything with a pillow over your face, but there was no one else in the office," Marwin answered, incredulous.

"Again, did you see Dr. Shoehorn fire the gun? Yes or no?"

"No, but—"

"No further questions, Your Honor," Wellborn said, turning away.

Marwin was dismissed and moved slowly back to his seat, his previous vigor gone. He sat down dazed and watched as Simon called Destiny to the stand.

Destiny strode confidently to the stand, was sworn in, and sat looking expectantly at Simon with her beautiful hazel eyes. As Simon prepared to question her, Destiny took a few deep breaths, readying herself as she had never been on this end of the questions.

"Miss Lawson, how did you become a patient of Dr. Shoehorn?" Simon began.

"After Marwin discovered that Shoehorn had given Madeline chlormethiazole, we devised a plan to see if we could get him to give it to me in such a way as to try to induce suicide."

"Objection!" Wellborn thundered, jumping from his seat. "There has been no proof that Dr. Shoehorn gave the aforementioned drug to Mrs. Montgomery."

"Sustained. Miss Lawson, please stick to the facts as we know them. If counsel asks for your opinion, you may then supply it."

Destiny tried to look abashed but smiled slightly and nodded her understanding to the judge. As the DA, she knew the jury had just heard her state that Shoehorn had given Madeline the drug. The fact that the theory hadn't been proven would likely be lost on them.

"Miss Lawson, did Dr. Shoehorn give you chlormethiazole?" Simon asked, cutting to the chase.

Murmurs flew through the courtroom as Destiny answered, "Yes, he did."

"Did he tell you what drug he was giving you?"

"No, he said he was using a regimen he reserved for his 'special patients.'"

"Special? What made you a special patient?" Simon inquired.

"I pissed him off by telling him how much I love Marwin and what a great sex life we shared before I developed menopause," Destiny said, placing air quotes around menopause.

"Did you receive chlormethiazole every time you saw Dr. Shoehorn?"

"No, initially he gave me a bag full of vitamins and herbal supplements. After I made him mad by praising Marwin as a pharmacist and a lover, he gave me the packets with chlormethiazole."

"OK. Did he continue to give you the packets on each subsequent visit?"

"Yes, but only after requiring me to have a pelvic exam each time," Destiny said, glaring disgustedly at Shoehorn.

"So, Dr. Shoehorn made you get undressed and allow him to do a pelvic exam just to continue your therapy?" Simon asked, incredulous.

"Objection! Counsel is not a doctor; therefore, he doesn't have the right to insinuate whether a medical practice is questionable," Wellborn roared.

"I will allow it. You may answer the question, Miss Lawson."

Destiny looked downward, paused briefly, and said softly, "Yes, he made me have an exam just to get the medication that he thought I was interested in."

Before Simon could ask another question, Destiny straightened and said, "That way, he could feel me up while trying to kill me, too!"

The courtroom erupted, and Wellborn exploded from his seat. "Your Honor, the witness is sensationalizing for the jury."

"Miss Lawson, I warned you about giving your unsolicited opinion," the judge said sternly. "In fact, as a member of the bar, you know better. I will not warn you again."

"No further questions, Your Honor," Simon said amicably.

"Your witness, Mr. Wellborn."

Before Wellborn reached Destiny, the bailiff approached the judge and whispered something in her ear. "We will adjourn for the day and reconvene at 9 a.m. One of the jurors is feeling ill," the judge explained.

"I'm surprised they're not all feeling ill after listening to that," Jackson said a little too loudly.

* * *

As Jackson, Destiny, and Marwin left the courthouse, they met Bradley entering. "You guys done for the day?" Bradley asked, confused.

"Yep, one of the jurors became ill," Destiny replied.

"Probably from listening to Destiny's testimony," Jackson opined.

Bradley glanced curiously at Jackson and then said to Destiny, "Well, since I'm not testifying today, I'll head back to the office. There's a ton of work waiting for me."

"Have you got any ideas about how we can pursue the deaths of Jackson's patients?" Marwin asked.

"I'm working on it. I have done some digging and found a few oddities, but nothing substantial enough to open an investigation. I did get the analysis of the stomach contents for the patient that was autopsied, though."

"Anything unusual?" Marwin inquired, his brain instantly alert.

"Not really, summer sausage, crackers, grapes, and cheese. His blood alcohol was 0.04 percent, and there was a red tint to the food, so he likely drank a glass of red wine before he died."

"Crap! I was hoping they found amphetamine tablets and ammonium chloride capsules in his stomach," Jackson interjected sourly.

"'fraid not," Bradley said. "I gotta go. I'll let you know if I come up with anything."

As Bradley walked away, Destiny asked, "You guys want to grab a drink and an early dinner?"

"I don't think so," Jackson replied. "I need to go by the office and check on things. Thanks for the offer, though."

"OK, see you tomorrow. How 'bout it, Mar?" Destiny said.

Marwin didn't answer. He just stared after Bradley. "Hello, Earth to Marwin," Destiny said, nudging his shoulder.

"What? I'm sorry. What did you say?" Marwin asked, escaping his fugue.

"I asked if you wanted to get a drink and an early dinner."

"Sure, that sounds great. Let me text the kids and let them know I'll be home a little later. You want to go to Northshore Brasserie?"

"Yeah, sure, I guess. I wasn't thinking anything quite that nice, but let's go."

"Cool. I'll meet you there," Marwin replied, kissing Destiny softly.

\* \* \*

JACKSON WORKED HIS WAY down Hill Street to Henley and finally over to Cumberland Avenue, which was moving passably at that hour. Staring into the brilliant sunshine as he headed west, he called Helen to let her know he was coming by.

"I'm glad you called. Tracey at Forever Young phoned and told me they found Ruth Westmoreland dead in her bed this morning."

"Damnit! Another one? I can't understand what is happening. Ruth hadn't been feeling well lately. She had lost some weight and was fatigued. I checked her out and ordered a bunch of bloodwork last week. Can you check to see if it ever came back, please? I'll be there in about twenty minutes."

"Fuck!" he swore aloud, slamming both hands on the steering wheel. *I don't know what the hell is going on, but I am definitely getting an autopsy,* he thought sadly.

\* \* \*

200

MARWIN AND DESTINY SAT at the white tablecloth-covered table, sipping wine and talking. They had ordered a dozen oysters on the half shell and a charcuterie tray as appetizers and hadn't decided if they would get an entrée.

"You were walking a thin line in court today," Marwin observed.

"Yeah, I almost pushed it too far." Changing the subject, Destiny said, "You killed it today! Wellborn was sure he could discredit you, but he actually verified your expertise."

"Thanks," Marwin replied proudly. "I was nervous at first, but once he started quizzing me on drugs, I settled down," he continued, placing prosciutto and cheese on a cracker.

"Honestly, even I was impressed at how quickly and effortlessly you answered the questions."

The appetizers stimulated their appetites, and Destiny ordered steak Au Poivre and Marwin the lamb chops. Marwin's phone buzzed, signaling a text as the waiter removed the remnants of the appetizers.

Glancing down, Marwin said, "Holy shit! Jackson lost another patient today."

"Oh, my gosh. What is going on?"

"I don't know, but something is not right. This is way too many patients dying in such a short time. There's no way it is just natural causes," Marwin suggested.

"Was this an elderly patient, too?"

"I don't know. He didn't give me any details."

Running her hand through her hair, Destiny said, "We need to let Bradley know."

"Know what? That Jackson had a patient die? It could have been natural."

"Or it could have been another patient that was murdered," Destiny shot back.

"Hey, what were you thinking about in the parking lot outside the courthouse? You were a mile away," Destiny asked.

"Uh, I was just thinking about the stomach contents he told us about."

"Summer sausage and cheese. Is that mystifying?" Destiny asked, smiling.

"Not really," Marwin admitted. "Look, none of this makes much sense. The man died from severe hypertension, secondary to serotonin syndrome. His normal meds made that seem unlikely, but he had amphetamines in his system. Plus, he had ammonium chloride in his system which makes it seem like he was probably poisoned. I've been kicking around some ideas in my head. Every time I go down the list of causes of hypertensive crisis, I come back to the monoamine oxidase inhibitors. However, this patient was not taking a MAOI."

"I still don't understand what you were thinking so hard about."

Marwin took a large sip of his wine and responded. "When Bradley stated the stomach contents contained summer sausage, cheese, crackers, and the evidence of wine, my mind went immediately to a list of foods that are high in tyramine content."

"Why? My mind went to date night," Destiny said playfully. "Plus, what is tyramine?"

"It is a substance found in many foods and drinks," Marwin explained. "It causes the body to release chemicals that raise the blood pressure and heart rate. It isn't normally important. Some migraine patients experience more headaches if they ingest too much, but otherwise, it rarely causes problems."

Taking another sip of wine, he added, "Unless the patient is taking an MAOI. That combination could kill them."

"Are you saying that if Jackson's patient was on one of those, uh—"

"MAOIs," Marwin supplied.

"Yeah, one of those MAOIs, the patient's food could have killed him?" Destiny asked, stunned.

"Well, in school, that's what we were taught. I'm not sure if a simple meal of cheese and crackers would really kill someone, though. Plus, only certain kinds of cheese and aged meats are really high in tyramine. Not to mention, he wasn't taking an MAOI. It's just where my mind went, that's all," Marwin said with a shrug, digging into his lamb.

"Could someone have slipped the man a MAOI?" Destiny wondered.

"Maybe, but it doesn't seem likely to me. For one thing, MAOIs are not commonly found in pharmacies any longer as they are rarely used in practice. They are only available as oral tablets, so the patient would have had to swallow them. It seems unlikely that the man would be taking another medicine that he was prescribed without asking questions. The last thing is that the toxicology didn't show any MAOIs in his system."

As Marwin took a forkful of garlic mashed potatoes in his mouth, he suddenly stopped, sat up straight, and his eyes widened.

"What's wrong?" Destiny asked, alarmed.

"Remember Wellborn asking me about the drug Parnate today?" Marwin said.

"Yeah, why?"

"Parnate is actually an MAOI," Marwin said excitedly.

"OK. So?" Destiny asked, obviously confused.

"When I was in school, I was taught that Parnate was metabolized into amphetamines. As I told Wellborn, though, later studies refuted that."

Destiny shook her head slowly, then drained her wine glass. "I still don't see where you are going with this."

"That's OK. You're not the drug expert," Marwin said, smiling.

# CHAPTER 33

"Court let out early today?" Helen asked, following Jackson into his office.

"Yeah, a juror became ill, so they dismissed until in the morning." He waved his hand dismissively. "Did you get a chance to check on Ruth's lab work?"

"We should have it soon. The tech I spoke to gave me some BS about the lab being out of some of the necessary reagents, but I suspect someone just dropped the ball."

"I can't believe we lost another patient," Jackson lamented.

Helen laid her hand gently on Jackson's arm. "I know. I'm sorry."

Jackson glanced at Helen's hand on his arm, momentarily unsure what to say. "Can you please check the computer for her labs again?"

Helen gave Jackson's arm a gentle squeeze before turning to leave the office. She returned just moments later carrying a computer printout. "Got 'em," she said.

Jackson quickly scanned the pages and sat down in his chair heavily. "Damnit," he said wearily.

"She had cancer, didn't she?" Helen asked.

"Yep, it sure looks like it." He rubbed his eyes and stared at the paper again. "Her CEA, RBP, and 1-antitrypsin are all through the roof. Her ALK phosphate is also over 300. It appears that she had lung cancer and it had probably already metastasized to her liver and bones. That would explain her weight loss and fatigue."

"Poor thing," Helen commented. After a brief pause, she gave a wan smile. "At least this death appears natural."

Jackson didn't reply at first but then realized. "No, it doesn't. The lung cancer would have caused her a slow, agonizing death. No way she should have died suddenly. Please get her family on the phone. We're getting an autopsy."

\* \* \*

Marwin and Destiny finished their meals, shared a glass of cabernet, and headed off to their respective homes. They kissed softly, promising to spend some time together during the upcoming weekend.

Marwin drove west on I-40, fully sated. Traffic ground to a halt just before the West Hills exit, but Marwin hardly noticed.

He rifled through his mental filing cabinet. The fledgling idea that had formed the previous night had blossomed into a full-blown hypothesis over dinner.

Buffeted by the wine, Marwin used his Bluetooth to make a phone call.

"Coroner's Office. This is Josh. Can I help you?" said the voice in a monotone.

"Yes, Josh," Marwin said congenially. "My name is Marwin Gelstone. I'm a pharmacist in Knoxville, and I work closely with Dr. Jackson Montgomery. You guys did an autopsy recently on one of his patients, Wilson Stanford. I was hoping you might answer a couple of questions about the results."

"Uh, I'm not sure, Mr. Gelstone. I think you need to talk to Vince—I mean—Dr. Adkins."

"Is he available this late in the day?"

"Let me check," Josh said, placing Marwin on hold.

After several minutes, the music Marwin listened to disappeared, and a gravelly voice said, "Dr. Adkins."

"Hey, my name is Marwin Gelstone. I'm a pharmacist—"

He cut Marwin off. "I know who you are. What do you want?"

Nonplussed, Marwin said, "I wanted to ask you a couple of questions about Wilson Stanford's autopsy results."

"What the hell for?"

"I'm looking into the unexplained deaths of Dr. Montgomery's patients," Marwin said.

"You're a pharmacist, not a detective. Why don't you stick to pushing pills and leave the investigating to the Dick Traceys down at Knox County?"

The insinuation that Marwin just pushed pills dissolved his demeanor instantly. "Look, Mr. Stanford died an unexpected death with an unusual diagnosis of serotonin syndrome. Nothing in his chart suggests he should have died that way."

"You're not familiar with amphetamines, Hot Shot?"

Marwin bit back a retort. "Why all the vitriol, Dr. Adkins? I would think that you would like to have such a strange death explained, also."

"Look, Gelstone, I don't have time for amateur detectives. I got a whole cooler full of people who ain't breathing. I need to get back to them before they start missing me."

"Would you prefer if Detective Jinswain contacted you instead?"

"I've already talked to him."

"But he didn't have my questions, "Marwin complained.

"So, give your questions to him," Adkins said, prepared to hang up.

"It will save you time if you just answer them from me."

"Yeah, but then I would miss an opportunity to talk to my favorite dick," Adkins said sarcastically.

Adkins wasn't going to cooperate, but Marwin tried one last time. "Can you just tell me if the toxicology report listed desmethylselegiline? I know you reported amphetamines, but were they specifically levomethamphetamine?"

Silence filled the airwaves for several seconds, stretching out so long Marwin began to wonder if Adkins had already disconnected. Adkins sighed heavily. "Hold on. Let me get the report."

Upon his return, Adkins delivered a surprise apology. "Sorry it took so long. I had to ask my dumbass tech where the report was since it wasn't filed in the correct spot."

"Here it is. Let me see what we got." Time dragged on again. "I'll be damned. The toxicology did show desmethyl selegiline and levomethamphetamine. I noticed the amphetamines, but I didn't remember seeing the selegiline metabolite. I assume the patient was taking selegiline?"

Marwin considered telling Adkins that the patient's medications were privileged information but decided against it. "Actually, no. He wasn't taking selegiline."

"Well, how the hell did it get in his system?" Adkins wondered aloud.

"I don't know, but I'm sure as hell gonna find out."

\* \* \*

THE MAN SAT IN his plush chair behind his dark oak desk, a look of concern on his face. One of his many employees had just sent him a text. While the text was not unexpected, it was troublesome all the same.

He pondered the text and how he should deal with it. The man made a rapid checklist of the entire Knoxville operation. Typically, one of his operations was scheduled to run for about three years, but the Knoxville project was only eighteen months old. He didn't want to shut Knoxville down so soon, as there were plenty of other profitable clients. Additionally, the next site had not been finalized and would take months to get up and running. Closing Knoxville prematurely would leave a large void in the business.

The man twirled his Montblanc ink pen across his fingers as he re-read the text.

*I wanted to let you know that one of your clients is being investigated. As far as I know, the police are not involved yet, but a local pharmacist is digging around. This guy is supposedly some drug guru that helped the cops solve a big case last year. I will let you know if I get any other info.*

The man wasn't overly concerned about a pharmacist digging around. He had the utmost faith in his operative and her methods. Still, the operative had been very active in a relatively short period, so he could not ignore the potential risk. The man sent a text back to his employee asking for any available information on the pharmacist. The response was almost immediate.

*The pharmacist's name was Marwin Gelstone.*

\* \* \*

JACKSON STOPPED AT KFC on his way home and sat at his kitchen table eating fried chicken and potato salad. Wiping grease from his fingers, he turned the TV on.

The local weather woman told everyone it was hot outside. Thinking miserably about the patients he had lost recently made him wish he had gone into meteorology rather than medicine. No one ever expected the weatherperson to be accurate.

Jackson's cell phone interrupted his thoughts of a different profession with an incoming call from Marwin. "What's up?"

"I wanted to let you know that I got some more info on Wilson Stanford," Marwin replied.

"What did you find out?"

"Mr. Stanford had selegiline in his system when he died."

"What? He wasn't taking selegiline," Jackson said, confused. "That's a drug for dementia, and he didn't have dementia."

Letting the unnecessary explanation pass, Marwin remarked, "Well, someone was giving it to him. Could he have been seeing another doctor?"

"He never mentioned it, and he didn't update his med list at his visit recently, so I'm pretty sure he wasn't taking selegiline."

"There is only one way he could have gotten it," Marwin told him. "Someone is poisoning him."

"How? Why? I don't understand."

"I'm not sure, but I think we are dealing with a very dangerous person. Let's assume that Mr. Stanford wasn't seeing another doctor, and someone was really poisoning him."

"OK, but selegiline seems like a weird choice to use to me," Jackson said, completely perplexed.

"On the surface, yes, but if you look at the whole picture, you find a complicated, intricate plan."

"I'm not seeing it, so how about you help me out," Jackson demanded.

"All right. Hear me out before you say anything. Selegiline is a selective monoamine oxidase, Type-B, inhibitor, so the dietary restriction about tyramine doesn't apply to it like it does to the older, non-selective ones such as Nardil, Marplan, and Parnate. However, at high doses, selegiline loses its selectivity and inhibits Type A, MAO, also. This can lead to severe hypertensive episodes if dietary restrictions are not followed closely.

"Mr. Stanford's stomach contents revealed summer sausage, cheese, and wine," Marwin went on. "The foods and wine have high tyramine content and could lead to severe hypertension if Mr. Stanford had ingested selegiline in some way. He was also taking carbamazepine and citalopram, which interact similarly with high-dose selegiline."

Jackson sat, dumbfounded, his chicken long cold. He ran a hand through his thinning hair. "That's crazy!"

"It is pretty wild, for sure," Marwin agreed.

"What about the ammonium chloride that was in his system?"

"That's the real clincher," Marwin said. "Whoever is behind this knows pharmacy and a good bit of chemistry, too. The ammonium chloride would hasten the urinary excretion of the amphetamine metabolites, most likely in hopes of the poisoning going undetected."

"That's crazy," Jackson reiterated.

"I agree. Look, we've got to get Bradley involved."

"I guess, but the whole thing seems crazy," Jackson reiterated.

"Jackson, someone murdered your patient. It's possible the other patients were murdered. We've got to get the police involved."

Marwin paused. "You could be in danger, too."

# CHAPTER 34

When the court reconvened the following morning, Destiny returned to the stand for Wellborn's cross-examination. She wore a sleeveless, high-neck pale yellow dress, her autumn hair hung loosely on her shoulders, and her make-up was almost non-existent.

"Miss Lawson," Wellborn began. "You were a patient of Dr. Shoehorn's. Correct?"

"No, not really. I pretended to have a medical condition to prove he gave Madeline Montgomery chlormethiazole."

Willborn picked up a folder and handed it to Destiny. "Is this not your chart?"

Destiny glanced at the folder, handed it back to Wellborn, and shrugged.

"Please answer verbally for the record, Miss Lawson," the judge instructed.

"It is a chart, but I was not really a patient of Dr. Shoehorn's."

Wellborn flipped through the pages of the chart. "Here are the doctor's notes. *The patient is a thirty-six-year-old white female who presents with signs and symptoms of menopause. She complains of vaginal dryness, painful intercourse, inability to achieve orgasm, and night sweats. Hormone levels are within normal limits. Will begin supplement therapy to improve general health status. Will recommend the patient consult a therapist as sexual issues appear more likely related to a lack of desire for her fiancé rather than from a physiologic origin.*

"I'm sorry, Miss Lawson, but that sounds like you were a patient of Dr. Shoehorn's."

"As I have already said, I pretended to have the symptoms of meno-pause," Destiny said irritably.

"So, you pretended to be sick to get the doctor to give you a sedative?" Wellborn stated, looking directly at Destiny.

"Objection!" Simon shouted, rising from his seat.

"On what grounds?" the judge asked, clearly amused.

"Uh, counsel is accusing the witness of being dishonest in hopes of obtaining drugs," Simon stated without conviction.

"Overruled. Miss Lawson, please answer the question."

"I didn't want sedatives for myself. I wanted Dr. Shoehorn to give me chlormethiazole to prove that he used it to harm patients—like he did with Madeline Montgomery."

"Miss Lawson, you expect the jury to believe that you lied to Dr. Shoehorn to obtain sedatives you had no intention of taking?" Wellborn scoffed.

"Absolutely. That is the truth," Destiny replied, sitting straighter in her seat.

"I see. You lied then, but you are telling the truth now. Is that right? How's the jury supposed to know when you're lying and when you are telling the truth?" Wellborn asked sarcastically.

"Counsel is badgering the witness," Simon complained.

Before the judge could rule, Wellborn said, "Withdrawn. No further questions."

Bradley was called to the stand following Destiny's dismissal. He sat down, obviously comfortable in his surroundings.

Simon approached the witness stand, a small smile on his face. "Detective Jinswain, please tell us how you came to investigate a death that was originally ruled a suicide."

The detective glanced at the jury before looking back at Simon. "Madeline Montgomery was an outgoing, well-known socialite in the Knoxville community. She was a member of several committees and boards across the area and donated her time freely. She and Dr. Mont-gomery were preparing to celebrate their twenty-fifth anniversary. All reports suggest the Montgomery's had a normal, healthy marriage. There was no history of mental illness for Mrs. Montgomery, so suicide didn't fit.

"The day after her death, Dr. Montgomery received a call from a man posing as a reporter for the Sentinel. He had information that hadn't been released, so the department tried to contact him at the Sentinel and discovered that no such person worked there."

"I see," Simon said, rubbing his chin. "Can you take us through your investigation, please?"

"Dr. Montgomery discovered a packet of powder in his wife's purse and learned she had made several visits at regular intervals to the defendant's office. There was a specific schedule on her calendar on her computer. Dr. Montgomery works closely with a local pharmacist, Dr. Marwin Gelstone, and he asked him to look into his wife's medications in hopes of discovering some reason to explain her ending her life. Dr. Gelstone determined the powder in Mrs. Montgomery's purse contained chlormethiazole, a powerful sedative used to detoxify patients addicted to alcohol. Oddly, the drug is not available in the United States. Dr. Gelstone devised a scenario where Dr. Shoehorn used the drug to cause Mrs. Montgomery to commit suicide."

"Objection, Your Honor, the witness is postulating. We need facts, not opinions," Wellborn argued.

"Overruled. You will have your opportunity to refute shortly," the judge stated simply. "Please continue, Detective."

"Dr. Gelstone's hypothesis was confirmed by the lab, so we exhumed Mrs. Montgomery's body and ran a hair analysis to confirm she had actually ingested the drug." Bradley stopped and glanced quickly toward Jackson to see how he was handling the difficult review. Making eye contact, Jackson gave a small nod and then looked away.

"We researched and found several of Dr. Shoehorn's patients had committed suicide over the last couple of years, so we enlisted the help of District Attorney, Destiny Lawson. She agreed to go undercover and become a patient of Dr. Shoehorn's. We hoped that Shoehorn would give her the chlormethiazole, too.

"It took a few visits, but Miss Lawson finally got under Shoehorn's skin. He then gave her packets of powder identical to the one in Madeline

Montgomery's purse. Upon assaying, the packets contained very large amounts of chlormethiazole. Miss Lawson pretended to take the medication and reported to Dr. Shoehorn that it improved her symptoms. Dr. Shoehorn required Miss Lawson to submit to pelvic exams before giving her more medication.

"The last batch of packets Shoehorn gave Miss Lawson had no chlormethiazole but contained a drug that would cause the rapid removal of the chlormethiazole that he thought she had ingested. According to Dr. Gelstone, this rapid removal of the drug after taking high doses could precipitate suicidal ideations, or thoughts of suicide. Unfortunately, Mrs. Montgomery took action on those thoughts."

"What did you do after Dr. Shoehorn gave Miss Lawson the powerful drug?" Simon inquired.

"Miss Lawson, Dr. Gelstone, and I discussed the likelihood of a jury convicting Dr. Shoehorn based on the evidence I just presented. Ultimately, we decided we needed something more concrete to ensure a conviction, so we allowed Dr. Gelstone to wear a recording device. He confronted Dr. Shoehorn in his office in hopes of getting him to incriminate himself."

"Were you successful in obtaining incriminating evidence against Dr. Shoehorn?"

"Yes, we were."

"Your Honor, I would like to play the recording obtained by Dr. Gelstone in the defendant's office," Simon requested.

"Proceed," the judge allowed.

A hush fell over the courtroom as Shoehorn threatened to kill Marwin. Two jurors shifted uneasily as Shoehorn directed Marwin to lie on the exam table.

When Shoehorn said, *"The best thing about chlormethiazole is that it makes my patients disappear! No more disgusting women asking me to save their sex lives. Perverts, every last one of them! Speaking of perverts, your Destiny may be the biggest one I have ever encountered. She got so wet during my exams. I thought she was going to climax right there on the table."*

"Fuck You!" Marwin's voice roared on the recording as his hands shook with rage in the courtroom.

*"Sadly for you, she won't be fucking you any longer, Mr. Gelstone. I'm afraid she is likely to commit Hari-Kari any day now. Your demise at the hands of a mugger will further add to the depression that the chlormethiazole is inducing. She will likely be dead before your funeral is complete. Maybe you guys can get a two-for-one deal at the cemetery,"* Shoehorn's voice echoed over the recording.

Murmurs spread through the courtroom, causing the judge to bang her gavel on the bench and command order.

Once everything quieted down, Simon asked, "What did you find when you entered Dr. Shoehorn's office?"

Bradley glanced at Marwin and hesitated before answering. Turning his eyes back to Simon, he replied, "I found Dr. Gelstone lying on an exam table with his hands bound and tied to the door. A pillow was over his face, and there was a pool of blood beneath his head and shoulder."

"Thank you, Detective. No further questions."

"You may cross-examine, Mr. Wellborn."

The defense attorney remained seated, a look of bewilderment covering his face. The judge prodded, "Mr. Wellborn?"

Wellborn finally stood and slowly approached Bradley. "Detective Jinswain, did you see Dr. Shoehorn when you entered the office?"

Hesitating, already suspecting where Wellborn was headed, Bradley said cautiously, "No, he was not inside the office where I found Dr. Gelstone."

"So, to confirm, you didn't actually see Dr. Shoehorn in the office?"

"No, but my partner saw Dr. Shoehorn exiting the rear of the building. As you heard, he was just in the office talking to Dr. Gelstone. He spoke of killing him and many of his patients, including Miss Lawson."

Wellborn had nowhere to go, so he slumped back to his seat, dismissing Bradley from the witness stand.

\* \* \*

MARWIN'S SUV SAT, UNMOVING, on I-40, surrounded by hundreds of other miserable people. Dan Henley sang about *Wasted Time*, and Marwin considered his current situation just that.

Sighing, he called Bogie and asked him to order pizza from Mr. Gatti's for dinner. Briefly wondering how the pizza delivery person would traverse the nightmare rush hour traffic when he couldn't move at all, Marwin called Sam to check on the day at the pharmacy. It was almost closing time, and Marwin smiled, knowing Sam would be cursing at the thought of a patient or doctor calling at that time of day.

"Community Pharmacy," Sam answered hesitantly.

Disguising his voice, Marwin said, "Yes, I need to pick up my prescription. I called it in this morning, so it should be ready."

"How long will it take you to get here, sir?" Sam asked, barely hiding his disgust.

"Not long. Maybe fifteen or twenty minutes," Marwin supplied innocently.

"Well, we close in five minutes, sir. Can you pick it up in the morning?"

"Oh, no! It's for my Viagra, and my wife and I are having a date night tonight," Marwin deadpanned.

Silence filled the line as Sam covered the mouthpiece and swore out loud.

"Hello? You still there?" Marwin asked, trying not to laugh.

"Uh, yeah. I'm still here. Come get your Viagra—Marwin! Hope you and Destiny have a great night!" Sam said, laughing. "I didn't know you needed Viagra, though."

"How'd you know it was me? I thought I disguised my voice pretty well."

"You did, but you didn't disguise the caller ID," Sam replied, chuckling.

"Everything good today?" Marwin asked.

"Yep, as far as I know. "

"OK. Are you still good to work until the trial is over?" Marwin asked earnestly.

"Sure am, but it's gonna cost you."

"Don't worry. I'm going to pay you extra."

"I don't want any extra *money*," Sam replied. "I want you and Destiny to come over for dinner and games. This time, we can play corn hole and Rook on my home court."

"I don't think there's a home court advantage in corn hole or Rook, but we'll be happy to kick your ass in your own backyard," Marwin said, laughing.

"Doubt it," Sam teased. "Let me check with Dawn on a time and tell you tomorrow when you call to check on me."

"I wasn't checking on you," Marwin stammered.

"Uh-huh. Anyway, see you Saturday, if not before. I'll let you know the time and what you need to bring. Oh, and I'll bring some Viagra for you in case Destiny is in the mood." Sam cackled as he disconnected.

Traffic finally relented past the Papermill exit, and Marwin slowly picked up speed. He decided to call Destiny.

"Hey, Hottie," she answered after only one ring.

"Hey, Babe. What are you up to?"

"Just sitting here with Simon and Edna. We were discussing the trial."

"Who's Edna?" Marwin asked, confused.

Destiny giggled and said, "Edna Valley."

"Uh-oh. How many have you had?"

"Just one. We ordered appetizers and a glass of wine to wait out the traffic."

"That was a very good call, Counselor," Marwin affirmed. Marwin told Destiny about Sam's invitation for dinner and games on Saturday.

"Sounds like a challenge to me," Destiny replied.

"Me, too," Marwin agreed.

"Well, challenge accepted!" Destiny stated gleefully.

"I'll let him know."

"Make sure you tell him we want to make it an early evening," Destiny purred.

# CHAPTER 35

Marwin arrived home just as the pizza delivery person backed out of his driveway.

*How is that possible?* he wondered.

In the kitchen, he found Bogie loading his plate with multiple pieces of meat-laden pizza. Morgan was busy picking pepperoni off of her slices.

"Dad, why do we always have to have pizza with meat?" she complained for the thousandth time.

"Meat is healthy, Dimwit." Bogie supplied.

"What would you know about healthy, Mister I-Wouldn't-Touch-A-Vegetable-With-A-Ten-Foot-Pole?" Morgan fired back.

"Enough!" Marwin ordered. Bogie headed for the stairs but stopped when Marwin spoke again. "Let's all eat together tonight."

Bogie groaned and rolled his eyes while Morgan threw herself into a chair.

Grabbing a bottle of water and three slices of pizza, Marwin joined them. "Tell me about your day."

Neither kid spoke. Instead, they simultaneously stuffed pizza into their mouths. Marwin watched, amused. "How did softball go?"

Morgan's eyes lit up, and she talked with her mouth full of pizza. "It was awesome! We got to get on the field today. We did fielding, base running, and hitting."

While he chewed, Marwin motioned for Morgan to continue.

"It went really well, I think. I was pretty good at fielding but awesome at running the bases. Coach Dalton thinks I am the fastest girl in the tryouts!"

"How did the hitting go?" Marwin asked.

"Um, not as well." Morgan deflated. "I did OK when Coach Dalton pitched, but then we had to hit off one of the middle school pitchers. That was awful! They throw so hard! I couldn't seem to catch up to the speed of the pitch."

"I know, Kid, but you'll have to find a way if you are going to play competitive softball," Marwin said sympathetically.

Morgan hung her head and whispered, "I know."

Bogie felt the need to offer his unsolicited opinion. "She's got no shot."

Marwin shot eye daggers at Bogie. Before he could chastise his first-born, Morgan shouted, "Eat shit, Bogie!"

"Morgan!" Marwin yelled. After a breath, he continued, "While I do not want to hear that language from you, I believe I would have said the same thing."

Marwin turned to his son, "That was rude, Bud."

Morgan grinned while Bogie sat—mouth agape—shocked at how it had played out.

Marwin changed the subject, "How was your day, Bogie?"

In true teenage fashion, Bogie mumbled almost incoherently, offering nothing of substance.

"We'll find out who made the team in a couple of days," Morgan offered.

"I think we already know who *didn't* make the team," Bogie mumbled.

"Bogie! You should be supporting your sister, not tearing her down!" Marwin thundered.

Turning to Morgan, Marwin said, "Give it your all at every tryout. If you make it, great. If not, work hard for next year's team. No matter what happens, I am very proud you had the guts to try."

"Thanks, *Dad*." She glared at Bogie before turning her attention back to her father. "I have a project to work on, so can I head up now?"

"Sure, Bit. See you in the morning."

Bogie appeared ready to follow his sister up the stairs, but Marwin put a hand on his arm.

"Stop being an asshole to your sister. There's no need for that, and it certainly doesn't help the atmosphere in our house. You wouldn't like it if I picked on you every time you failed. Would you?"

"I don't fail like she does," Bogie retorted arrogantly.

"Really? Mister Groundball-Through-The-Five-Hole?"

The reference to Bogie's recent game-ending failure rocked him as if he had been slapped.

"Damn, Dad," Bogie said. He turned toward the stairs with his ego dissolving.

Watching his son trudge slowly up the stairs, Marwin felt a pang of guilt for hurting him but decided he had it coming. He hoped Bogie would think twice before picking on Morgan next time.

Marwin decided to add some bourbon to his water and call Jackson to discuss the latest patient's death. Just before the call went to voicemail, Jackson answered breathlessly.

"Hello?"

"Did I interrupt something?"

"As a matter of fact, you did. I was enjoying a pinot noir, a box of Cheez-Its, and Alan Jackson on the back deck."

"Next time, try taking your phone with you," Marwin suggested.

"Thanks for the great advice. Can I help you?"

Marwin adopted a gentler tone. "I was just wondering about the details of the latest patient you lost."

Jackson emitted a large sigh and visibly sunk into his seat. "She was an elderly lady who lived at Forever Young. She had been feeling ill for about six weeks. She lost a bunch of weight, grew lethargic, et cetera. I ordered a battery of tests, but she passed away before we got the results back."

"Was it a hypertensive crisis like most of the other ones?" Marwin inquired.

"I'm not sure. The nurse found her dead in her bed one morning after she failed to show up at breakfast. I had an autopsy done, so hopefully, we will get that back tomorrow if Vince isn't farting around."

"Sounds like she had some type of cancer," Marwin opined.

"Lung cancer, actually," Jackson confirmed. "We finally got her tests back today. Her CEA, RBP, and 1-antitrypsin levels were all extremely high. I'm sure the autopsy will show lung cancer with mets to the liver, most likely."

"Maybe, but why did she die suddenly in her bed?" Marwin asked.

"Damned fine question, Dr. Gelstone," Jackson replied.

\* \* \*

MARWIN'S WEEK TRUDGED ON slowly. Shoehorn's trial finally wrapped up, with the lawyers on each side doing their best to convince the jury to vote their way. Late Friday afternoon, the judge sent the jury to begin deliberations, and neither Destiny nor Simon expected a quick verdict.

Marwin went by the pharmacy to check on the consults and the general state of affairs. Finding nothing urgent or of any real significance, he headed out.

Stopping to talk to Miranda as he left, Marwin asked, "You keeping Sam straight?"

"Yes, sir. He's behaved pretty well this week. He's only thrown one patient out all week."

Taking the information in stride, Marwin turned to Sam, "What happened?"

"One of our new patients, who recently transferred here from another pharmacy, came in and wanted his Xanax filled. It was a week too early, so I explained I couldn't fill it yet. He told me not to worry about running it through the insurance; he would just pay cash for it."

"Oh, boy," Marwin interrupted, already knowing where it was heading.

"Yep, he became irate when I explained it wasn't legal for me to fill it early regardless of who was paying for it. He cussed me out, so I told him to get the hell out of the store."

"Good for you," Marwin said easily. "Pay attention when you leave, just in case he decides he wants to do something stupid."

"Don't worry. I will."

"OK. I guess I will see you tomorrow. I hope you and Dawn are ready for another ass beating," Marwin joked.

"Yeah, whatever. We'll see."

\* \* \*

THE WOMAN SAT ON the couch, sipping a glass of white wine. The week had been productive, albeit somewhat stressful, and she looked forward to a relaxing weekend.

As the woman ventured into the kitchen to top off her wine, her phone dinged with an incoming text. It did nothing to derail her trip, and she explored the freezer for something to eat after replenishing her wine glass. After a fruitless search, she settled on a Red Baron pizza. Once the pizza was heated, she headed to her bedroom to change into more comfortable clothes. Before she reached her bedroom, her phone rang.

"Damnit!" she exclaimed to her empty house. She briefly considered ignoring the phone but thought better of it and answered on the third ring.

"You better have a good excuse for ignoring my text, and I know you don't," the man said without a preamble.

"Um, sorry, sir. I was—"

"Shut up and listen to me. Meet me in Tyson Park in exactly thirty minutes. Don't even think about being late."

The woman shakily laid the phone on the table and stared sightlessly at the floor, momentarily unsure of what to do. Finally snapping out of her trance, she grabbed her shoes and keys and sprinted for her car.

\* \* \*

TWENTY-TWO MINUTES AFTER the call disconnected, the woman pulled into Tyson Park. She silently thanked the traffic gods and tried to compose herself for her upcoming meeting. She couldn't fathom what had necessitated the impromptu meeting, but it was nothing good. Before her mind searched through scenarios, a car parked next to hers, and the man stepped out.

"Come with me," he instructed.

As the woman exited her car, she looked around. No other vehicles were in sight, and dusk was rapidly approaching. Fear took over, and the woman's heart ticked up. Looking into the man's face, she broke out in a cold sweat despite the August heat as his steel-blue eyes looked through her.

"Take it easy. I'm not going to kill you," the man promised.

The man's statement did little to alleviate her fear, but the woman forced herself to not look away. The man led her to a covered picnic area, and a stream gurgled softly nearby.

"Sit," he commanded.

The woman climbed nervously atop the picnic table, her feet resting on the bench. Again, gathering her internal strength, she looked into the man's face and waited for him to speak.

"We have a situation," he began. "I have another assignment for you, but this one is more difficult and dangerous. The target is incarcerated and must be eliminated immediately."

"Incarcerated? Sir, how am I supposed to make contact with the target? I can't go visit him and shoot him in broad daylight."

The man turned an icy stare at his star employee. "First off, you could do just that if I instructed you to do so. However, I have no intention of losing you, so you will be using a different method. I believe I have a plan that should work."

Should *work*? the woman thought. *I am walking into a prison to kill someone with a plan that "should" work. Jesus!*

He expected her to say something, so the woman licked her lips. "OK, great. Tell me what you have in mind."

The woman listened intently as her boss laid out the plan. As he finished, her mind raced with a million questions and doubts.

"I think that might work," she said, hoping she sounded more confident than she felt. "The only thing is that I have never worked with that drug before."

"If you want to work with it again, I suggest you be extremely careful this time," the man replied earnestly. "Any questions?"

Silently debating, the woman finally answered, "Yes, can you tell me why I am doing this? It seems very risky."

For the first time, the man smiled. "I knew you would ask. I will tell you because I value your loyalty, and you deserve to know why you are putting your life on the line. The man is a doctor who is currently on trial for murder. According to a trial consulting firm we hired, there is an excellent chance he will be convicted. We cannot allow it, as the doctor is an employee of ours and he might want to discuss our operation in an attempt to save his skin. The doctor's name is Ernie Shoehorn."

The woman was indifferent to the name. She nodded to show she had paid attention.

"Everything you need is in here." The man handed the woman a black attaché case and walked away.

# CHAPTER 36

Marwin woke stiff and achy, which seemed to be a more regular occurrence. He stretched before pulling on gym shorts and trudging downstairs for his morning coffee.

In the kitchen, he caught movement through the window overlooking the backyard. Through the window, Bogie and Morgan threw a softball back and forth. Blinking, he shook his head as if to wake himself from what seemed like a dream.

Marwin thought briefly about going outside with his kids but decided to embrace the peace. Taking his coffee, a bagel, and iPhone into his study, he perused the morning news and last night's baseball scores. Seeing nothing of significance, he showered and dressed in khaki shorts and a yellow PFG shirt, then returned downstairs just as the kids came back inside.

"Hey, Dad. Bogie's been throwing with me this morning!" Morgan announced exuberantly.

"That's awesome," Marwin said, glancing at Bogie, who offered an embarrassed shrug.

"You guys can take your stuff to your mom's if you want."

"Um, I think she has plans for us," Bogie said hesitantly.

"I'll bring mine," Morgan said, directing a look at Bogie.

"Yeah, OK. I'll bring mine, too. I guess we can find some time to throw."

Marwin watched the strange exchange and wondered what the hell was going on. Checking the clock, he said, "Get all your stuff together. Your mom should be here in about fifteen minutes."

After the kids left with Lindsey, Marwin spent a few minutes straightening up the house before calling Destiny. "I'm leaving in ten minutes or so," he told her.

"Oh, OK. I didn't know you were coming over so soon."

"I can wait until later if I need to," Marwin said, sounding pitiful. "I just missed you and wanted to spend as much time as possible with you today."

Catching Marwin's tone, Destiny replied, "Nah, come on over now. I miss you, too."

"Cool, I'll see you shortly. Do I need to pick anything up to take over to Sam's? I have some beer and Pinot Grigio already in a cooler and ready to go."

"That sounds perfect. See ya soon."

* * *

THE WOMAN COLLAPSED ON her bed, completely exhausted. She was physically drained as she had been up for almost twenty-four hours, but her nerves were frayed, also. The preparation was tedious and required slow, steady hands working with tiny parts and a lethal drug. It had taken her three attempts before she was satisfied that everything was right.

Her eyes closed as the Sand Man threatened to win, so she forced herself off the bed and stumbled to the bathroom. Stripping her clothes off, she climbed into an icy shower. The frigid water ran over her body, but she tried to block the cold from her mind. Within seconds, her tired mind cleared and hyper-focused on the task ahead.

Turning off the icy water, she dried and quickly dressed in a black skirt with a conservative blouse. She seated a blonde wig atop her head and applied a light amount of makeup before inserting a pair of contact lenses that changed her brown eyes to a striking green. She studied her appearance in the mirror for a long moment, picked up the black attaché case, and headed for her car.

* * *

MARWIN LISTENED TO A SPORTS gambling show on satellite radio as he drove toward Destiny's place. The station was previewing the upcoming college football season, which caused Marwin to realize, yet again, that he had done no preparation.

It was a brilliant, late summer day, but clouds were already building from the west. Thunderheads rose into the sky, promising much-needed relief from the sweltering heat. Traffic was light on Saturday, and Marwin didn't encounter construction work on his trip. This, he considered a harbinger of a great day.

Pulling up to Destiny's condo, Marwin almost skipped to the door. Destiny greeted him with sparkling hazel eyes, and she was dressed in a lightweight, floral robe.

"Good morning, Handsome," she glowed, kissing him softly.

"Good morning to you, too, Beautiful," Marwin returned, pulling Destiny in for another kiss.

"I was about to get dressed. Come talk to me," Destiny said, turning toward her bedroom.

After three or four steps, Destiny stopped, loosened the belt on the robe, and let it fall to the floor, leaving Marwin to stare after her. When Marwin entered the room, he found Destiny in the closet, rifling through several sun dresses, pretending to be oblivious to his presence.

Marwin came up behind Destiny and kissed the back of her neck while encircling her with his arm.

"Umm," she purred, tilting her head away so he could have greater access to her neck and throat.

Marwin caressed Destiny's neck with his lips, and his hand roamed to her breast, gently pinching her nipple.

She moaned, arching her back and pushing her rear against the stiffening erection behind her.

A guttural sound escaped Marwin, and he spun Destiny around, kissing her deeply. He pulled back, looked hungrily into her eyes, and placed his hands on her shoulders. He pushed Destiny down to her knees, and she slid his pants off over his bulging member. Just then, Marwin's phone rang, but neither he—nor Destiny—paid any attention to it.

After Destiny teased and licked Marwin, he dropped to the floor beside her, kissed her deeply, and pushed her gently backward. He placed himself between her legs and lowered himself down on top of her. Destiny grabbed Marwin's erection and prepared to guide him into her, but his phone rang again.

"Shit!" he exclaimed, frustrated.

Marwin drew away from Destiny and said, "Sorry. It might be the kids. I'll be right back. Don't go anywhere."

Marwin's now-deflating member led him out of the closet and into the bedroom, where his phone was dancing across the dresser. Just as he picked the phone up, it went silent. Cursing under his breath, Marwin checked the call log and found the first call was from an unknown number, likely a telemarketer. The second call was from Bradley Jinswain. Marwin cursed again, knowing he would not have interrupted his activity if he had known it was Bradley calling.

Destiny peered out of the closet, dressed in a perky yellow sun dress. "Everything OK?"

"Yeah. It was a telemarketer first, then Bradley." Eyeing Destiny's attire, Marwin said, "Looks like we're done, huh?"

"For now," she replied, grinning. "We'll pick up where we left off after we kick some ass at Sam's."

Destiny went into the bathroom to finish getting ready, so Marwin called Bradley. "I missed a call from you. What's up?"

"I've been doing some digging into Jackson's patients. I may have found a link, but I wanted to talk to you to see if you discovered anything when you went through their charts."

"No, not really," Marwin conceded. "There was really no explanation for the sudden deaths except they were all elderly. The patient that had the autopsy died of a hypertensive crisis, secondary to serotonin syndrome. He also had large amounts of a drug in his system that Jackson had not prescribed. He had amphetamines, also, but that could have come from the drug. Lastly, he had ammonium chloride in his blood and urine, likely to mask the drug no one knew he was taking. In a crime show, it would suggest he was murdered."

"Well, maybe he *was* murdered," Bradley replied.

"Really? What kind of link did you find?"

"Look, all of this is unofficial. It appears all the patients had an insurance policy with the same company. One patient had a cancer policy, and the others all had long-term care policies."

"Huh, that's weird," Marwin said.

"I don't know exactly what it means, but my gut tells me it is important."

"Your gut was right about Madeline's suicide, and I won't doubt it now."

"We'll see," Bradley said. "I'm gonna call Vince Adkins and see if he has seen any other deaths similar to these."

"Good luck," Marwin said sourly. "I had a hard time getting any information out of him."

"He'll talk to me," Bradley spoke confidently.

"Hope so. Ask him if he has the results of the latest patient Jackson lost. I believe her name was Ruth Westmoreland."

"Will do. I'll be in touch."

* * *

THE WOMAN EXITED I-40 at Western Avenue, turned right on Henley Street, and traversed the rest of the way to the Knox County Jail. She parked her car a block away, checked her appearance one last time, and walked the rest of the way to the building.

Once inside, she was greeted by two guards who directed her to the metal detector and x-ray machine to her right. She placed her phone, purse, and attaché case on the conveyor belt and walked slowly through the metal detector. No alarms sounded, so she retrieved her belongings and followed the guard to a desk, where she explained the purpose of her visit.

She smiled. "Good morning. My name is Isabelle Snow. I work for Lawrence Wellborn. Mr. Wellborn represents Dr. Ernie Shoehorn, and I have some documents for Dr. Shoehorn to review."

The short-haired, plump guard at the desk tapped some keys and studied the screen. "OK. I see your name here. Sign in, please."

After signing the register, the woman was led into a room with a hard plastic chair in front of a long, scarred table. She was instructed to wait while the prisoner was retrieved. She opened her attaché case and removed several sheets of paper. She sat back easily in the chair, noticing the camera in the back corner.

Five minutes later, Ernie Shoehorn was led into the room, looking haggard. "Who are you?"

"I'm Isabelle Snow. I work for Lawrence Wellborn."

"I don't know you," Shoehorn stated warily. "I've never seen you before."

"I know. I'm one of the flunkies in the practice. Actually, the *only* one who is working on a Saturday." She laughed.

Shoehorn remained standing. "What do you want?"

"Sit down, Dr. Shoehorn," Isabelle said, pointing to the chair.

Shoehorn hesitated, obviously debating, before settling into a chair opposite Isabelle.

Isabelle glanced at the guard. "Can we have some privacy, please?"

The guard smiled and looked at the cameras mounted on the ceiling. "I'll be right outside."

After the guard left, Isabelle looked directly into Shoehorn's tired eyes. "The boss has some paperwork for you to review."

At the mention of 'the boss', Shoehorn stared at the woman, who gave an almost imperceptible nod in his direction.

Sliding the papers toward Shoehorn, Isabelle said, "Mr. Wellborn enlisted the help of a trial consulting firm for your trial. Based on their observations, they believe you will be convicted."

Shoehorn visibly shrunk in his chair, face clouded with confusion and worry.

"Dr. Shoehorn, Mr. Wellborn has outlined a couple of last-minute plea bargains for you to review." She tapped the papers with her blue pen.

When Shoehorn stared blankly at her, she tapped the papers pointedly again. The disgraced doctor finally broke his gaze and looked down at the papers. Instead of a plea bargain, the first page had a signature line and a paragraph instructing Shoehorn to sign the name Edgar Simpson for the preparation of a new driver's license and passport. Shoehorn glanced questioningly at Isabelle, who again gave the slightest of nods.

Shoehorn visibly relaxed.

Isabelle told him, "Please review all these proposals. Mr. Wellborn will be by early Monday morning to discuss them with you. He has requested that you initial and sign each proposal, thereby acknowledging they were presented to you. Please take a few minutes to look over them before signing."

Shoehorn nodded, then studied the papers. Page one was the new identification documents. Page two detailed how a not guilty verdict was expected to be returned. The last page detailed a large sum of money that had been deposited into an offshore account that matched the new identity.

Shoehorn smiled and reached for Isabelle's pen. Isabelle withdrew a black ink pen from her attaché case and handed the pen to the doctor. "Mr. Wellborn is confident the plea deals will be accepted. Please initial and sign the marked locations, Dr. Shoehorn."

Shoehorn placed the pen on the paper, but it wasn't open. He clicked the end of the pen with his thumb and initialed and signed the various lines. Twice during the process, Isabelle stopped him and reiterated the plan. After finishing, Shoehorn handed the pen back to Isabelle, but she pushed the attaché case forward, and he dropped the pen into it.

Isabelle placed the signed papers atop the pen and snapped the case shut. "Thank you, Dr. Shoehorn. Mr. Wellborn will see you on Monday."

When she opened the door, she said to the guard, "We're done."

Shoehorn watched Isabelle walk away with eyes that were already beginning to blur.

\* \* \*

AT SAM'S HOUSE, THE four friends spent the afternoon playing corn hole and sipping beer. When the anticipated rain came, they moved inside to play cards. Dawn brought out a tray of cheese, crackers, thinly sliced meat, and spinach dip, and the four munched while playing cards. The guys stayed with their IPAs while the girls changed to Pinot Grigio. The conversation was light, and they talked as if they had been friends for years.

Several times during the card game, Destiny used her bare foot to rub Marwin's feet under the table. She gave him her best *I want you* look each time he glanced her way. When Destiny took a restroom break, Marwin nonchalantly slipped his hand into his pocket and withdrew a small, blue tablet which he took while no one was looking.

When a new hand was dealt, Marwin related how Bradley had discovered an insurance link between all of Jackson's deceased patients.

"I wonder if Memi's boyfriend was one of those with a policy with that company?" Dawn asked.

"I'm not sure. Bradley didn't give me specifics. Her boyfriend was the one that died differently from the rest. Correct?"

"Yes, he died of organ failure due to severely low blood pressure. You said the others died of a hypertensive crisis."

The card game continued, with Sam and Dawn leading throughout. Destiny looked curiously at Marwin. "Mar, you OK? Your face is flushed."

Marwin had noticed the warmth spreading through his face and the congestion building in his nose, so he was pretty sure he knew what was happening.

"I guess I'm just steamed that Sam has the Rook up his ass today," Marwin joked.

"I can't help it if you don't know how to play," Sam poked.

"Bite me."

"You talking to me?" Destiny asked, giggling.

"Destiny's right, Marwin. Your face is lit up. Are you sure you are feeling all right?" Dawn asked.

"I'm good. Let's finish the game," Marwin replied, eyeing Destiny across the table.

"You know, Memi said her boyfriend's face was really flushed right before he collapsed," Dawn offered.

"I'm fine. Let's just get this debacle over with."

The game mercifully ended with Sam and Dawn trouncing Marwin and Destiny. Marwin grumbled about Sam's lucky horseshoe he kept up his butt and vowed the four would play Hearts next time.

"I can beat you at whatever you would like," Sam said, laughing.

"We'll see, but not tonight. I think I am about ready to go," Marwin admitted.

"Can I have just a little more of that delicious cheese before we leave?" Destiny asked Dawn. "Where do you get it?"

"I have to order it. You can't buy it in a store around here. My grandmother loves it, so I order it for her periodically."

"What kind of cheese is it?" Destiny inquired.

"It's called Borsault. It's a French cheese."

"Huh. I've never even heard of Borsault cheese. Well, it sure is to die for."

"I agree. It is delicious. It's too expensive and hard to get for my liking, but since my grandmother loves it, I get it for her. Nothing's too good for Memi," Dawn affirmed.

Marwin, face now completely aglow, stared strangely at Dawn. He rifled through his mental filing cabinet. He finally located the folder he was searching for and was stunned by what he read in it.

"Earth to Marwin," Destiny said, laughing.

"What? I'm sorry, I was off somewhere," Marwin said slowly.

"Was it somewhere cooler?"

"Not exactly. What did I miss while I was away?" Marwin asked, making light of the situation.

"Dawn asked if you wanted to play another game," Destiny supplied.

Marwin looked at Dawn, smiled, and said, "I think I'm ready for a different kind of game, so we'll get together again soon."

"Well, for Destiny's sake, I hope you're better at that game than you are at Rook," Sam interjected, getting the last jab in.

"Yeah. Me, too," Marwin agreed, giving Sam a fist bump.

Marwin and Destiny said their goodbyes, each vowing to get revenge at the next meeting.

"You sure you're OK?" Destiny asked as Marwin drove. "Your face was really red, and you had a strange expression before we left."

*You know, come to think about it, Memi said her boyfriend's face was really flushed right before he collapsed*, Marwin remembered.

Dawn's words echoed in Marwin's mind. Marwin knew what had caused his face to flush, and Marwin wondered if Memi's boyfriend had taken a little blue tablet, too. Scanning his mental files again, he found no listing of Viagra on the patient's chart. The patient was on nitrate medication which could have caused major problems if he had taken Viagra. Marwin decided to contact Jackson to see if he might have given the patient some samples of Viagra.

Destiny placed her hand on the inside of Marwin's thigh, allowing her pinkie finger to squeeze between his right testicle and leg. It broke Marwin's reverie and snapped him back to the present.

"So, what's up?" Destiny asked playfully, allowing her hand to roam.

"Uh, nothing really, but if you keep doing that, something will be up," he replied, thrusting his pelvis upward to meet her hand.

"Bullshit, you're thinking hard about something," Destiny replied but didn't stop rubbing.

"Apparently, you're thinking about something hard, too."

"I am," she replied, trying to unzip his shorts. With Marwin's help, Destiny finally freed his engorged member.

Taking her seatbelt off, she said, "Don't wreck."

Destiny placed her head in Marwin's lap and slowly licked. Marwin moaned and reached for her, finally able to work her sundress up so he could smack her butt. An animal sound escaped her throat, and she intensified her efforts. The two rode down the road this way like two horny teenagers on a date.

Marwin struggled to focus on the road in front of him. "You better stop."

Destiny pulled up and looked hungrily at Marwin. "You sure you want me to stop?"

"No, not really, but you better," he panted.

Destiny buckled her seatbelt back but pulled her sundress off her shoulders and teased her nipples—first with her fingers, then with her tongue. "Hurry home," she said, looking into Marwin's eyes.

Minutes later, the two lust birds flew into Destiny's condo and completely disrobed before the door was shut and locked.

Marwin ravaged her mouth with his tongue and pushed her onto the couch. Tongues and fingers flew in all directions as the two tried to devour each other. Destiny bent over the arm of the couch, and Marwin plunged into her from behind. He pounded away, pulling her hips against him. Destiny moaned and thrust, too, and soon shook all over as the spasms spread through her.

Realizing Destiny had finished, Marwin withdrew. Destiny turned over and said sheepishly, "You shouldn't have stopped me in the car."

Normally, Marwin would have said, 'It's OK. You can owe me one,' but instead, he held his rock-hard member and pleaded, "Come on, Des."

Destiny forced Marwin onto his back and straddled his member. He immediately grabbed her butt and slammed her up and down. They continued bucking wildly, and soon Destiny was sweating profusely. She climbed off, sweat-soaked and exhausted.

"Damn, Mar. You still going?"

"Don't leave me hangin'," he implored.

Eyeing Marwin's straining penis, she said, "OK, but you better get there quick, or you're gonna have to take a trip to the bathroom."

Again, Destiny straddled his exaggerated member, this time facing away from him. As she rocked back and forth, Marwin thrust deeply. She rose almost to the point he slipped out but dropped down, forcing him deep inside her. A moan came from his throat, and he smacked her hard on the ass. This caused a tingle to start in Destiny again, and she rode Marwin with all the strength she had left. As the tingle turned into spasms again for Destiny, Marwin emitted a loud moan and grabbed her hips tightly before finally emptying himself, too.

Climbing slowly and painfully off Marwin, Destiny smiled weakly and said, "Don't ever take Viagra again."

# CHAPTER 37

Marwin and Destiny showered together, tenderly washing each other's backs. Lust was temporarily replaced by love as they murmured to each other and paused to hug and kiss softly.

Once out of the shower, Destiny ordered P.F. Chang's, and Marwin opened a bottle of Biltmore Pinot Grigio. The two finished the sesame chicken and sipped their wine, now completely sated and content.

They talked about everything and nothing, too, just relishing the day and the time they had spent with one another. As their eyes grew heavy from the wine and the day's events, Destiny's phone rang. Simon's name popped up on her phone and caused Destiny to sit straight up, startling Marwin.

"Has the jury returned a verdict?" she asked.

"No, they haven't, Destiny," Simon replied wearily. "It doesn't matter now, anyway."

"What? Why not?" Destiny's eyebrows drew together, and she grabbed Marwin's hand.

"Because Shoehorn is dead. He died in jail this afternoon."

"How? What happened to him?" Destiny asked Simon while mouthing that Shoehorn was dead to Marwin.

"We don't have all the details, but it looks like he died of a drug overdose," Simon explained.

"I don't understand. How could he have gotten drugs?"

"As I said, we don't have the details, but apparently, he was murdered."

"Simon, what are you talking about?" Destiny asked, exasperated.

"Shoehorn was murdered?" Marwin asked from behind her.

Destiny nodded to Marwin and said, "Hold on, Simon. I want to put you on speaker so Marwin can hear, too."

"Go ahead, Simon. Tell us what you know," Destiny instructed.

"We know that Shoehorn was visited by a woman named Isabelle Snow this morning. She claimed to work for Wellborn's office and had papers for Shoehorn to review. Her name was on the available visitor's list, interestingly enough. We are in the process of tracking down who called and added her name to the list. Anyway, she met with Shoehorn and presented paperwork to him.

"She told him Wellborn had hired a trial consulting firm, and he was likely to be convicted. Supposedly, Wellborn had drafted a last-minute plea deal for Shoehorn to review. Shoehorn took a few minutes to read the papers and signed them.

"Snow left, and Shoehorn was taken back to his cell. Right before he reached his cell, he stumbled sideways into the guard and claimed he was dizzy. The guard placed him in his cell, and he crawled up on his bunk and laid down. At lunch, they found him unresponsive and took him to the clinic, but he died before they could examine him.

"Holy shit!" Marwin exclaimed, overwhelmed by a myriad of emotions. While Marwin despised Shoehorn, he was a colleague with whom he had interacted on numerous occasions. It seemed surreal that Shoehorn was actually dead.

"Yep, that about sums it up," Simon agreed.

"Any idea how the woman was able to drug him?" Destiny asked.

"Maybe," Simon said slowly. "The Snow woman—if that's even her name—made him use a different pen to sign the paperwork from the one she was holding. When Shoehorn finished signing, he offered the pen to Snow, but she wouldn't take it. She had him drop it into her briefcase instead."

"The pen must have been coated in a powerful opioid or depressant," Marwin opined.

"Could enough be absorbed through his skin to actually kill him?" Destiny wondered.

"I don't know for sure," Marwin admitted. "There are nut-jobs out there coating inanimate objects with fentanyl and leaving them for people to find. I believe there have been some deaths reported from this type of accidental exposure."

"Geez! That's scary," Simon said. "The Snow woman did hand Shoehorn the pen, though. So, wouldn't she be at risk, too?"

"Was that the only time she touched the pen?"

"Yes, she had another pen in her hand, but she handed him a different one from her briefcase when he was ready to sign the papers."

"So, she did touch the pen briefly. That seems very risky to me on her part," Marwin said. "She would have no idea how much of the drug she might have absorbed in the short period of time her fingers were in contact with the pen."

"Hold on, guys. I need to get this call," Simon interjected.

Marwin and Destiny sat lost in their thoughts.

"Sorry, guys. That was Wellborn. He doesn't have anyone named Isabelle Snow working for him, and he doesn't know anything about a trial consultant or a plea deal. This confirms what we suspected. Ernie Shoehorn was murdered."

After hanging up with Simon, Marwin and Destiny replayed their conversation. They offered scenarios about who would want to kill Shoehorn so bad they would conduct the murder in the riskiest place possible. No reasonable conclusion presented itself.

Marwin sat up and said, "Oh, my God! I wonder if Jackson knows?"

Destiny quickly dialed Jackson and asked casually, "Hey, Jackson. How's it going?"

"It's going, I guess," Jackson answered, sounding normal.

Eyeing Marwin, Destiny said, "Marwin and I were just wondering what you were up to tonight?"

"Nothing, really. I'm just sitting here reading. Another exciting Saturday night in Knoxville. Why? What's up?"

Destiny shook her head at Marwin and said, "Would it be all right if we stopped by for a visit?"

"Sure. Is he so boring that you need to visit someone else?" Jackson asked with a chuckle.

"Nah, he's plenty exciting enough for me," Destiny said, smiling across at Marwin. "We just thought we would stop by and catch up on things with you if you are home."

"Sure. You're welcome anytime. Bring that grumpy old fart with you if you want."

Destiny hung up. "He obviously hasn't been told."

"Crap. I guess we better go break the news to him."

The two made the short drive to Jackson's house quietly, each likely playing out how they would break the news to Jackson. As they pulled to the curb in front of the house, Destiny asked, "So, what was up with you right before we left Sam's this afternoon?"

Marwin hesitated, rubbing his hand across his chin, before finally saying, "Look, Des. I'm not sure I want to verbalize this right now. Some things happened at Sam's that caused my brain to make some connections. I need to sort it out before I start spouting crazy shit."

"Why? Your crazy theories are usually correct. Aren't they?"

"Yeah, sometimes, but if I'm wrong this time, I could end up hurting some good friends, and I don't want to risk that."

"I can understand, but you can tell me. I won't share your crazy theory with anyone."

Marwin smiled lovingly at Destiny. He took her hand and gave it a comforting squeeze. "OK. Let's get this over with, and I'll tell you what I'm thinking."

Destiny leaned forward and gave Marwin a soft, gentle kiss. "All right, let's go, Dr. Gelstone."

\* \* \*

THE WOMAN SAT ON her couch, the energy flowing rapidly out of her. She was physically tired—but mentally—she was completely exhausted.

After leaving the jail, she drove to a secluded park where she removed the license plate cover on her car. She stripped out of her clothes and blonde wig and changed into casual attire. She carried a bag containing the wig, clothes, and license cover to a hidden area, where she doused it in lighter fluid and set it alight. She watched it burn until it was all unrecognizable and then scattered the ashes around the area. Looking over her handiwork, she seemed satisfied and drove home.

The woman had no problem with responding to her alias. In fact, she couldn't remember the last time she'd heard her birth name. She adopted a new identity every time she performed a duty outside the usual requirements set by her boss, even if she only altered her last name.

The people who thought they knew her were clueless. She was careful not to mix acquaintances at work and in her private life, but when it happened, she was safe from discovery by the terms of endearment that blanketed the South, like "Honey" and "Sweetie". Her name was rarely spoken.

Once home, the woman scrubbed the New Skin off of her hands. She had felt no ill effects from the powerful drug that coated the pen, so apparently, the New Skin provided an adequate barrier. She scrubbed her hands until they were a bright pink, trying to ensure no residue remained on her hands.

Satisfied that her hands were clean, she went into the bathroom and took another icy shower—just on the minuscule chance that the hot water would aid in any accidental exposure to the powerful opioid. Shivering, she exited the shower and dressed in shorts and a tee shirt before sitting on the couch.

As her energy rapidly dissipated, the woman thought about going to bed but lay over on the couch and fell instantly asleep.

* * *

"So, what brings you two love birds out on a Saturday night?" Jackson asked, closing the door behind them.

"We're out visiting the elderly," Marwin quipped.

"Yeah. Kiss my elderly ass!" Jackson returned, grinning up to his eyes.

"Have you heard from Simon?" Destiny asked, interrupting the teenage barbs.

"No, why? Has the jury returned a verdict?" Jackson asked nervously.

Before Destiny could answer, Jackson's phone rang. He ignored the phone, waiting for Destiny to answer his question. When no answer came, he picked up the phone and answered distractedly.

"Hey, Jackson. It's Bradley."

Destiny's question—paired with Bradley's call—accelerated Jackson's heart rate, and a sense of dread swept over him. His knees buckled, and he swayed slightly into the table.

"Jackson? You still there?" Bradley asked.

Steadying himself, Jackson answered shakily, "Yeah, Bradley. I'm here. What's up?"

"Have you heard from Simon?"

"No, I haven't, but Destiny and Marwin are here, and Destiny just asked me the same thing. What is going on? Is the verdict back?"

"No, there isn't a verdict, and now there never will be." Before Jackson could ask for an explanation, Bradley continued, "Shoehorn is dead. It looks like he was murdered in jail today."

Jackson rocked back, wide-eyed, and stammered, "M-Murdered? How? Who?"

Bradley relayed the information Simon had just given to Destiny and Marwin. When he finished, Jackson murmured, "I can't believe the son-of-a-bitch is actually dead."

"I also have some information on the patients you have lost recently, but I'll let you digest Shoehorn's death first. I'll give you a call tomorrow if it's all right."

Jackson's mind raced with thoughts of Shoehorn and Madeline, and he barely heard Bradley's last statement. "Yeah, sure. Call me anytime." Almost as an afterthought, he added, "Thanks for calling me."

Turning to Destiny and Marwin, Jackson said, "I guess you heard?"

Placing a hand on Jackson's shoulder, Marwin said, "Yeah, that's why we came over. We were gonna let you know in case you hadn't been notified yet." Marwin gave Jackson's shoulder a gentle squeeze. "You OK?"

"Yeah, I think so. It'll probably take some time to sink in, but I think everything's gonna be fine. If you guys don't mind, I think I'd like to be alone tonight. You're welcome to stay as long as you like. Just lock the door when you leave."

As Jackson ascended the stairs, Marwin said, "We'll see you tomorrow. Don't hesitate to call either one of us if you need us. Anytime, day or night."

"I will," Jackson mumbled, continuing his climb.

At the top of the stairs, Jackson turned. "Thanks for coming over. You guys are the best, and I love you both."

# CHAPTER 38

Climbing back into Marwin's SUV, Destiny noted, "Shoehorn's death really rocked Jackson."

"Yeah, it did," Marwin agreed. "I can understand, though. Even though I couldn't stand the quack, his murder is unsettling."

Destiny ruminated. "Yes, it is, but you have to remember he caused multiple women to commit suicide and tried to kill you, so in the end, he got what was coming to him."

Marwin tried to refute Destiny but realized he would be defending Shoehorn, so he said simply, "True."

The two rode quietly in silence without bothering to turn on the radio. Eventually, Marwin stated, "I'm worried Dawn may be involved in the deaths of Jackson's patients."

"What? Why?" Destiny exclaimed, turning in her seat to stare at Marwin. "You can't be serious!"

"I am serious, or I would never mention something like that. You wanted to know what happened at Sam's, so hear me out," Marwin said sternly.

Destiny started to protest the ludicrous idea but bit her tongue and waited for Marwin to continue.

He took a deep breath. "First, she is a pharmacist. From everything I have seen and Sam has said, she knows her drugs very well. Second, the cheese she served us—and she ordered for her grandmother—is called Borsault. It has one of the highest tyramine contents of all cheeses."

"OK, so?"

Ignoring her interruption, Marwin continued, "Third, Mr. Stanford had a soft cheese that could have been Borsault in his stomach contents, with wine and summer sausage, both of which are high in tyramine. Fourth, Mr. Stanford had amphetamines and metabolites of an MAOI in his system when he died. If he was given that MAOI in a high, non-selective dose and ingested the cheese, wine, and summer sausage, he could very easily have developed serotonin syndrome and a hypertensive crisis."

"Uh, OK," Destiny said slowly, obviously trying to choose her words carefully. "It is still a huge jump to say Dawn was involved because she had access to a cheese that may or may not have been in the man's stomach."

Deflecting the rebuttal, Marwin said, "There's more. She recognized I had taken Viagra by my face flushing. She told us her grandmother's boyfriend's face was very flushed just before his collapse."

"Um, OK. So what?" Destiny asked, bewildered.

"What if Dawn didn't like the boyfriend and wanted him out of her grandmother's life? She is at Forever Young several times a week, too, so everyone there knows her, and no one would think anything about her visiting other residents."

"What? You think Dawn is some Angel of Death or something?" Destiny asked incredulously.

"No, I don't think that for sure. I just see several links between Dawn and two of the patients that died."

"Well, if I were a lawyer, I would say you are throwing shit at the wall in hopes that some of it will stick," Destiny said unpleasantly.

"Look, I certainly don't want to be right about Dawn. I just want to find out who's killing Jackson's patients."

"I suggest you take your detective skills down a different path," Destiny said vehemently.

Marwin spoke in soft tones. "Easy, Des. I'm not the bad guy here."

"Seems to me you might not be the good guy either." She sat back in her seat and crossed her arms.

"Damnit! I knew I shouldn't have said anything to you."

No response came from Destiny, and the two finished the trip in stony silence.

* * *

MARWIN AWOKE EARLY SUNDAY morning, feeling tired and out of sorts. He had slept fitfully. He was in the kitchen pouring coffee when Destiny entered.

"Morning," she said, kissing him softly on the cheek.

"Look, Des, I'm sorry—"

"Marwin, stop. I'm sorry I reacted the way I did. Your theory caught me completely off guard." She shrugged. "Maybe I was still affected by Shoehorn's death? Maybe I just acted like a crazy woman? I don't know. Anyway, I'm sorry. I want you to dig into your theory, just *please* do it so no one knows you suspect Dawn."

Marwin took Destiny into his arms, hugged her gently, and felt the tension drain out of himself. "Thanks, Des. I will do my best Dick Tracey detective work, and no one will know but you." Breaking the embrace, he asked, "You want to go to church?"

"Yes, but no. Why don't you put on your detective hat and see what you can find out," Destiny suggested with a smile.

"OK, but I really don't know where to start," he admitted.

"Well, I'm not a detective like you, but I think you should maybe visit Forever Young, where all the action has occurred."

Marwin pulled Destiny back into his arms. "You know, you're pretty smart for a lawyer."

* * *

MARWIN DROVE TOWARD FOREVER Young as the day heated up. He didn't really have a plan in mind or even much of an idea about what he hoped to find. He decided to try to talk to an old friend who worked there as a nurse.

244

Using his Bluetooth, he called Jackson. "How're you doing this morning?"

"Actually, I'm good," he responded huskily. "I went to bed after you guys left and cried like a baby. I guess I cried for Madeline and myself. Hell, I might even have cried for Shoehorn, but I would hate to admit it. I eventually dozed off and slept like a dead person. This morning, I feel better than I have since Madeline died."

Shocked at the rarely-seen softer side of Jackson, Marwin said, "I guess crying can be therapeutic."

"Yep, and also knowing that the son-of-a-bitch paid for what he did to Madeline," Jackson agreed brusquely.

Laughing, Marwin said, "There's the man I know and love."

"So, what's up with you this morning?"

"I'm headed over to Forever Young and was wondering if you had gotten the autopsy results for Ruth Westmoreland."

"Wow! The boss doing chart reviews on a Sunday morning? Did you lose a bet with Sam?"

"Yeah, something like that," Marwin said evasively.

"I haven't gotten the results yet, so let me call down there and see if I can get anything out of the grumpy, old curmudgeon."

"Let me know if you get anything."

"Will, do. Oh, thanks for calling to check on me, Marwin."

Marwin laughed. "No problem. My mom taught me to try to take care of the elderly."

* * *

JACKSON SMILED AS HE waited for the phone to be answered. *I am so lucky to have such good friends*, he thought.

"Vince Adkins," came the voice, breaking Jackson's thought process.

"Hey, Vince. It's Jackson Montgomery. How're you this morning?"

"Just peachy. I'm surrounded by four dead bodies on a Sunday morning. What could be better? What can I do for you, Jackson?"

"I was checking to see if I could get the results of the post on Ruth Westmoreland."

"Yeah, I was actually gonna call you. I just haven't been able to find the time. People keep dying around here. Plus, every time I turn around, my technician is in the shitter. I have to do everything myself, like answering your phone call."

"Yeah, I noticed that part. Since you're so busy, could your tech give me the results? I don't want to take up any more of your time," Jackson said, taking a soft approach.

"I doubt it. The phone won't reach the toilet. I needed to talk to you about it anyway. Hold on while I pull her results up." Following a brief pause, Adkins continued, "Here it is. Your patient died of a massive stroke and heart attack, consistent with a hypertensive crisis."

After he heard the almost identical autopsy report of one of his previous patients, Jackson was stunned. "Oh, that's surprising. She didn't have blood pressure problems."

"That you knew of," Adkins remarked.

"I had just examined her recently as she had been feeling poorly. She was lethargic and had lost quite a bit of weight. Her BP was normal in my office. There's no way she suffered a hypertensive crisis."

"OK, Hotshot," Adkins fired off. "Why don't you come down here and slice and dice? Then, you can come up with your own cause of death."

"I didn't mean that I thought you were wrong, Vince. I mean it doesn't make any sense."

"OK, whatever. Anything else?"

"Yes, just one more question. Did you find evidence of lung cancer?"

"Yep, she was eaten up with it. Her lungs and liver were like Swiss cheese. There was also a suspicious spot in her brain, but I would have to send that to pathology to find out if it was a metastasis."

"Damn, I was afraid of that. Her labs came back the day after she died, and all her cancer markers were elevated. Still, that wouldn't cause her to drop dead suddenly."

"No, but a massive stroke and heart attack secondary to a hypertensive crisis would," Adkins confirmed again.

Ignoring the jab, Jackson said, "Just one more question."

"Really? You've already asked 'one more question,'" Adkins quipped.

"Stop being an asshole, Vince!" Jackson thundered. "I'm just trying to find out what happened to my patient."

"I understand," Adkins said, nonplussed. "Go ahead, ask all the questions you want. I'll be here until five."

Jackson bit back a retort. "Was there anything unusual in her stomach contents?"

"No, her stomach was basically empty. I did find a soft, cheesy substance under her dentures, though."

"Was there any selegiline, amphetamines, or ammonium chloride in her system?" Jackson asked, running with Marwin's theory.

"No selegiline, but there was a large amount of tranylcypromine in her blood. That is likely what triggered everything," Adkins postulated.

"What? She wasn't taking tranylcypromine!" Jackson exclaimed.

"Well, I don't believe it is naturally found in the human body, but I could be wrong," Adkins said sarcastically.

Jackson was dumbfounded. He finally said, "Thanks, Vince. I'll let you go."

"Thank God!" Adkins said and slammed the phone down.

* * *

"WHAT'S UP, OLD GIRL?" Marwin asked the nurse seated at the desk.

"You're older than me, so you tell me," Tracey replied, looking up.

"I was just passing by and thought I would check on one of my *old* friends," Marwin said, grinning.

"Uh-huh. I bet. You know the first liar doesn't stand a chance," Tracey said, returning Marwin's grin.

"Yeah, I know. Actually, I was hoping you would be here. I wanted to ask you some questions."

"Sorry, I already have a date for the prom," Tracey deadpanned.

Marwin chuckled. "Whoa! You win! No way you have a date for the prom."

"Very funny. What you need, Marwin?"

"I'm not really sure, Trace. I'm looking into the deaths of several of your residents over the last couple of months. I thought you might be able to shed some light on the situation."

"What? Are you Alex Cross now?" She raised her eyebrows.

Marwin ignored the barb. "Look, Trace. There are some strange circumstances surrounding Ruth Westmoreland, Wilson Stanford, and Tom Richardson's deaths. I was wondering which pharmacies supply these patients' meds."

"Uh, ever hear of HIPAA?"

"Come on, Trace. No one cares about that shit, especially now that they are all dead."

She posed a question instead of answering Marwin's request. "What kind of *strange circumstances?*"

"I-I don't really want to get into it until we have more information," Marwin stammered.

"Really? You want me to violate HIPAA and lose my license to help you, but you won't even tell me why?"

"OK, I get it. You want a little quid pro quo."

"Did you learn that from John Grisham?" Tracey asked without smiling.

Marwin sighed and ran his hand through his hair. "Wilson Stanford died with amphetamines in his system. The coroner said he died of serotonin syndrome, but he wasn't on any drug to cause that to occur. He also had selegiline in his blood, but he wasn't taking it either. Lastly, he had ammonium chloride in his blood and urine, and unless he ate licorice by the foot several times a day, there's no explanation for its presence."

Tracey said nothing and just stared at Marwin. Finally, she clicked some keys.

"Mr. Stanford was not taking selegiline. Neither did he have any as-needed orders for pseudoephedrine which could have shown up as amphetamines in a toxicology report. I've never seen him eat licorice, but I can't be positive he didn't."

Before Marwin could comment, Tracey clicked more keys. "All three patients received their meds from Bi-Lo on Kingston Pike."

"Wow, really?" Marwin asked, mind whirling. *That's where Dawn works,* he thought sadly.

"Could you check to see if Tom Richardson had any orders for Viagra, please?"

With HIPAA already tossed, Tracey clicked the keys again and said, "Nope, no Viagra or any of those drugs listed. Actually, now that I think about it, we joked that he is the only man in here not on Viagra."

"Yeah, but if all the other male residents take it, Tom could have easily gotten some if he wanted it," Marwin opined.

"True story."

"I don't suppose Tom's stuff is still here. Is it?" Marwin asked hopefully. "Or Mr. Stanford's or Mrs. Westmoreland's?"

"Nope, 'fraid not. The families cleaned out their rooms shortly after they passed.

"Shit. I was afraid of that," Marwin lamented. "Can you think of any link between these patients?"

"Why do you think there might be a link? Did Tom and Ruth die the same way Mr. Stanford did?"

"No, Tom died in the exact opposite way from Mr. Stanford. He died of organ failure, secondary to severe low blood pressure. I'm not sure how Mrs. Westmoreland died. I am hoping to get the autopsy results later today. She had lung cancer, but the cancer wouldn't explain a sudden death."

"I don't know, Marwin. It seems like you might be searching for something that isn't there, "Tracey said gently.

"Yeah, maybe, but there's one more link I didn't mention. All three patients had an insurance policy with the same company."

"OK, so? I imagine lots of people use the same insurance company, especially in an assisted living facility. I know we have several patients who have a long-term care policy, and I think there may only be a handful of companies that still write those."

Before Marwin could respond, the door opened, and a young woman stepped inside.

"How are you this morning?" Tracey asked the woman.

"Oh, I'm OK, I guess, considering I'm here on a Sunday morning."

"Who are you here to see today?" Tracey inquired.

"I'm checking on Gladys again."

"I haven't seen her yet this morning, so let me know how she's doing," Tracey told her.

Turning back to Marwin, Tracey said, "I gotta get back to work. It was good to see you out and about."

"Thanks. It's good to get back to normal."

Tracey took one more cheap shot. "I didn't say anything about normal. You haven't ever been normal."

"True. I used to like you, so that made me abnormal right off the bat," Marwin returned, smiling. "Let me know if you think of anything else that might help."

As Marwin walked away, Tracey called after him, "Hey, Marwin! I just realized all of those patients were seen by Geri Assist."

"What's that?" Marwin asked. "Never heard of it."

"It's actually a really cool agency. They send someone out to interact with the residents. They play games with them and help them with small household chores if needed. They're kinda like geriatric babysitters, but the residents love them. In fact, the woman who was just here is one of their employees."

"Really? That's interesting. I've never heard of anything like that before."

"The coolest thing about it is that our facility actually pays for their services," Tracey offered.

"Wow! An assisted living facility pays for babysitters?" Marwin asked, perplexed.

"Yep, the theory is that the residents will be happier and more content, so they are more likely to live longer lives and will remain in our facility much longer," Tracey explained. "Obviously, that generates a lot more revenue."

"Seems crazy to me."

"Yeah, I was skeptical, at first, but now that I've seen how the residents respond, I think this company has really hit on something. Maybe you should talk to her. I'll be glad to introduce you."

Marwin hesitated, then realized he had gained very little except for the pharmacy and Geri Assist link, so he shrugged and said, "Sure, why not."

Tracey knocked on the door of Gladys' apartment. The Geri Assist employee opened the door, and Gladys was seated at the table eating breakfast.

"Come in, Tracey," the woman said, stepping aside.

Tracey spoke in Gladys's direction. "Sorry to interrupt your breakfast, but I have someone here that I would like to introduce to your friend."

"Sure, Honey. No problem."

Tracy gestured to Marwin. "This is Marwin Gelstone, a local pharmacist and an old, old friend of mine. He is here looking into some of the unfortunate deaths that we have had lately."

"Marwin, this is Gladys and Isabelle. Isabelle is one of the many Geri Assist employees who visit our patients."

"Nice to meet you, Gladys," Marwin said, extending his hand.

Marwin turned toward Isabelle and found her eyes pouring over him. Hesitating briefly, he finally extended his hand to her. "Nice to meet you, too, Isabelle."

The woman broke her stare and looked over Marwin's shoulder. "Yes, it's nice to meet you, also."

Marwin stared at her. "I was wondering if I could ask you a few questions."

"I guess so. What kind of questions?"

"I don't want to interrupt your visit with Gladys, so maybe you could give me a call later, at your convenience," Marwin suggested.

"Uh, yeah, sure. I can call you when I finish here," the woman replied slowly. "Could you tell me what this is about?"

"I was hoping you could tell me a little about Wilson Stanford, Ruth Westmoreland, and Tom Richardson. I understand you worked with all of them," Marwin said pleasantly.

"Yes, they were all on our service," the woman admitted.

He handed the woman a business card. "Here's my number. Just give me a call whenever you have the time to talk."

Reaching for the card, the woman turned an icy stare on Marwin. "OK, I'll be in touch later."

# CHAPTER 39

The woman exited Forever Young, climbed into her car, and sent a simple text.

*I need to talk to you, please.*

Placing her iPhone in the cup holder, she closed her eyes and leaned back against the seat with her mind spinning. Before her brain could form a tangible thought, her phone rang.

"What's wrong?" the man asked.

"Thank you for calling me so quickly."

"Cut to the chase," the man instructed.

"Yes, sir. I just met a pharmacist at Forever Young. His name is Marwin Gelstone, and he wants me to call him about some of our clients—the ones who are no longer in our service."

The man was silent. Finally, he said, "Call him, and report back to me immediately after you are through speaking with him."

\* \* \*

MARWIN LEFT THE FACILITY, picked up a sub from Sam and Andy's, and headed home in hopes of getting some stuff done before the kids returned from Lindsey's. As he drove, Don Henley sang about *The Boys of Summer,* and Marwin silently prayed summer would end soon.

His thoughts turned to Forever Young and what he may have learned. All the deceased patients used Bi-Lo as their pharmacy, which happened to be the pharmacy where Dawn worked. All the patients were seen by Geri Assist, and all had an insurance policy with the same company.

Not wanting to focus on Dawn's potential involvement, Marwin thought about the insurance link. It didn't seem unusual that the patients all used the same insurance company as not many companies wrote long-term care policies any longer. Maybe they were life insurance policies, but he doubted it as most elderly people didn't carry life insurance. The premiums were exorbitant. Auto policies also seemed unlikely as most elderly patients in assisted living were no longer driving a car. Marwin made a mental note to ask Bradley about the specifics of the insurance policies.

Just before Marwin reached his house, he received a call from Jackson giving him the detailed findings of Ruth Westmoreland's autopsy. At the mention of tranylcypromine and cheese, Marwin's mind put the pieces together. He thanked Jackson and smiled as he pulled into his driveway.

\* \* \*

BRADLEY SAT ON A bench in Third Creek Greenway Park, toweling himself off. He was drenched in sweat after finishing five miles in the blistering August heat. Drinking Gatorade and trying to cool down, he was interrupted by his phone buzzing again. He received a text from Marwin while running and now his boss was texting him.

*Damn, people! Can't I even enjoy a peaceful Sunday morning?* he thought irritably.

He sat quietly, deciding which person to contact first. It was doubtful that either his boss or Marwin had texted to invite him to dinner. He flipped a mental coin and called Marwin.

"Hey, Marwin! What's up?"

"Not much. I'm just trying to get some stuff done around the house before the kids get home. What about you?"

"I just finished a five-mile run and I'm returning everyone's messages. I never knew I was so popular."

"Yeah, sorry about bothering you. I just wanted to talk about Jackson's patients."

Ignoring Marwin's apology, Bradley asked, "Do you have new information?"

Marwin relayed his visit to Forever Young and the pharmacy and Geri Assist links to Bradley.

"Sounds like babysitting for old folks," Bradley said.

Marwin laughed. "Yep."

"I've never heard of anything like that before. Let me do some digging into Geri Assist when I get home. I'll also pull up my notes and give you the specifics about the insurance policies. I'll be in touch with you later."

"Sounds good," Marwin said. "I'm going to be talking to one of the employees of Geri Assist today, so I will let you know if she has anything to add to the puzzle."

Bradley made a note on his iPhone, then called his boss. His boss informed him that the initial findings in Shoehorn's autopsy showed he died of an opioid overdose, specifically sufentanil. Bradley hung up, made another note in his iPhone, and sat back against the bench.

*It's amazing how a day can go to Hell so quickly,* he thought.

\* \* \*

MARWIN FINISHED CLEANING THE house, at least as much as he was going to do. He marinated some chicken breasts he had gotten out of the freezer. He was sure Bogie would complain about eating chicken 'again', but Morgan would hardly eat red meat, so it was easier to make chicken frequently than to try to fight with them.

After placing the marinated chicken breasts in a bag and putting them into the fridge, Marwin washed his hands as his phone rang. He managed to answer it on the fourth ring.

"Mr. Gelstone? This is Isabelle from Geri Assist. Is this a good time for you to talk?"

"Yes, this is fine. Thanks for calling me back."

"No problem. What can I do for you?"

"I'm looking into the deaths of three patients from Forever Young, specifically, Ruth Westmoreland, Tom Richardson, and Wilson Stanford," Marwin explained.

"OK, but I'm afraid I don't understand, Mr. Gelstone. Didn't you say you're a pharmacist?" Isabelle asked, seemingly perplexed.

"Yes, ma'am. I am. I work closely with Dr. Jackson Montgomery, who was the primary care physician for all the patients. He asked me to look into their deaths as they all died suddenly and unexpectedly."

"Well, we're talking about patients that reside in an assisted living facility," Isabelle said. "I'm sure Dr. Montgomery has experienced sudden deaths with his patients before."

"I'm sure he has, but these deaths occurred very close together."

"They say people die in threes," Isabelle said flippantly.

"Maybe," Marwin replied slowly. "But two of them died from hypertensive crisis and the other one died of severe low blood pressure that led to organ failure. They were all three insured by the same insurance company, and they all used the same pharmacy. Lastly, they were all patients in your service. That's quite a few coincidences," Marwin surmised.

"Are you implying Geri Assist might be involved in the deaths?" Isabelle asked, trying to sound offended. "I believe you said they were all patients of Dr. Montgomery, so you might want to look in that direction rather than at a company that provides entertainment for the patients," she finished indignantly.

"I'm not implying anything," Marwin responded equitably. "I'm trying to find a reason as to why three seemingly healthy patients died suddenly under strange circumstances."

"I hardly think blood pressure issues are *strange circumstances* in elderly patients, Mr. Gelstone. Anyway, I have paperwork to do, so unless you have any questions for me, I need to go."

"Before you hang up, could you give me an overview of your activities with these patients, please?"

Exhaling loudly, Isabelle replied, "I made sure they took their meds on time, helped them get dressed, if needed, brought them snacks, played games with the ones who were interested, et cetera. I showed them com-passion—unlike most of their family members."

Marwin thought for a moment. "Could you tell me if Tom Richard-son ever took Viagra or other erectile dysfunction drugs? There were none of those listed in his chart and Dr. Montgomery had not prescribed any of them to him, but I have reason to suspect he may have died from mixing Viagra with his normal medications."

Isabelle rocked back, instantly glad they were not on FaceTime or a Zoom call. "Uh, no. I don't recall him ever talking about Viagra. Although, it wouldn't surprise me. Tom was a feisty old guy! In fact, the last time I visited with him he said he had a hot date with Gladys. He basically threw me out of his room! Who knows? Maybe he took a Viagra before he went to see Gladys."

"Where would he have gotten one?" Marwin inquired.

"Hell, he could have gotten one from any male resident he knew in Forever Young," Isabelle laughed. "They pass pills around like candy in a bag."

"Yeah, I thought that might be the case," Marwin conceded.

Changing directions, he continued, "Do you know anything about Wilson Stanford using illicit drugs?"

"*Illicit drugs?*" Isabelle asked, incredulous.

"There was evidence of amphetamines in his system," Marwin explained.

"I can't imagine that. Mr. Stanford was one of my favorites. He was like a grandfather to me." After a brief pause, Isabelle continued, "Could he have been taking Sudafed?"

"You tell me, Isabelle. Sudafed wasn't on his med list, but oftentimes, patients don't list over-the-counter drugs. They don't think of them as actual medications. Do you recall ever seeing Sudafed with his meds?"

"Now that you mention it, I do remember Mr. Stanford having Sudafed in his medicine cabinet," Isabelle responded immediately.

"Well, that could explain the lab results for the amphetamines," Marwin said simply. "But it wouldn't explain the presence of selegiline metabolites in his system."

Again, Isabelle rocked backward as if struck. "Selegiline? I-I don't know what that is," she stammered.

"It's a drug used to treat Alzheimer's and depression. However, Mr. Stanford wasn't taking it as far as I know."

Isabelle's mind raced as she tried to assimilate the best response. Finally, she blurted, "I don't know anything about Mr. Stanford taking that drug. I know I never gave him any when I gave him his meds, though."

"I thought you didn't know what it was?" Marwin asked pointedly.

"Oh, I don't, but I knew all the meds he was on. There were no unknowns when I gave him his meds," Isabelle explained, recovering.

"OK. How about Ruth Westmoreland? She died of a stroke and heart attack, apparently induced by tranylcypromine ingestion."

Isabelle anticipated Marwin's pharmaceutical knowledge and calmly replied, "Tranyl- what? I have no idea what that is."

"Yeah, OK. Tranylcypromine is an old antidepressant that is very rarely used today due to various drug interactions and dietary restrictions," Marwin said and listened closely to her response.

"Oh, well. I guess I'm too young to know about that," Isabelle laughed.

"All right. That's all I have for you, Isabelle. If you can think of anything that might help, please give me another call."

"I sure will," she said sweetly.

"Oh, one last question. Did you ever take cheese to any of these patients?"

# CHAPTER 40

The woman leaned back on her seat, drenched in sweat despite the car's air conditioning. Her mind and heart were both racing. Taking a couple of deep breaths to try to calm herself, she prepared to call her boss. Knowing she couldn't wait any longer, she dialed the number.

"What did he say?" the man demanded without a greeting.

"He asked about our services and what services I had provided to the patients who recently left our care."

"All right. I assume you answered his questions and satisfied his curiosity effectively?"

"I think so," the woman said, but she knew she'd have to divulge all the details eventually.

"Thinking so is not acceptable! You better damn well be sure you answered sufficiently to make him go away."

"Y-Yes, sir," she stammered.

As the woman tried to find an easy way to disclose the details of her conversation with Marwin, the man asked, "Is there something you need to tell me?"

"Well…yes, sir," she replied shakily. "The pharmacist knows how the patients died, and I believe he has a realistic theory on how their deaths came about."

"How could he know? Did you make a mistake?"

"No, sir!" she responded immediately. "Everything went flawlessly on my end."

"Undoubtedly not," the man said simply.

"But, sir—"

"Silence! I will be in touch," he stated angrily and terminated the call.

The woman slumped in her seat, skin clammy and heart and mind continuing their race. She replayed the brief conversation, wondering what she could have said differently. Waves of nausea rolled over her as her mind turned to the previous employee she had visited in jail the previous day. *He was deemed dispensable, a loose end,* she thought in horror. *Just like me.*

* * *

MARWIN GRABBED A BOTTLE of spring water, a notebook, and a pen and retired to his study. He quickly listed the facts as he understood them and wrote theories to explain them. He crossed some off, added new ones, then crossed some of those off, too. Bradley could provide a large piece to the puzzle, so Marwin decided to call him before exploring any further theories.

Before he could dial Bradley's number, Bogie and Morgan burst into the house, bickering loudly. Exiting the study, Marwin caught up to the kids as they were halfway up the stairs.

"Hey, guys. It's nice to see you're home."

"Hey, Dad. Bogie's being a butthead again," Morgan stated.

Marwin glanced at Bogie, who shrugged and continued his climb to his room.

"Go put your stuff away and come back down," Marwin instructed the kids.

"I've got stuff to do," Bogie complained.

"Well, don't waste time getting back down here then," Marwin returned dryly.

Morgan smiled and almost skipped to her room. Bogie mumbled something under his breath before trudging upstairs.

Marwin was seated at the kitchen island when the kids resurfaced. "How was your weekend?" he asked.

"It was awesome!" Morgan answered, smiling broadly.

"What about yours, Bogie?"

"It was OK," Bogie replied non-committedly.

Marwin started the ritual of pulling information out of his kids. "What did you guys do?"

"Mom took us to the park yesterday," Morgan offered. "We took our gloves, and Bogie threw with me, except we kept getting interrupted by a bunch of text messages, so we finally quit."

Bogie shot eye daggers at Morgan but remained silent.

"You know, your teammates can wait until you are through doing what you are doing," Marwin chided.

"Oh, I don't think it was his teammates texting him," Morgan supplied.

Bogie took a step toward Morgan but knew better than to say anything.

"No? Who was so important that you couldn't finish playing with your sister?" Marwin asked, even though he already had a suspicion.

"Just a friend," Bogie replied vaguely.

"A friend that happens to be a girl." Morgan grinned, confirming Marwin's suspicion.

Marwin smiled. "Does this *friend that happens to be a girl* have a name?"

"Just a friend," Bogie replied, looking for an escape.

"Her name is Laney. She and Bogie are going out now," Morgan announced proudly.

"We are not!" Bogie yelled in Morgan's direction, but his face turned bright red.

"Take it easy, Bud. There's nothing wrong with having a girlfriend."

"She's not my girlfriend!" Bogie asserted. "Morgan is just trying to get me in trouble."

"Now, why would Morgan try to get you in trouble?" Marwin turned a questioning gaze on his daughter.

Neither child offered any answer. Marwin looked from one to the other. "OK. Out with it."

Bogie stared at Morgan, who, in turn, stared at the floor. The silence stretched thin before Morgan decided to speak. "Mom will tell you anyway."

Marwin's anger fired up immediately. "Tell me, what?"

When Morgan didn't answer, Marwin turned to Bogie. "What's your mom going to tell me, Bogie?"

Bogie shrugged but didn't answer.

"I asked you a question!" Marwin thundered.

Before Bogie could decide whether to answer, Morgan said, "Mom will probably tell you I got caught making out with Patrick."

"*Making out with Patrick?*" Marwin inquired, incredulous.

"Patrick met us at the park. Mom let the two of us go for a walk. She saw us kissing goodbye," Morgan confessed.

Bogie breathed a huge sigh of relief, knowing he was completely forgotten.

Marwin stood, staring at his precocious daughter. "Bogie, go to your room."

"I didn't do anything, Dad!"

"I didn't say you did. I need to talk to Morgan in private, please."

Marwin collected himself as Bogie exited. "Honey, I'm afraid you are trying to grow up too fast."

"Dad, I'm not," she rebutted.

"Just listen. Don't talk. We just had a conversation about the smoking incident. You're too young to smoke cigarettes and make out with a boy. I will talk to your mom, but I don't think I can support your relationship with Patrick right now."

"Dad! It wasn't Patrick's fault. I *wanted* to kiss him."

Marwin stifled a comment that flew into his mind. "Go get your homework done—if you have any—and get ready for school tomorrow. We'll talk more later."

* * *

BRADLEY SAT IN HIS chair, stunned. He had read and re-read the information multiple times, each time failing to help him believe it. He had completed three hours of research on Geri Assist. Not knowing exactly what he was looking for, he looked through the company's history, the officers, the financials, and the current employees. Initially, nothing jumped off the page to him, so he did a random internet search of the company.

He found numerous articles related to Geri Assist and their place in the ever-expanding field of geriatric care. Finding nothing of importance, he was ready to close his search when he came across a photo that caused him to double-take.

It showcased Ernie Shoehorn as he received the Employee of the Year award from a handsome young man. Confused, Bradley opened the attached article and learned Dr. Winston Ernest Shoehorn had been recognized for his outstanding care of the citizens of Knoxville.

The mention of Shoehorn in such a positive light was shocking, but the connection to Geri Assist—which was possibly linked to several deaths recently—caused warning bells to sound in Bradley's head. He quickly bookmarked the article and opened the Shoehorn file on his desk.

Scrolling through the list of victims possibly attributed to Shoehorn, Bradley saw a solution unfold. As he tried to determine his next step, he was overcome by the enormity of the evil he had uncovered.

* * *

MARWIN FIRED UP THE Big Green Egg, diced some potatoes to roast, and chopped vegetables for the salad. He dialed Lindsey as he waited for the smoker to reach the optimal temperature.

"Well, it didn't take you long to get the juicy details out of the kids," Lindsey said tiredly.

"Why did I have to pull it out of them? Why couldn't you just tell me?" Marwin asked bitterly.

"I wasn't keeping it from you, Marwin. I didn't think it was that big of a deal. I knew we'd eventually have this conversation."

"Eventually? So, you were going to wait until I found out before talking to me about it? That's bullshit, Lindsey."

"Calm down, Marwin. Morgan is twelve years old. It's completely normal to have an interest in the opposite sex."

"Maybe, but her interests lately seem more like an eighteen-year-old instead of a twelve-year-old," Marwin suggested.

"Really? How old were we when we first kissed? I believe I was fourteen, and you were seventeen."

"That's different," Marwin said, but he knew his words sounded stupid.

Lindsey was silent. She knew Marwin understood more than he had admitted.

Marwin finally said, "She's our baby, Lindsey. I don't want her to grow up too fast."

"I know," Lindsey said softly. "Neither do I, but we can't keep her from growing up. We just have to try to guide and be there for her when she ignores our advice and gets hurt."

"Should we ground her?"

"Seriously! For kissing a boy I gave her permission to hang out with?"

"Yeah, OK. I get it. But she isn't old enough to smoke, and I am not backing off on that," Marwin replied sternly.

"I agree. Our kids will never be old enough to smoke."

"Thanks for listening to me, Linds. I gotta go finish supper."

"Me, too. Remember, we have to cut the cord eventually."

* * *

MARWIN AND THE KIDS made it through dinner with no further mention of the weekend's activities. They discussed school, baseball, and softball.

The kids rinsed their plates and loaded the dishwasher before Marwin said, "You guys go put in your swings on the tee, then get ready for bed."

"Morgan is gonna hit off the tee, too?" Bogie gasped.

"How else is she going to get better? You can help her, and she can help you," Marwin suggested.

"Awesome! I'll meet you out there." Morgan practically flew out of the room.

"Work hard, Bud," Marwin said to Bogie before answering his ringing phone.

"What's up, Bradley?" he said after Bogie slumped after his sister.

"I was hoping we could get together tonight to discuss some new information I found about Jackson's patients' deaths."

"It would have to be over here. I can't leave the kids tonight. Could we just discuss it over the phone?"

"No, I think it's better to discuss this in person. Could you see if Destiny could be there, too?"

"Let me check with Des and see if she can make it. How about nine o'clock?"

"Cool. I'll see you then," Bradley responded and hung up.

Destiny wasn't thrilled with the late hour of the meeting but agreed she would be there. After hanging up with Destiny, Marwin finished cleaning the kitchen, checked on the kids, and returned to his study to retrieve the notebook he had been working out of earlier.

He poured a glass of merlot, turned Amos Lee on Pandora, and looked over his notes again. Fifteen minutes later, his doorbell announced the arrival of his friends.

Opening the door, he was greeted by Destiny, Bradley, and Jackson. He stood dumbly in the doorway, caught off-guard by Jackson's unexpected appearance.

"Hello, Handsome." Destiny kissed Marwin lightly.

Marwin stepped back, and Jackson said, "What! No kiss for me?"

"No way. I don't think you could handle kissing something as fine as me," Marwin said, regaining his composure.

As Jackson worked up a retort, Bradley said, "Let's get started. We have a lot to go over tonight."

The four found seats in the study, and Marwin said, "OK, Bradley. What's this new information we all need to hear in person?"

Bradley ran his hand through his short hair. "After I talked to you, I did some research on Geri Assist. It appears to be a very successful company with strong financials. Actually, the financials are *too* strong, in my opinion, but let's come back to that later."

"While I scrolled through articles on the internet, I came across a picture of a doctor receiving the Geri Assist Employee of the Year Award. The doctor's name was Winston Earnest Shoehorn."

"Shoehorn worked for Geri Assist?" Marwin and Jackson asked simultaneously.

"Yep, apparently so," Bradley acknowledged.

Jackson shook his head. "How's that for irony? A doctor who killed his patients was awarded Employee of the Year. Crazy!"

"I know, right?" Destiny chimed in.

"That is amazing. Did you find anything else, Bradley?" Marwin inquired.

"Yes! Geri Assist's CEO is a man named Julio Vandam. His grandfather is Malcolm Vandam, CEO of Clinical Care Insurance."

Marwin's brain immediately made the connection. "I assume all of the Forever Young patients who died had a policy with Clinical Care?"

"Yes, either a cancer policy or a long-term care policy," Bradley affirmed.

"Holy shit!" Marwin said. "This is like the book Robin Cook wrote. I don't remember the title of the book, but it was about an insurance company that killed its insured clients to prevent paying out claims."

"That's crazy!" Jackson offered.

"Nothing really surprises me anymore," Marwin said sadly.

"Not the book, the fact you can't remember the name of the book," Jackson said, cracking up.

"Very funny," Marwin leered.

The levity quickly dissipated. Destiny asked, "Did any of Shoehorn's patients have a policy with Clinical Care?"

Bradley eyed Marwin and Destiny. "You guys are all over it! So far, I have found five patients who committed suicide under Shoehorn's care, and they had a policy with Clinical Care."

"Oh, my god!" Destiny remarked, horrified.

Bradley, Marwin, and Destiny chatted about the new information before Jackson interrupted. "Madeline wasn't insured by Clinical Care. Why would Shoehorn want her to kill herself?"

266

No one offered a hypothesis, and the silence stretched out painfully. "I just don't understand," Jackson said, his voice breaking.

\* \* \*

AFTER HIS GUESTS LEFT, Marwin returned to the study, and he added notes about Clinical Care and Shoehorn into his notebook. Re-reading everything, he came to the same conclusion as earlier. He was ninety-five percent sure he knew who had murdered Jackson's patients and how they had done so.

He felt he needed one more piece of the puzzle to be certain. He considered calling Bradley but decided to wait until the morning and handle the job himself.

Marwin was horrified by the level of evil in the world. *What will it be like when Bogie and Morgan are on their own?* he wondered.

Thinking of his children caused Marwin's mind to go to Destiny. He had planned to propose to her last October, but Madeline had committed suicide. After that, he had almost been killed by Shoehorn and spiraled downward, almost forcing Destiny out of his life. Thankfully, she stayed with him throughout his stupidity and rescued him from going into the abyss.

He was desperately in love with Destiny and wanted to spend the rest of his life with her. He vowed to take action as soon as possible before anything else happened.

# CHAPTER 41

Monday morning was chaotic, as usual. Marwin hustled the kids off to school, got ready for work, and jumped into the irritating commute east on I-40.

Sportstalk radio rattled on about the upcoming football season, and Marwin wondered if he was ever going to have time to do calculations. Deciding it was unlikely he would get anything done before the season started, he turned off the radio and asked Siri to dial the Knox County Coroner's Office.

Steeling against the upcoming push-back from Vince Adkins, Marwin listened as the phone rang repeatedly. He wondered if Adkins hadn't come in yet. Marwin was about to hang up when the gruff old goat finally picked up the phone.

"Dr. Adkins! This is Marwin Gelstone. I'm sorry to bother you so early this morning."

"Obviously, not too damned sorry or you wouldn't have called."

Marwin ignored the jab and tried to keep things civil. "I won't keep you. I just had a couple more questions concerning the autopsies of Wilson Stanford and Ruth Westmoreland."

"Really? You doing Jinswain's work for him now? If he has any more questions, *he* will have to ask them. I don't have time for this, Mr. Gelstone."

"It's Dr. Gelstone, and Bradley is in court this morning," Marwin quickly lied. "He asked me to call you since you were kind enough to share the information with me previously."

"Bullshit. I know bullshit when I hear it, *Dr.* Gelstone. Look, I told you I don't have time for this. Apparently, the gangs had a get-together this weekend and I have two new visitors this morning," Adkins growled.

"I understand. I just need to know if the cheese found in Ruth Westmoreland's cheek could have been the same kind that was found in Wilson Stanford's stomach," Marwin rushed on.

"Damn. You really are dense, aren't you?"

Marwin didn't reply. He waited in hopes the coroner would answer his question. The seconds stretched out.

"This isn't a James Patterson mystery. I can't tell you what type of cheese was in Mr. Stanford's stomach as it was just a bunch of goo. As for Mrs. Westmoreland, the cheese in her cheek had a creamy consistency. It is possible they were the same type of cheese, but it is also equally possible they were not."

"Could a lab test determine the type of cheese?"

"More than likely, yes, but I'm not sending them out. Now, if you'll excuse me, *Dr.* Gelstone, I need to attend to my assistant. He's staring at me like he just shit his pants."

Marwin leaned back in his seat and let out a heavy sigh. He had learned nothing new from calling Adkins—other than to confirm the man was a total asshole. Marwin turned Hair Nation on the radio to help him think of his next step.

* * *

THE MAN SAT AT his mahogany desk with an unfamiliar feeling of uncertainty. He prided himself on making quick decisions and had never been unsure of actions to take in the past. However, for the first time in his career, he was perplexed. He had spent the weekend weighing the pros and cons of the situation but had not reached a conclusion.

He was not ready to shut down the Knoxville operation as the next site was far from opening. He did not want to dispose of the woman as she had been one of the most valuable and productive employees on the payroll. Still, without the woman, there was little or no chance his operation would be discovered.

The strange indecisiveness had unnerved him, and he stared at the wall. The ping of an incoming text message broke his reverie, and he swiped the phone off the desk. Reading the text, he swore aloud. He placed the phone back on the desk and his hand trembled.

The man closed his eyes and allowed his mind to go blank. After several minutes, he opened his eyes, and a calm spread over him. The decision was made. A degree of sadness washed over him as he prepared to send the woman on her final mission before she had an unfortunate accident.

* * *

POLLY WOKE GROGGY AND tired. She had slept poorly the night before and needed to be at Forever Young early. She had trouble getting motivated as the combination of chardonnay and Ambien was finally working.

She stumbled to the bathroom, sat down to pee, and nearly fell asleep on the toilet. Slapping her face, she turned on the cold water and climbed into the shower. As the icy water attempted to break through her fog, she tried to find a solution to her problem.

Covered in goosebumps, Polly stepped from the shower, and someone knocked on her door. Wrapping a towel around herself, she opened the door and found Kristen holding a Starbucks bag and two cups of coffee.

"Am I interrupting again?" Kristen asked, grinning.

"I wish," Polly replied, stepping aside.

"I brought you breakfast. Since I haven't seen much of you lately, I thought I would grab us something to eat. I was afraid you might already have gone to work, so I was glad when I saw your car in the parking lot."

"Thanks," Polly said, taking a coffee from Kristen. "I'm actually supposed to be at Forever Young already. I can't seem to get it together this morning, though."

"I'm going by there this morning, too. I don't have to be at school today. You want to ride together?"

"I would like to, but I have to visit another facility after I leave there."

"Bummer. OK. Maybe we can get together for a glass of wine or three and catch up on life," Kristen suggested. "Maybe you could even bring out some of that special cheese, and we could eat, drink, and be merry."

A plan formed in Polly's mind and a smile crossed her face.

"What are you smiling at?" Kristen asked curiously.

"I was thinking how your impromptu visit had made my day. What seemed like it was going to be a shitty Monday, just became the perfect day!" Polly replied, hugging Kristen.

"Do you want to come to my place around six? I have plenty of wine and some meat if you want to bring the cheese."

"Sounds good. I'll see you tonight around six, but I may see you at Forever Young, too, if I can get my ass in gear and not get fired."

\* \* \*

THE INTERSTATE TRAFFIC EVENTUALLY eased up and Marwin made it to work with fifteen minutes to spare. After talking with Adkins, he called Bradley to see if he could have the two cheeses analyzed.

Bradley informed him that he was making a presentation to his boss about the whole case. He desperately wanted to open an official investigation. Bradley also hinted he might be able to go through outside channels if his boss wasn't willing to accept his proposal.

Thoughts of cheese and murder quickly evaporated as the cacophony of the pharmacy swallowed Marwin. Endless phone calls, patients, and prescriptions caused the hours to fly by.

Marwin looked up as Sam counseled a patient and realized it was after lunch. He also noted zero calls from Bradley, and he hadn't peed since getting to work.

"I'll be right back," he announced to Miranda.

"Thanks for the warning," she quipped, never breaking stride on the stack of prescriptions she was working on.

After emptying his bladder, Marwin headed to the office to call Bradley. Before he reached the door, Miranda called him back to the phone and the pharmacy engulfed him again.

Two hours later, the pace slowed to a stop and Marwin retreated to his office to call Bradley. He grabbed some peanut butter crackers from his desk and a Mountain Dew from the mini fridge as he waited for Bradley to answer. The call went to voice mail, so Marwin was forced to leave him a message.

Sighing, Marwin stood and stretched his back, preparing to return to the pharmacy counter. As he passed his cell phone, he saw an incoming call from an unknown number. Debating whether to answer it, he finally hit the green button.

"Mr. Gelstone? This is Mitchel Dalton from Cedar Bluff Middle School. Do you have a minute?"

*Oh, shit!* Marwin thought.

"Yeah, sure. What can I do for you, Mr. Dalton?" Marwin said with trepidation.

"If you're available, I hoped we could get together this afternoon to talk about Morgan."

"What's wrong with Morgan?" Marwin asked, fearing the worst.

"Nothing's wrong. She's fine. If possible, I just wanted to talk to you briefly."

Glancing at the clock on the wall, Marwin sighed. "I can be there in twenty minutes."

"That would be great. Come to the softball field. We will be getting ready to practice."

"OK. See you, shortly," Marwin replied, suddenly feeling very tired.

Marwin's phone flashed a text from Bogie. *Morgan made the team!!!*

*Holy shit! I can't believe she made the team.* Marwin thought, some of his energy returning.

\* \* \*

SECOND CHANCE TO DIE

THE WOMAN'S PHONE PINGED with an incoming text. *Call me in five minutes.*

She cursed as she tried to maneuver through the morning traffic and find a place to pull off the road. Pulling into the Brown Squirrel parking lot, she dialed the number as her heart rate ticked upward.

The man answered before she heard the first ring. "We have a problem," he stated immediately. "It seems our pharmacist friend is continuing to poke his nose where it doesn't belong. It is also apparent you have made mistakes that allowed him to figure out your methods."

"But, sir—"

"*But* nothing," the man snapped. "It is of no consequence now. We must deal with it."

"Yes, sir. What do you need me to do?" the woman asked, voice trembling.

She listened quietly as the man told her the plan. Her mind screamed in protest, but her mouth remained silent, fearful of his reaction if she suggested another plan.

"Do you understand?" he asked when he had finished.

"Yes, sir," the woman replied meekly.

The man heard the hesitation in the woman's voice. "You made this mess. I suggest you clean it up—unless you want me to get involved."

"Y-Yes, sir. I-I will take care of it right away," she stammered.

"Sooner rather than later," he instructed and hung up.

Despite the building heat, the woman sat drenched in a cold sweat. Terror swept through her as she replayed her boss's instructions. Closing her eyes, she took several deep breaths as her mind weighed her options.

*I could pack up and leave town. I have plenty of money, and I could try to disappear in St. Somewhere. If I go through with his plan, I will likely get caught and end up in jail. He may see the need to eliminate me even if I'm successful.*

She sat with her head back against the headrest, her brain searching for solutions when a horn blew and startled her. A Knox County cruiser was parked next to her car and an officer peered at her. She reached slowly for the window button and forced a smile onto her face.

"Is something wrong, Officer?" she asked easily.

"I'm not sure. Are you all right, ma'am?"

"Yes, sir. Why?" she asked innocently.

"I noticed the way you were sitting in your car, and you appeared to be in some kind of distress. You were leaning back in your seat with your eyes closed. I was afraid you needed assistance."

"Oh! I was driving to work, and I developed a terrible headache. I pulled over here to see if it would get better," the woman lied.

The officer studied the woman's face and glanced into the empty back seat. "Uh-huh. I see. Is your head feeling better?"

"Truthfully, not much. I think I may have to call in sick today," she replied, frowning.

"I can give you a ride home if you need one," the officer offered.

"No, that's not necessary, but thanks. I really need to crawl into my bed and turn all the lights off. The headache usually goes away pretty quickly if I do that."

"OK. Be careful going home," the officer said as he rolled by her car after stopping briefly to check out her license plate.

* * *

MARWIN ARRIVED AT CEDAR Bluff Middle School and debated checking in through the office. Deciding against the formalities, he walked the short distance to the softball field. He had never met Coach Dalton, so he didn't know how to locate him. Morgan had said her coach was 'really cute', but Marwin wasn't sure that would help him identify him.

Approaching the field, Marwin spied a young woman in the outfield. She was encircled by a group of young girls, all dressed in green. The girls spread out and did a series of stretching exercises as they counted in unison. Marwin located Morgan, who was intently doing her exercises and counting with the rest of the team.

Turning away, Marwin continued his search for the head coach. He assumed a man wearing a green tee shirt lettered with *Giants* on the front of it was the man in question. The man pulled an L-screen across the infield to a position in front of the pitcher's circle.

"Coach Dalton?" Marwin asked through the chain-link fence.

"Yep. Mr. Gelstone, I assume," the man said, dropping the screen.

"Yes, sir. Do you need a hand?"

"That would be great. Two of my assistants are out today, so I'm setting up by myself."

Marwin slipped onto the dirt, ignoring his dress shoes and clothes, and helped the coach set the screen about twenty-five feet in front of home plate.

"So, what did you want to see me about?" he asked.

The coach turned to Marwin, revealing his dark-brown eyes and ruggedly handsome face. "I wanted to talk about Morgan and then present a proposition to you afterward."

"What about Morgan?" Marwin asked tensely.

"As I'm sure you know, I took a chance putting Morgan on the team. She has no experience and little knowledge of the game."

"I know. I can't understand why you took her," Marwin admitted.

Dalton scrubbed his chin. "There's something about her. She gives everything she's got on every play. Many of the girls at this age only give an effort when they want to. Morgan is different. She busts her butt every time."

"She better," Marwin stated. "There's no reason to be out here if you're not going to give it your all. It doesn't take talent to hustle."

"I agree. Unfortunately, not many girls subscribe to that theory yet. Anyway, I'm really impressed with Morgan's work ethic. Plus, she has blazing speed and is very athletic. I guess you could say I am betting on the come," Dalton said with a smile.

"I appreciate you taking a chance on her. Hopefully, you won't be disappointed."

"As long as she continues to work the way she is, I won't be disappointed. Uh, I do have some concerns, though. I have seen her hanging out with an older boy before and after practice recently. In fact, I walked up on them making out behind the batting cages last week before tryouts. Of course, she was horrified and would hardly answer me when I addressed her during the team's workout. She worked hard that day—which is impressive after having been embarrassed by her potential coach."

"M-Making out?" Marwin stammered, completely floored.

"They were kissing. Necking, in my day. Nothing more, but I assumed you wouldn't approve."

"No, I most definitely do not approve!"

"I wouldn't like it either. Look, I'm not here to tattle on the girls, but I am responsible for them and their actions, especially while they're on campus. I don't want them to make poor decisions and get in trouble."

"I appreciate the heads up," Marwin said as his eyes shot daggers at Morgan in the outfield.

"No problem. The other thing I wanted to talk to you about is considering the lay coach position this season."

Marwin continued to stare at his precocious daughter stretching in the outfield. "I'm sorry. I was thinking about her punishment. What did you say?"

"I asked if you would be interested in being our lay coach this year. I prefer for it to be someone without a daughter on the team, but I think you will be fine. I'm not worried about you trying to play *Daddy Ball*."

"Why? You don't even know me. I might not know anything about softball," Marwin argued, looking curiously at Dalton.

"You're right. I don't know you, but I have seen your son play on numerous occasions and he is a great ball player. He has solid fundamentals and knows the game very well. I doubt God did all of that by Himself. I imagine you helped."

"Where did you see Bogie play and why?" Marwin asked, a little on edge.

"My nephew, P.C., plays on the same team as Bogie," Dalton explained.

Marwin rifled through his memories, but he could find none of a time when Dalton was at Bogie's games.

*Of course, I didn't go to Bogie's games for a few months*, he thought sadly.

"Um, OK. Thanks for the offer, Coach Dalton. Could I discuss it with Morgan tonight? She might not want me to be one of her coaches."

"Sure, if you can, let me know tomorrow. We start playing in two weeks and I need to get everyone—players and coaches—on the same page."

"OK, I'll call you tomorrow. Thanks, again," Marwin said, turning to leave.

"Marwin? Can I call you Marwin?" Dalton asked.

"Sure."

"Don't be too hard on Morgan. She's just a kid trying to figure things out," Dalton suggested with a wink.

* * *

KRISTEN ANSWERED THE DOOR with bare feet and in gym shorts and an orange Vol tee shirt. Her curly hair hung damply on her shoulders.

"Aw, you cleaned up for me," Polly said, moving past Kristen into the apartment.

"Yeah, well after visiting with Mr. Chamberlain this morning, I needed a shower. What a dirty old man!" Kristen replied disgustedly.

Polly laughed. "He's really harmless once you put him in his place. You're the new girl, so he looks at you like fresh meat."

"Gross," Kristen shuddered, heading to the kitchen.

"Here, take this with you," Polly instructed, holding out a Bed, Bath, and Beyond bag.

Eyeing the bag, Kristen asked, "Since when do I need to take my bath supplies to the kitchen?"

"Look inside. It's not bath supplies."

Reaching into the bag, Kristen withdrew four containers. "What's this?"

"It's some of the cheese you like so much," Polly said, smiling broadly.

"Wow! When I asked you to bring some cheese, I didn't mean enough to feed an army. I think it's just the two of us tonight."

"I brought you some extra. Why don't you take Mr. Chamberlain some the next time you visit him?" Polly suggested. "He loves it!"

277

"Ugh! I dread seeing him again. He was undressing me with his eyes today." Kristen shivered.

"Start taking him some cheese when you go, and in no time, I guarantee he won't bother you anymore."

"Enough about that dirty old man. Let's get some wine."

After securing glasses of chardonnay, the two ate snacks and talked easily, catching up on the last several days. Kristen affirmed nursing school was going well, so far, and despite her interaction with Mr. Chamberlain, she was enjoying her time at Forever Young. With the advent of the four-day school week, she had been able to work for Polly's company on Monday at Forever Young every other week. She was also doing her student nursing at Forever Young on the weekends. While she was exhausted frequently, she was enjoying interacting with the residents. She was allowed to take their vital signs and weight, and she played some games with the clients and helped them do small chores. Mostly, she asked them questions related to their health and well-being.

"I can't believe they're paying me twenty dollars an hour for what I do," she voiced, amazed.

"That's a drop in the bucket for my company," Polly confirmed. "I told you, we keep the residents happy, and they live longer. The facilities are paying us big bucks to make the residents active and alive."

"Yeah, that's what you said. It still seems crazy to me, though."

"Just enjoy it now," Polly advised with a smile. "Once you become a nurse, you'll be covered in puke and shit most of the time."

"Well, that's comforting," Kristen said, toasting Polly.

* * *

As MARWIN BATTLED THE afternoon traffic, his thoughts turned to Morgan and his conversation with her coach.

*I'm not ready for this. She is too young to be doing this crap!*

Running through different scenarios on how best to handle Morgan, Marwin was interrupted by his phone. Bradley's number popped up, so he hit the answer button on his car's screen. Bradley's voice erupted from the speakers.

"Hey, sorry I haven't gotten back to you before now. I ended up having to go to court unexpectedly. Did you get in touch with Vince Adkins?"

*Well, at least I didn't lie about Bradley going to court today,* he thought with a smile.

Marwin laughed. "Oh, yeah. I started my day in a great way."

"He's a joy, all right. Did you find anything out?"

"Nope, I got nothing new," Marwin admitted.

"Did he not have the information, or did he just refuse to give it to you?" Bradley asked.

"I'm not positive. He wasn't interested in talking to me, but I doubt he held anything back. He said an independent lab might be able to answer my questions, but he wasn't going to bring them in."

"Tell me exactly what your theory is. I'll get Vince to do whatever needs to be done."

"I don't know, Bradley. This would be a very serious accusation. I would rather have proof before I fired off a wild theory."

"No offense, but you are not responsible for proving anything," Bradley replied matter-of-factly. "You're a pharmacist. I'm the detective, and it is my job to prove who did what."

"You're right," Marwin agreed, sounding like a chastised child.

Taking a deep breath, Marwin laid out his scenario.

* * *

"HAVE A GOOD NIGHT," Helen said with a wan smile. She locked the door behind the last patient of the day.

"Geez! What a day!" she exclaimed to Jackson.

"Yep! Days like this make me want to retire regardless of my financial situation. I think someone put crazy drops in the Knox County water supply."

"I know," Helen agreed. "I don't know what was wrong with our patients today. Everyone wanted pain meds. What the hell did they all do this past weekend?"

"Beats me. Half of them want pain meds and the other half wanted anxiety meds. I couldn't deal with this on a day-in, day-out basis. I'd hang it up and spend my day losing golf balls in the woods," Jackson admitted.

Helen grinned mischievously. "Let's get outta here. How about I buy you dinner since your financial status isn't the greatest?"

"Where did you get all of your money?" Jackson asked, returning the grin.

"Oh, my boss pays me more than I am actually worth."

Jackson looked away. "I don't know Helen. I should probably go home."

"Just as friends, nothing else," Helen promised. "I wanted to talk to you about my niece, Kristen. We might as well do it over a nice glass of wine."

Eyeing Helen, Jackson finally relented. "OK. Where do you want to go?"

"What about Ruby's? They have decent wine and it's casual," Helen suggested.

"OK, I'll meet you there."

* * *

MARWIN MINDLESSLY CHOPPED ASPARAGUS and broccoli while Pandora played Billy Squier. His mind was a whirlwind, but he was able to sing along to *The Stroke* as he diced potatoes.

He wondered if he had made a mistake by letting Bradley in on his theory. He had basically accused a person of being a serial killer. *What were the ramifications if his theory was wrong?*

Bradley seemed to take his hypothesis in stride, not commenting much. He had agreed to try to get the cheese found in Wilson Stanford's stomach compared to that which was found in Ruth Westmoreland's cheek. If the cheese turned out to be the same, he would be much more confident in his theory. However, if the cheeses didn't match, it meant there was more going on than he suspected.

As Pandora rolled with the changes, Marwin's mind rolled to Morgan. *When had she gotten so boy-crazy?* he wondered.

*Probably while you were searching for answers at the bottom of a bottle,* his conscience offered.

Marwin placed seasoned pork chops on one end of a baking sheet and tossed the potatoes on the other end. Placing it all in the oven, he set a timer and started to clean up the kitchen.

"Hey, Dad," Morgan said, as she bounced into the room.

"Hey! I hear congratulations are in order. I'm so proud of you!"

"Thanks. I still can't believe I made the team," Morgan marveled.

"You obviously impressed the coaches with your hard work and potential," Marwin suggested. "How was the rest of your school day?"

"It was really cool. We started reading *Oedipus* in Language Arts. It's absolutely gross to marry your mother!" she exclaimed.

"Yep! It would be like you marrying me," Marwin offered with a grin.

"I know. Gross!" Morgan reaffirmed. "Coach Dalton told me he offered the lay coaching position to you today."

"Yes, he did. I told him I needed to talk to you about it before I could give him an answer. Would it bother you if I was one of your coaches?"

"That would be *awesome!*" Morgan said, firing off her favorite adjective.

"You sure? I'm pretty tough as a coach," Marwin admitted.

"I know, but it's because you want your players to get better," Morgan answered with wisdom beyond her twelve years.

"Did Coach Dalton tell you that?"

"Yep, he sure did," Morgan said, grinning.

Knowing it wasn't the optimal time, Marwin decided to plunge in anyway. "Did he also tell you he told me he caught you making out after school?"

"I wasn't *making out*," Morgan said, blushing. "Patrick just kissed me goodbye after he walked me to the field."

"Look, Honey," Marwin said gently. "I'm not sure you are ready for boys, yet, but I know *I* am definitely not ready for you to be ready for boys."

Morgan looked forcibly at Marwin. "I know, Dad. I promise I'm not getting carried away. I just like hanging out with Patrick. He's cool."

"That sounds great on paper, but once hormones get involved, kids lose their minds. Actually, adults do, too," Marwin said with a big grin.

"We're just kids trying to figure out how to grow up."

"Coach Dalton again, right?" Marwin said, smiling.

"No, Mom told me that. She said this is the start of a crazy time in my life. She told me there is a ton of stuff to learn, and I should take my time and learn it slowly.

Eyeing his pubescent daughter, Marwin started to offer a different view, but instead pulled her into a tight embrace, kissing the top of her head.

"You can always come to me, your mom, or Destiny if you ever have questions, a problem, or just need someone to talk to. Don't try to figure everything out on your own. It can be very painful. Take advantage of the old people who have already made the mistakes. I love you. Please don't grow up too fast."

"I won't. I promise. I'll be doing my homework. Call me when dinner is ready, *Coach*," Morgan said and skipped away.

\* \* \*

BRADLEY SAT AT HIS desk, idly rolling the worn baseball between his fingers. His desk was covered in notes regarding the deaths at Forever Young. After speaking with Marwin, he now had a suspect. While the scenario seemed somewhat crazy, it was also plausible. He needed evidence to prove the hypothesis. Vince Adkins possibly could supply that evidence but wasn't in the mood to offer it willingly.

The suspect's phone records would be useful, but it would require a subpoena to get them, and without more evidence, it seemed unlikely he could obtain one.

Bradley started to make a profile of the suspect, but nothing he had found pointed to a serial killer designation.

Continuing to roll the ball through the various grips, Bradley finally reached a decision. He dropped the ball back into the drawer and dialed a familiar number.

\* \* \*

JACKSON AND HELEN SAT in a booth at Ruby Tuesdays, just two booths removed from where Jackson tried to strangle Dr. Ernie Shoehorn several months prior.

Jackson was uneasy initially, looking around the restaurant like a cheating husband. Helen ordered a pinot grigio and Jackson opted for a Dewar's on the rocks. The conversation was slightly awkward until the drinks arrived, but both parties relaxed after taking a few sips.

"So, what's up with your niece?" Jackson inquired.

"I'm not sure, really. Maybe nothing. She just hasn't been herself lately."

"How so?"

"Well, you know she is in nursing school at UT, right?"

Jackson nodded for Helen to continue and sipped his scotch.

"She really seemed to be settling in well. She was very enthusiastic about school, and she called me almost every day. She made some friends and learned her way around the big city. One of her friends had even helped her get a job at Forever Young as a sort of babysitter for elderly residents. The extra cash never hurts, you know?"

Jackson cringed at the mention of the assisted living facility. Helen sipped her wine, seemingly oblivious to his discomfort.

"Everything was going great—until it wasn't," she continued.

"What happened?"

"I don't know. She stopped calling me, so I started ringing her at night. She either didn't answer or was short on the phone and didn't want to talk."

"Does she have a boyfriend or girlfriend?" Jackson asked sheepishly.

"Not that I know of."

"Sounds like she is pretty busy. Maybe she's just stressed out right now," Jackson offered, finishing his drink.

The two ordered food and talked more easily than expected. The conversation eventually turned to Forever Young and the patients they had lost.

"Have you come up with anything that explains our deceased patients?" Helen inquired.

"Yeah, they're dying!" Jackson snapped. Seeing the hurt on her face, he added, "I'm sorry, Helen. I didn't mean to bite your head off."

He took a deep breath, picked up his empty glass, and frowned. "Bradley has found a link between all the patients we have lost. They all have an insurance policy through the same company."

"Huh, that seems a little weird."

Jackson signaled the waiter. "He also discovered Shoehorn was an employee of Geri Assist. It's a company that provides services to the residents of Forever Young. It is heavily associated with the insurance company the patients have policies with."

"What? Are you sure?" Helen asked, dumbfounded.

"Yep. According to Bradley, Shoehorn received the Employee of the Year Award a few years back."

"A doctor who caused his patients to commit suicide was given the Employee of the Year Award?" she asked incredulously.

Jackson looked as if he had been struck and automatically reached for his glass. Lowering his hand, he said quietly, "Apparently so."

"I'm sorry, Jackson. I didn't mean to open old wounds," Helen apologized.

Jackson stared at Helen. "That wound will never grow old and will never heal."

"Jackson, I'm—"

"Forget it, Helen." He stood up and tossed a hundred-dollar bill on the table. "I gotta go. Take my food home with you if you want."

Leaving Helen to stare sadly after him, Jackson walked out the door.

# CHAPTER 42

Marwin woke before his alarm sounded, feeling surprisingly refreshed. His sleep had been much better over the last several days. Maybe it was getting back into the work routine, or the surprising lack of turmoil with his children. Coaching kids had always been a passion, so perhaps his return to the coaching ranks was helping him rest better.

The main reason was likely found inside a small square box that rested on his dresser. Inside it rested a beautiful diamond ring that paled only in beauty when compared to its intended recipient.

Between work and helping with the softball team, he had not been able to have alone time with Destiny. Taking a chance, he made a reservation at The Melting Pot for Saturday night.

He showered, grabbed coffee, a bagel, and got the kids off to school before heading to work. Sam had agreed to let him open the store every day during softball season so Marwin could make the practices and games in the afternoon.

*Sam is a lifesaver*, he thought as he entered the freeway.

Marwin started turning Pandora on to start his day with rock and roll but decided to call Destiny. Her job had been crazy over the last week, so he had hardly talked to her, much less spent any time with her. Ever the rule-follower, he used his hands-free system to dial her.

"How'd you know I was naked?" she asked when she picked up.

"I didn't, but since you are, I'll be right over."

"Afraid I won't be by the time you get here. I gotta go to work. No play for me today," she added sadly.

"I understand. I'm in the same boat today, too. But we have Saturday to look forward to," Marwin extended cryptically.

"We do? What's happening on Saturday?" Destiny asked, intrigued.

"We are going to The Melting Pot, and we're gonna spend three hours and probably three hundred dollars enjoying great fondue and some much-needed alone time."

"Ooh! That sounds delicious!"

"Which part? The fondue or the alone time?"

"Yes," Destiny said simply. "Why don't you come over Saturday afternoon?"

"How about I come over Saturday morning and stay all afternoon?" Marwin replied huskily.

"You think you got it in you, Big Boy?"

"Probably not," Marwin chuckled. "But I love a challenge."

"OK. I gotta get dressed. Go save some lives. I can't wait until Saturday. I love you."

* * *

THE WOMAN CLIMBED OUT of her bed, finally giving up on her pursuit of sleep. Her body ached as she had dozed little, if any, during the night. She had been on edge, expecting a text from her boss at any time.

She trudged to the bathroom and glanced at the mirror. The image that greeted her looked only vaguely familiar. Bags resided under her tired eyes and her face appeared swollen and slightly misshapen.

*Oh, well. I have to put on a different face anyway,* she thought apathetically.

She had dressed in her disguise the previous day, but the pharmacist had already left for the day. She had phoned the pharmacy and asked to speak with the pharmacist. She was told her target would be in the following morning.

She had gone to Forever Young to work but found she couldn't concentrate. Her heart raced, and she appeared too nervous to function. Finally giving up, she went home and packed her belongings, debating briefly about which items to leave behind.

The woman planned to remove the pharmacist and then disappear in the wind. She was sure her boss would try to find her, but he would likely have his hands full after the pharmacist died. The pharmacist had figured out what she had done at Forever Young, and she was sure he had shared the information with the authorities.

If, perchance, he had not shared the information, everything would die down with his death. In that case, the boss would likely let her go after a short search. However, if the pharmacist had told the authorities about her activities at Forever Young, the police would descend quickly on her boss and the company would be shut down.

Hopefully, the latter would be the case and the woman could slip away and start a new life in another world. Everything was out of her control, except for the removal of the pharmacist. After that, she would disappear and see how it all played out.

She showered in cold water. The woman stepped into the icy spray and forced herself to breathe calmly. As the cold water sluiced over her, her mind cleared, and the aches dissipated. She used no soap as she couldn't risk altering her skin's permeability.

She stepped from the shower with only the slightest chattering of her teeth. Drying off quickly, she didn't dress but applied New Skin to the fingers of her right hand from the knuckles down. The liquid seared as it crept into tiny cracks in her skin, but the woman paid no attention.

After the liquid was completely dry, she applied a new face. She rubbed on creams and bases to alter the color and used a pen to create unobtrusive freckles. Using a marker, she changed the color of her eyebrows, before inserting contacts that altered the color of her eyes. She placed a red wig on her head and studied her appearance in the mirror for a long minute. Satisfied, she finally dressed in a bright red dress with a plunging neckline, which accented her bra-boosted cleavage. A pair of wedges finished her ensemble, and she gave herself one last look.

Her own mother wouldn't recognize her at first glance.

The woman reapplied the New Skin to her fingers. She gathered her needed items and slipped out of her apartment, desperately hoping no neighbor was looking out.

* * *

MARWIN DETOURED SLIGHTLY ON the way to work. He swung onto Kingston Pike and picked up two dozen doughnuts from Krispy Kreme. Once at work, he made a pot of coffee, set out the doughnuts, and had everything ready to open when Miranda entered fifteen minutes early.

Miranda glanced at the sweets and coffee, then back to Marwin. "Is there something I should know?"

"Yep! It's a beautiful day to save some lives!" Marwin replied enthusiastically.

"Have you been drinking already?" Miranda asked, wondering who was impersonating her boss.

"Nope. I'm just happy to be alive. I am blessed to have great employees, so I thought I would help them develop diabetes so my business will continue to prosper." He chuckled.

"Community Pharmacy," Marwin said as he answered the phone.

"Is Dr. Gelstone in?"

"This is he."

"Hey, Dr. Gelstone. My name is Abigail Howser from South College of Pharmacy. I was hoping I could stop by to talk to you for a few minutes this morning."

"Maybe. Can I ask what this concerns?"

"I'll tell you when I get there," Abigail said excitedly.

"OK. Come on by around ten. I never know when I will be busy and when I won't, but I'll make some time for you."

Marwin turned on the lights and the pharmacy sprang to life. Three retired pharmaceutical reps were seated at the table, eating doughnuts and telling lies. Marwin shared a doughnut and popped in and out of their conversations as time allowed.

The phone rang steadily with calls from patients requesting refills. The morning shift always handled more refills while the afternoon shift received the bulk of new orders.

Marwin answered phones, filled prescriptions, swapped a few lies with the drug reps, and picked on Miranda as the morning flowed easily along.

Promptly at ten o'clock, the bell above the door tinkled, announcing a new patron. Marwin glanced up from his prescription, and a young woman dressed in a bright red dress that showed way too much cleavage entered. Her red hair seemed to blend in with the dress, leaving only pale skin showing. She carried an attaché case as she approached the counter.

*I wonder what drug company she works for,* Marwin mused to himself.

Pharmaceutical reps used to be mostly male and were often pharmacists, too, just like the three old geezers sitting at the table. Recently, though, companies had hired young, beautiful women with no medical background. They dressed well, showed off their God-given talents, and hawked products based solely on what their company gave them to memorize.

"Dr. Gelstone?" the woman asked.

"I'll be right with you," Marwin said before returning to the prescription he was checking.

"These are all good," he said to Miranda referring to the bottles lined up on the counter.

"Hi. I'm Marwin Gelstone," he said, extending his hand across the counter.

"I'm Abigail Howser from South College," the woman replied, shaking Marwin's hand.

"Nice to meet you, Miss Howser. What can I do for you?" Marwin asked, trying to force his eyes to remain on her face.

"I have exciting news, Dr. Gelstone. You have been nominated for Preceptor of the Year!"

"Really? That's awesome," he said, standing a little taller.

Marwin loved precepting fourth-year pharmacy students and sharing his vast knowledge with them. He took great pride in proving to them that they did not know everything and were not ready to practice just because they had finished their classroom work. He continually hammered away at the students with random question after question while they were trying to perform their daily pharmacy duties. Students often complained it was difficult to answer questions while working. They whined that they were used to multiple-choice questions rather than rapid-fire ones.

"Multiple-choice?" Marwin often scoffed. "Do you think Dr. Montgomery is going to ask me what the starting dose of semaglutide is and then give me four options to pick from? You really think that I only get questions when I am not busy and have plenty of time to think about the answer? A pharmacist must be able to multi-task and supply information on demand. This is the real world, not a cozy classroom with Scantron sheets for you to bubble in your answers."

"Is now a good time?" Abigail asked, breaking Marwin's reverie.

"Sure! I've got a few minutes. Why don't we sit at the table? If you'd like one, there may be a doughnut or two left."

"Wow! You know the way to my heart," Abigail replied, smiling.

Marwin started to reply but was stopped by something in Abigail's eyes. He looked intently at her, thinking he knew her. He shook his head when he realized it wasn't possible.

"I'll be right over," he told her. Turning back, he instructed Miranda to call him if she needed him.

Marwin made his way to the table where the doughnut count had dwindled substantially. Abigail sat with her attaché case open in front of her on the table.

Marwin remained standing. "You want some coffee with your doughnut?"

"Let's get my work out of the way and then maybe I'll take you up on your offer."

"All right," Marwin said, taking a seat across from Abigail.

Abigail had noticed Marwin's stare, so she looked down at her open case. She glanced up but didn't make eye contact with Marwin.

"I have a form for you to fill out and a few questions for you to answer if that's OK with you."

Abigail pushed a piece of paper with the pharmacy school's logo on it across to Marwin and retrieved a pen from her case just as he reached for the ubiquitous pen in his shirt pocket.

"Thanks," he said, taking the pen.

"If you wouldn't mind filling out your personal information at the top, please. Since your degree is from a different school, we want to make sure we have your bio correct," Abigail explained.

Marwin filled out the form. It consisted of personal information and the dates during which he had attended Mercer Southern School of Pharmacy.

"This is a really neat pharmacy," Abigail commented as Marwin wrote. "I see blood pressure kits, blood glucose machines, and tape measures. Do you use this stuff every day?"

Marwin stopped writing. "On most days, we do. We are definitely a hands-on pharmacy, and we work closely with doctors and patients in the management of their health. That's the main reason we are classified as a clinical rotation for your students even though we're a retail pharmacy. I'd be happy to show you some of the stuff that sets us apart from other pharmacies."

"That would be great!" Abigail said excitedly.

Marwin resumed filling out the information and was almost finished when Abigail commented, "I hear you actually do the dosing for your patients. The doctor gives you the diagnosis and you pick the drug and dose. Is that right?"

Marwin looked up from the page. "We do that for some of our patients but not all of them. We have a collaborative agreement with some physicians in the area that allows us to do what you mentioned. Sometimes, the doctor will pick the drug and ask us to select the dose. Other times, they will let us pick the drug and the dose. The doctor usually sends us the patient's labs and pertinent medical history so we can make the best choice for them.

"After starting the patient on therapy, we have them come by here to monitor their progress. The patients love it as they can come by any time without an appointment. Plus, they don't have to pay for an office visit either."

Abigail nodded along.

"We communicate the information back to the doctor and work with them regarding any calendars—I mean changes—that might be needed," Marwin explained, starting to slur his words.

"That is super cool!" Abigail announced, ignoring Marwin's difficulty speaking.

"Yeah, it's pretty st-stool," he agreed, suddenly unable to focus on the form in front of him. His vision doubled, then momentarily cleared as he shook his head.

"Are you OK, Dr. Gelstone?" Abigail finally asked.

"I feel shaky. I sh-shink I need to eat sumphin," he slurred.

"Let me get you a doughnut," Abigail offered, rising.

Marwin's head swam. "'s OK, I guess."

Abigail placed the doughnut in front of Marwin and picked up the form and pen and returned them to her case.

"Would you like some water, Dr. Gelstone?" she asked after latching her case.

"Uh, yeah. Or no. I don't know."

Marwin pushed the chair back, knocking it over. He swayed and lurched into the table causing it to almost tip over.

"Easy, Dr. Gelstone," Abigail said, steadying Marwin by the arm.

Miranda saw Marwin stumble and called out, "Marwin, what's wrong?"

Marwin tried to turn in the direction of Miranda's voice, but his vision darkened. He fell head-first into the counter, catching the bridge of his nose on the edge. He hit the floor with no attempt to break his fall.

"Someone call 911!" Abigail screamed as blood pooled around Marwin's head.

# ACKNOWLEDGMENTS

I would like to thank my editor, Courtnee Turner Hoyle, who was taxed with correcting innumerable redundancies and improper grammar. She held my hand through the entire process and showed no irritation (outwardly) with my lack of technology acumen. Without Courtnee, this book would be a mess.

Also, to my loving wife, Dana, who listened tirelessly as I read and re-read chapter after chapter to her. She will likely have no desire to read this book as I have probably ruined it for her. Hopefully, someone will tell her how good it is!

# ABOUT THE AUTHOR

Mike Grindstaff is a pseudo-retired pharmacist from East Tennessee. He received his Doctorate of Pharmacy from Mercer Southern School of Pharmacy in 1989. Mike practiced independent as well as specialty pharmacy in the Atlanta area for almost 30 years before moving back to the hills of Tennessee.

Mike resides in Unicoi, Tennessee, with the love of his life, Dana, and two annoying dogs. When not golfing, cooking, watching sports, or playing with the grandkids, he writes fiction. *Second Chance to Die* is the sequel to his previously published novel, *Moon Over Knoxville*.

# MOON OVER KNOXVILLE

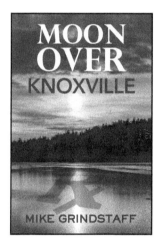

Marwin Gelstone, a divorced pharmacist with a unique practice, tries to get through the daily grind of pharmacy while simultaneously trying to understand his adolescent children. His life takes a drastic turn when his partner's wife commits suicide. Madeline Montgomery is a well-known socialite in the Knoxville community who abruptly ends the life that so many have longed for. The senseless nature of her suicide leads Marwin to search for an answer to the age-old question of why a person takes their own life. As he explores, Marwin becomes entrenched in a twisted plot that could cost him everything, including his life.

Printed in the USA
CPSIA information can be obtained
at www.ICGtesting.com
JSHW011258110823
46356JS00005B/17

9 781954 978942